Cyclone Blues

Chris Cocks

Cyclone Blues

Chris Cocks

COVOS DAY

By the same author:

Non-fiction
Fireforce – One Man's War in the Rhodesian Light Infantry
Survival Course

Published by Covos Day Books, 2000
Oak Tree House, Tamarisk Avenue,
P.O. Box 6996, Weltevredenpark 1715, South Africa

Cover design by JANT Design
Design and origination by JANT Design
E-mail: j.design@mweb.co.za

Printed and bound by United Litho.

ISBN 0-620-25438-6

For Jacky

"*'Tis life, whereof our nerves are scant,*
Oh life, not death, for which we pant;
More life, and fuller, that I want"

Tennyson

One

The green car broke down about halfway up the Zambian side of the escarpment. It had been a reasonable prediction that it would. Mike had warned the others that it had been overheating and perhaps it wasn't such a good idea to take it to Zambia. But Melvin and Oscar had overridden him—and anyway their cars were out of action. Melvin's red Datsun Pulsar was at the panelbeaters again and Oscar's ageing VW Combi just wasn't reliable—it was certainly guaranteed to break down before it had even departed the Harare suburbs.

So Mike had reluctantly bowed to the pressure of the other two muzos, and in spite of his wife's protestations, had crammed all the music gear into the little 1400 Pulsar. As usual they'd had a row, her standard complaint that he was never at home—owing to either his work or music. And what about the baby? Little George needed a father too, y'know! And he was too old to be rushing around like some kind of hippie—after all, he was well into his 30s. Time to settle down. They'd parted without saying goodbye.

The car had been crammed to the gunwales with 2,000 watts worth of speakers, amplifiers, analogues, mikes, stands, drum boxes, guitars and all the other accoutrements of a muzo roadshow. Mike had been slightly niggled by the fact that he had to go and collect all the gear from the hire shop. And he had to

---

put down the $800 deposit on the equipment because both Melvin and Oscar said they were out of money—as usual.

But he'd shrugged it off and rationalized that they were muzos, and muzos were always broke because they were so irresponsible. Talented, but hopeless with money. The fact that Melvin earned more than he had been brushed aside. Melvin was the guy who was going to make or break the tour, wasn't he? He was the guy with the charisma, he was the 'name'—without which the roadshow would have been nothing …

And now here they were, 40 odd kays inside Zambia in a broken-down Datsun Pulsar that was hissing and spluttering itself to death. Melvin had been driving as he'd insisted he was the only one who was sober enough, competent enough and the least doped-up. Oscar had shrugged—who cared? And at any rate he was quite happy strumming Van Morrison in the back seat and making the jays. Mike had tried to make a stand by saying that it was his car and he should take responsibility for it. And anyway he knew Zambia—he"d driven up the escarpment a hundred times.

But in the end Mike had succumbed. Melvin was persistent and Mike could see that he just wasn't going to give way. He would win at all costs. Besides, Melvin had said that Mike could be in charge of the tapes—albeit his choice. Well, that was something.

"Bloody hell Melv, why weren't you checking the damn gauge? Couldn't you see it was overheating?" Mike felt the whine in his voice, but Melvin wouldn't have to face the wife and tell her that he'd cooked the cylinder head. If that's what it was. Melvin just didn't have that kind of shit in his marriage. And who was going to pay for the repairs—if they ever got it back to Harare? Mike wondered briefly if he could perhaps try to deduct the costs from the concert earnings, but then decided he'd cross that bridge later.

"I've been checking out the gauge ever since Chirundu and it's been fine—the needle hasn't moved since the border,"

Melvin replied forcefully, trying to suppress any further accusations. "I reckon your gauge is a goner."

Mike sighed, already beaten. "So ... now what?" He took another slug of the ready-mixed cane and Coke. He passed the Mainstay bottle over the back seat to Oscar whose eyes were very red. Being the shortest, Oscar always had to sit in the back. He'd been a back-seater all his life.

"You can stay as you are for the rest of your life—or you can spend the night on the escarpment," Oscar tried to strum the tune to the Mainstay ad, as he took the bottle.

Melvin thought this was very funny and arched back in the driver's seat, tossing his head with laughter, clapping the steering wheel with the palms of his hands. "Stop crying Mike," he laughed, rolling the "r" of the crying for effect. "We're on holiday, we're having a gas—we can sort this out—not a snag." Always the optimist.

Mike got out of the car and noticed how greasy Melvin's long blonde hair had turned. It must be the heat, but Melvin was like that. Spend hours washing and preening and then behave like a baboon and end up looking like a drunken lout. His hair was one of his greatest assets, adding substance to his skinny frame. But they were all like that—lots of talent going nowhere. Or perhaps it was a symptom of their generation—the lost white tribe of Africa.

It was about three o'clock in the afternoon and still very hot; at least 40° centigrade in the shade. But where was the shade. Melvin had pulled over when Oscar first noticed the steam coming up from under the bonnet. Like wisps of fire coral the heat from the tar road was almost palpable. Mike put on his sandals and the gravel crunched underfoot as he went round to the front of the car and popped the bonnet. The tape was still blaring out *The Pretenders* inside the car as Melvin and Oscar lit up another joint.

"Hey Mike," Melvin shouted, leaning out around the driver's window. "Whatever you do, don't open the radiator cap." He adjusted his Raybans that were scratched and smudged, and leaned back to take the smouldering reefer from Oscar. For a brief moment Mike wondered what on earth he was doing in that place. It was bizarre. *The Pretenders* on volume ten, Melvin with the Band-Aid on the corner of his Raybans, and Oscar about set to break into the second cob of the day. Did the man have no threshold?

He peered into the engine that was frothing like a volcano and dropped the bonnet with a clang. There was nothing to be done for a good half-hour or so. Perhaps Melvin or Oscar had a plan. Oscar had worked on a farm and reckoned he was okay with these mechanical-type problems. Melvin was hopeless with motors but wouldn't admit it.

The sun was starting to cook as it threaded its way relentlessly through the mountains. Three o'clock was always about the hottest time of day in the Zambezi valley.

Harsh was the word that described the terrain. Hot, dry, arid, inhospitable. A Scania truck came trundling round the bend, hurtling controllably towards the valley floor and the border post. The black driver in the cab glanced only briefly at the green Pulsar. He was gripping the wheel, all the while battling his air brakes and the 28 tonne payload on the inter-link about set to overtake him. In a cloud of dust and burning rubber he negotiated the next corner and was out of sight.

"Wouldn't want that job in a month of Sundays," Mike stated flatly, leaning through the passenger window.

"Yeah, but those dudes can drive, man," said Oscar. "And they get well paid."

"And fuck their butts off," added Melvin.

"Well, wouldn't you?" Mike asked.

"Not with AIDS. These dudes spread it around like butter." Oscar tossed the empty Mainstay bottle out onto the side of the road where it shattered on the sizzling gravel. Where's the rest of the cane?"

"Under the seat, but we're out of Cokes," replied Melvin.

"Hey Mike, why don't you mix up some orange and water?"

Mike complied and decanted about a third of a bottle of cane into an empty. He poured in an inch or so of Mazoe orange juice and then topped up the bottle with cold water from the Coleman's. "So okes, what's the plan?"

"Well, there's not a lot we can do until the motor cools down, old son. So we may as well take five and enjoy the view," said Melvin, his left foot up on the dash. "And then I reckon all we can do is top up the radiator with water every five minutes and hope like hell we can make it to the nearest town."

"You'll crack the head if you do that," warned Oscar, "and then we're up the creek." He took a drag of the joint, sucking long and hard and exhaled several seconds later, clouding the inside of the car in a pall of sweet, blue smoke.

"Where is the next town anyway?" Melvin asked.

"Kafue," Mike replied. "But I guess it's 50 – 60 kays from here, and all uphill."

The Pretenders came to an end and a few minutes later the cassette popped out. No one bothered to change it and no one bothered to switch off the tape. The engine was still making gurgling noises under the hood as if it was in pain, now that the fury had started to dissipate. Mike wandered across to the other side of the road and looked down the valley. It was heavily wooded with spindly, sentry-like mopani trees claiming the territory as far as the eye could see. A bush fire had been through a couple of weeks before and the veld was black and smooth. But the mopanis were accustomed to bush fires and stood undaunted.

In the distance Mike noticed a cluster of huts. A village, he thought, and wondered vaguely how the people earned a living. There must be water somewhere down there. He decided to walk awhile up the hill, following the road. Perhaps around the next bend, or the one after, there might be a truck pulled over, gathering its strength for the final run down the escarpment towards Chirundu. He trudged slowly up the gradient for a few hundred metres but saw nothing. He expected as much. At this time of day the trucks would be through the border and halfway towards Harare—probably somewhere near Chinhoyi or Banket.

He stopped at a gravelled lay-by that the engineers had chiselled into the mountain face. It was littered with shredded bits of tyres and used condoms. Down the slope across the road lay the mangled remains of a rusty orange shipping container—a 20-footer by the looks of it—that had come to grief some time back. Mike pondered curiously whether the truck had gone over with it, but saw no signs. Perhaps a recovery team had hauled the horse out.

The sun slipped over the mountain as he turned and made his way back to the car. It felt as if someone had switched the heat off.

Melvin and Oscar were both out of the car now, sitting on a rock in the lee of the mountain. Oscar was strumming a Jackson Browne number and singing softly in that raspy voice of his. Mike had grown to like Oscar's style. He hadn't at first, as he'd felt the voice tended to jar. But Oscar sang good songs and he played a fine guitar. Melvin was half listening to the song but concentrating more on the fat reefer he was rolling. Mike shook his head as he watched.

"Man, Melv, when are you ever going to learn to roll a joint properly? You don't empty out a cigarette and pack it up with dope. It burns too quickly."

Oscar laughed, swaying his head from side to side in slow resignation. "I tried to tell him man, but the dude just won't listen."

The bonnet of the car was open and Melvin had taken off the radiator cap. The steam had stopped and only the occasional grumble could be heard from the guts of the engine.

"Totally outa water," said Melvin, as he vigorously shook the end of the cigarette in an attempt to tamp down the marijuana. "We're gonna have to get some water from somewhere."

"What about the Coleman?" asked Mike.

"Finished. Oscar used the last bit with the cane."

"You mean, you've finished the bottle I did just now?" said Mike.

"Yeah. We were starting to dehydrate man," retorted Oscar, chuckling. His eyes were now blood red but they didn't seem to bother him. The curly black hair more tousled.

The mountain shadows were lengthening further as they discussed the possible options. Melvin was all for one of them, or rather—one of the other two, hiking down to the village to locate some water for the radiator. But it was finally agreed that the five-litre Coleman, being their only container, wouldn't make much of an impact on the radiator.

Before the light faded totally, Oscar spent some time scrutinizing the engine. His diagnosis was that there weren't any apparent cracks in the head, but then sometimes the cracks were only hairline, and to drive like that was just as dangerous. Mike was starting to get tired of *The Pretenders*, tired of Jackson Browne. The cane, orange and water had left a sickly, sweet taste in his mouth that had made him thirsty.

The crickets started up somewhere across the valley and a couple of lilac-breasted rollers were whistling at each other through the gloom and Mike had more or less resigned himself to the fact that they were going to spend the night on the mountainside, when they heard the sounds of a vehicle approaching in the distance. They could see the beams of the headlights picking their way through the ravines and around the bends.

Melvin put on the flashing hazard lights and stood in the middle of the road as the pick-up truck from Lusaka jerked to a halt.

Two

She'd woken early that day, just after dawn. Perhaps it had been the atmospheric pressure that had been intensifying over the past few days—slowly and inexorably. Even the old-hand residents of the city were complaining. Without doubt, a cyclone was imminent. Pray to God it wouldn't be a repetition of the beast that had struck in 1995. That had surely been the hand of the Lord. It had struck without prior warning, sending entire villages of wicker and daub huts in torrents down on to the Pungue Flats, which turned into one vast lake that stretched as far as the eye could see.

She remembered that well. How it had rained every day for eleven and a half weeks. The people had been driven on to the higher ground of the roads. Some 20 feet above the floodwaters, these island ribbons had become so congested that the governor had sent in the soldiers to clear a passage for the vehicles to pass.

It had taken another eleven weeks for the flood waters to subside. Beira had become one massive festering sponge. Once the fury of the cyclone had abated, it had left in its wake a legacy of cholera, typhoid and starvation.

She smiled without humour. It had been good for business. Good for business as a *puta*. A whore. The deluge following the cyclone had been the international relief agencies, bringing with it the legions of European aid workers for whom 50 US dollars a trick was of no consequence. 1995 had been a boom year.

The years following had not been that bad either. Mozambique was slowly picking herself up off the floor and the trickle of foreign investors was gradually becoming a steady flow—in spite of the monolithic and bureaucratic administration.

She studied her naked body in the full-length mirror that took pride of place in her bedroom. She was beautiful—of that there was no doubt. Not beautiful in the classic western mould, not beautiful like some of the Mozambican girls of mixed race, with their traces of Arabic or European blood. She smiled. Some of the white men, particularly the South Africans, preferred the mulattos. With their aquiline features and their lighter skin, they were somehow less than black. There was less of a stigma.

Hers was the blackness of the peoples that had settled across the northern band of the African sub-continent seven or eight centuries before. Not the full blackness of the central Africans—the Ugandans and the Congolese. Neither the paler brownness of the Xhosa and Zulu peoples of South Africa. Somewhere in between, it was the wholesome pigmentation of the Shona, the Shangaan and the Chinyanja races. There was a softness about it that was complemented by the fullness of her lips and the flare of her nostrils. Sensual features that were wholly African.

She had worked hard for that mirror and remembered the day she had ordered it from the downtown Asian bazaar around the corner from the Banco Comercial de Mocambique. The little Indian trader had demanded a large deposit, but she'd thrown caution to the wind and paid him in full—in advance. It would take six weeks for the mirror to arrive from South Africa, he'd warned. On the sixth week to the day, she'd returned to the bazaar and the mirror was waiting for her. Salim and his shadowy *guarda-costa* had not been necessary on that occasion.

It was a simple mirror, framed by a plain Oregon pine border. It captured the simplicity of her beauty and made her feel good. After all, her body was her living and therefore her life. She slapped the top of her thigh and was satisfied to note the firmness. She knew that she had left another five years or so. With luck and care, maybe seven, even eight. She thought no further than that, after which there was no future. Therefore it was not worth consideration.

Cupping her breasts, she examined them carefully—for lumps, for any loose skin, for any sagging—as a routine. She pouted in approval. They were fine. She laughed out loud, an involuntary girlish tinkle, as she thought back to the early days when she'd sat for hours in front of a shard of mirror, practising that pout. At the time it was important to a girl of 16. Or was she 15? Like the walk, which had to be slow, sensual and hip-driven. It had worked and she'd never been short of clients.

And that had pleased Salim. She was happy that Salim had been pleased—and he still was, wasn't he? After all, had it not been Salim who had taken her out of the camps and had turned her into what she was? Had it not been Salim who had arranged for her to move into this state *apartamento*? Without Salim she would not have this freedom, this independence, would she now? It was only three rooms—a bedroom, a bathroom and a kitchen. But it was hers. She did not think of it as the state's. The state was something far away to the south in Maputo.

She dressed. Today she chose a pair of blue jeans and a white T-shirt. She decided she would not wear a bra. She slipped on a pair of white sneakers. Tossing her long black hair up into a bun, she pinned it loosely in place with a chunky wooden comb, exposing her slender neck. She liked to wear her hair up, but from experience she'd found the Westerners preferred it down—like a black Jezebel, an ebony temptress. For a while she had worn her hair in braids, interlaced with brightly coloured beads. But it had proved an exasperating and time-consuming business and she soon tired of the effort. Now she simply let it run, free and wild and wavy. The original tightness and curliness had long since been combed away.

She tossed her head in the mirror and grunted approvingly. A mirror was necessary for her trade. For the finishing touches, for the final overall effect—the outward appearance. But of late she'd been learning from its image. Her moods, her body language, her soul—her karma. One could hide nothing.

Today was market day. No clients until nightfall. It was her time. She always enjoyed her time at the market—that squalid collection of makeshift pole and *dagga* stalls amid the putrefying waste, where a visitor could buy anything and everything. For her, it was the heartbeat of Beira.

Even after the cyclone of 1995 when most of it had been washed into the sea, it came back through the stench and the filth as a triumph of humanity. It was not there to serve the aid workers, nor the party bureaucrats, nor the desultory tourists. It was there for the people, and as such the prices were realistic—unlike those in some of the Asian bazaars and the government *inter-franca*, the so-called duty-free shop where you could buy South African wines and French perfumes—only with US dollars, naturally.

She went to the kitchen table and took out a handful of *meticais* notes from the wooden vase, carefully replacing the plastic daffodils when she'd done. She would buy a pineapple, some fresh line fish and that Martha Viera cassette tape she'd been thinking about. She liked Martha Viera. It was good, strong Brazilian music. With soul.

She was about to stuff the notes into her pocket when she heard a vehicle pulling up outside on the street. Her heart sank. For a brief second she thought about sneaking out the back into the alleyway. But the children playing football on the pavement would tell the Toyota Hilux driver that the woman had not come out yet—certainly not by the front door.

Peeping through a slit in the curtains, she recognized Salim's white 4 x 4. A burly bodyguard, a *guarda-costa,* in a dark suit slammed the car door as the crowd of children scattered in front of him. A bony dog creaked itself to its feet and hobbled away as the big man kicked the sodden ball of sacking across the street from *2B Apartamento, Rua de Julius Nyerere 86*. To the jeers of his friends, an urchin scampered over the street to retrieve it.

Pre-empting the *guarda-costa*, she opened the front door. She did not greet him and neither he her.

"Salim has called for you," he grunted, scanning her up and down like a piece of horseflesh.

"Tell Salim I am busy today. I have made plans," she retorted, her hands on her hips.

The man turned away, smiling with infinite patience. For a second she thought he was preparing to backhand her. He said nothing. It was not necessary.

"What does he want of me?" she asked less defiantly.

He shrugged and nodded towards the Toyota.

"*Una momento*," she tossed her head. She went back inside where she returned the money to its hiding place amongst the plastic flowers. There would be no requirement for money at the Hotel Beira. She had long since learned that on the streets of Beira it was wiser to carry the bare minimum. Nothing, if possible—no packets, no handbag, no jewellery.

They drove in silence down the *Rua de Julius Nyerere*. The man drove very fast as did most in the city, oblivious of the children and the dogs. Weaving his way through the potholes, he swung into the roundabout at the end of the street. She glanced at the Catholic Church to her right. In spite of the fact that she had seen it a thousand times before, she never failed to marvel at the grandeur and style of the old Portuguese architecture. That the building looked tired and worn and was in desperate need of a coat of paint, did not detract from the solemnity of its pureness.

The church was like most of the buildings in Beira—soundly crafted and constructed, internally solid—but superficially dowdy and disreputable. She had been told that in the days of the one-party state, one was required by law to seek permission to paint a house, because all the houses were owned by the state. As permission could only come from Maputo, it could sometimes take months, or even years to gain the necessary approval. And even then, when the house had been painted, some officious bureaucrat could come along and order the house to be stripped and repainted—for the simple reason that perhaps he might not like the colour.

"So, you are the *guarda-costa* who does not speak?" She cast a mischievous glance at her driver, baiting him.

He ignored her, his attentions on the road ahead, and more particularly the Tata omnibus that was hogging the road. Beads of sweat had built up on his brow. It was already very humid, but it was one of Salim's rules that his male employees should at all times wear suits. An inane and archaic legacy of the colonial days, perhaps. But in Africa, men of substance wear suits.

"So *Senhor* Salim not only has your soul, he has your tongue as well?" she continued.

He grunted angrily as he pulled out past the Tata. "Silence, *puta.*"

"Ah-hah," she squealed. "It talks … it talks." She clapped her hands in delight.

The 4 x 4 pulled into the reserved parking bay in front of the hotel, as the gaggle of resident street children loitering on the pavement, fled across the road. Lurking in the shadows of a row of mango trees, they warily surveyed the big *guarda-costa* and the woman as they got out of the vehicle. A few recognized the woman and whistled and whooped at her. She smiled and waved back at them. One of the boys, braver than the rest, cartwheeled into the middle of the road, clowning about in a puerile display of braggadocio. She tilted her head to one side, acknowledging his courage.

★   ★   ★   ★   ★

She felt the big man's grip on her elbow as he steered her into the foyer. The lobby was empty. It was still early. That Goanese girl, Martha, was behind the desk, sallow and insipid under the yellow sheen of her skin. Glancing up from her tallying, she nodded at the woman and the *guarda-costa* with the thin trace of a smile.

"*Senhor* Salim is waiting in his office," she bobbed her head in the direction of a closed door, off to the side of the reception counter.

Salim was at his large expensive desk that gleamed darkly from the countless layers of polish. Unbidden, the woman sat down as Salim came around to greet her, kissing her lightly on each cheek. She did not withdraw, nor flinch, as she felt his breath against her face. She smelt the cigars and the cologne. As usual, the hotel manager was dressed in an expensive flannel suit of the finest imported fabric. It hung casually from his slight neat frame, as if moulded for his body alone. A fresh carnation peeked out discreetly from his lapel, a few tiny beads of water still glistening on the delicate petals.

"Ah, my Phoebe," he greeted. "How are we today? As usual, you are looking *tres chic*. Very relaxed. It becomes you." There was a hint of genuine fondness that did not pass unnoticed. Over the years the two had built up a relationship of relative trust and respect. Of course they had had their differences—not unnatural in a pimp and prostitute combination. A crude description. Salim would have preferred to describe it as a manager and hostess arrangement. But they had always resolved their differences and Salim had only raised his hand to her on two occasions—a long time ago.

He nodded to the *guarda-costa* standing awkwardly at the door. His signal to leave.

"I am well, Salim," she smiled easily. "But I was planning on going shopping today." She noticed his hair shining in the subdued burgundy lighting of the office. Lightly oiled, it was swept back off his forehead, accentuating the handsome, almost boyish face. The perfect foil for his rich ochre complexion. The ideal match for those searching black eyes.

"Ah, *ma cherie*," he consoled. "You know I do not like to call on you at such short notice. It is only when there is a very important visitor. And you are one of my best girls. I am a perfectionist. I offer only the best."

The flattery was routine, but nonetheless it was of comfort to the woman, if only by its routine. She knew she would do what Salim asked of her. She always did. It was inconceivable that it could ever be any other way. After all, did she not owe Salim an eternal debt of gratitude for rescuing her from the camps? That was nearly ten years ago. Was it not Salim who had taken that sore-infested starving waif in rags into his bosom? Was it not Salim who had fed her, cleaned her, clothed her and turned her into a thing of loveliness?

Salim had given her self-respect. He had given her hope. He had given her life. There had been only despair, when as a wide-eyed and hunted 13 year-old she had fled the deprivations of the UNHCR camp at Chimoio in the Manhica Province.

She remembered how the UN team had tried to repatriate her to Zimbabwe. Many times she had joined the endless queues at the Machipanda border post, and many times she had been turned back. She had not understood. Was she not a Zimbabwean? Had she not grown up as a child in the bush camps of the *chimurenga* fighters—the Zimbabwean guerrillas fighting the liberation struggle? Many times they had told her that she must be proud to be a part of the heroic struggle for Zimbabwe. She did not understand why she was turned back.

"What is the business?" she asked of Salim, pulling herself back.

He stroked her hair, almost paternally. "He is a visitor. A very important man."

"Who?"

"He is a senior Zimbabwean cabinet minister," he replied. "He is in room 416."

"When?"

"Now. He is waiting for you. He phoned me at five o'clock this morning, demanding a woman."

"Why did he not take a woman last night ... like everyone else ... to take a woman at night? That is the correct time." She wanted more detail. It was dangerous to go in blind.

"*Ma cherie.* You know how it is with these government people. They have important meetings at all times of the day and night. Who understands these matters of state?" She noted he was avoiding her gaze.

"And what about my fee?" she persisted. "These people do not carry cash."

"It is taken care of. It has already been added to the account. You will be paid by the hotel."

"And a tip? These important people do not give tips. They are so important that they do not understand kindness any more." She did not suppress the sarcasm.

"Okay, Phoebe," Salim sighed with infinite patience. "I shall include a substantial tip as well. *Não problema.*"

She knew there was something he wasn't telling her. She could tell that he was uncomfortable. The faint twitch at the corner of his mouth had returned, and still he was not looking at her.

"What is it Salim? What is it about this man that makes you uncomfortable?"

She'd always had that disarming directness that even Salim could not avoid. It was a strange mix of naïveté and gentleness, hardened against the background of her deprivation. She could read people. She could look inside their souls. Perhaps that was the consequence of having witnessed humanity at its depths on the streets of Beira.

"He has been drinking ... all night. There were no meetings." His mouth twitched as he loosened his tie. Even with the airconditioner on full, the heat from the street was infiltrating the confines of the office.

"Hah! And what else? He has had women in the room ... last night?" She knew.

"Yes. There were women." He looked down at the richness of the carpet.

"How many? Two? Five? How many Salim?" She would not let up. She had experienced these so-called VIPs. Their sordid appetite for women and drink was renowned. Especially the Zimbabweans.

Salim looked at her, embarrassed. "I don't know. Two, perhaps three."

The telephone rang and he snatched at it. She could hear that the voice on the other end was loud and aggressive. "Yes, *Senhor* Minister …." Salim was nodding. "She is here … she is on her way to you now, *Senhor* Minister."

She sighed as he put down the phone. Salim was beginning to get annoyed.

"Okay, " she lifted her hand in compliance. "I will go now."

Salim showed her to the door. Ignoring Martha's obvious sneer of distaste, she made her way to the elevator, preparing herself for the unsavoury prospect waiting for her on the fourth floor. It was a standard preparation that had become second nature.

Take the mind and soul from the body. The body is simply the vessel. And it is the body that they want. The heat and the energy of the flesh. That is all. They will never be able to buy the mind or the soul. Never. When you die the earth will take your body, the fire will consume it. But it cannot take that which is not physical, that which is not of matter. It is simple.

But of course, there was always the fear of AIDS. It was a primary concern—particularly with such people as these Zimbabweans. For the men, it was a cultural insult to have to wear a condom. It took away the sensual pleasure of what they called the 'skin to skin' sensation. Normally her clients would happily acquiesce to her demands of protection. But such people as this minister—well, they were different. Not even the regular monthly check-ups with that Red Cross nurse were of any solace. It would be too late …

She made a mental note to discuss this with Salim. It was unacceptable. Surely he would see that?

In the corridor, she brushed past the cleaning women who anxiously backed out of the way, in deference. Taking a deep breath, she knocked on the door of room 416. She heard a toilet flushing inside and a shuffling. The door opened to reveal the minister, wearing only a white hotel towel draped under his bulging stomach. He looked her up and down, critically, as if inspecting a heifer.

"Heh! My little *musikana*. Come." He flashed her a smile, revealing the absolute whiteness of his teeth. His lips were fat and loose, almost purple. Yet the face was not unhandsome.

She felt her heart jump. She didn't know why. Perhaps there was a familiarity about this man. It was nothing. He was a client. Nothing more. She had not spoken Shona for many years, but she recognized the *musikana*. Girl. Yes, she was a girl.

She followed him into the room. The white towel, contrasting against his blackness, had slipped down, revealing the flabby cleavage of his buttocks. He waddled, rather than walked. It was awkward, yet there was an arrogance about him that was plain. Possibly in his early 50s, his obesity had developed apace with his career, as was often the case with African politicians. It was a symbol of position and affluence. She had learned long ago that obesity did not necessarily equate to physical weakness. Looking at the man as he poured himself another neat whisky, she could see that he was powerful—strength begotten by his sheer bulk.

This man would wear no condom. That was plain.

The room was a mess and smelt of alcohol and stale sex. Empty beer bottles lay scattered over the crumpled bedclothes, limp and stained with damp patches. The man downed the whisky and belched loudly.

"What is your name, *musikana*?" he leered.

"Phoebe," she stated flatly. "What is yours?"

"Huh!" He lurched forward as he poured the last of the whisky into the glass. "You don't know me? I am surprised, *musikana*. You do not know who I am?" He stared at her, his eyes hooded.

"No, I do not." She stared back. "Should I?" She knew she was playing a dangerous game. This man's arrogance knew no borders.

"You are talking to the Zimbabwean Minister of State Security, *musikana*."

"Oh, I am? And does the Zimbabwean Minister of State Security always drink whisky this early in the morning?"

She was vainly hoping that her insolence would put him off—that he would chase her away.

"Hah!" he almost shouted, looking through her. "The Zimbabwean Minister of State Security can drink whisky all day and all night. He can take many women—all day and all night. That is the power of the position. That is my power." His gut heaved and the towel finally succumbed and dropped to the floor, revealing his sex, hanging heavily.

She closed her eyes for an instant, willing the soul away.

"Take off your clothes, *musikana*," he slurred. "You will now feel my power." He approached her, his penis engorging. "Like the others, you must feel the power." He laughed, a deep rumbling growl and his belly shook.

As she started taking off her T-shirt, she felt the surging explosion of pain across her cheekbones. She had not seen the flash of his fist. It had been remarkably fast for a man of such bulk. She fought back the tears. Tears, more of frustration than of pain. She should have known. He was such a man. The cruelty had been there in his eyes when he had opened the door.

She opened her eyes and willed herself to look directly at him. He was smiling as he threw her onto the bed.

Three

It was mid-morning on a Saturday in the city of Lusaka. The freshness of the early morning was beginning to wither as the citizens of the capital went about their business in their never-ending conflict with poverty. Oscar was as usual sitting in the back seat of the Pulsar as it made its way south down Cairo Road, the city's main thoroughfare. He was gently strumming a riff he had put together the previous evening—around the braai at Connelly's house. Every once in a while he added some lyrics as they came to him—about cruising down Cairo Road—about being stranded on the escarpment—and about a state of well-being. His contentment was apparent.

The car drew stares from the curious citizens, which wasn't surprising. It wasn't every day that they saw a Zimbabwean car loaded up with white muzos and musical equipment. Black muzos—yes. Cool rasta dudes with dreadlocks tucked under those saggy, beret-type affairs, coloured in gaudy reds, yellows and greens. Or the more common traditionalists wearing jeans and teardrop shades, like the Congolese rumba muzos from across the border. But white muzos! There weren't enough whites in Zambia to form a half-decent audience.

Mike smiled at the thought and concluded that a guitar was like a second passport in Africa. A muzo, be he black, white or the shades in between, was royal game. No trouble at border

20

posts or police roadblocks—he was someone without any political or ulterior motive. He was uncomplicated—there simply to provide music and soulfood to the people. He was integral to the psyche of African society. He was venerated.

Mike remembered the times journeying through Africa as a travelling salesman, without his guitar, merely his product samples. These were construed as 'goods' and as such were dutiable, or better still, provided the bribeability angle for a customs man. Without a guitar or a wadge of cash tucked less than discreetly between the most recently stamped pages of a passport, travelling in Africa was an exasperating, time-consuming, pain-in-the-ass experience. Unless you assumed the mood.

This had been reaffirmed the previous night when the green Pulsar had rolled over the top of the escarpment onto the open savannah that swept up towards Lusaka. There was a permanent customs checkpoint just before the bridge over the Kafue. With soldiers in reserve, leaning idly out of the blockhouse, the customs official in his white peaked cap with a green band had approached the car.

"Ahh ... you are musicians?" he asked, noticing the bulky Peavey speakers on the roof rack. He flashed a grin at Melvin. "You play geetarra?" He strummed an imaginary guitar, singing a tuneless 'chinka, chinka, chinka, chinka'.

"Yes, my friend, we are professional musicians," Melvin replied, somewhat pompously. Melvin always called black people 'my friend'. The way he said it immediately demonstrated a lack of aggression. He also prefixed the word 'musician' with 'professional', believing it added a certain amount of respectability to the profession. "You want a cigarette, my friend?" Melvin proffered Mike's packet of Madison.

"Where are you going to?" the customs man asked, taking a cigarette as if expected.

"Lusaka."

"Where are you coming from?"

"From Harare."

"Ohhh…" The customs man acknowledged in a singsong 'oh', that intimated he had now learnt something of extreme interest. "You singing at putty in Lusaka?"

"No, brother," Oscar leaned forward from the back seat. "We're doing a concert at a farm near Chilanga."

"Ja," interrupted Melvin, "we're singing at a rhinofest."

Mike found this irritating, knowing that Melvin's unasked details would surely complicate the issue and confuse the man further. But that was Melvin—he always knew best. Mike toyed with the idea of butting in and settling the matter with one loud straightforward explanation that the customs man would understand. But he held his tongue, figuring Melvin wouldn't let go. Another interruption would only compound the confusion.

The customs man was confused anyway. "What?"

Melvin laboriously tried to explain that a rhinofest was like a beerfest, with lots of music and drinking. And the reason these three white muzos were in Zambia was that they were providing the music for the rhinofest so that money could be raised to save the rhino. But he simply confused the man further. He had no concept of 'fests', least of all protecting endangered species.

"Brother," Oscar explained loudly, trying to assert himself over Melvin's protracted explanation, "it's just a very very big party—plenty music, plenty beer, plenty *mahoris*, plenty jig-jig."

The customs man laughed. Now he understood. Now they were talking his language. "These putty, is for *mulungu*, or for black people?"

Both Melvin and Oscar hesitated. It was important to answer carefully. They couldn't very well say that this was to be an exclusively whites-only party. Connelly had gone to great pains to warn them before they'd even left Harare, that the rhinofest angle was purely a front for getting a licence—and the requisite ministerial approval. Such a large congregation of whites in one place at the same time would have been regarded with extreme suspicion by the minister of law and order and would undoubtedly have been banned. The country was still jittery over the recent coup attempt.

"No, no, no, no, my friend," said Melvin expansively. "It's for everyone—black people, white people—brothers altogether." To Mike, the insincerity was obvious, but then that was a part of Melvin's style. He could lie with such charisma and conviction that only the absolute cynic would disbelieve him.

Melvin gave the customs man another pack of Mike's Madison as they were ushered on their way. They hadn't been asked for their papers. As they crossed the Kafue, Mike noticed the customs man in the rear-view mirror, two-stepping across the road towards the soldiers in the blockhouse, chinka-chinging an imaginary guitar.

"That was close," Melvin breathed heavily as they pulled away. "If he'd searched the cab he would have found all the dope." Melvin's tone hinted that they'd all be languishing in the Kafue police cells by now if it hadn't been for his smooth talking and quick thinking. He studiously assumed an exaggerated posture over the steering wheel, sitting erect, concentrating heavily into the darkness ahead.

Oscar's laugh of derision went unnoticed as Melvin detached himself from the other two and assumed responsibility for getting them all safely to Lusaka. His body language was saying "You guys, go ahead and get stoned. I'm a mature leader-type person. Just let me get on with the task at hand."

Mike found this irksome, but said nothing and cracked open another Mosi beer. "You wanna beer Oscar?" he asked, pointedly ignoring Melvin, stiff at the wheel.

"Ja. Are they still cold?"

Mike nodded and popped another Mosi. "Y'know, we're incredibly lucky that Jumbo stopped for us and fixed the car. Otherwise we would have been the night on the escarpment."

"Bloody amazing," agreed Oscar. "You break down in the middle of nowhere and a good buddy who you haven't seen for ten years just *happens* to be going fishing down at Chirundu for the weekend. *And* he's a qualified mechanic. I mean … I ask you!"

Mike was shaking his head slowly, still unable to grasp the reality of their good fortune (which Melvin believed he'd engineered). What's more, not only was Jumbo a qualified mechanic, but he also had a full set of tools—sockets, torque wrench, the lot. *And* he had that gasket cork stuff. In no time at all, he'd whipped off the head and had fashioned a new gasket. He'd stated that he didn't think the head was cracked—maybe warped, but it should hold until Lusaka. Just keep an eye on the water level. There was nothing wrong with the gauge, he'd said. Oh ja! And take this jerry can of water—just in case.

The only downer, Mike thought, was that Jumbo wouldn't be at the rhinofest where they could repay his hospitality with some replacement Mosis. And return his jerry can. But Jumbo was obviously a purist and fishing came first. Oh well, it had been good to see him. Perhaps next time.

Melvin had maintained his frosty air of responsibility all the way to Lusaka, which was okay for Oscar and Mike. If that's what he wanted, then that was his buzz. Lusaka had crept up on them. Firstly the occasional twinkling lights on the outskirts, increasing in intensity as they neared the city. Mike noticed that most of the properties on the road were walled—big eight or ten-foot unpainted walls made out of cement blocks, with broken glass cemented in on top.

"Crime's a major problem here," Mike stated to no one in particular.

Oscar had been born in Zambia and considered himself an authority. "Yeah, these Zamboons. If they can't eat it, they either fuck it, steal it or break it."

This was Oscar's way of saying that the heady glamour of independence had vanished nearly a generation before in the face of poverty, corruption and mismanagement.

A minibus taxi rumbled past them at speed in the face of an oncoming cement truck, which didn't dip its headlights. Melvin took evasive action and jerked the wheel hard to the left, forcing the Pulsar over the one-foot cliff-face that marked the edge of the tarmac. The car crunched onto the gravel, scraping and grinding in a hail of dirt.

"Well, there goes the sump," said Oscar matter-of-factly.

"BASTARD!" Melvin hollered out of the window at the fast-fading taillights of the minibus.

Mike closed his eyes, as Melvin forced the car back over the ledge onto the road. A minute later Melvin hit a pothole and again the car bumped and jarred.

"You're gonna crack the CVs—and they've just been reconditioned," Mike snapped. The trip was fast losing the final remnants of any romanticism it had once held.

Melvin muttered an inaudible reply—something about the bloody roads and that it wasn't *his* fault. The roundabout at the southern end of Cairo Road approached and with it the first real glimpse of the city at night.

At a glance it looked like any other city at night—lit-up high-rises, neon lights, people cramming the sidewalks. Colours and brightness and noise. But through the buzz, the keener observer would see the decay and the hopelessness. He would smell the poverty and the filth. The high-rises were empty shells in which the lifts didn't work and there was shit on the stairways. The neon lights didn't flash and had dropped more letters than held. And the people were milling with nowhere to go, hoping against hope that something might miraculously turn up on the pavements and change their lives forever.

Melvin and Oscar had an argument about who gives way at a Zambian roundabout. Oscar said in Zambia you give way to the left and Melvin told him he was being stupid—because that meant you would have to give way to cars approaching the roundabout—whilst you were *in* the roundabout. Mike knew, correctly, that Oscar was getting confused with Mozambican roundabouts where you *do* give way to the left. Something of an old Portuguese legacy. But in Zambia, with its British influence still evident, you give way to the right.

Mike didn't say anything. They were both too stubborn to listen, and at any rate he didn't want to give Melvin the satisfaction of knowing he was right. Memories of the cylinder head and the CV joints were still too painful. Melvin somehow managed to weave his way through the roundabout, refusing to give way to anybody—taxis, diplomatic limos, four-by-fours, cyclists, pedestrians. Anybody. Melvin was angry and Mike could see his jaw was set.

They arrived at Connelly's townhouse around ten—16 hours after leaving Harare—to find that the welcoming braai was in full swing, and the bunch of white Zambians were all more than half-drunk. Evidently Jumbo had phoned through from Chirundu to tell Connelly that the muzos had been delayed, but were on their way.

There were two genres (three including the diplomats and aid workers) of whites in Zambia—the ex-pats (generally British) and the born or naturalized white 'Zambians', formerly Northern Rhodesians. The latter, including a sprinkling of Afrikaners, were closely related to the white 'Rhodies' south of the Zambezi. Although they would strongly proclaim their own identity, there were many cultural similarities in dress, accent, way of life and racial attitudes.

Connelly had lived all his life in Zambia, having been brought up on his father's farm in the Mkushi district, east of the Copperbelt. His upbringing had been austere. During his school holidays he was put in charge of the cattle and had to account for every single beast after the weekly dipping. If any animal was missing, Connelly was forbidden to return home until he had found it. As a result, he found himself scouring the 20,000-acre ranch for the larger part of his holidays, surviving off the veld as best he could.

During the brief intervals he was actually at home, he would be punished by his heavy-drinking Irish father for the slightest misdemeanour. His normal punishment was to be locked in a cupboard for several days.

He'd once told Mike that when he returned home after six years of soldiering in Rhodesia and South Africa, he and his father had had their final confrontation. Father and son had fought it out in a gun battle in old man Connelly's living room. Young Connelly had left Mkushi, never to return. The old man never bothered to fill in the bullet holes over the mantelpiece and would tell his friends, "There's the proof … that bastard son of mine."

There were both ex-pats and white Zambians at the braai, and as usual the conversation was about farming and the blacks. Connelly was hurting with laughter as he described the night he caught some of them trying to climb over his wall into his yard. He'd let the rotties loose and they'd chased the bastards up into the fir trees on the edge of the property.

"There were three of them. Two of them went swinging through the trees like chimps and escaped into the vlei across the road," Connelly chuckled at the memory. "But the other was so high up the tree, hanging on like a vervet, that he couldn't get down in time."

The wind direction changed, enveloping Connelly in billows of smoke from the braai. The boerewors and the steaks smelled good. "I could see what had been happening from the kitchen window and I knew there was still one zot stuck up the tree. So I took out ol' Bertha here," he patted the Magnum on his hip, "and went over to the tree to see what tasty morsel the rotties had got for themselves."

Connelly's friends had heard the story before but it was a good story, so they listened intently, if only to impress upon the muzos that it was worth paying attention.

"So I peered up the tree, but it was helluva dark and the bastard was right at the top—hiiiigh up like a Christmas fairy.

I could sort of make out his shape but the top of the tree was swaying a lot in the wind. I shouted at Joyce to bring the torch but the damn batteries were flat. Meanwhile the rotties are going crazy, jumping up and down, trying to get up the tree ... hey, Thinus... gimme a Mosi." Connelly paused as Thinus passed him a beer. He squirted some over the braai as the flames started to get out of hand.

"Anyway, I thought this was a great opportunity for some night shooting, so I started popping away with Bertha. But it was bloody difficult trying to shoot vertically above. *And* the branches kept swaying and every time the zot moved about, he showered me with all sorts of leaves and shit."

"So, did you get him?" Melvin asked, intrigued.

"Dead right. After seven or eight shots, I got him straight through the poophole. I reckon the shot must have come out of his mouth 'cause he didn't even yodel. Just plummeted like a sack of mealies and nearly landed on top of me."

"Ja, I reckon the coon didn't half shit himself," Thinus interjected loudly.

"Hell, talk about a dead ringer!" a young English mechanic with a Scouse accent chipped in from the back of the braai. The assembly recognized the pun and screamed with laughter.

"Ja, like a seven hundred mile-an-hour vertical enema!" Thinus added, not to be outdone. The laughter became hysterical.

"No. Anal envelopment," Connelly concluded. The laughter reached a crescendo.

"And then what happened?" Thinus prompted. "The rotties get stuck in?"

"No ways...they don't eat coon. They're fussy." Connelly replied to further laughter.

"No, seriously. I had to call the cops. Couldn't chuck the body next door—even though they are bloody Bulgarians—or something like that. But—normal story, the cops didn't have transport, so I had to go'n collect Inspector Mulenga myself."

The wind direction changed again and Connelly shifted his position. "Anyway, he was chuffed. Didn't even open a docket. Said it was a good thing that the citizens of Lusaka were assisting in crime prevention. But it was a bit embarrassing 'cause the rotties wanted to chomp him as well."

"Ja, he's a good kaffir. Don't take no shit from the coons," said Thinus.

Oscar had pulled out his guitar and was tuning up next to the trestle table that was the makeshift bar. Connelly, still chuckling to himself, was turning the meat. It was about ready. One of the wives, a plumpish woman in her late 20s came up to Mike and started making small talk. Mike thought her name was Lilette, or something like that. There was a hint of an Afrikaans accent and Mike guessed that Thinus was probably her husband. He was standing next to Oscar, waiting eagerly for the sing-along to get going.

"Hey Oscar," Mike heard Thinus say. "D'you know *Me an' Bobby McGee*'?

Lilette was quite pretty, but she was drunk and had whisky on her breath. She was swaying gently next to Mike and occasionally bumped against him—either oblivious or deliberate. Oscar had ignored Thinus' request and started with John Denver's *Grandma's Feather Bed*. Lilette picked up the beat and began moving clumsily to the rhythm. Mike always admired how well Oscar played *Grandma's Feather Bed*. He had it down pat—snappy chord changes, fast tempo and he knew all the words—well.

Lilette over-compensated and crashed against Mike who staggered a bit, but did well to hang on to his brandy and Coke. He glanced over at Thinus, nervous that he might misconstrue the situation and come over and belt him a shot. But Thinus was fully engrossed in *Grandma's Feather Bed* and was clapping and singing along loudly. Lilette's arm was now around Mike's waist. Embarrassed, he didn't reciprocate, but she hung on tightly anyway.

Over by the braai, Connelly was telling Melvin about the time he'd shot the neighbour-from-across-the-road's dog. "Think he was a Yugoslav—probably a Serb."

Oscar had started on *Me and Bobby McGee* to Thinus's whoops of delight.

"A whopping Great Dane that was always barking. Used to stand on the balcony and bark all damn night—at nothing. So one night—it was Christmas Eve actually—I took out the rifle with the night sight."

Freedom's just another word for nothing left to say
An' nothing aint worth nothing, but it's free
Feeling good was easy Lord when Bobby sang the blues
Feelin' good was good enough for me ... good enough for me an'
Bobby McGee

"So I propped myself comfortably in my armchair next to the lounge window, pulled the curtain aside and rested the rifle on the burglar bars. *What* a perfect shot! The dog was *perfectly* silhouetted on the balcony."

Oscar modulated.

From the coal mines of Kentucky to the California sun
Bobby shared the secret of my soul
Standing right beside me Lord in everything I done
An' Bobby she done kept me from the cold.

"One shot only. Got the bugger right through the mouth. He must have been right in the middle of a bark when his mouth was wide open. Blew him right back into the Serb's bedroom. Blood, shit'n brains all over the place."

Lilette wasn't listening. Her arm had dropped down to Mike's backside. He felt her kneading the left buttock and let her, for a while.

"Saw the Yugoslav the next morning. He was furious. 'Some

bastard, he killa my dog.' Told him he better be careful—pretty violent neighbourhood. Anyway, no more dogs barking all night." Connelly laughed and began forking the meat into a big stainless-steel serving dish.

Melvin had helped himself to a piece of boerewors off the grill and was talking with his mouth full. "So Connelly, what's the story for the rhinofest?"

"Well, just an excuse for a piss-up. 'Bout time we had some white humour in this country. Bugger the rhino anyway. No one's too sure how many rhino are left. National Parks say there are only two left in the country, but others reckon there are five of them."

"How come?" asked Melvin, bemused.

"Who knows—maybe some farmer's got three stashed away somewhere," replied Connelly.

Lilette had disengaged her arm from Mike's butt and was now cramming a steak roll into her mouth. The grease was dripping out of the bread roll onto her floral frock. Thinus and Oscar had gelled and Thinus was singing a useful harmony to *Where have all the flowers gone?*

The rhinofest was to be *the* event of the year. The whites were coming from all over the country—from the Copperbelt, from Mkushi, from Livingstone, even a few from Chapata on the Malawi border. And of course a massive crowd of farmers was coming up from Mazabuka. Not since Independence in 1964 had there been one white assembly of more than 100 people. Now they were expecting over 800—perhaps 1,000.

A venue had been a big problem. You couldn't have it in a municipal hall or a country club—otherwise you'd get the blacks in off the street. Just to be nosy and let the whites know who really had the power. Bloody typical.

Lilette had now entwined herself around Melvin who was telling her to 'show us yer tits'. She was delighted with the attention and unbuttoned the top of her dress, somehow unclipping her bra at the same time with her other hand. She manoeuvred the two pendulous breasts out of their prison and held them up proudly for all to see. Connelly made some growling noises and attacked them, landing his mouth on one gigantic nipple. Lilette squealed like a banshee, pretending to try to throw him off.

In the end, an Afrikaans maize farmer, named Blignaut, had offered his Chilanga farm as a venue and the problem had been solved. Chilanga was ideal. It was a small town about 20 kilometres south of Lusaka. The town depended on the cement factory for its existence, but there were several affluent white farmers in the area, one being Blignaut.

Mike felt weary. He downed the brandy and Coke and made his way to the caravan that Connelly had organized for them in the back garden. He stripped off to his underpants and wriggled into the sleeping bag. From the other side of the house came the intermittent screeches of Lilette. Melvin had obviously taken out his guitar and had joined Oscar. They were into some standard rock 'n roll and the party was on.

Mike lit a cigarette in the darkness. For no discernible reason, he felt empty. He tried to analyse it, but found he couldn't. After all, these were the kind of people he'd grown up with. This was their culture. His culture? They would never change. Why should they? They had established their niche in Africa, and it was working for them. Perhaps that was it—he was still looking for his particular niche. Their culture was open to him. It always had been. But somehow he knew he didn't want it. He didn't know why.

He couldn't put his finger on it. After all, had he not been brought up in a privileged environment? The golden years of his youth? A golden age, they said. A middle class upbringing with plenty of sport and sunshine. His parents were middle class immigrants from England and mildly 'liberal'. But it wasn't something they used to shout about. Life was too good for that. And then the war had come along, and like a sheep he'd followed his friends into the army—the white army of Ian

Smith. To fight for right, to fight for morality against the black heathen hordes—against the cowardly murdering communist terrorists. To fight for the maintenance of standards. Something the world just couldn't understand. And neither could he. But what could he do? Only 18, he couldn't vote. Only 18, he was made to kill. For right.

His wife was one of them. The 'Rhodies' with their manufactured synthetic traditions. Perhaps that was part of the problem. Perhaps the marriage had been a desperate attempt to integrate into their world? To become one of them. But it wasn't working, was it?

It was like a hollowness, or perhaps a loneliness. He flicked the stub out of the window and curled up.

★ ★ ★ ★ ★

The Pulsar turned into Blignaut's farm. The gateposts were built out of rock, with a wagon wheel embedded into the stonework on either side. An ornate arch completed the entrance, and welded out of wrought iron was the name of the farm—El Dorado. Oscar wanted to know why every other farm in southern Africa was called either El Dorado—or Maranatha. A long avenue of jacarandas in full flower led up to the homestead. On either side of the driveway were the wheat lands, now harvested. Massive John Deere tractors were working in the dust, ploughing up the wheat stubble, preparing the lands for the summer maize crop. In time for the rains.

Four

She'd said nothing to Salim when she came down the stairs from room 416. She hadn't needed to. The deadness in her eyes told it all. Norman Mubvunduku ... the Zimbabwean Minister of State Security ... the cruel one.

Salim had handed her the envelope, but not before he'd shuffled her inside his office, like a pariah—away from the public eye. She had wanted to scream. What was he so afraid of? That the concierge would see her? That Martha, that sallow wench, would see her? What was he protecting? His reputation? Hah!

"*Ma cherie ...*" Salim had started, but she'd cut him short with a swish of her hand. As if swotting a fly.

"You are angry, *ma cherie*. I was not aware that he might be this kind of man."

"Enough, Salim," she'd replied, flatly. "Get me to my *apartamento.*"

The same *guarda-costa* had driven her back to *Rua de Julius Nyerere 86.* In absolute silence, which gratified her. There was nothing to say. Without switching off the motor, he'd pulled up outside *2B Apartamento* and she gingerly climbed out. The pain was beginning to tell.

That was this morning. She had slept for over six hours and had woken to the sound of a football thumping against the front door. She screamed out of the window at the urchins, who fled in a flurry of dust and squeals. They had never seen the woman as angry as this.

It was then that she felt the pain in her loins. It was a scalding, rasping pain that cut into her private parts like a hot knife. Wincing, she undid the zipper of her jeans and carefully put her hand on the pain. She felt the blood, partially congealed and tacky—like the blood from a joint of meat not quite cooked. Too afraid to explore further, she made herself a cup of black coffee and counted out the money from the envelope that Salim had given her.

There was more than she'd expected. A lot more. Cramming it into the wooden vase with the plastic daffodils, she slowly got to her feet and made her way to the bathroom.

Blood money, she thought. Salim had known all along what that man was like. That was why he'd paid her more. To salve his conscience. Blood money. Blood money for the cruelty. But had he known of the extent of the cruelty? Or the method of the cruelty? Had he known that Mubvunduku would use his fist? Had he known that Mubvunduku would lose his erection because of the whisky, because of the excesses he'd already indulged in with the other women? No, he wouldn't know that. He wouldn't know that Mubvunduku would become insanely angry, furious at his own impotence. And that he'd hurl the woman to the bed and use his fist so brutally that she bled.

No, he wouldn't know this. The matter would have been closed when he handed over the envelope.

Holding back the tears, she forced herself to get into the bath. It was too hot, but that was how she wanted it. Perhaps the heat would purge the pain and the foul taste of cruelty. Of course, it had happened before, but never like this. Never with such venom.

After a while the soothing effects of the hot water kicked in and she felt better, if only marginally. The intensity of the heat made her feel light-headed, yet it was a good feeling. She closed her eyes and drifted away, uncaring. Oblivious to the pinkness in the water, oblivious to the dullness of the pain, now ethereal and unconsuming.

She thought about the pineapples at the market. And about the Martha Viera casette she had been planning to buy that morning. Fleetingly, she considered going to the market later to buy these things. If she ever recovered the energy to get out of the bath. Yes, it would be a good thing to go to the market—almost as if the whole interlude with the Zimbabwean had never happened.

His face came back to her, the boyish features and those full, soft lips. He had talked a lot. Not to her. Just talking. He talked about the war, as if it had happened only yesterday. It was as if he were boasting.

But she knew he was drunk. She didn't listen. He'd hit her again because she hadn't been listening. So she tried to pay attention, although the words were blurred and meaningless. About how he was a political commissar during the struggle and that PCs were very powerful people. That they controlled the war effort against the white settler regime of the fascist Ian Smith. That the PCs controlled the minds and bodies of the cadres and that he could, and did, have any female cadre he wanted.

She vaguely remembered the camps. She vaguely remembered the name Ian Smith. But that was 20 years ago. Nearly a generation.

She had not known of the commencement of the *Chimurenga* war of liberation that the black Zimbabwean nationalists had initiated with the first shots at the Battle of Chinhoyi. The volleys that echoed across the veld of the then Rhodesia in 1966. Neither had she known that during the next ten years of sporadic warfare, the Rhodesians would practically decimate the fledgling guerrilla movements.

The ill-equipped and poorly trained cadres had been gunned down in their dugout canoes as they attempted to cross the

Zambezi River into Rhodesia—from their havens in Zambia. The few who made it across were soon hunted down in the inhospitable Zambezi valley—long before they ever had the opportunity of reaching their targets—the highveld, with its teeming peasant masses and scattered white farmers.

It all changed in 1974. A socialist coup in Lisbon saw to that. Within weeks the incoming Portuguese regime had divested itself of its African colonies—Angola, Mozambique and Guinea-Bissau. For over a decade in all the three territories, the depleted and weary Portuguese Army had been fighting the respective nationalist guerrilla movements in protracted and bitter struggles.

Mozambique was handed to the dominant liberation movement, Frelimo, the Front for the Liberation of Mozambique. Samora Machel, a one-time semi-literate male nurse, became the new president in 1975. Following his inauguration, he opened his doors to the renegade Zimbabwean nationalist, Robert Mugabe, and his embryonic liberation movement, Zanu (PF), the Zimbabwe African Nationalist Union.

The letters 'PF' referred to the tenuous alliance the party had maintained with the other member of the Patriotic Front, Joshua Nkomo, and his predominantly Ndebele Zapu (PF) movement. The Patriotic Front was a poorly-conceived ploy to convince the Frontline States of the OAU, the Organization of African Unity—primarily Tanzania and Zambia, that unity did in fact exist amongst the rival Zimbabwean liberation movements.

Within a very short time, Mugabe had established a necklace of training and logistical camps within Mozambique, facing the 1,000-kilometre border of Rhodesia. Under the able and intelligent leadership of the charismatic general, Josiah Tongogara, Zanla, the armed wing of Zanu (PF) was able to flood the eastern border areas of Rhodesia with thousands of dedicated and highly motivated guerrillas. Within months the guerrillas had infiltrated the hinterland and were politicizing the masses in the very heart of the country.

By 1977 the tide of war had begun to turn. The Rhodesians, under-equipped and under-manned, in desperation began resorting to cross-border raids—to strike at the guerrilla bases in Mozambique in an effort to eliminate the freedom fighters before they had a chance to infiltrate the country. The slaughter escalated, as the Rhodesians accounted for thousands upon thousands of guerrilla and civilian casualties. But their external military operations were beginning to embarrass their only remaining ally, the South Africans, who gradually began to withdraw their support.

By the late seventies, the writing was on the wall for the beleaguered Rhodesians.

Casualties were mounting and emigration had reached alarming levels. United Nations sanctions were becoming increasingly effective—and the guerrilla juggernaut became unstoppable. In late 1979 the British Government finally persuaded all the warring parties to sit around a negotiating table and the Lancaster House Agreement was born—the framework for an independent Zimbabwe, with a black majority government.

In April 1980, after 14 years of civil war, peace came to the war-ravaged country. But not before the Rhodesians were able to play their last cruel card. Renamo, the Mozambican National Resistance Movement, was secretly conceived by the Rhodesian Central Intelligence Organization, the CIO.

With no political party line, other than to destroy Frelimo and the Mozambican economy, Renamo was to become one of the most brutally effective counter-revolutionary movements on the African continent. Supported by the South Africans after the demise of the Rhodesians, Renamo embarked on a fearful civil war of attrition that was to bring Mozambique to its knees. In spite of the fact that Frelimo was shored up by the Zimbabwean National Army, its erstwhile allies, the former guerrillas of Zanla, there was little the inflexible and bureaucratic regime could do to stop the waves of rebels.

For fifteen long years the war dragged on, until eventually in 1993 Frelimo was forced to declare multi-party elections. After a generation of bloody guerrilla warfare, peace had finally come to the country.

It was in this cauldron of deprivation and death that the young Phoebe had grown up. She knew little of the history. She knew little of any other way of life to that she had lived. She was a product of that generation—lost and confused. The bath had cooled. Her feet and fingers were pink and wrinkled. But the pain had dissipated, as had the blood in the water.

She got out and still wet, stood naked in front of the mirror. She stood like that for a very long time, oblivious of the water dripping from her body onto the floor where it lay in a pool at her feet. The parquet tiles were turning white from the water, as she tentatively put her hand to her face, to where Mubvunduku's fist had caught her the first time. She winced, but noticed the skin wasn't broken. Puffy and bruised and swollen, but not cut. That was something. As it was something he'd used his fist and not his penis. You couldn't get AIDS from a fist? Hah? She laughed out loud at the irony.

No, she would not forget Comrade Minister Mubvunduku. She would not forget.

Five

Back in Harare Mike was feeling irritable. He couldn't quite put his finger on it. It was just so—and he accepted it. It was almost as if there was an external force driving his life, though just right at that moment he felt as if this force had deserted him and that his life was drifting. In the doldrums. But it was often like that when things weren't happening ... well things just didn't happen. Yet he was not resentful. He'd long since learned that life owed him nothing. Not even life. And if his life was wallowing in nothingness, well ... so be it. Another cycle would come by, undoubtedly.

He therefore understood his irritability. Irritable at the fact that he was not in control. Oh how he envied those people who seemed to have their lives in order. He'd heard Lionel talking in the pub once, after work, about his five-year plan. At first he thought he was talking about some kind of communist five-year plan, like the one the Soviets used to try to implement back in the 30s. He'd listened in to the conversation, intrigued that someone like Lionel might actually know a bit of history outside of the Limpopo and the Zambezi.

But it wasn't so. Lionel was actually talking about a five-year plan for his own life and pretty well on the same grandiose scale as the Soviets ... back in the 30s. And the Chinese ... and the North Koreans. Even the Zimbabweans.

Mike decided that people who talked about five-year plans, particularly their own, were obviously idiots. Who the hell could predict what would happen tomorrow? Who particularly could predict what would happen in Africa tomorrow? Africa—the one-day-at-a-time continent. Well ... obviously Lionel could. Perhaps it was all only guesswork, and Lionel's guesswork had been minimized because he had a father who was a wealthy farmer who would always bale him out when things got tough—in the rough and tumble world of business.

Mike felt his irritability rising again and pulled himself back. It was futile getting all het up over someone like Lionel. Okay, so the jerk had been born with a silver spoon in his mouth and had been spoilt rotten all his life. But that wasn't his fault, was it? The same as it wasn't his fault that he was unaware of his own arrogance.

What galled Mike though, was the fact that there were many whites like Lionel in Zimbabwe. Whites who believed that they had some kind of inalienable right to the privileges that they'd inherited. He'd given up trying to argue this point with his contemporaries. They all assumed he was a socialist—or a lover of blacks. Their logic was simplistic. If you were white and didn't agree with their *raison d'être*, then you were either a TWoG or a lover of blacks—who was generally a Third World Groupie anyway ... either that, or mentally unstable.

He took another sip of his drink. His wife hadn't bothered to top up the fridge with Cokes or ginger ales on his return from Zambia. He had become superfluous in her life, so it seemed. Little George was in bed and she'd gone out at seven. Some pretext about a charity function at some school. She knew he would have checked up with the school, which he had, and that he would find there was no charity function at the school that night. Seemingly, she felt some necessity to give him some flimsy excuse for her infidelity. Going through the motions. Either that, or deliberately antagonizing him out of his inaction.

He had tried, or so he told himself. He finished his drink and felt faintly nauseous. It was the combination of too much alcohol with the sweetness of the mixture. With no Cokes, he'd had to use orange juice. Brandy, orange and water didn't go too well.

"Bugger Lionel," he muttered out loud. "Bugger them all. Have they forgotten already that there was the war? And life must just carry on … as if nothing ever happened?" He got up and went to the kitchen, where he poured himself another drink. It was the last of the orange juice. Well, down to straight brandy and water next.

He became bitter, which he didn't like in himself. But it was something he allowed occasionally—as a treat. A little self-indulgent bitterness. He knew it was the frustration of his wife's affair, combined with the cheap brandy.

"Hah!" He looked at the brandy bottle. The bastards even had the balls to put 'VSOP' on the label. It wasn't VSOP. It was recycled cane spirit. Like the gin in Zimbabwe. Like the whisky. Recycled. Wasn't that what they made that ethanol petrol out of as well? The entire country ran on cane spirit. His liver included. He laughed out loud at his own humour.

"VSORCS," he muttered to himself, still chuckling. "Very special old recycled cane spirit."

The Germans had a word for it—*ersatz*. It was a great word. Very appropriate. It even sounded like a cheap substitute. He'd read it once in a World War II book … somewhere about captured British pilots drinking *ersatz* coffee in the German PoW camps. He'd never forgotten, and all through the UDI years in Rhodesia, when international sanctions had been biting, the country had survived on *ersatz* home-made products. And they were proud of it!

And the damn country was still running on *ersatz*. It had become an inbred status quo. He went back to the living room and switched off the TV. Some re-run from the 70s Well … after all, that proved his point. *Ersatz* TV as well.

He put on a record and turned it up loud, but not so loud as to wake the baby. But Joe Jackson didn't suit his mood, so he changed it for Handel's *Messiah*. The sheer power of the music superseded his mood that wasn't particularly classical at that moment. Classical music he found, was always a great leveller. It kind of put things into perspective … well at the least it put you back in your place—in the grand scheme of things.

Drifting away with the music, he vaguely wondered what time his wife would be home. Hardly likely before midnight. At least he'd have a couple of hours alone with his thoughts. It was a rarity. And thank goodness little George was now sleeping through. It had always been he who had to attend to the baby when he'd woken at night. When he was home, that is.

"Your turn," she'd grunt. "Go'n. Get out of bed."

And he'd attend to the baby. But the baby didn't know him and it always took forever to nurse him back to sleep. And then during the day he never saw the child. Either he was away out of the country on business, or at the office. Or if he did try, she'd come up with some pretext that she was trying to get him down and she didn't want him disturbing the baby. He didn't understand it. It was almost as if she was deliberately using little George against him. For what? But then again, he was away so often that it was difficult for him to measure what was normal and what wasn't.

So, there it was. A part-time, night-time father.

Zambia had been okay. In fact, apart from the problems with the car, the trip had turned out reasonably well. Connelly had paid them in cash—US dollars. They'd all had to stash the money away when they came back through the border. Along with the dope. Of course, Melvin had been melodramatic and had insisted on cramming his greenbacks into one of the hubcaps. He'd tried to bully Mike and Oscar into doing the same, but they told him to get lost and stowed the cash in their underpants.

It was because Melvin had ostensibly 'made' the rhinofest, that he felt he could behave in such a manner. So … he probably had, but that didn't give him the right to act the main *man*.

Mike smiled to himself. Melvin would never change. People just didn't. It was as Oscar had said once after he'd been to an old school reunion. "Y'know, I hadn't seen old whatsisface for 20 years. He was my senior at school and he was a real ass. I see him at the reunion ... and y'know what? After 20 years, he's still a full-on ass."

Just as it was in Melvin's make-up that he should score with a chick at the concert. Oscar didn't. Mike didn't. But Melvin did. The funny thing was that Melvin hadn't even remembered who had given him the blow-job round the back of the stage.

"Can't remember who the bitch was. All I remember was that she klunked of whisky. Had whisky all over my dick."

"You should have dipped it in some soda water," Oscar had quipped.

"Nah. A true Scotsman takes it neat."

They all laughed. It had been good. Then Oscar told Melvin that it was Lilette, that Afrikaans chick, who had given him the blow-job.

"How do you know?"

"Because she gave me one the night before at Connelly's boogie an' said how she digged giving head."

"Don't talk shit. You're talking crap." Melvin was seriously concerned that his reputation might become tarnished. It was unheard of that he should ever take 'seconds'.

"S'true," Oscar was almost crying with laughter. "An' y'know what else? Her husband Thinus saw her ducking round the back to check you."

"Bullshit."

"I'm telling you. An' he knows you're the dude, because Mike and I were on stage."

There was a momentary silence while Melvin absorbed this. "You mean ... Thinus ... that big Dutchman?"

"The very one. Connelly told me that he was looking for you, but he was so *frot* drunk. Why d'you think Mike and I wanted to hit the road so early the next morning? To save your ass—that's why."

Oscar's explanation was partially true, but Mike hadn't expanded, that the real reason was that he was worried about the car and didn't want to take the chance of breaking down again in the middle of nowhere. Anyway, it was always good when Melvin felt he owed you. Not that it lasted for too long.

There had been 800 whites at the farm in Chilanga that night. Connelly had said they'd be talking about it for years. They'd boogied until dawn, with Melvin discovering early on in the evening that the lowest common denominator was alcohol and vulgarity. Never before in the history of either Zambia or Northern Rhodesia had 400 white women all bared their breasts simultaneously.

Not wanting to be outdone, Connelly himself clambered up on to the stage and had drunkenly attempted to sing a duo with Melvin. Mike thought it had been *The Wild Rover*, but couldn't remember. What he did remember though, was that at the end of the song, overcome by the sudden fame, Connelly had resisted Melvin's efforts to leave the stage and instead performed an impromptu strip. Outraged, Connelly's wife Joyce, had also clambered up on to the stage and dealt her wayward husband a series of severe blows. Melvin on stage, and Mike and Oscar in the wings, collapsed with laughter.

A car's headlights swung through the kitchen curtains and Mike knew his wife was back. He hadn't attended to the Pulsar since his return, but it seemed to be running fine. He hadn't told her about the problems in Zambia. What for? Certainly she'd said nothing and he'd been using it daily.

As a matter of course, he stood up and went to greet her at the door. More conditioning than manners. If he didn't, she'd want to know why, and was there a problem? And he'd say, yes, there was a problem, and the whole merry-go-round of recriminations would start. And they'd end up in a slanging match and she'd holler like a banshee that he was the one who'd always been unfaithful—what with his singing and those scum-bag muzo mates of his. And then the baby would wake up, and he'd end up trying to get him back to sleep, because she would have stormed off to have a bath. To wash away the traces of sex, no doubt. He didn't feel he could handle a scene. The confrontation. Always the confrontation. And anyway, there was little George to consider … So he got up. As he opened the door for her, she glared at him, her face flushed. He noticed a fresh red mark on her neck but said nothing. She noticed him noticing and glared again.

"Hi. The meeting go on a bit late?" The charade began.

"Yes …. you know these fund-raising people." She brushed past him and deposited her handbag on the kitchen counter, pretending to busy herself with the contents.

"So … who was there? Anyone I know?"

She didn't look up. "Oh, you know … the usual."

He hadn't moved from the door, which was still open. Tactically, he didn't know where to position himself. In fact, tactically, he had no idea what to do or say next. He knew that now was the perfect opportunity to get it all out in the open. But of course, she would lie and deny 'til the cows came home.

"Was … whatsisname there?" he asked, not wanting to say his name.

"Who?"

"That friend of yours … your confidant." He couldn't keep the sarcasm from his voice.

She turned on him, her eyes ablaze. "Listen … I'm sick and tired of your jealousy. It's so … so … ugly. D'you know how hard it is to live with someone who's always jealous? Honestly, Mike. I wish you'd grow up. Now … if you don't mind, I'm going to bed. It's been a long day and I'm exhausted."

"I want to talk to you. It's important."

She turned halfway down the passage. "That's your problem Mike. It's always important. Maybe you should have thought of that before, when you were having a good time with all those groupies. You've had your fun. Now it's my turn." She slammed the bedroom door behind her as little George whimpered softly in his cot.

Mike froze. "Please, please, don't let him wake up," he whispered to himself.

The bedroom door snapped open a few inches. "And turn that shit down. Why don't you ever listen to normal music?" And slammed again.

He sighed. Round one thousand and whatever to her—again. Collecting his empty glass from the lounge, he went back to the kitchen, catching sight of his reflection in the window. He studied himself for a while. His physique wasn't that bad, was it? It wasn't totally unattractive? Okay, he wasn't tall, but he wasn't short either. Five ten was an okay height. He still had all his hair and it wasn't grey, although he had noticed the occasional whitish hair in his moustache. Sandy hair. Would he be more attractive to her if he were blonder?

Nah. She didn't want him. Period. It wasn't his body. He didn't work out, but he was in good shape. Not trim—but no paunch, no gut. Not like a lot of other guys in their mid to late 30s who had monstrous beer-bellies which spilled out over their boxer shorts.

Was it his face? It wasn't a classic, rugged, good-looking face. The nose was maybe a fraction too big—or rather too long. But did that warrant infidelity? Did the Adam's apple, which protruded a fraction too much warrant infidelity?

No loose flesh, no bad breath, no obvious deformities. Just ordinary. Perhaps that was it? There was nothing about him that was out of the ordinary. He was simply mediocre.

And his mind? Did that not count for anything? He was brighter than most, but perhaps she saw that as a threat. God had got things the wrong way around for him. He should have given him a stunning physique and an ordinary mind. Well, to get anywhere with a woman in Zimbabwe, like her, that is.

But it hadn't always been like that with her. Had it? I mean, there'd been good times too. Think back to when you first met her. That time at the battalion dance. You'd been smitten by her. It was love at first sight. And how you had laughed with her.

Not always bad times. Not always. But when did it start to go wrong? And even now, she wasn't a bad woman. They'd just gone down different paths, that's all.

"Enough, Mike," he chided himself softly. "There you go again on one of your analytical, self-pitying, waste-of-time jaunts."

Handel was ended, so he put on Mozart's *The Magic Flute*. You had to balance the volume settings right with the *The Magic Flute*. The opening stanzas were so soft that it was tempting to turn the volume up. And then just as you had sat down, Mozart would hit you with a crescendo and blast you out of your chair. He'd learnt this.

The brandy and water tasted bitter, but it didn't worry him. It wasn't the taste he was after. Sinking into the armchair, he tried to clear his mind, to think rationally and unemotionally, in order to make some decisions—and to plan. For a second he thought about putting a five-year plan together. If you had a five-year plan, then perhaps you would have a set of clearly-defined goals and objectives. Simple. Then you couldn't deviate.

He gave it up. To understand the future meant understanding the past. And how could you understand anything if you didn't understand yourself? Work on what you know. Work with tangible realities.

The first reality, that had been staring him, unseen, in the face for some while, was that his marriage was finished. That was a tangible reality. Don't try to understand why it is finished. Don't try to analyse the effects of the war. The fact that you got married too young. The fact that you are a heavy drinker, that you take drugs. Don't. One step at a time. It is pointless even to attempt to resolve all the extraneous issues. Point One is Step One is that the marriage is dead. Address that first. It is tangible. It is comprehensible. As it is a reality that she is no longer interested in resolving anything. How can two people come to an agreement if one of the parties won't even come to the table?

He felt better. Of course it would be painful. There was little George to consider. But that was unfortunate. Kids or not, the relationship with her was gone forever. Further, the so-called paternal bond just wasn't there. She'd seen to that, hadn't she?

The music came to an end as the record continued to turn mindlessly with a gentle shh-shh-shh. He resolved to confront her in the morning and fell asleep with the unfinished brandy still in his hand.

He awoke that morning with a stiff neck. She had gone. God knows where. Probably shopping, or aerobics ... or to see old lover-boy. Guiltily slugging back the half-glass of brandy, he decided to have a shower. He would go to Mozambique. Some pretext about a business trip. Away from it all.

The resolve of the previous night had dissolved. He'd known that it would.

Six

The woman had an old towel wrapped around her waist and up over her breasts. It was to keep the baby in. She was barefoot, following the edge of the tide out. Mike had been sitting in the sand for over an hour now, watching her every move. His mind was in neutral, blown empty by the offshore breeze that came across from the Pungue estuary. It was a good feeling, like being suspended in time's own momentum.

The woman was hunting for little molluscs in the wet sand—or periwinkles as Mike remembered from his childhood. She was an expert. Or so it seemed to Mike, judging by the heavy bulge in the grey plastic packet she carried in her left hand. She'd had a good haul.

He watched her move quickly, yet unhurriedly after a retreating wave—or rather the spent residue of a tame ripple. It seemed that timing was the key to the exercise, when the small frothy bubbles of the periwinkles were visible for a few moments, before the sheen of wetness vanished in a twinkle into the sand. She obviously mapped out the target area before the attack. In an instant, making a mental note of a dozen or so spots, for the tell-tale signs would be gone before she'd finished scooping out the first mollusc. And then she'd move on to where the next one had been, and deftly flick the little animal into the plastic packet.

He wondered whether she was doing this for the family meal that night, or was it perhaps to supplement the family income—if any? He realized how little he knew of these people. Of their lives. He assumed they had never known anything other than poverty and tyranny. So to them that was the norm. That was the yardstick by which they measured happiness and misery. But surely such people could not afford the luxury of philosophizing? To fill their bellies—that was what life was about.

He felt guilty. His crass, superficial judgement was unasked for. He'd been arrogant enough to assume he could even begin to analyse—to judge. He stood up and dusted the sand off his shorts. He walked down to the water's edge and watched the woman from a few feet away. The baby on her back was asleep, unbothered by the shifting and sliding as the mother bent over and stood, bent over and stood. Again and again and again. Dried mucus, laced with sand, was crusted under the baby's nose.

The mother glanced briefly at the white man next to her, unfazed. She had a job to do. Mike thought that maybe she was thinking: "What does this white man want? Is this job really so interesting to him? Why is he not up there on the esplanade, drinking *cerveja* with those other white people?" And then he thought that perhaps she didn't think anything—and that was worse.

He considered opening a conversation with her, but didn't. He wanted to ask her so many questions. Did she do this every day? For how long? Did she like eating molluscs? And how did she cook them? But it would have come across as patronizing. His questions would have made no difference to her life. Respect her as she was. No more, no less. That was how it was in Africa.

It struck him that she had achieved an important reckoning point. To his inexpert eye she was an expert. She was unquestionably the best periwinkler he had ever seen. She was without peer. Could he say that about himself—not periwinkling—anything? He wasn't a good salesman, even though everyone said he was. He was a reasonable guitarist, but not an expert. Not like her and her periwinkling skills. Was it okay to be just okay? Perhaps. Why were white people so damn get-ahead competitive?

He looked at the woman again, still engrossed in her work. The hem of her ragged dress was wet. The blackness of her legs shone with the wetness, but he noticed her skin was dry and lifeless and uncared for. Of course, that was it—she couldn't afford petroleum jelly. He was briefly surprised. Surely petroleum jelly was a part of their culture? He smiled at the woman and half-waved as he turned and walked slowly up the beach to his spot. The soft white sand felt good and comforting between his toes. He sat down and pulled out the pack of Marlboros. Beira was Marlboro country. He always smoked Marlboro in Mozambique. Just as he always smoked Camel plain in South Africa. Or Chesterfields in Zambia. Or Madison in Zimbabwe. It was a thing with him. The associated flavour of the country.

He bit the filter off the Marlboro and spat it out. He'd picked up the habit from an American buddy in the war nearly 20 years ago. At first he did it because it was cool; it was different. But the habit stuck. Anyway you couldn't buy Marlboro plain in Mozambique.

He heard a shout from farther down the beach and saw the scampering black figure of João coming towards him. He smiled. The little urchin had found him. Like a faithful dog, João flopped in the sand beside Mike, grinning broadly. He had been swimming with a bunch of street kids. His hair was still wet and droplets of water clung like diamonds to the tight black curls. Distractedly, Mike thought that João's hair was an irritating length—or height. It was sort of in-between. It was not short and it was not long. In-between and scruffy. Like the street kid he was.

He smiled at the boy and offered him a Marlboro. João never asked, but when he was offered, he took. Mike lit it, cupping the Zippo. The boy inhaled loudly, showing off. He held the cigarette between the thumb and the forefinger of his one hand. He had probably seen that James Dean poster outside the downtown cinemas, on the wall alongside the crudely daubed revolutionary graffiti.

"Why aren't you guarding the truck?" Mike asked out of formality, more than concern.

The boy took another long drag and shrugged. "*Não problema*. I go."

"No, it's okay. Later."

The woman had packed up for the day. Mike hadn't noticed her go and chided himself for his lapse in observation. But that would have been how she had wanted it. To get on and away, unobtrusively.

"I come to Zimbabwe?" João asked Mike the daily question. "Zimbabwe is good, huh?"

"You haven't got a passport. How can you come?"

"*Não problema*. I jump off truck before *fronteira*. Walk, walk, walk." Joao walked the fingers of his one hand purposefully in the sand, as if he was walking across the border. "Walk to Zimbabwe. Wait on road. You come. We go together." He made it sound as if he'd thought over this strategy for a long time.

Mike laughed. The boy made it sound so simple. Perhaps it was. He had been tempted before and on the last trip had very nearly done it. It would be easy—as João said. Just drop him off on the side of the road before the border post and meet him on the other side. And so what if he didn't make it? He'd find his way back to Beira and try again next time. But at the last minute Mike had felt hesitant and the boy had stayed behind. It wasn't so much a question of caution, but rather a matter of why. What were his motives for doing something like that? For the boy, it was obvious—a new life. But for Mike? João wasn't his possession. He had his own life. What would he do in

Zimbabwe? His servant? His lackey? His *thing*? He pictured some of his Rhodie mates in that position. 'Hey, you okes! Come check my pet *munt*,' they'd boast.

Mike stubbed the cigarette out and poked it deep into the sand with his forefinger.

"Maybe João, I'll take you sometime," he said lamely.

"Tomorrow? When you go?" It was apparent to Mike that the boy had thought no further than simply getting to Zimbabwe. It was as if this was the end in itself, and having achieved that end it wasn't even a consideration that life wouldn't be okay after that. Almost incomprehensible.

Like all the other millions of homeless on the continent of Africa. Always moving, always migrating, as they'd been doing for thousands of years. East, west, north—but mainly south. To the magnets of Harare and Johannesburg, the city of gold. A mobile, teeming, seething continent—dynamic and volatile. Ever changing, regardless of the illogical colonial borders, those vestiges of the white man's greed and arrogance.

"No, not tomorrow. I'll tell you." Mike closed the subject and João was content.

The sun was out of sight now and the sky had turned pink. The breeze was noticeably cooler, but still pleasant on the skin. Apart from Mike and João, the beach was deserted.

"Come João," Mike stood up. "We go to the hotel."

João went racing off up the beach, his tattered clothes streaming like pennants behind him. Everything in his life was a new adventure.

It was his ritual. Even if he hadn't been guarding the pick-up truck, it was his responsibility to make sure he was there, on duty, when Mike arrived.

★　★　★　★　★

The Hotel Beira was one of two hotels in the city that was 'suitable' for foreigners. When Mike had first met Salim, the manager, he had gone to great lengths to explain to Mike that the hotel was owned by private investors. Businessmen from Maputo, he'd said. But everyone knew that the hotel was owned by the president's wife and that Salim was the front man. He belonged to the party.

Mike didn't like Salim and Salim didn't like him, although they both extended a frosty politeness to the other. On Mike's part, it was more a matter of mistrust. He found Salim obsequious and condescending, and although he could never prove anything, he was sure Salim read the faxes that he used to leave for Martha, that Goanese girl at reception, to send for him. He'd stopped sending his faxes from the hotel during the previous trip and preferred instead to make use of Colin's fax machine at the shipping office down by the docks. It was inconvenient, but less of a risk.

"Evening Salim," Mike nodded to the manager who was going through a pile of papers behind the reception counter.

Salim looked up briefly and returned the greeting with a slight bow. As always he was dressed in a black suit and bowtie. No doubt he was wearing his shiny black patent leather shoes below the counter. Image was important for Salim, thought Mike.

Two black prostitutes were sitting in the foyer. They were dressed in shimmery lamé outfits, obviously set for the evening's trade in the hotel night-club upstairs. One caught Mike's eye as he waited for his room keys. "Hi," she offered, lowering her gaze flirtatiously. The opposite end of the racial and moral spectrum, when compared to some of the white women in Zimbabwe, Mike thought briefly. Poles apart, cultures apart. Just so apart.

Mike noticed Salim smiling and felt irritated. "Martha … Four One Zero, *por favor!*" he demanded loudly.

Martha slid the keys across the counter. Out on the pavement the *porteiro* was chasing João away from the hotel front. It was an important duty for doormen in Beira, keeping the trash away from the establishment. João swore at the man and scampered off into the darkness of the vacant lot next door.

The lifts were working tonight as Mike swung open the wooden door of the cage. He pressed four and hoped he would arrive on the fourth floor. He did. The corridor smelt slightly dank. Mike opened his door and immediately scanned the room to make sure everything was still in place as he'd left it that morning. It was a habit of his. Watch your back! A legacy from Zimbabwe. Nothing seemed to be remiss and he tossed his briefcase onto the bed. He opened the large sliding windows and breathed in the warm sea air. It was humid tonight. João had said there was another cyclone on the way.

He decided to leave the windows open awhile before switching on the airconditioner. Opening the wardrobe, he pulled out a bottle of brandy from under his clothes and poured himself a drink—neat—into one of the tumblers from the bathroom. He'd long since given up on room service. There was always the language problem and anyway the drinks were so ridiculously expensive.

The liquor burned as it went down his throat, but he'd become accustomed to the sensation and liked it. He switched on the TV and decided the talk show on the Portuguese TV channel was preferable to the French football. If anything, it might improve his Portuguese. That first slug of brandy in the evening had become a ritual for Mike, his symbolic end to the stresses of the day, and a foretaste of the night ahead.

The phone rang and Mike jumped. He hated the telephone. It always meant bad news. Apart from his boss, and his wife back in Zimbabwe, who knew he was here? Anonymity was fast becoming part of his make-up and he resented the intrusion. He took another swig of brandy and made sure his cigarettes were close at hand, in case it was a long call.

"Hello," he answered, guardedly.

"Hi, Mike?" a long-distance voice crackled over the line. "It's me … Oscar. I'm phoning from Zim. Can you hear me?"

"Oh, yes. Hi, Oscar," Mike gulped at the brandy, more out of relief. "I can hear you fine. What's up?"

"I'm coming down to Mozambique next week. Are you still going to be there?"

Mike paused. He didn't know if he was still going to be here next week, but more to the point, he didn't want any Zimbo coming back into his life, just as he was beginning to achieve his anonymity. "Uhh ... I dunno, Oscar. I haven't made any plans. By the way ... how did you know I was here?"

"Phoned your wife. But she didn't have the number. I had to go through directory enquiries. Major hassle man."

"Oh, right," Mike said lamely. "So what are you coming down for?"

"Just to have a look around. D'you know I quit my job?"

Mike wasn't surprised, but acted so. "What? You quit? But why?"

"Long story, my buddy. I'll tell you about it next week." Oscar spoke as if he knew Mike was still going to be in Beira. "If you're still there, will you still be staying at the Hotel Beira?"

"Maybe, I dunno," Mike was trying to sound non-committal. "There's a Danish guy here who has offered me his caravan... " Mike wanted to kick himself. It wouldn't be difficult to track down a Danish man with a caravan in Beira. You'd just have to ask a couple of people at Club Nautica and they'd soon enough tell you it was Kurt you were after.

"Yeah, bloody farming," Oscar continued. "Who needs it? I'm never going farming in Zimbabwe again... but that's another story. I've got a couple of brilliant schemes for Mozambique. You might be interested."

"Yeah, maybe Oscar." Mike tried to sound enthusiastic. Here we go again, he thought. Another dumb idea that his friends wanted to drag him into.

"Mozambique's so buggered they'll accept anyone ... even me. Even you, Mike."

"Yeah, sure Oscar." Oscar was right.

"Okay Mike, hang loose and see if you can stick around 'til next week. Okay man?"

"Yeah, right. We'll see you." Mike hung up. He clenched the brandy glass and thought briefly about hurling it at the TV. But his anger was gone. He was left only with the feeling of futility as he raised himself to close the windows. He was sweating and the cotton shirt felt clammy against his skin. Oscar had spoiled his mood. Well at least it wasn't his wife or his boss who had phoned. That was something.

★   ★   ★   ★   ★

He suspected that Oscar knew he didn't want to go back to Zimbabwe. It was no secret that he and his wife were having problems.

"Huh! Problems? Is that what you call it? How 'bout fucking my husband's buddy?" Mike spat loudly to himself. "Bloody bitch!" But the invective was of no use. It didn't even make him feel better. Just useless. Deep down he knew she wasn't really a 'fucking bitch'. It was all circumstantial. An 'events in motion' philosophy. She knew he knew what was going on, but either didn't care—or worse, wanted him to know. Almost as if she was torturing him, like getting her own back for all those years he'd been on the road, having a good time with all those useless drunken yobo muzo mates of his. There'd never been any time for the marriage, she'd said. She had a point, of course. And now the events were in motion. So be it.

Mike finished the tumbler and poured himself a refill. She'd never understood that he'd had to do it. For the money—yes of course, but it was also something he just had to do. Couldn't she see that? Then he saw that he was losing her, that they were drifting apart. It was almost as if she didn't care anymore and that was worse than the anger. He'd stopped playing the guitar and had tried to settle into a formal job. He'd really made an effort. Didn't she see—he had done it for her?

But she hadn't and didn't see and carried on carrying on with that hairy macho rugger-bugger who thought he was a Ted Danson look-alike. So he'd started on the guitar again which had perpetuated the whole unhappy issue into an irretrievable downward vortex. Even little George seemed to sense what was going on, or at the very least, sensed the discord in the house. Perhaps that was why he didn't sleep; maybe he was pretty screwed up. But she couldn't see that either. Or perhaps she did, and laid that guilt trip on him as well. As well as being able to use the child as some kind of leverage against him. She was cunning, or was he just over-imaginative?

He finished the second tumbler of brandy, uncaring that he'd flattened half the jack and it wasn't yet seven o'clock. He changed channels on the TV. M-Net, the South African satellite channel had come on. An American soap was showing. He switched the television off. He had enough *soap* in his own life without having to watch some contrived, puerile load of drivel.

He took the briefcase off the bed and stashed it under the mattress. He'd been meaning to do some work when he returned to the hotel, like writing up his marketing report. He planned to do that every night, but somehow never got round to it.

"Bloody job," he muttered. "Bloody job, bloody wife, bloody Zimbabwe. To hell with them all." He stripped off his clothes, kicking them under the desk and took a shower. Perhaps he'd go down to Club Nautica tonight and get blasted. The hot water still wasn't working. Bloody Salim. He'd reported it three days ago. The bastard had probably deliberately ignored him. And there was still no plug for the basin. Bloody typical!

He felt better after the shower and dressed into his jeans and his black T-shirt. Sandals would be okay as well. There were no problems with dress regulations in Mozambique, not like Zimbabwe where they still insisted on archaic and obtrusive dress requirements in the hotels and restaurants. Some kind of perverted throwback to the self-righteous Calvinistic days of the Rhodesians. The golden years. Hah!

He switched the aircon onto full so the room would be well chilled on his return. Stashing a fistful of *meticais* into his back pocket, he took a final slug from the brandy bottle and walked down the stairs to the lobby. The two whores were still there, chatting up a fat slimy Portuguese businessman. Life seemed simpler here in Mozambique. You want a woman? Simple. You pay. Straightforward, cut and dried. No analysing, no agonizing.

He looked briefly for João on his way out, but didn't see him.

★ ★ ★ ★ ★

Jean-Paul was the manager, or possibly the owner, of Club Nautica. In its prime, Club Nautica had been the trendy venue of Beira, the chic yacht club where all the wealthy ex-patriate and local Portuguese used to meet. Then overnight most of the Portuguese had left and the club closed down and was vandalized.

No one knew where Jean-Paul had come from. Some said he was a deserter from the Legion. He certainly looked like a legionnaire, short cropped hair and tattoos on his bulging forearms. But no one ever asked. It was not important. And any rate, he'd done a grand job in getting the club back into some sort of order. Not the whole club mind you, just the restaurant and the salt-water swimming pool.

Mike had never really had a conversation with Jean-Paul. Just the odd 'hi' here and there and yes, the food was fine. But he liked Jean-Paul. There was a mutual respect. He could tell by the way they smiled at each other when he came in. He also liked the way Jean-Paul didn't fraternize with the diners. He kept himself to himself, except when he was supervising the waiters or playing backgammon with his blonde South African girlfriend at the corner table.

Mike sat at his table at the front of the verandah, next to the low sea wall that kept out the beach and the high tides. He ordered an Olsen's beer and a plate of prawn rissoles from the waiter. Jean-Paul's chef made the best prawn rissoles in Beira.

With hot chillies, they were dynamite. The candle on the red-checked tablecloth fluttered in the breeze and went out. He lit a Marlboro and carefully put the butt into the glass ashtray, which had water in the bottom. The waiter brought the beer and the rissoles and Mike started to feel more relaxed.

He was onto his second beer when Kurt and Colin joined him. Kurt, the Dane with the surplus caravan, was an engineer on contract to the City of Beira. Some UN project to start the water sanitation working again in the city. But Kurt had said it was a losing battle and the city just couldn't cope with the massive influx of refugees from the rural areas. He said the city had a quarter million people too many.

"Zat's why, zey shit on ze side of ze roads," he'd said. "Zere's no place for zem to shit. And zen zere's all zis fockin' dysentery and typhoid and zat shit, ja?"

Kurt pulled up a chair next to Mike and slapped him on the back.

"So my friend, when you want my caravan, ja?"

"Maybe next week, Kurt. Nothing definite yet. Can I buy you a drink?"

"Ja, I haff a double whisky. To kill all zat smell of shit." He laughed loudly and infectiously.

"What you having Colin?" Mike asked the Englishman across the table.

"I'll have a beer, thanks Mike. Olsen's," Colin replied. Colin was a tall balding softly-spoken Yorkshireman. He now had permanent residence in Mozambique and was struggling to get his freight-forwarding business up and running, in between desultory bouts of air-charter flying.

Mike ordered from the waiter, as attentive as ever. Jean-Paul would have seen to that. "So are you fellows joining me for dinner?" Mike asked.

"No, no," said Kurt, "we haff just escaped from ze fockin' wimmin for a quick drink." He slapped his thigh with gusto. "You know, I leave Denmark because ze fockin' wife is driving me fockin' crazy. Now I'm here in Mozambique an' what I do? I marry a fockin' black woman. She no fockin' different from ze white woman—fockin' nag, nag, nag. An' now I haff a bunch of fockin' mulatto kids running all over my house, ja!"

They all laughed warmly. It was plain to Mike that Kurt was very proud of his new wife. He was obviously very happy with his new circumstances and Mike felt a pang of envy. Colin was also married to a black Mozambican woman. He wondered briefly why they never brought their wives to the club. Perhaps it was a cultural thing. The men go drinking and the women stay home and cook and look after the kids.

"So, Kurt, what would you charge me for your caravan, if I took it?" Mike asked.

"Ag, my friend. I give it to you for 25 US a week." Kurt replied. It was cheap at the price and they both knew it. Mike had been worried about the blue UN logo still emblazoned on the side of the caravan, but Kurt had assured him that it was all above-board. He said he'd bought the caravan from the municipality on a used-equipment tender. And as he'd been the tender adjudicator, it hadn't been too difficult. Mike had also asked him about the property where the caravan was parked. Kurt had said it was his house-in-town and that all the workshop activity in the garage was part of a private business he had started. Those graders and Caterpillars were only there temporarily. Mike had shrugged. At least the place would be quiet at night.

The talk on the caravan brought Mike's nagging dilemma to a head. It hadn't been a dilemma until now, but suddenly it was a massive reality. What on earth did he think he was playing at? Had he gone out of his mind? Here he was negotiating the rental on a caravan in Mozambique, as if he was going to stay. What about his job? What about little George? What about that two-timing bitch of a wife?

It was an escape route, an option. Nothing more. Simply an insurance policy. Simply a dream. Perhaps that was it, the aura of Beira had gone to his head?

Kurt ordered another round. Mike hadn't been listening.

"You know, ze whole fockin' city of Beira is sinking," Kurt stated.

"How do you mean?" Colin enquired.

"Well, zere's so many fockin' people, zat zey are cutting all ze trees down for firewood. An' ze city is sinking because zere are no trees to hold ze sea back."

"So why did you go and buy that farm and fix it up?" Colin continued.

"Ag, I have to give ze wife some security. Anyway, it's not a farm, it's a smallholding."

Mike knew that Kurt wasn't too concerned about Beira sinking. He had done a lot of work on his smallholding. It looked as if he planned to be there for the rest of his life.

Kurt swallowed his third double whisky in one throw. "Well, gentlemen, I haff to return to my duties as a husband. I shall see you tomorrow." He slapped Mike on the back. "You tell me about ze caravan tomorrow, ja?"

Mike nodded. Colin took his leave as well and Mike said goodnight to them both. Jean-Paul brought him a menu and he ordered prawns. What the hell, it was still on the company expense account.

"*He, pa!*" a young voice sounded from the blackness of the beach. Mike turned and peered into the gloom. João had found him.

Seven

João banged on the roof of the cab. "Okay. We go!"

Mike put the truck into reverse and backed into the road, narrowly missing a stray dog. Hey! Fock off!" João shouted after the dog, proudly showing off his English. For good measure, he threw a stone with his one hand at the animal, which fled yelping towards the casuarina trees lining the beach. João kept a stash of stones in the back of the truck for just such occasions.

Mike smiled to himself. João was a good boy. He had a lot of spunk. He'd never asked João about his missing hand, assuming he'd lost it playing with a grenade or something like that. God alone knew how many thousands upon thousands of stray grenades and landmines littered the countryside. Or perhaps it had been hacked off by a machete. Who knew? There were legions of *deslocados* in Beira, the cripples and amputees from the war. You saw them everyday on the streets, some with no arms, some with one leg, some with none, dragging themselves along on their stumps using a piece of cardboard as a base. João had never made mention of his disability. It was a part of his life and he'd long since learnt that pity meant nothing. Survival on the streets was more pressing.

João stuck his head inside the cab, through Mike's open window. "We go to One-Two-Three Rock?" His teeth flashed in the darkness.

"Yes, but you are the *guarda*. You have to stay with the truck," Mike shouted through the wind. "You are not permitted in the nightclub."

"*Não problema*," João retorted. He started singing loudly in the back, a tuneless shouting more than a song. Today he had succeeded in his mission of life. He'd swum with his friends in the sea, his belly was full with the Cokes and *pregos*, the steak rolls, that the white man had given him—and he had a responsible job, guarding the truck. Life was good today. Perhaps life would be good tomorrow as well.

Mike pulled up at the One-Two-Three Rock and parked on the pavement in front of the verandah. The place was nearly full and in the beam of his headlights he saw there were only a couple of tables still empty. He switched off his lights before he drew too much attention from the patrons inside. A crowd of street kids was swarming around the truck, selling cigarettes and wooden carvings. João was furiously trying to fend them off, kicking at them over the sides of the truck.

"*Não, não, não*," Mike shooed the urchins away, banging one on the head with the side of the car door as he got out. João cackled victoriously. His turf had been marked.

Mike went into the nightclub, elbowing his way through the phalanx of whores hanging around the entrance. The purple neon light above the doorway didn't flash anymore, but it glowed out ONE T-O-HREE R-CK like a beacon. There were a lot of cars parked outside, which usually meant ex-pats. Locals didn't have cars, except perhaps party officials and cab drivers.

There was always a party of five or six prostitutes outside the door, normally shepherded by their pimp, who was in this case a uniformed policeman. Mike had tried before to work out the system. Why weren't they inside where the custom was? After all, there were other whores inside. Perhaps it worked on a quota system, in which management, or a more important pimp inside, would allow only a certain number of girls in at any one time. Mike smiled inwardly. Perhaps it was a question of supply and demand—controlled economy. Not flooding the market.

He found an empty table and sat down. A waiter appeared and he ordered a beer. The band in the corner had just taken a break and a crackly disco had started up. Dire Straits' *Money for Nothing* swamped the verandah on about volume ten. Mike took in the crowd through the smoke. It was the usual cross-section—a cosmopolitan bunch of black Mozambicans, mulatto Mozambicans, white Mozambicans, Scandinavians, white South Africans, Canadians, Germans, Italians, Koreans, Philippinos … they were all there. All except the Rhodies—the white Zimbabweans. Mike was thankful for that. It was better they drank with their own kind at that newly thatched pub opposite the American compound.

A few months back, Mike had brought his boss to the One-Two-Three Rock for a drink. He should have known better, although he'd secretly enjoyed his boss's discomfort. Particularly when that black whore had come and sat down next to him and asked him to buy her a drink. Lionel's reaction—shrinking embarrassment—had been predictable, and he'd shaken his head dumbly. So Mike had bought her a drink and the boss had looked at Mike as if he was mad.

"How can you do that Mike?" he'd hissed. "You're only encouraging it."

"Encouraging what?" Mike was stunned.

"Prostitution. These people are the dregs of society."

Mike had got angry, though he tried not to show it. "She's a *person*, Lionel. A human being. Just like you and me. She also deserves a bit of respect."

"*Respect?*" Lionel asked, incredulous. "These people have *no* self-respect. Can't you see? That's the problem!"

"She's just trying to *live*! Is that a crime?" Mike felt himself shaking inside. "She's a human being too, you know." But he knew it made no difference. Lionel would never change. Never. He was just grateful that the girl couldn't understand English.

That night had left a sour taste with Mike. What should he have done? Clouted the bigot? For the honour of a hungry black whore? But it was bigger than that. The feelings of unease had stayed a long time and Mike wondered whether it had been something to do with the fact that Lionel was his boss. Was it a cop-out? Perhaps. But more importantly for Mike, he was able consciously to admit to himself and come to terms with the fact that the black hookers of Beira were women with normal feelings, just like hookers anywhere—a part of humanity. Of course, he'd always known this and, if anything, he'd always felt an empathy towards them. He liked them and in some strange way, felt he could identify with them. In fact he was curiously envious of them—the straightforward, unashamed honesty of their craft. Just … just that he'd never had the guts to admit it openly … to the world, or to himself.

Of course, Lionel wouldn't have known this. Lionel had packed up his elephant-skin briefcase the next day and flown back to Harare on the Beira Corridor Group flight and told the managing director that Mozambique was a seedy place to do business and he didn't understand why that fellow Mike kept on going back.

The band was tuning up which jarred against Dire Straits. He noticed that the lead guitarist's B string was slightly out and wondered whether he should interfere and tell him. It wasn't that important. Any rate, it was not surprising. How could they hear anything above the disco? The crowd started clapping and whooping in anticipation of the coming set.

The waiter brought Mike another beer. He flicked his cigarette butt onto the concrete floor. There were no water-lined glass ashtrays here. He felt himself leaning forward across the table, like the crowd, expectantly waiting for the music. There was nothing to beat a live band. These guys were obviously local. He could tell by the battered equipment. Where in hell had they got it from? The bass guitarist's hundred-watt Peavey speaker took pride of place, centre-stage. Some of the other speakers looked homemade.

Someone switched off the disco as the keyboard man began a seventh chord sequence. His timing was slightly out, but it didn't matter. He was very young, about 17 or 18. He was having a fine time. Good for him, Mike thought. Good for him. He recognized the intro for *The Girl from Ipanema*, as the drummer came in, smooth and gentle with his brushes, tapping out the subtle samba rhythm.

Mike felt his foot tapping. He spotted the fat Portuguese businessman from the hotel on the other side of the room, chatting up a black woman. He was leaning over her chair with his arm draped over her shoulder. He was smoking a cigar which irritated the woman, but the businessman didn't seem to notice.

Tall and tanned and young and lovely,
The girl from Ipanema goes walking
And when she passes, each one she passes
Goes ... Aaaah.

The bass man was doing the singing. His voice was deep and husky, almost throaty, but it worked for the song. The trace of his African accent came through the words. Mike wondered if he could even speak English. Probably not—probably the only English he knew was from the songs he sang. It was something to be admired.

A few couples had got up to dance and were swaying softly in the cleared space in front of the makeshift stage. The fat businessman had finally pulled his whore onto the floor. He rocked from side to side, pretending to whisper the words of the song into the woman's ear. Now and again the gold medallion on his open-shirted chest caught the light from the rotating mirror ball above. The lead guitarist slid into a break and his fingers danced like velvet across the frets.

Mike noticed that most of the women seemed to be prostitutes. In that place it seemed right, almost natural. The few who weren't were obviously married. A white girl approached him and he felt himself tense as she sat down, unprompted, at his table. She was in her early 20s and had long blonde hair, almost bleached. She was very tanned, dressed like an overlander.

"Excuse me," she asked with the hint of a Scandinavian accent, "do you speak English?"

Mike asked himself if he looked like an English-speaker. "Yes."

She was very attractive, but he saw her legs and armpits were unshaven. She seemed dirty, but Mike thought that was probably an unfair generalization that he'd picked up from the Rhodies. TWoGs, they called them—Third World Groupies—or Dirty Danes. Young Scandinavians who came out to Africa with Danida or DAPP or Norad or SIDA—on aid programmes, but in reality to screw niggers, so they said. He caught himself. How instinctive, how judgemental. Was that the Rhodie in him, the conditioning?

"Please, you can help?" she stated, greatly relieved that she had finally discovered a fluent English speaker. "My friend, she's a Canadian. She's very ill. She has a very very bad fever. We come today on the boat from Nampula. I take her to hospital. They say she has very bad malaria …." The girl looked through Mike.

He had the sudden feeling that they were truly hemispheres apart. She had come into the black world. Why now did she want to come back to the white? Where was this heading? Why him? She would have noticed his accent and would have assumed he was a Rhodie, the same way he had assumed she was a TWoG.

"What do you want of me?" he asked.

She leaned closer to make herself heard above the music, but there was no familiarity, no friendliness. Her sweat smelt acrid. She wants something from me, thought Mike.

"We have very little money. We used it all on the boat trip from Nampula and now we cannot pay for a hotel. Do you know any guest houses or backpackers' lodges? We can only pay maybe ten US a night …, " she trailed off.

"I don't," he answered, honestly. One very rarely saw backpackers in Beira, possibly the occasional Aussie or Brit. "Ummm… " he was thinking about Kurt's caravan, but told himself to keep his big mouth shut. "I always stay at the Hotel Beira, but it's very expensive … maybe you could speak to Jean-Paul at Club Nautica. He will know of a place." He felt better. He had tried to help, albeit in a pass-the-buck fashion. "But your friend, surely she will have to stay in hospital tonight? I mean … they won't discharge her if she's as bad as you say?" He felt he ought to say something else, but the girl had already lost interest in him and was looking distractedly into the crowd.

"Pardon? Oh! No…. she does not stay at the hospital tonight. She will die if she stays there. Okay, thanks." She stood up and threaded her way through the throng to a cluster of black Mozambicans over by the corner. They seemed to know her well. One of them passed her a beer and she was soon laughing with them. Back into their world, the black world she had infiltrated—or so she thought.

Mike wondered whether she did in fact have a Canadian friend who was desperately ill in hospital with malaria. He felt relieved he hadn't made any concessions to the girl. It was some kind of set-up, and normally he was the sucker.

He ordered another beer as he felt something brush against his leg under the table. The band was playing a lambada now and the space that was the dance floor was bustling with sweating, swaying couples. It was humid and stuffy. It was noisy and smoky. The smell of the stale beer and urine from the overworked toilets combined with the vapours of seafood and garlic from the kitchens to produce an aura of musky eroticism.

The same thing brushed his leg again as he looked under the table. It was a *deslocado*. This one had no legs from the buttocks down. Or possibly from the waist down. The wizened young man looked up at Mike with a sheepish grin, as if embarrassed to approach him in such a manner. His teeth were sparkling white. Mike was intrigued. The man was riding on a homemade platform apparatus, about a foot square, with what looked like castors from a supermarket trolley as the wheels. It was ingenious—better than the standard scrap of cardboard that most used. And here he was, wheeling himself around the nightclub, under the tables.

Mike dug into his pockets and gave the man a few dirty *meticais* notes. The *deslocado* responded by grasping Mike's calf.

"*Obrigado, senhor,*" he beamed. Beneath the rags of his shirt, his muscled arms sought purchase from the concrete floor and propelled him off to the next table.

It was about then that Mike happened to notice the girl. He hadn't come to the club to find a girl—simply to have a few beers and enjoy the music. Or so he told himself. His gaze stopped dead. There was something about her. He couldn't define it, but in a way he felt as if he had known her for a long time. Perhaps that was the chemistry. He tried to deny it. He was white, she was black.

She was sitting with a friend and they were laughing. Were they whores? Probably, but that didn't seem to matter. He felt himself foolishly fixated as he stared at her. She was undoubtedly beautiful. One of the most stunning women he'd ever seen. Although she was sitting with her legs crossed demurely, he could tell she was tall. Her long black hair tumbled carelessly over her open shoulders down onto her back. She was wearing a very short white dress. It was sleeveless and cut low at the back. The shimmery lurex seemed moulded to her body and the whiteness offset perfectly the soft sensuality of her black skin.

His throat was dry and he knew then that she was someone special. As if in response to his innermost thoughts, she tossed her hair, glancing around the room. Their eyes met for a brief moment as often happens in clubs and bars. She smiled at him for a second and then returned to the conversation with her friend. Mike had tried to smile back at her, but it felt as if his face was frozen. That smile—it wasn't flirtatious; perhaps a mite coquettish. It wasn't the crude leer of a drunken whore. It was no come-on, simply a warm happy 'it's nice to be here and I hope you're having a good time because you look like a nice person too' type of smile. Nothing more.

And that to Mike made her all the more desirable. She wasn't a slut, he convinced himself. She couldn't possibly be. Certainly some class there. He had that stupid feeling in his lower gut; a feeling he dimly remembered from his days as a teenager. He was smitten and he knew it.

He tried to analyse her smile again. What are you doing for God's sake? Behaving like a lovesick youth. And anyway, what are you going to do about it? Nothing. You never do do anything. You always were the gooseberry, getting yourself drunk because you were too much of a coward even to talk to a woman. And you told yourself that you were unattractive to women. *They* never told you. You told yourself. And now you'll stand back with the excuse that's she's black, so therefore you cannot go to her. Y'know, it's a cultural thing. And anyway, what language would you speak? Be honest with yourself. Is it a black - white thing? Or is it because she's a woman? A black woman? A black whore? Perhaps it's a combination of both. Perhaps, number one, you haven't got the balls, and number two, you're too afraid what others might think.

And that's why, aged 18, you paid a dirty, skinny coloured whore with a bunch of missing teeth two dollars to take your virginity in a filthy shebeen in Pioneer Street, just around the corner from the Jameson Hotel in downtown Harare. If only your Rhodie mates had known. But you were very very careful and kept it a tightly guarded secret. Well locked away in your sordid little closet. Oh, how you'd lived with that one. How you'd explained it all away. Some pathetic excuse that the white girls weren't interested in the cropped haired soldiers. And how the macho cropped haired soldiers didn't have the time, in between the man's business of killing, to be bothered with the inane civilian niceties of a bunch of vacuous schoolgirls.

So whore-shagger, what's the problem now? She's only a puta, isn't she? Probably cost more than two bucks now—but so what, she'd be worth it, wouldn't she? You've done it before, haven't you? And Lionel would sign the expenses claim form. Entry: Entertainment—US$50.00. Or perhaps: Entry: Fucked another black prostitute—US$50.00 for staff welfare. The idiot would probably want to know where the slip was.

He felt the panic rising as he saw the fat Portuguese businessman sidle up to the two girls. He was pawing them and he saw that she was shaking her head whilst politely attempting to push him away. Mike was pleased. She obviously *did* have class. The businessman eventually gave up and took the other girl off to dance.

She was now alone at the table, watching her friend and the businessman dance a rumba. She was laughing all the while and her friend was giggling back at her over the fat man's shoulders. She was clapping to the beat and her eyes danced with merriment. She uncrossed her legs and Mike felt his breath catch imperceptibly. They were the most beautiful legs he had seen. Long, firm and shapely, with finely turned ankles of exquisite grace. The skin was like a sheen of sheer silk.

He closed his eyes and took a deep breath. Now was the moment. Do it. Go to her.

You may not have another opportunity. She's alone. Go on—before someone else does. But he knew he wouldn't. He just couldn't. What would he say? Some corny one-line come-on? There was a wall of fear that came down like the blade of a guillotine.

That's it. He would go back to the hotel. He could not prolong this torture any longer. She was too good for him. She would only laugh at him, wouldn't she? As she'd laughed at the Portuguese businessman. Well, after all ... she was black ...

He swilled back the last of his beer and put his cigarettes in his shirt pocket. He stood up to leave.

Perhaps it was this movement in the corner of her eye, or perhaps it was a feeling, but at that moment she turned and looked to him. Longer this time, but with the same warm smile. Mike forced a half smile as their eyes met, then dropped his gaze and walked away.

He didn't notice the trace of disappointment in her eyes. Well he did, but he told himself it was something else. He couldn't turn back, could he? Not now. Not now that he'd committed himself to leaving. It wouldn't seem right.

He strode purposefully to his truck and banged the side hard with his fist. João woke in the back with a start and rubbed his eyes with the stump of his arm. He smiled wanly at Mike as he huddled up against the cab.

"*Não problema.* All okay," he mumbled.

Mike revved the truck and reversed noisily, scattering a horde of street kids in his path. He slammed the gears into first and drove angrily back to the hotel. Martha was still on duty at reception and silently passed him his room keys and a message from Oscar.

★　★　★　★　★

Phoebe had seen the white man go and was disappointed. She had noticed the look of disgust on his face. At what? And who was he? Where was he from? She had tried to guess his nationality, but found she couldn't. He was fair, so obviously not Mediterranean. European? South African? American? Perhaps. Not Zimbabwean. They rarely came here.

And earlier he'd talked to that white girl, that Swedish trash who hung out with those small-time pimps who were often there in the corner, hustling and drinking and swearing. She had to admit that she'd been pleased when she saw that he'd managed to palm her off and get rid of her.

She'd even smiled at him and noticed how he'd tried to smile back. But still he would not come to her. What was his reticence? Was he shy? Did he not like black women? What? But what was her interest? Was it that there was something a little bit different about him? That perhaps he wasn't just after sex? Naturally if he had asked ... and if he had the money ... But she knew she wasn't up to it tonight. The traces of pain in her groin were still evident.

In the morning Salim would want to know why she hadn't scored a trick. Well ... damn Salim! She would tell him the truth. Damn him! She would no longer stand for this ... this slavery. There was no other way to describe it. There was a limit to what a girl could take. Damn him!

She'd felt the anger rising. And then the man had picked up his cigarettes and left, and in dismay she'd tried to bring him back with her eyes. To talk, just to talk. That was all. Nothing more.

But he went. Somehow, she had a feeling that he would come back. Only a feeling. She put a hand to her face. The swelling had subsided and the bruising almost gone. Scanning the club, she instinctively went through the motions of identifying potential clients. But she was tired.

"Damn you, Salim!" she muttered, as she finished off her drink. She scooped up her handbag. "I will dance to your tune no longer."

And she went home.

Eight

It was Saturday morning in Beira. Already the humidity was oppressive and it was not yet nine o'clock. Banks of mauve cumulus nimbus were marshalling on the eastern horizon, as they had been doing for days now. With each day, the intensity and depth of the clouds had increased marginally as the cyclone moved irrepressibly westwards across the Mozambique Channel.

Mike was snoring loudly, splayed out over the bed sheets, drenched in sweat. He'd switched off the aircon the night before when he'd got back from the nightclub. The room had been ice-cold.

There was a knock at the door and Mike grunted. Before he even opened his eyes he knew he had a hangover. He felt faintly nauseated by the smell of his own breath. Stale cigarettes and brandy. Lifting himself onto an elbow, he instinctively wrapped a sheet around his body. He reached over and lit a cigarette.

"Who is it?" he called out, his voice husky.

"*Bom dia, camarada,*" a voice answered from the passage. "It's me ... Oscar."

Mike tossed aside the clinging sheet and put on a pair of shorts. "Oscar? What are you doing here? Your note said you were only arriving tomorrow."

"I was. But I got a lift with Colin," Oscar returned. "Now open the bloody door!"

Rubbing the sleep from his eyes, Mike unlatched the door. Oscar, guitar in hand and duffel bag slung, stood beaming.

"Howzit my buddy?" his eyes sparkled. "Got any coffee going?"

"No. Only brandy and Beira water."

"*Não problema, camarada.* Let me just dump my gear an' I'll organize some." Oscar pushed himself in and tossed his guitar and bag onto the bed. "I'll just pop down to the dining room and order some. Maybe you should have a shower." He looked Mike up and down and laughed, "Have you been razzing it up … or what?"

"Just go'n get the coffee," Mike said, remembering the girl.

Oscar gave Mike a friendly slap on the back, which stung. "It's so good to see you. We've got a lot to talk about."

Mike closed the door behind Oscar as he left. A clutch of cleaning maids was in the corridor, giggling. As was his custom, he went to the window and looked down on the street below to check on the truck. It was still there, with a bunch of street kids swarming and romping in the back. He picked out João, sitting atop the cab like a king. Flicking out his cigarette stub, he watched as a flock of squabbling gulls flapped niggardly in the direction of the docks to meet the incoming catch from the previous night. He closed the windows and switched on the aircon.

He took a cold shower. Salim still hadn't sorted out the hot water.

His life was a mess, he mused, as the tepid water trickled over his face. Out of any control he seemed to be able to impose upon it. And now Oscar was here. He didn't know whether he was pleased or irritated—perhaps a bit of both. Was Oscar going to complicate his already complicated life? Undoubtedly. Oscar never had any money, and now here he was in Beira—without a car. How in the hell was he going to get around? Bum off him? No question.

Finishing the shower, he decided against shaving. Waste of time shaving on weekends. He'd been toying with the idea of going back to Zimbabwe. There was little to be achieved business-wise in Beira over a weekend. He'd have to face his marital situation sooner or later. It was coming to a head. Couldn't go on in self-imposed exile in Mozambique forever. And then there was Lionel, his boss. There seemed little doubt that sooner or later, things would come to a head between them. Why did it all have to happen at once? Was there no autonomy in his life? Apparently not.

And here was good old Oscar, bright as a button—no money, no car, no job, no woman. How did he do it?

"I dunno," he sighed to himself. He let in Oscar, who put the tray of coffee on top of the TV. "So, tell me about your big plans."

Oscar poured the coffee. Mike took his black and sweet, like the Mozambicans. It was almost a sacrilege to add milk. Mike thought back to when he'd given Lionel an espresso, and how he'd spat it out, whining about how bitter it was and how can you drink that shit?

"My friend," Oscar stated importantly, as if building up to something of magnitude. "You ... and... I ... have got a two o'clock appointment ... with ..... wait for it ..... ," he smiled mysteriously at Mike to add to the suspense, "...with ... *Senhor Presidente.*"

"What? Which president?" Mike was confused.

"With *Afonso Dhlakama,*" Oscar replied, smugly.

"You mean ... the president of Renamo?"

"The very one."

Mike sipped on his coffee. It wasn't as hot as he liked it. It never was in the Hotel Beira. Oscar was complicating his life big time. But nothing about his friends surprised him anymore. They all had these bizarre ideas—stupid, crazy ideas most of the time. Like the time he'd driven from Jo'burg to Harare with Melvin who had insisted they drive at night to avoid being caught driving drunkenly. Melvin had said he had inside information that the highway police worked only during the day. Twelve hundred kilometres in the dark with only the sidelights on because Melvin was adamant that the wild animals on the road would be hypnotized by the car's headlights.

And now this? The same kind of shit. Mike knew that if he was to reject the idea, now was the time to do it. He felt instinctively that whatever it was that Oscar was on about, it was unlikely to be a winner. He felt irritated that Oscar had gone ahead and set up this meeting without consulting him but also felt flattered that Oscar had automatically included him in his grandiose, if hare-brained, scheme.

"What for?" Mike followed, cautiously. Immediately regretting it. He'd opened the door.

"What d'you mean 'What for?'?" Oscar was stunned. "To offer our services. That's what for."

"What services, Oscar?" Mike heard himself asking with a trace of annoyance. His friends—all of them—had this irritating trait of assuming that he knew where they were at, at any specific point in their lives. "Tell me from the beginning. I mean ... you just pitch up in Mozambique on a Saturday morning and tell me we've got a meeting with the president of Renamo. I mean... I was thinking about going back to Zim ... still am. Gotta lot of personal problems to sort out."

Oscar was horrified. "You can't!" He shuffled earnestly towards Mike on the bed. "This is big Mike. Very big." His cigarette ash fell unnoticed onto the sheet. "This could change everything. Bugger Zimbabwe. Mozambique is where it's happening."

"What's happening Oscar?"

"Everything!" Oscar's voice was raised. "Just promise me you won't go back ... at least until tomorrow."

"Pour me another coffee," Mike passed his cup to Oscar, deliberately trying to antagonize him. It was his way of getting him to slow down. A bit childish, he thought, but nevertheless effective.

It was one of those split-second decisions that could alter your life forever. Despite all his doubts, he was wary that if he refused, he might lose out on an exciting opportunity. If anyone could open doors in central Mozambique, then surely it had to be Dhlakama? Conversely, what about his job? His family? The thought of little George … abandoned by his father …?

"Promise me," Oscar persisted.

Mike felt his friend's power. He hated his own weakness at that moment. Why could he never say no?

"Okay. I'll stay."

A light squall hit the city, softly lashing the hotel windows. Mike glanced outside. The sun was still shining, but the horizon across the estuary was purple. Subconsciously, he registered that the cyclone would soon be here. Probably tomorrow … or the day after.

"Has this cyclone got a name?" he asked distractedly.

"What cyclone?" Oscar looked puzzled.

"I dunno. Normally they give cyclones girls' names. Or is that hurricanes?"

"What are you on about? Let's go'n have some breakfast. I'll fill you in," replied Oscar. He was thinking about the meeting.

★   ★   ★   ★   ★

Oscar had smoked a joint on the way to the *Senhor Presidente's* house, which Mike thought was really dumb, but said nothing. Oscar was big enough to make his own decisions. The only thing though, was that Oscar's eyes were always a dead give-away after he'd been smoking. Blue, blue eyes encased in pools of blood-redness, like targets. And his curly black hair seemed to curl more haphazardly.

Of course João had come along for the ride. It was interesting that his master had this new friend.

It was João who had noticed the white 4 x 4 Hilux that had been trailing them from the hotel. Was it following, or was it just coincidence? After all, the route they were taking was a common thoroughfare from the docklands, through the CBD and across the old golf course towards the residential area up near the beaches.

João thought briefly about banging on the roof and warning his *patrão*, his master. But then, surely his master would not be that stupid? His master would know if they were being followed, would he not? His master was a man who had seen the world—and such men knew these things.

It was unfortunate for João that he did not bang on the roof. But he was distracted by the throngs of small children defecating on the side of the road between the market and the canal. He hurled a shower of stones at them, scattering the urchins in squeals of panic. It was not right that these children should do such things in public places.

Inside the cab Mike and Oscar were laughing.

"Are those little peccies crapping?" Oscar snorted.

"Ja," Mike replied. "They've nowhere else to shit. The parents won't let them crap near the shacks. So they do it here."

"Terrific!"

"Ja, and then the rains come and wash all the turds into the canal and everyone wonders why there are typhoid and cholera epidemics."

"Phew!" Oscar wrinkled his nose. "It's ripe, man."

"There was that light rain this morning, so most of them have been washed away. This is the new crop."

They drove on towards the beaches, traversing the causeway that bisected the once grand old golf course, now an overgrown marsh. Vast pools of invading water sat putrefying amongst the rankness, a perfect home to the millions of resident mosquitoes.

Senhor Dhlakama's house was like any other suburban Beira house—run-down and only a few steps ahead of the creeping decay, kept at bay, in the main, by the solid workmanship of the Portuguese builders of two generations before. Like the most, it was in desperate need of a coat of paint.

In the road, parked under an avenue of mangoes, was a motley array of vehicles. Four-wheel drives, sedans and a few of the ubiquitous scooters—or Velos, as they were commonly known. That the vehicles were old and worn was not important. A vehicle of any standing was a mark of influence.

Pulling up behind a Land Rover, Mike swung his pick-up into the shade and switched off. Almost immediately he was accosted by a black man at the window. A young man with teardrop sunglasses, a brown open-necked shirt and what appeared to have been at one time, camouflage-pattern trousers. Without a word he ushered the two white men through the pedestrian gate, picking their way through a jungle of overgrown hydrangeas to a lean-to verandah.

He indicated that the two men should sit on the two upright wooden chairs. Shutting the door behind him, he disappeared inside, presumably to announce to *Senhor Presidente* that his guests had arrived.

"Is this his house?" Mike asked quietly, unsure whether talking was permitted.

"Yeah," said Oscar. " His HQ is over by the esplanade, near that thatched Rhodie pub. Oscar made no attempt to speak quietly. Perhaps it was the dope.

"So why aren't we seeing him at his HQ?"

"Dunno. Reckon cos it's the weekend. The dude's gotta have some time-off."

Oscar was about to light up a cigarette when the man in the faded camo trousers came out. Pointing at the pack of Madisons in Oscar's hand, he shook his head and vigorously waggled his forefinger.

"*Não, não. Senhor Presidente* ees okay you see. Come."

They followed the man into a lounge that Mike thought was surprisingly airy, with an almost homely feeling about it. A picture of the Pope hung crookedly on one wall, next to a set of bridge prints—Sydney Harbour Bridge, London Bridge, Golden Gate Bridge and a few others Mike didn't recognize. It was weird. What did the president of Renamo want with pictures of bridges in his house?

Again the usher invited them to sit down. The green rexine lounge suite took pride of place in the room, but as was the custom, the armchairs were crammed up against each other as in a doctor's waiting room.

A short bespectacled man in his early 50s came in, presumably from the kitchen area. Hand extended in welcome, the genial president shook hands with the two white men.

"Sit down, please. You are welcome." He nodded to the usher, who left the room. From behind the tortoise shell glasses, Mike got the feeling that those smiling eyes were assessing and dissecting the two men. Yet he was not uncomfortable with it and decided he liked the little black man.

"So, you are from Zimbabwe?" The little president sat down on the settee across the coffee table. Mike noticed how he sat in the middle of the three-seater, at ease and relaxed, as if secure and unafraid, like a sleeper splayed out on a bed, unthreatened. It made Mike like him the more for his confidence. It was very natural. Mike let Oscar take the lead.

"Yes, we are from Zimbabwe, *Senhor Presidente*. We are agriculturalists."

The man's eyes twinkled behind his spectacles. He was smiling. Was it embarrassment, or was it that he had the measure of the two? Perhaps he was smiling at Oscar's pretentious 'agriculturalists'.

"*Desculpa*. I am sorry. I am not a good ... how you say ... *dono da casa*?" House.

Casa meant house, Mike was thinking. "Host?" he prompted.

The president slapped his thigh. "Host. *Exatamente*! Exactly! My English ... is not so good." There was a tinge of embarrassment in his voice. "I am not a good host. You have no drink?"

Mike and Oscar laughed politely and the president beamed back at them.

"You like Fanta?"

"*Obrigado, Senhor Presidente,*" Mike answered. It was polite to accept hospitality.

The president returned directly with three bottles of Fanta orange juice and a bottle opener. Putting the bottles on the coffee table, he uncapped the tops, but did not remove them.

"Drink, my friends," he indicated expansively.

Mike was touched by his kindness and drank gratefully. Even inside, with a creaking air conditioner rattling down-wall from the Pope, it was still excessively humid.

After the requisite period of silence, in which the three men drank their Fantas, the black man opened the discussion. One could not rush these things. Protocol was important.

"So, gentlemen. You are here to discuss *agricultura*?"

Mike and Oscar nodded.

"But is Zimbabwe not the place of good *agricultura*?"

Mike and Oscar again nodded. It was obvious where the president was leading. Of course Zimbabwe was a good place for agriculture. But it was not a good place for white farmers. The ruling party had seen to that. Politics were more important than productivity.

The president's eyes were twinkling again. He was enjoying this. Not at the white men's expense, but at the Zimbabwean government's. After all, he had spent over a decade fighting Frelimo and its allies, the Zimbabwean National Army.

Oscar felt it was time to say his piece. He cleared his throat as the president studied him. "*Senhor Presidente,* there is no future in Zimbabwe for the white man. We are not wanted. Simple. The government says, 'Yes, we want you white farmers to stay', but the ministers only say this when they know the World Bank is listening."

"So why you think is different in Mozambique? Frelimo is government in Mozambique and Zanu (PF) is the same for Zimbabwe government. Both *socialista, não*?"

"Yes, *Senhor Presidente,*" Oscar agreed. "But in Mozambique, there is democracy. You have had genuine free and fair elections. In Zimbabwe, no one votes anymore. For what?"

The president laughed easily. "Hah! Frelimo declare elections in Mozambique before Renamo win all the country with the gun. It is no decision. In Zimbabwe, there is no Renamo. All the opposition is killed, or frightened like rabbits. So, of course, no one votes. It is natural."

Mike smiled. It was so simplistically true. So self-evident.

Oscar was becoming increasingly earnest. He was not here for a political discussion. He cut to the point and Mike flinched. Perhaps it was too soon. "*Senhor Presidente,* we are here to offer our services as agriculturalists. We would like to work together with the people of central Mozambique and develop farms as joint ventures—for the people … with the people."

The president considered this for a while. His demeanour was serious. The frivolity of political discussion was now over, yet he was not affronted by Oscar's presumption.

He was nodding deliberately, "Yes. It is important. Renamo has been fighting the war for many, many years. Now we must fight for the votes of the *povo* in the next elections. We fought the war for the people—to liberate them from the *communismo.* Now we must fight to liberate them from the hunger. The people are very hungry. There is no food." There was a look of genuine sadness in his eyes.

He continued, more to himself than the two white men. "I am very powerful. Renamo, it controls 75 *por cento* of Mozambique. Is only in the north, near the border to Tanzania where we have no control. But these people are Muslim people. And of course, in Maputo Province. The party in power must always control the capital city. For the World Bank people when they come to visit, *não*? And for the diplomats, *não*?"

Oscar nodded agreement and was about to say something, but the president continued.

"But it is the masses, the *povo,* who control the power. Frelimo forget the teachings of their own Mao and Lenin. They are too worried about their privileges. That is why I allow the South African farmers to come to Niassa Province. It is me who gives them the land—not Frelimo. I give the land to the Boers because I know they are good farmers and they give jobs to the *povo*. Now the *povo* have money to buy food and because they are no longer hungry, they will vote for me, because they know it is me who gives the land to the whites."

"But surely, *Senhor Presidente*," Mike asked pointedly, "for the South Africans to come to Mozambique, they must have the authority of the government? That is Frelimo?"

The president laughed, "Of course. It is necessary for the bureaucrats in Maputo to stamp the papers. But they have no choice. Already I have been to the World Bank to tell them of this project. If Frelimo does not permit the settlers to come, the World Bank asks many embarrassing questions. Why, Frelimo, do you not permit development? And I say to the *povo* that Frelimo will not permit development."

Mike found the logic irrefutable. It was something to be admired.

"So, gentlemen. Frelimo is of no consequence in central Mozambique. They are the puppets with the rubber stamps. That is all."

Leaning forward, ever earnest, Oscar asked, "So how do we proceed, *Senhor Presidente*? What is the next step?"

"It is simple. You must go to the places I tell you where the development is necessary. You will take with you my ... how you say ... my *ministro de agricultura*. You will stay one week in this place with my *ministro*. He will educate the *povo* that you are farmers for development and then you choose the land for your *agricultura*."

"Where is this place, *Senhor Presidente*?" Mike asked. It all sounded too simple.

"You go in Zambesia Province. Zambezi River. It is important because Frelimo is now talking with the Italians to develop the big sugar estates. These that were destroyed by Frelimo in the times of the Portuguese. I cannot permit Frelimo to develop this place. His sense of urgency came through. It was important that they beat the Italians to it, in order to take the credit for Renamo. It came to Mike that they had been unwittingly politicized. If he and Oscar were to follow this through, they would clearly be seen as Renamo supporters. No question about it. Well, so what of it?

The meeting was coming to an end. Mike could sense it, though Oscar was trying to thrash out some of the finer details. The president stood up.

"*Desculpa,* gentlemen. You must excuse me. I have another meeting."

Mike and Oscar stood up and shook hands with him.

"You will make the necessary arrangements with my *ministro de agricultura* for the visit. You know his office, *não?*"

"We know it, *Senhor Presidente. Obrigado.*"

★   ★   ★   ★   ★

The *guarda-costa* looked at Salim. "It is the truth, *senhor.* They were engaged in this meeting for 90 minutes."

"Are you sure? How do you know?"

The *guarda-costa* ignored the girl sitting in front of Salim's desk. It was the same girl he'd had to collect from the *Rua de Julius Nyerere* the previous week. And again this morning. Another of Salim's *putas.* "Of course, *Senhor* Salim. I followed the white man's truck from the hotel. When I saw that it turned into Dhlakama's road, I pulled over into the ditch near the end of the causeway ... near the golf course. I could see the truck from that position. It was for a period of 90 minutes."

"And the other white man? You say there were two?"

"Precisely, *senhor.* The other was that short one ... with the curly hair. The one who has the guitar."

Salim glanced briefly at the girl. But she was not listening. He nodded his dismissal to the *guarda-costa* and picked up the telephone.

Phoebe sighed impatiently. Who was Salim talking to now? She had not come here to listen to such things. Always it was the same. Salim barking out instructions and that *guarda-costa*, that gorilla, lurking always in the wings. She was studying her fingernails as Salim talked. Trying not to listen, she could nevertheless tell from the tone in his voice that he was uptight. Perhaps now was not the time to bring up the subject.

But no. It was time. It could not wait any longer. She took a deep breath, sensing that Salim was coming to the end of the call. Her palms were sweating.

Yes, there had been a moment of uncertainty this morning. Life wasn't that bad, was it? After all, she had the *apartamento*, didn't she? And her time was more or less her own, wasn't it? She could come and go as she pleased. She could go to the market when she wanted. She could sleep when she wanted. She never went hungry. The work? Well that had become routine, apart from the occasional bad one … like that Mubvunduku. But then, surely in any job, in any profession, there were ups and downs? Good times and bad times, *não*?

She looked at herself in the mirror. But there were no answers there. Only herself.

Her vacillating had been cut short when the *guarda-costa* arrived in the white 4 x 4 and grunted some instruction that *Senhor* Salim wanted to see her urgently. Well, that had done it.

"Phoebe, *ma cherie*," Salim tilted back in his chair, his arms clasped behind his neck. A thin film of sweat covered his brow. "Where were we, before we got interrupted by all this mundane trivia?"

He knew very well what they'd been talking about prior to the arrival of the *guarda-costa*, thought Phoebe. She would not prompt. Damn him and his arrogance. But she was nervous. She knew it and found herself sitting more erect. She wiped the palms of her hands on the front of her jeans.

"Ah, yes!" Salim smiled, her nervousness not unnoticed. "We were talking about your 'returns', weren't we?"

"Yes. And I was about to tell you, Salim …" she tailed off. What was she going to tell him?

Salim leaned forward across the desk, intently. "What were you going to tell me, Phoebe? I am waiting." The hint of menace in his voice was unmistakable.

She felt herself swallow, but looked at him directly, her chin to the fore.

"Phoebe," he glowered, his voice low. "I want to know why I have not had any returns from you for five days now... no six! Nearly a week, Phoebe, and I have had nothing from you. Not even one lousy *meticais*! He slammed his fist on the desk and she felt herself jump.

"I ... I .. have been recovering, Salim. It was very bad with that Zimbabwean. That Mubvunduku." She was willing herself to stay calm, detached. Tell it as it happened, Phoebe. Do not be afraid, Phoebe.

Salim's voice subsided as quickly as it had erupted. "Of course, you have been to the nurse?"

"Yes," she lied, "but she said there was nothing that could be done. It was all a question of bruising.... and that it would take some time to heal."

"Can I see her medical report? She always gives you a report, doesn't she?"

"I ... I ... did not bring it. It is at the *apartamento*," she lied again. She felt herself shaking inside, but still she willed herself to look at him. Do not turn the eyes away. Do not. He will know.

Salim again leaned back in his chair as he lit up a cigar. "I do not believe you, Phoebe," he said evenly. Challenging her.

"Believe what you want, Salim!" she snapped. Immediately she regretted it. But there! It was said. It was done. She prepared herself for the violence that would follow. For the barrage of abuse. For the strike of the fist. But now she was not afraid. Inside she was calm, in control.

Slowly, deliberately Salim came to his feet, the cigar hanging limply from his mouth.

"What did you say to me?" he whispered. Never. Never before had Phoebe spoken to him in such a manner.

Now she was standing, her legs braced, her body taut. "You heard me, Salim. I am not your piece of meat. I am not your … your commodity that can be bought and sold at the market … and then tossed away when it has been used. I have served you well. I have served you faithfully for many many years now Salim. And this is the thanks I get!" She pointed at her groin. "From your filthy Zimbabwean *camarada*!" She was shaking, but now from anger.

"Be silent, woman!" Salim barked. "You have taken leave of your senses!"

"*Não*! I shall not be silent!" She felt herself shouting. "Do … you .. know … what that man did to me? Huh? Do you know?"

"No, Phoebe. I do not know," he said quietly.

"You know!" her voice caught. "You know. That is why you paid me more than was normal." She leaned across the desk at him, boring into his eyes, her voice low and ominous.

"He … used his fist, Salim. He used his fist … to fuck me, Salim. He fist-fucked me, Salim." She raised both her hands, fists clenched, in front of his face.

"I … I had no idea," Salim was whispering.

She collapsed on the desk, sobbing uncontrollably, her face buried in her hands.

"Martha!" he shouted out to the reception. "Bring a glass of water here. Quickly!" He went round to her, unsure of how he should handle her. Censure her? Comfort her? What?

"Sit, *ma cherie*. Sit." He took her arm and guided her gently back into the chair. She was still sobbing, her body heaving.

"I … am … very tired. I am so tired," she sniffed through the tears.

"Yes, of course you are, *ma cherie*. You must sleep."

She pulled away from him angrily. "*Não*, Salim. You do not understand. I am tired of it all. I am tired of the business. It is too much. I can take it no longer."

Martha brought in the glass of water, glancing curiously at the woman in the chair.

"Drink this, Phoebe," Salim said, passing her the glass. "Of course. I have been unreasonable. Unthinking. You need a break. It will be arranged. Do not worry. I will arrange it. Yes."

She was shaking her head slowly as he wiped the tears away with a tissue. "No, Salim. That is not it. Still you do not comprehend." Her voice was tired, with resignation. "How long do you expect your girls to carry on doing this, Salim? What is the normal working life span of a *puta*, Salim?"

Salim flinched. He hated that word '*puta*'. It was so coarse. So crass! "Perhaps you have a fever, Phoebe. You are not yourself. Yes. A good rest—away from it all. That is what is required." He was fumbling. He was grasping, unsure of what to say to placate her. It couldn't happen. It was inconceivable. He couldn't lose her. After all, the revenue? It was significant.

"Phoebe. You are still young and strong. You have many years left. Many many years."

She turned on him, her eyes ablaze, "And then what, Salim? When you have finished with my body? Will you give me a pension? Will I be able to stay for the rest of my days in the *apartamento*? Hah!"

She was becoming irrational. She was not thinking straight, thought Salim. He felt the irritation rising. He had more important issues to deal with. Matters of state. And now here he was trying to pacify an angry whore! Get a grip of yourself, Salim. Finish this.

"Enough!" he snapped. "I will hear no more of this nonsense."

She looked at him, disbelievingly. Nothing she had said to him had registered. Nothing!

"I own you Phoebe," he said, his face inches from hers, his teeth gritted. "Do you understand that, Phoebe? Do you? Huh?"

She met his glare. "You own nothing, Salim," she hissed.

He hit her, a smarting slap across the face with his open hand. "You will do as you are told, woman. I will tell you when I am finished with you. No one else! Not you. No one! Is that clear?"

She looked at him in silence, her face stinging.

"Now get out of here," he breathed, "before I get really angry. I will not suffer such ingratitude. GET OUT!"

She stood up unsteadily, breathing heavily, her nostrils flaring and her eyes on fire.

"OUT!" he screamed, pointing to the door.

She turned her back on him and without a word, left the room.

Salim was shaking violently as he closed the door behind her. He re-lit the remains of the cigar and inhaled quickly, in short sharp sucks. The bitch had spoiled everything! Why? Why did she have to go and screw it all up? Things had been just fine up until now. Just fine. They'd had a good relationship. And now she went and did this?

It was incomprehensible. There was no accounting for a woman. There simply wasn't. Well so be it. If that's the way she wanted to play it, well, that was fine. Let her ... she would soon see... she would see soon enough.

He went to the door and opened it a fraction. "Martha! Get me my *guarda-costa*. This minute!"

Yes, she must be watched. Carefully. Can't have her behaving like this. So ... so unpredictable. Most unprofessional. The other girls might follow suit. And then what? A rebellion? Uh uh! It must be nipped in the bud. Now. Before it gets out of hand.

Nine

Mike came away from the meeting with Afonso Dhlakama in high spirits. Yes, he was realistic about all the uncertainties, but the proposal sounded good and as Oscar kept saying, it was loaded with potential. Potential—that word again. Mozambique, the country with so much potential, they kept saying, and had been saying for years. Just that no one ever seemed to realize it; the potential seemed never to come to any kind of fruition.

Cynicism aside, he did feel that the project had merit. And what was wrong with feeling optimistic about it all? Couldn't do any harm, could it?

"C'mon, my buddy," Oscar said, slapping Mike on the back. "Let's go'n celebrate. I think we made an impression on the ole *senhor* back there."

"Hmm, didn't like your 'agriculturalists' though, did he?"

"Agh! You gotta talk big to these dudes. It impresses them."

Mike thought otherwise, "Ja, so much so that they think you're going to fund the whole thing. I mean, who's going to pay for the trip expenses? The fuel and all that?"

"For Pete's sake, Mike. Think big! You're getting bogged down in petty details already, man. You gotta think big!"

Still arguing, they pulled up in front of the Hotel Beira. The banter was good-natured and Mike allowed himself to be carried along by the wave of enthusiasm emanating from the meeting. So what if it was only a dream? There was nothing wrong with dreaming, was there?

The dream came to an abrupt end in the hotel foyer when Martha handed him a message. 'Your wife phoned from Harare. Phone her back URGENTLY.'

Mike passed the note to Oscar. "So much for Zambesia."

Oscar's shoulders slumped in disappointment. "Blast!" he spat.

★   ★   ★   ★   ★

The Zimbabwe customs man passed Mike his passport and gate pass. "Welcome home, sir. Have a nice journey?"

Back home. Back to Zimbabwe. He smiled thinly at the black official.

He'd phoned his wife back—dutifully, of course, thinking maybe there was a problem and something had happened to little George. But it was all okay with George. So what was the problem then? And she'd told him very calmly that unless he got back to Harare immediately, she would sue for a divorce. Enough was enough, she'd said. This was the last straw. She'd been expecting him home by Friday and how in hell did he expect her to live like that? As if she could waste her whole life hanging around, waiting for him! In your dreams Mike, in your dreams.

He was stunned. How had he ended up being the guilty party? She wouldn't let up. And what about his son? Growing up without a father. No wonder little George just wasn't bonding with him. No bloody wonder! And it was all his fault.

He had listened, dumbfounded. Was this how a common cuckold was meant to react? Was this how the unfaithful party was allowed to behave? He'd been very confused and in his confusion he'd agreed to come back—'to clear the air', as she'd said. It was worth a shot, he rationalized to himself. One last chance. One final, supreme effort. And then if it didn't work out ... well at least he could walk out with a clear conscience. He would have done his best.

And then to add to his confusion, Oscar had become resentful when he told him that he was heading back.

"I have to Oscar. Can't you see? I have to finish this. Once and for all."

With that Oscar turned to him with that that faraway look in his eyes, as if he couldn't care less, which angered Mike intensely.

"What kind of mate are you anyway, if you can't understand that this is something that I just have to do. It's my future, Oscar. One way or the other."

But Oscar was hardly listening and simply shrugged. Well, Oscar got like that when the dope was wearing off. He'd get over it.

Mike hadn't intended to, but half way up Christmas Pass, on the western side of the border town of Mutare, he pulled out the bottle of brandy. He switched the tape off and slugged back a gulp—neat. He gasped as the liquor coursed down his throat.

The brandy loosened his memory and his inner emotions and he allowed himself to become melancholic. It was the thought of losing George that was nagging away at him. Not that he had any overly affectionate feelings for the child. More a case of picturing the poor little fellow growing up without a dad.

Ever since the war, that ghastly civil war that had taken so many children, a kid in distress would bring back all those images of suffering and death.

He was finding that as he grew older, death was becoming an increasing preoccupation. Was it because he had given life to a child, little George? They always said it was easier for a child to lose a parent than for a parent to lose a child. Huh? Equating death with being 'easy'.

There was a famous photograph of a German soldier shooting a Jewish woman and her child somewhere in the

Ukraine. The photo was a black and white and it was blurred. But the image returned to Mike pretty much every day since he'd seen it. One young Jewish mother clutching her baby, back turned away from the soldier to protect her child. You couldn't see if it was a boy or a girl, but that was unimportant.

Even though the photo was a black and white, you could see that it was a bright sunny day. The soldier in that field had his rifle levelled, taking aim at the woman from about five paces. How many split seconds later had he fired the shot? How many shots did he fire? What was the woman thinking just before she undoubtedly died? Was she screaming, or was she silent? Did he shoot her first—and then walk up to the dead or dying woman as she lay on the ground and shoot the baby? Perhaps even in death the mother was hugging her baby to her bosom, trying to protect it?

An event that happened over 50 years before. A couple of weeks before, Mike had been in a bookshop buying some stationery. As was his want, he'd found himself drawn to the book section, and more particularly the war section. There was a book on the Holocaust that he hadn't seen before, so he picked it up and wandered through the pages. The picture on the Ukraine was in there. He knew he would buy the book even though he couldn't afford it. As it was, there was a problem with his credit card at the checkout counter and he didn't have enough cash for the book and the stationery. So he left the book.

He thought vaguely that perhaps that was some kind of omen, but couldn't quite figure what. So he'd left it at that, but it still puzzled him. Would it be of any succour to that Jewish woman on the Ukrainian plain to know that someone was thinking of her? He decided to pray for her and her child, there and then in the shopping mall. And he got angry at all the shoppers, the wealthy white housewives, their trolleys bursting at the seams with all sorts of things that they didn't need. They didn't give a damn for that woman, did they?

But his anger was short-lived. It wasn't their fault. Yet it was always the children. He'd sat down near the fountain in the mall and pulled out his cigarettes and watched the people going by. Was he the soldier on that Ukrainian steppe?

She was waiting for him at the front door, her lips white and drawn, her arms crossed. She smelt the brandy on his breath.

"You've been drinking," she accused.

He ignored her and pushed past her, lugging his bag after him. "Where's George?"

"Asleep. An' I don't want you disturbing him. I've just got him down."

They sat at the dining room table, one at each end. Her arms were still folded.And then she told him that she'd had to phone the office to find out where he was and when he was expected back. Someone called Lionel had told her that he should have been back on Wednesday.

"Look what you've gone and done now, Mike. Now you're in the shit with your job. That Lionel sounded pretty fed up."

He got angry. Now she was butting in on his work. Interfering with the boss. "Well, bugger Lionel!" was all he could say.

"Oh, ja. Easy for you to say. So what if you lose your job? So what if we haven't got any money to live on? Easy, huh?"

He hated her when she was sarcastic like that. He retaliated. "Since when have you started worrying about when I get back? Why? Is it because of your sordid liaisons with that wanker?"

"Don't start with that, Mike! I bloody well knew you'd drag that in."

"Well, isn't that what this is all about?"

"Don't be ridiculous. Honestly!"

"You're screwing this guy, aren't you?" he remembered himself saying.

"I am not ... he's just a very good friend," she retorted aggressively, trying to bully him into believing it. "Since when is it illegal for a woman to have male friends? Huh? Huh?"

He felt almost detached from his body, as if he was a spectator on the ceiling. "I .. I just want to know the truth… that's all." He felt weak. He felt sick. There was an emptiness in his gut he couldn't describe. He could hear little George waking up in his bedroom, whimpering softly.

"I'm sick and tired of your questions," she was shouting now. "I don't want this subject ever brought up again. EVER."

"I … I … just wanted to ask …"

"EVER. Do … you … understand me?" She was shrieking, almost hysterically. Like a she-wolf, he thought.

He said nothing. He knew he had a choice to make—there and then. Another ground-breaking, life-making decision. He was staring vacantly at the coffee cup on the table. Perhaps death was like this. A void of nothingness. George was now crying very loudly, fully awake. An anxious, pitiful cry.

"I'm leaving," Mike heard himself say, almost inaudibly.

There was a long silence before she spoke. "What are you saying, Mike?" Her voice was now low and menacing.

"I'm leaving."

"You will do no such thing … how dare you even think about that … I mean, you have a child. He is your responsibility. I mean, you can't just walk out." Her voice was a mixture of anger and fear. Of incredulity … through the snarls.

He made to stand up, all the while his gaze fixedly on the coffee cup.

"SIT DOWN!" she was almost howling. In a frenzy. She clawed at his arm and shoved him back into the chair. Tears were beginning to well.

Mike stood up and looked at his wife. He knew then that he had made the right decision. He picked up his car keys from the dresser. "I'll come back later to collect my stuff."

Like a robot he unlocked his car and climbed in, all the while hearing his wife wailing and shrieking inside the house. She'd made no attempt to follow him out and he was grateful for that.

He drove for a long long time.

★ ★ ★ ★ ★

Like the Jewish mother on the sunlit Ukrainian steppe, the image of his child, desperately crying, came to him. He was the soldier. Jewish children, white children, black children. Children all. His child.

He drove around Harare for what seemed like hours. He didn't know where to go. Finally he wound up at Melvin's house and Melvin took him in. The first thing he did was give Mike a double brandy and Coke. And then another, which took the edge off. And another and another. And Mike was crying and laughing at the same time.

He'd done it.

Mike slept on Melvin's couch that night. He had vomited a lot and Melvin had said that was okay. Under the circumstances.

He woke late the next morning, feeling like death. Melvin was out, so Mike wandered through to the kitchen and made himself some tea. Melvin's wife had left a note for him next to the toaster, saying that they had gone out to Lake Mac for the day and that he must make himself at home, take it easy and not do anything foolish.

"Huh!" Mike grunted to himself. "And life goes on."

★ ★ ★ ★ ★

Twenty years before in another era, a little girl was collecting water from a river when she heard the fighter-bombers come. She was only six but she knew something was wrong. She dropped her bucket and started running frantically back to the camp. She was confused. She'd heard the grown-ups talking. The camp was far inside Mozambique. The white men and their aeroplanes would never dare come this far.

But they were here.

The planes screamed overhead and she heard the bombs whistling. The world went white and she collapsed into the earth in terror. The explosions rumbled and roared and the ground shook. The very world was being torn apart. She scrambled frantically under a fallen tree and huddled into a ball, squeezing her eyes shut and blocking her ears with her little hands.

And then the heaving subsided and the earth stopped shaking. Slowly uncovering her ears, she listened. She could hear the people from the camp screaming. Then they were running. She cowered lower into the refuge of the tree trunk as she saw the hordes of frightened people rushing blindly away from the camp. Anywhere—anywhere away from the camp.

She saw her mother in the throng. She always recognized her mother even though she wore the same combat fatigues as everyone else. She was running wildly, her arms flailing to her front, desperately trying to seek safety through the clinging bush.

The girl scampered out from the tree-trunk. "AMAI, Amai," she shouted, frantically waving her arms in the air. "I am here. I am here." To the west she heard the dull throb-throb of helicopters.

The mother recognized the girl in the madness and ran to her. They fell to the ground, clutching each other with tears of joy and relief.

Then, like demons, the white soldiers came. In a long line from the bush. A wraith of men with black paint smeared on their faces. Quickly and silently they approached the mother and her child as they clung to each other. A soldier, his eyes aflame, stopped a few paces in front of them, his rifle in his shoulder.

The little girl was screaming. She knew what was happening. The soldier squeezed the trigger and she squeezed her eyes shut. There was darkness and she felt her mother's arms go limp. She felt the warm blood on her face. She tasted it in her mouth. She was squeezing her eyes so tightly that her whole body was shaking violently.

"Leave the girl," she heard someone say. And when she opened her eyes, the white men were gone.

Ten

Mike sat polishing outside Melvin's kitchen porch. It was hot and languid. Like a zombie he'd sat on his haunches all day, polishing the brass belt buckles that Melvin had made. It was one of Melvin's many businesses—all good ideas, but all under-capitalized—rather zero-capitalized. Melvin said he had a mega contract with one of the town's leading boutiques but Mike saw little evidence of Melvin having an infra-structure of coping with such a contract, if—and that was a big if—the "mega contract" was real.

The bottle of brandy on the grass was about two-thirds gone. He'd run out of Cokes at the halfway mark and had been too bothered to walk down to the Greek cafe on the corner for a re-supply. Melvin had been out since eleven o'clock that morning. He knew Melvin's routine. Wake up late—towards midday normally, wander around the house in a towel looking for a Coke, a cigarette and some Syndol painkillers. Take a bath for about 40 minutes and then blow-dry the hair for another 20.

Melvin had said he was going out.

"In the meantime Mike, why don't you get stuck into this box of buckles? It'd really help me out. I've got a big order to deliver on Friday."

"I ... I'd rather not, Melv. I'd kinda like to hang out ... and do nothing ..." Mike finished lamely.

"Hey man, it'll sort the pip out. Take your mind off all the hassles." Melvin was being his persuasive best. "Just park off in the sun an suck on a bottle of dop and rub the odd buckle with a bit of Brasso. No major sweat."

And with that he'd left. Mike had gone to the mukwa bar in the living room and had found an unopened bottle of brandy. There were a few unfinished bottles of Coke, mostly flat and without caps, lying around the place. He decanted some into what looked to be the most promising bottle and was gratified to see that the fizz wasn't totally gone. He salvaged a bottle-full and found a clean glass under the counter. The ice trays in the freezer box were empty, so he decided it was unimportant. He'd do without.

A fluffy white Persian cat was lying on top of the perspex lid of the stereo turntable. Mike picked it up and plopped it onto the sofa. Wiping the white hairs off the lid, he put on a record. It was The Temptations' *Masterpiece*. The record was only slightly scratched, which he thought was fortunate, as most of Melvin's record collection lay scattered about the house out of their sleeves. He turned the volume up loud as 'Ma' came on. It was a good song. Lots of guts, and it made him feel better immediately. He poured himself the first brandy and felt better still. The day wasn't going to be so bad after all.

He polished and polished, rather enjoying the mindless, physical nature of the work. An uncomplicated life, that for those few hours held an allure on a long-term basis. The music kept on rolling.

By mid-afternoon he had retrieved all of the records from about the house and had found the sleeves for most of them. He knew that in a couple of days they'd all be strewn around again, but it didn't matter for now.

He pretty well knew the whole of Melvin's collection. They'd grown up on records and had spent many long hours together, exploring each other's musical tastes, which were diametrically opposed, yet intrinsically similar.

Mike had introduced Melvin to Motown, the blues and southern rock—Marvin Gaye, Smokey Robinson, Sonny and Brownie and The Allman Brothers. In return, Melvin had taught Mike the wonders of mainstream rock n' roll—The Beatles, Elvis, The Everly Brothers, The Doobie Brothers, Bachmann-Turner and Queen. But also the songs of the old music halls and the traditional Irish and Scottish ballads. Nothing was irrelevant.

They even began listening to the *kwela* music of the townships and found they liked the rhythms and the syncopations. They didn't understand the words but that didn't matter. Their white contemporaries would sneer at them—even their women. "How can you listen to that kaffir music? It's *so* repetitive."

The sun slid down behind the neighbours' tall fir trees and as the daylight folded so did Mike's feeling of bonhomie. Twilight had become an increasingly difficult time of the day for him. He felt guilty as he so often did when he realized he was already drunk. How could he face the night if he was drunk? He lost interest in the buckles and packed them back in the box.

Melvin's red Pulsar came into the gravel driveway. The drive shafts were shot and rattled like a machine-gun. Mike smiled as he looked at the car—even the panel beaters had given up. The passenger seat was missing, the driver's door was jammed stuck and the fuel cap, long since lost, had been replaced by the remnants of a pair of underpants.

Melvin was impressed by the amount of polishing Mike had accomplished, but his mind was on the gig ahead. The buckles would have to wait until tomorrow. He began gathering up his music gear. Another cat was asleep on his battered guitar, oblivious of the two broken strings prodding into its fur. Melvin kicked the cat off and hurriedly started to replace the strings.

"Give us an E, Mike," he ordered.

Mike took his own guitar, a Yamaha, out of the case and obliged. Melvin had a thing about tuning up, imagining after every song that his guitar had gone out. Satisfied that he was in tune, he dumped the guitar in the back seat of the car, promptly knocking the pegs out of tune again.

He rushed back into the lounge and gathered up the remains of his gear—sheet music, leads, mike stand and all the other bits and pieces which he crammed into the blue suitcase that didn't close properly. He had an 'octopus' for that, an elasticized strap with hooks at the ends.

"Pull in later, Mike," Melvin shouted, as he clambered into the car through the passenger door. "But don't come too early … nothing happens 'til about ten or eleven." With that he fired up the motor and reversed out the drive. Mike winced as the drive shafts ground metal and threatened to snap. He knew Melvin didn't like his buddies to come along to his gigs too early. He was never at his best with a crowd that wasn't fired up. Mike respected this.

Mike timed it right. He jostled his way through the crowd of young whites, who were singing and shouting above Melvin's slightly distorted music. Mike sensed Melvin was overdoing it on the bass, but that didn't worry the crowd. Melvin was in full stride, in the middle of Kevin 'Bloody' Wilson's *Do you fuck on first dates?* which had become his signature tune. That and *Up against the wall motherfucker*. Mike shook his head and smiled. Melvin somehow always got away with it. The hotel management would ban him from time to time in a token gesture of piety, but would soon woo him back when they noticed the drop in bar-takings.

Mike felt light-headed and faintly nauseous from the joint he'd had in the car on the way to the hotel. But that was all part of the buzz.

He bumped into a girl he vaguely knew, a divorcee, who spilt her beer down his shirt. She was drunk and swayed against him, clumsily trying to apologize. Her eyes were hooded. She was shouting in his ear that all men, except him of course, were bastards, and she was going to get even. She had a weapon that no man could ever hope to match.

"I c'n get inny fuckin' man I want—with this!" She rubbed her groin to emphasize the point. "Wash your name again, sweedhard?" Her eyes were red from the smoke.

"Mike."

"You wan' it?" She slurred.

"No thanks," Mike replied, thinking about it briefly.

"Well, damn you. Y'aint gonna bloody geddit anyways!" She smiled triumphantly, a victory for her feminism. Or so her eyes seemed to be saying.

Mike elbowed his way past her, towards the small stage where Melvin was singing in the corner. Melvin must have had at least a dozen double cane-and-Cokes lined up on top of the amplifier. Do you fuck on first dates? had come to an end and Melvin was in the middle of organizing a wet T-shirt competition with the bunch of groupies around the stage.

Four or five of the girls were standing in a line facing the audience, thrusting out their breasts, as a young bearded fellow doused them with beer. They had taken off their bras, and their nipples showed clearly through the wet fabric. The crowd roared in appreciation and amidst the whoops and catcalls, Melvin noticed Mike.

"Hey, Mike," he bellowed above the din, "come pull in with the harp."

Mike groaned inwardly, but was nevertheless pleased that Melvin had asked him. It was a charade they always went through. Melvin taking the limelight with the rowdy sing-along songs, and when he was weary, or had run out of material, he'd get Mike up to come and play the harmonica.

Mike played a mean blues harp.

"There you go—you *are* an expert at something," Mike muttered under his breath, thinking back to the periwinkle woman on the beach at Beira. He waved at Melvin who was gesticulating impatiently for him to get up on stage. "Okay, Melv. I'm there in a minute." He felt the familiar kick of adrenaline inside—a good warm feeling. As the muzos said—he was in the key.

His wife, little George ... Lionel and the job ...were now distant memories.

The wet T-shirt girls had done their thing and Melvin was distractedly wrapping up the judging.

"And ... the winner of ... The Miss 'Soggy-Tits' Wet T-shirt competition ... iiiisss ....," he flicked a knob on his drum box which gave out an impressive drum roll, "... iiiisss going to be announced in a few seconds ...." Another drum roll, finished off by some loud cymbals. He gulped at the nearest cane and Coke and lit up a Madison.

Some of the crowd were beginning to get impatient, shouting at him to move it up.

"Laaaadies and gentleman," he silenced them all by turning the volume up a notch on the microphone, "before I announce the winner, I have been requested by the management to confirm that the first prize, most generously donated by Crest Chickens, is one year's free supply of chicken!"

The girls looked at each other askance. Clearly no modelling contracts this time.

"Yes, you heard me correctly. ONE YEAR'S FREE SUPPLY OF CHICKEN!" He took another slug of his drink, revelling in the anticipation of the crowd and the power he held over it. "The winner will get to suck my dick for one whole YEAR! ... Why? BECAUSE IT TASTES FOWL!" He shouted the punchline to make sure it wasn't lost and then convulsed into fits of laughter, spluttering his cane and Coke over the blonde in front of him. She turned to him, feigning anger. It wasn't cool to get pissed off with the muzo, although she was.

"AND the winner is ..." no nonsense this time. He lent over to the blonde, "What's your name, darling?"

"Chantelle."

"AND the winner, by the briefest of a purple nipple ... with the biggest tits south of the Zambezi, IIISSSS ... CHANTELLE. SHOW US YER TITS, DARLING."

Chantelle shrieked, blushing violently and then lifted the sodden T-shirt to reveal her statuesque breasts for a few seconds. The crowd roared with delight.

Mike remembered the black girl in the Beira nightclub and found himself wondering what her breasts were like. He pushed past the girls on to the stage. Melvin was still chuckling to himself.

"Stupid bitch … probably believes me. Hey Mike, grab one of those cane and Cokes and get that harp out. We're gonna blow these Rhodies away with some *serrrious blues*."

Mike pulled out his little harmonica. Not many people could play a blues harp in Harare like him. Perhaps one or two of the coloured dudes from Arcadia. But certainly no honky.

He blew the key to Melvin, who had to bend down close to hear above the noise. It always took some time to get the key right. The harp played a different key to the guitar and Melvin had to work it out. After a while of blowing, sucking and twanging, they were ready. Melvin set the drum box to a fast 12-bar blues and away they went. It was complete unstructured free-style. Mike started slowly and softly, building up to a crescendo and then bringing it down again, with Melvin instinctively following, working it well.

Mike noticed out the corner of his eye, that the divorced woman had jostled her way right up to the front and was clapping along merrily, the hooded eyes almost closed in rapture.

After about ten minutes, perhaps more, Mike felt they were done and began winding down. But Melvin would have none of it and started sliding into another chord sequence, softly growling unintelligible jazz-type lyrics. And Mike again clasped the harp to the microphone and started over.

Finally, after 20 minutes or so, Melvin began to slow it down, adding more sevenths in the run-up to the ending. Mike followed suit and they finished off tightly in a lengthy flurry of drums and vibrato strumming. The crowd screamed and whistled for more, but they were both done. Sometimes an encore would kill it all.

Mike felt drained, flushed from the exertions. He was sweating from the intensity of the stage lights and flattened his drink.

Melvin was hugging him. "Brilliant Mike. Bloody brilliant … give me about ten minutes to finish this set and we can flick out to the car park for a jay."

Mike nodded. He would like that.

Presently, they were sitting out in the car park, dragging on a joint. The divorcee had followed Melvin out, not wanting to miss out on an opportunity to be alone with two celebrities, small-town that they were.

"I can't hang about for too long," said Melvin, passing the joint to the divorcee. "I gotta start my next set in five minutes. Are you coming back for another session Mike?"

Mike shook his head, "Uh-uh, I've had enough. I need to hit the sack."

"Okay, we'll check you tomorrow." He climbed out of the car, ignoring the divorcee, and disappeared into the darkness.

The divorcee spread herself out on the front seat of the car, puffing hard on the tail of the joint. Her legs had carelessly flopped open, with her short skirt riding dangerously high towards her lace panties. But she was oblivious of this.

"Here, mouth-organ man," she slurred, handing the smouldering tail to Mike. "D'you wanna finish this?"

Mike took the jay. He sucked on what was left of it, more resin than actual marijuana. He felt dizzy and thought about being sick. It had been a very long day. He considered making a 'snifter' out of the tail, but changed his mind and tossed the butt-end out of the window.

"Are you going back in?" he turned to the woman on the seat next to him.

She shook her head slowly, without answering, and shuffled across the seat towards him. Her skirt had now ridden up about her waist and Mike could plainly see her panties under the folds of her slight paunch. She groped clumsily at the zipper of Mike's trousers. He did not resist, although he was thinking about it. Perhaps she would take it as an insult. Perhaps it was the gentlemanly thing to do, to let her get on with it. After all, he didn't want to hurt her feelings.

Her head was down on his crotch as she extricated his now-erect penis from the trousers. He winced as she caught it against the toothed metal of the zipper. But he was beyond caring, forcing himself to relax as she took him into her mouth. Her head moved languidly up and down and he began to warm to the sensation.

His left hand found her crotch, forcing his fingers into her wetness, prising her panties aside. He felt her hips move to receive his hand, as he roughly plunged his fingers into her. He felt himself coming and his body tensed violently as he emptied himself into her mouth. She was moaning softly, her pelvis grinding angrily against Mike's hand. He clenched her hair with his right hand. It felt clammy, almost greasy and he didn't like himself much at that moment. He wanted to be away from the situation.

He hauled her head off his crotch as she turned up to face him. She smiled at him drunkenly, and for a moment he thought she might vomit. Her face was smeared with his semen, her eyes closed. He could see she still had a mouthful of the stuff that she hadn't swallowed. She dragged herself up towards his face and tried to kiss him. He panicked at the realization of what she was trying to do and roughly thrust her away. She swallowed the mouthful of semen, making noisy gulping sounds and laughed, revelling in his repulsion.

"I'll take you home," he muttered, zipping his flies. "Where d'you live?"

"Dunno. Just drive, Mr. Mouth-Organ." She was fingering herself, squelching loudly "Mount Pleasant … that's where. Just drive…"

"Where in Mount Pleasant?"

"Dunno. Just drive … I'll tell you."

He fired up the engine and slammed the door shut. He switched on the car radio, but it was after midnight and all the radio stations had shut down for the night. Bending forward, he found an old Status Quo cassette and popped it into the tape. The woman attempted to smear her middle finger under his nose and he pulled himself away. She cackled, and sucked on the finger. She smelt.

"Mmmmm … You don't want some? There's plenny more where that came from." She cackled some more.

She tried to play a game with him—giving him the wrong directions to her house. He was becoming angrier. Why did he always end up with trash like this?

"If you don't tell me where you live, I'm going to dump you on the side of the road," he tried to sound forceful. It irritated that this stupid little charade had become the preoccupying event of his life at that particular moment. Did Eric Clapton or Phil Collins have to put up with this kind of crap? He almost laughed out loud at the ridiculous analogy.

Perhaps it was the tone in his voice, yet more likely the tension of his body language, that persuaded her to stop the game. The car finally turned into the driveway of her house. He didn't want to switch off the engine as she might construe that as an invitation. But it made no difference and she leaned across the steering wheel and turned off the key herself.

"One last suck Mr. Mouth-Organ?" she pleaded in a little-girl voice.

Mike heaved a sigh, "No. I gotta get home."

"Pleassse," she whined, "it won't take a minute…"

Mike was about to capitulate as a way of getting rid of her, when he heard an horrific wailing from inside the house. Almost a screech. For a second he thought it was a cat being strangled, but on closer inspection recognized it as the sound of a small child in severe distress. The faces of the war children flashed in front of his eyes.

"Bloody brat," the divorcee snarled, hitching up her skirt and pants.

"Is that your child?"

"Ja, an' I'm gonna wring her neck."

"How old is she?

"Four, but if she carries on like this, she's never gonna get to five." She grabbed her handbag from the floor of the car.

"Don't you have a nanny?" Mike was allowing himself to become concerned, involved.

"Oh, ja! But she's probably pissed. Bloody kaffirs!" She spat the words, got out of the car and slammed the door behind her, storming off towards the house. Mike knew he should just start the car and get out of there as fast as possible.

Yet for some reason he dallied. Was this how his wife would turn out? With little George? He saw the lights going on in the house—first the lounge, then the passage, and then presumably the bedroom where the little girl was crying. He heard the mother screaming with rage. He heard the dull thumps. Thump, thump—it pounded in his brain.

The soldier, the Jewish mother. Leave her ... leave the girl.

He tried to block out the terrified screams of the little girl and when he could take no more, he started the car and reversed furiously on to the road.

He was breathing heavily when he pulled over a few hundred metres down the road, finally succumbing to the combined smells of the cheap sex, stale tobacco and marijuana that swamped the inside of the cab. He opened the door and retched violently, gagging and spitting. But it was what Melvin called, 'a dry run', which was the worst, his stomach empty and contorted.

"This is the last, Mike," he vowed to himself. "The last time. Get a grip, Mike. You're gonna kill yourself if you don't. Get out of this sleaze, for Christ's sake. Can't you see what it's doing to you?"

He knew in himself then, hanging out that car door with all his dignity stripped, that this was as low as he was going to sink.

If he could just hang in there for a bit longer, a few more days, then he could start pulling himself out of the trough of despair he had found himself in.

He made the resolution to himself, no more alcohol, no more dope, no more white trash, no more guitar, no more … self-pity.

Somehow, he knew he was serious. There was no choice anymore.

★　★　★　★　★

Phoebe had never been so afraid in her whole life as she was now, sitting there on the derelict quayside. Not even the distant memories of her mother's death had seemed as bad.

The sun was setting up the Pungue estuary, its muddy waters, tinged golden bronze in the fading light, sliding silently to the sea. A tugboat chugged upstream towards the modern, gleaming, state-of-the-art docks, gently scattering a swarm of dugout canoes out of its path. A lone fisherman, crouching on his haunches below at the water's edge, pulled anxiously at his handline, uncaring of the woman above on the stonework.

She felt the coldness of the concrete through her jeans. She had been sitting like that for many hours now, her knees pulled into her chest, her arms around her legs. She was alone. It was better like this.

The tears had gone. No more would come, in spite of her efforts. Resting her chin on her knees, she watched as a stray dog approached, nervous, cringing, its head tilted sideways, askance. She made no effort to acknowledge it and merely regarded the creature with a dull indifference. The dog came within a couple of metres and craned its snout to her, sniffing at her with a mild curiosity. There was nothing of interest. It turned and wandered away a few paces and then lay down, its face on its forepaws.

Her life was in danger. She knew it was an outside possibility. Anything was a possibility with Salim. She had seen the way he could change. One minute, the picture of serenity and gentleness. And the next, an erupting volcano. Such behaviour was not normal. Yes, this pattern had always been in him, but never to such an extent.

She had fled from the hotel after Salim had hit her. She had fled for her life, running wildly away from that place. All she had known was that she should not return to the *apartamento*. The *guarda-costa* would surely be waiting for her. So she had run, stumbling blindly through her tears, in the other direction, towards the docks. The docks where she had first started plying her trade when Salim had brought her to Beira, more than ten years before, before the new port was built.

It was with a certain amount of equanimity that she addressed her situation, in spite of her fear. There was a level of candour in her thinking that was borne out of her past, her life on the streets. There was nowhere to run. Where could she go? Her world was that narrow strip of corridor that ran from Beira to Chimoio. That was all.

Yes, she could hide for a while, but it would not take long for Salim to find her. And how could she live? To find the right sort of clients would mean frequenting the clubs controlled by Salim's pimps. All the clubs and bars were controlled by Salim and his pimps. There was no escaping it.

She stood up, as the dog flinched nervously. The decision was simple. Facing the estuary, she breathed in deeply, the air clammy in the evening sun. She would go back to the hotel and face Salim. With humility. She would apologize. She had not been herself of late. And yes, she had not been attending to her duties. She would see to that. Perhaps he would strike her again. Well, if so, she would cower. After all, he was a man, was he not? It was necessary for his honour that he should be seen to have the power.

It was a solution … for the moment. Things would change in time.

She turned on her heels, her back erect, as the dog slunk off into the shadows.

★   ★   ★   ★   ★

Martha knew that the *puta* would come crawling back. What else could she do? She had intimated as much to the *senhor*, but he had merely grunted and retreated into his office, slamming the door behind him. She also knew that it was a waste of time sending the *guarda-costa* off to her *apartamento*. The *puta* was not stupid. She would not go there. Better to wait and do nothing. She would be back before nightfall.

The woman had returned as she'd predicted. And, as she'd known, the *senhor* had forgiven her. All too easily. But such were the ways of men. Martha held her tongue. It would not be prudent to speak just then.

She buried her head in the petty cash ledger as the *senhor* and the *puta* emerged from the office. He was smiling benignly, his arm around her waist. She could not make out the *puta's* face, hidden beneath her hair, dishevelled and matted.

No, that *puta* was not stupid. Not by any means.

Eleven

Mike went to work the following day. Lionel wanted to see him, urgently. The previous night had been packaged away into the ever-increasing 'waste box' in his brain as was his habit. Not totally forgotten, but now superfluous to the matter at hand. He'd always had a knack of being able to do that but it hadn't been like that in the old days, when a morning following a night of drunkenness and whoring had always been wracked with self-recrimination. But in time he'd learned how to deal with his feelings—simply a question of putting it all in the past.

But today was different, wasn't it? It was now time to address these issues, face on.

He turned left off Samora Machel Avenue onto Sir James MacDonald, as a minibus taxi loaded with black commuters, veered across his front and pulled over on the side of the road to disgorge a few of its passengers. For a moment he thought about getting angry and shouting out the window at the driver. But he dismissed the thought. It wasn't worth the effort, and anyway the driver had deadlines to meet, targets to reach.

"There you go again—rationalizing everything," he said aloud. His loins felt tender from the oral sex the previous night and he forced himself to think not only about that debasing experience but also the events of the last few days. His wife, little George … and always, always there was the alcohol. Even in that night-club in Beira he had been half-drunk.

"Admit it, Mike," he said to himself. "You cannot function without alcohol. You cannot face the world. You cannot face yourself…without it. This must change."

He pulled up at the traffic lights near the milk depot. The minibus taxi that had cut him off earlier, raced past in the left-hand lane through the red light. Midway through the intersection, it almost collided with a Peugeot 504 station wagon that was also running the red light from the opposite direction. At the last second the minibus veered to the right to avoid the oncoming car. Both drivers slammed on their horns but not their brakes, waving their fists and showering each other with futile invective. Mike smiled at the normality of it all. He felt tender all over, shivering and held up his left hand, outstretched, to see if it was shaking. Not a quiver.

But he was shaking inside. Was it the alcohol, or was it the nerves? Nervousness of what lay ahead at the office? Nerves or nervousness? His mind was spinning out of control, trying to deal with his life's problems at that intersection. But deal with them he would, one way or another. The car behind hooted impatiently and he started. The lights had changed to green.

It was hot already. Hot and dry. A wind was blowing erratically in warm gusts that buffeted the car intermittently. The lack of uniformity in the pattern irritated Mike. It was untidy. Like the old newspapers and empty plastic milk packets that were being swept across the tarmac, getting trapped against the sagging mesh fence on the side of the road. A line of ice-cream vendors, with their unwieldy bicycle carts, pressed crab-like into the wind.

Rush hour in Harare's light industrial sites was like a race. It seemed important to the drivers that they get ahead, if only by one car-length. Mike could see in front that the lights at the Coventry Road intersection were red. He slowed down, pacing the rusty Morris Minor doing about 40 kays an hour in the next lane. Almost immediately a dam of infuriated drivers built up behind him. Mike again smiled.

He knew the Coventry Road traffic lights took forever, so he tapped out a Madison and lit up. The car was enveloped in smoke as he wound the window down a fraction. Like a vacuum cleaner, a gust of wind immediately sucked the smoke outside.

He turned the radio on, tuning in to Radio One. A Bellamy Brothers' song was playing—*If I said you had a beautiful body, would you hold it against me?* Standard fare for Zimbabwean listeners, and here they were, heading for the millennium.

Then there was 'The Saying of the Day'—some inane cliché, today sent in by a Mrs Mavis Someone from Hatfield, who had kindly donated her winning dollar to the SPCA. He remembered the 'Saying of the Day' from a generation before. How many pearls of wisdom would that be? Three hundred and sixty-five times 25. And still only for a dollar.

The traffic lights changed and he turned right into Coventry Road, the main access into the industrial sites. Seeing the opportunity, the dam of cars furiously overtook him on the inside lane, racing ahead to get to work first.

As he pulled up at the gates, the security guard recognized him and routinely swung open the boom. He looked for a parking place and with irritation noted that the car park was full. Maliciously he thought about pulling into one of the managers' undercover bays, most of which were still empty, but decided against it. No point in adding fuel to the fire.

"They want us to come to work, but there's no place to park," he shouted loudly out the window at a black sales rep who was locking his car. It was Innocent and Mike liked him.

"Oh, hi Mike. When you get back?" Innocent replied.

"Yesterday," Mike lied, "back to this." He waved his arm generally, indicating the full car park. He knew he was being petulant, but couldn't stop himself.

"Ja, I know. We were complaining again at Monday's sales meeting, but Lionel said we should just park outside." Innocent was making conversation.

"Well, bugger Lionel," Mike spat. "And then the cars get pinched outside…."

Innocent shrugged. "What can you do? … I'll see you later."

Mike reversed and decided to park on the patch of unkempt lawn outside the showroom. The grass was dry and half-dead, so what did it matter? He'd noticed Lionel's car wasn't in its bay and was grateful. It would give him time to sort out his briefcase in the sales office and have a cup of coffee. The roses outside the entrance still hadn't been pruned and were woody and diseased. He'd pruned them himself last winter, but no one had really noticed. Although someone had vaguely asked what the pair of secateurs was doing on his desk.

The showroom was already a buzz of activity, with the ranks of the black counter salesmen preparing their order pads, their invoice pads, their delivery-note pads, their receipt pads and the yards of carbon paper for the day's trading. They waved at Mike, smiling cheerfully. He waved back in acknowledgement but recognized the worry behind their eyes. There had been some retrenchments last month. He wondered if they greeted him because they genuinely liked him, or was it because he was white and therefore one of the bosses, even potentially?

He plonked his briefcase on an empty desk in the communal sales office, adjoining the showroom. Pulling up a chair, he lounged, waiting for the tea tray to arrive. It was late today. Maybe the tea-boy's commuter omnibus had broken down.

"Howzit Mike? Good trip?" It was Wayne, one of the white sales managers. His desk was in the corner and Mike hadn't noticed him when he'd walked in. Wayne and Mike didn't like each other, although Wayne extended to Mike a frosty respect because he had also been in the war. Perhaps it was the fact that they had absolutely nothing else in common.

Wayne was, as far as Mike was concerned, the epitome of a 'Rhodie' in its worst interpretation—not overly intelligent, belligerent and innately racist. It wasn't so much his clipped Rhodesian accent that grated, but more so his dress-sense that mirrored his attitudes. Like a relic out of Federation, a time warp. Today he was wearing his sky-blue, crimpolene slacks that were slightly flared and an inch and a half too short. Even the safari suit was better than this.

"Oh … morning, Wayne. Sorry, I didn't see you there. Ja, it was okay," Mike replied, noncommittally.

"D'you do any business?" Wayne asked, testing.

"Ja, some."

"Any orders?" Wayne persisted.

"Ja, a couple. Nothing major. But lots of possibilities." Mike was wanting to kill the conversation, sensing Wayne gratuitously trying to dig out information.

"Ja, y'know I've always said that Mozambique has heaps of potential."

"It has, but it's going to take a long time," Mike added.

The tea-boy came in with the tray and smiled nervously at the two white men.

"Ja, y'know. That's the problem with these okes," Wayne pointedly indicated the tea-boy as a prime example of the entire black race. "Give 'em one of the richest countries in Africa … and they still manage to destroy it."

Mike started to pour himself a cup of tea. Wayne was on to his pet subject and nothing would distract him.

"Y'know, we should have buggered them up proper in the *hondo*. I mean it was war! That was the problem—the politicians sold us down the river, before we could finish the job," Wayne continued.

Mike didn't reply. He felt he should challenge him, but knew he'd be there for another hour, slugging it out. And Wayne just wouldn't understand. In a million years he could never comprehend how someone like Mike had actually fought in the war, but didn't necessarily agree with it.

Seeing that Mike wasn't rising to his diatribe, Wayne changed course marginally. "Lionel was telling me about his trip to Beira with you … an' about that black bitch that asked him to buy her a drink." He laughed lewdly. "I'd have loved to have seen his face."

"It was embarrassing," Mike said flatly, but Wayne misunderstood him.

"Bloody right it must have been. Having some black bitch trying to chat you up." He ignored Mike's ineffectual interruption to put the record straight. "Y'know, at least here in Zim, the kaffir still knows his place. Except the government … bloody clowns. I dunno why we put up with it."

"So why are you still here?" Mike couldn't resist the jibe. "Why don't you leave?"

Wayne missed the point. "Agh, it's still a good lifestyle here, y'know … if you ignore all the bullshit. I mean, I was born in this country. So I'm as much an African as these okes. I've also got a right to be here…." The telephone rang at his desk, cutting him short. "Hello … Oh, howzit, Lionel … ja, he's here…" He laughed loudly at something Lionel had said. "Ja, we were just talking about that … Okay, I'll tell him … Ja, okay. Cheers."

"Is he looking for me?" Mike asked. The nerves had returned and his mouth felt dry.

"Ja. Wants you up in his office. Now."

Mike closed up his briefcase, having extracted his trip report. "See you later," he said, stowing the briefcase under the desk.

"Ja, check you around." Wayne got back to his sales figures.

Lionel's office was on the second floor of the building, wedged in between the boardroom and the managing director's office. Mike greeted the phalanx of secretaries as he walked down the corridor. His palms were sweating and he was telling himself to keep cool. His biggest concern was that his voice might waver. He knocked softly on Lionel's open door.

"Ah, come in Mike," said Lionel, looking up from his laptop. "Shut the door behind you, will you."

"Morning Lionel," Mike tried to say with confidence.

"Have a seat." Lionel closed the lid of the laptop and leaned back in his chair, his arms clasped behind his head.

This is it, Mike thought. Lionel's body language said it all. It was the hint of a smile on his face that Mike read—somewhere between awkward, embarrassed and patronizing.

"Mike..," he began. "I don't quite know how to say this ... but there's a problem ... and we've gotta deal with it."

Mike took a deep breath, but said nothing. He wasn't going to make it easy for him.

"What I'm trying to say ... at this point in time ... is that this company has a business culture we've taken many years to develop ... "

Mike knew what was coming next, but at that moment was wondering why they all used that meaningless and pretentious phrase 'at this point in time'.

"What I'm trying to say," Lionel was building up the courage to say it, "... is that you've got your own ideas on doing business ... which are fine, don't get me wrong. It's just that ... they aren't always necessarily compatible with the company's. D'you know what I'm trying to say ... Mike?" Lionel looked down at his desk.

Mike took another deep breath. "Am I right in saying that I don't fit in?" He didn't know if the tremor in his voice was audible.

"Well ... not exactly, although that's part of it. I mean, we have the greatest respect for you Mike, and what you've achieved for the company," he added quickly.

"What then? What is it?" Mike asked coldly. He felt the anger rising inside. "Is it personal? Be honest with me."

Now it was Lionel's turn to take a deep breath. "Okay. I'll give it to you straight. And this is from the MD, you understand? Firstly, we're aware of your alcohol problem. And secondly, we're very worried about some of your ... social habits." He raised his hand to stop Mike from interrupting.

"Look … your personal business is your own business. We're a strictly non-racial company … affirmative action and all that crap. But regrettably some of our most important clients are the old-school Rhodesian types. I mean, you know that some of them won't deal with black reps. They won't even deal with whites who they reckon are too …buddy-buddy with the blacks."

"Go on Lionel. Say it. Say it all," Mike heard himself say softly.

"Okay, Mike. Cards on the table. And I'm telling you this because you're a good guy. I mean, you're a mate. The first thing is that your drinking has become an embarrassment to the company …"

"And the second?" Mike prompted.

"There are stories going around that you're sleeping with black women … I can't tell you where we've heard, but bottom line Mike, we can't afford to have rumours like this flying around."

Mike was silent for a while, aware of Lionel's acute discomfort, but uncaring. He knew that Lionel knew there were no such stories. This was all about that incident with the black hooker in Beira, wasn't it? His drinking? Well, yes, that was a problem. But it hadn't affected his work performance. Had it?

"Are you firing me, Lionel?"

"I'm saying Mike, we want to let you go. We're very sorry it had to come to this. But you know how it is? I mean, business has to come first. Please understand … it's nothing personal. It's purely a straightforward business decision."

"Ja, sure." Mike tried not to sound sarcastic, but didn't succeed.

"Look Mike," Lionel went on, "let's not part ways on bad terms. We'll sort you out with a generous severance package. You'll get three-months' salary in lieu of notice. We'll let you keep the car for three months and we'll take care of your medical aid as well."

It was generous. Blood money. Mike made a decision. "Okay Lionel. I'm not going to take it further. No point flogging a dead horse. We leave it at that?" He stood up.

Lionel also stood up, very relieved. He extended his hand. "My secretary has your envelope for you. If you can collect it on your way out. Oh … and if you could hand over all your files to Wayne. He'll be taking over your duties." He smiled thinly.

"Okay, no problem," Mike shook hands with Lionel. "See you."

"Ja. Go well."

Mike turned and stepped out into the corridor. The secretaries looked away, busying themselves in their computers.

The wind was still blustery outside and a layer of dust and soot had settled on the car. The security guard at the gate flashed Mike a broad grin as he lifted the boom.

"See you tomorrow, Mister Mike."

Mike smiled back at the man and swung out into Coventry Road.

"What!" Melvin almost choked on his cane and Coke.

"Ja, the bastard fired me."

"The bugger! What the hell for?" Melvin still couldn't believe it.

Mike had toyed with the idea of a brandy, but had resisted. It would have been justifiable under the circumstances. Drowning your sorrows and all that. But instead, he'd made himself a cup of tea. Melvin had noticed this, but said nothing.

"Ja, he said I had an alcohol problem and that I was fucking niggers."

Melvin slowly put down his glass and looked directly at his friend. "Well, are you?"

"What?"

"Fucking niggers, of course? We all know you've got a problem with the grog."

The barb sank home. "It hasn't affected my job," he said, indignantly.

"It damn well has, and you know it. It's just that you're too smarmy for them and you know how to get away with it."

Mike felt a twitch of anger. He hadn't asked for Melvin to be so brutally direct.

"You haven't answered my question, Mike."

"What?"

"Are you fucking black chicks?"

"No."

"So what made him think that? D'you think he made it up?"

This wasn't the reaction Mike had expected from his friend. Shit, man! Melvin was behaving as if he was the guilty party. "On our last trip to Beira a black hooker came and sat at our table and asked Lionel to buy her a drink. He got all huffy about it and said it was disgusting. That's all."

"Well, what d'you expect? He's a Rhodie," Melvin followed.

"I know. It just pissed me off."

Melvin sighed. "Mike, Mike. For crying out loud. Rhodies don't change. You should know that. That's why he fired you. You're a threat to him, an unknown quantity."

"So, what crime have I committed?"

Melvin sighed again, more impatiently. "Hell, you can be naïve sometimes. You still don't get it, do you? You don't fit into his simple little macho world. He doesn't know how to control you. "

"But he's being so hypocritical," Mike continued.

"No, no, no, he's not. Not in his eyes. He's too stupid to be a hypocrite."

They were silent for a while, though Mike knew Melvin hadn't finished. He was gathering his thoughts.

"So, Mike. You're up the creek, aren't you? No job, no wife, and a reputation for shagging black honeys. You'd go down a treat at the sports club."

Mike laughed, in spite of himself. Melvin always had that ability.

"So what are you going to do? May as well piss off back to Mozambique?"

Mike nodded slowly, "I was thinking of that. I kind of knew this was all coming, y'know. Even got a caravan lined up."

"And a couple of black chicks, no doubt," Melvin joked.

Mike was silent for a while. "Maybe."

Melvin said nothing for a long time and then, very quietly, "Tell me about it, Mike."

So Mike told him about the woman in the night-club. Of course, at this stage it was only an infatuation. In fact it might never come to anything. But it was playing on him, drawing him back, pulling him back like some sort of primeval urging. Melvin listened closely, without interrupting.

Mike finished, and again there was a long pause.

"Mike, you're a good mate," Melvin breathed heavily, after much deliberation. "I'm not a racist. Neither is Oscar. We all think alike. We play the same music, drink the same grog, smoke the same dope, know what I mean?"

"Ja," Mike nodded, wondering where Melvin was heading.

"Your marriage is dead. Okay. No big deal. You've just joined the other half of every marriage in Zim. You've lost your job. No big deal. You're bright, you'll get another tomorrow."

"What are you trying to tell me, Melvin?"

"Don't get me wrong. I mix with black chicks and there are some I really dig. Even one or two I wouldn't mind giving a shot. But I wouldn't. Ever! Y'know why?"

"No, why?"

"Because I'm white and I live here. That's why. Can you imagine pitching up at the club with a black chick on your arm? Shit, man! Can you?"

"Ja, but then I wouldn't go to the club, would I?"

"So where you gonna go? To the black clubs? They're just as bigoted. It's not in their culture, man. And what about little George when he grows up? All the little Rhodie kids at school are gonna mock him that his old man's married to a nanny!"

"But, Melvin. What about the principle? It's … it's just so wrong …" Mike tailed off.

"Of course it's wrong. But that's Zim for you. I mean, you've just had first-hand experience of it. That's how it'd be. You wouldn't even be able to get a job!"

They talked for a long time. Mike knew exactly what Melvin was driving at, but he also knew that he would follow his instinct.

Melvin knew this as well. "Hell, Mike, you can be a stubborn bastard sometimes," he sighed resignedly. "I'm not going to stop you, am I? You're going to bulldoze your way into Mozambique, aren't you? I'm not saying what you wanna do is wrong…it's not, and I admire you for it. But … just think about your position if you ever came back here. That's all I ask."

Mike finished the last of his tea. It was cold. "You're a good buddy, Melvin. I appreciate your honesty."

Melvin smiled, "Forget it, man. But I am right about your drinking," he added, almost as an afterthought. "If you don't knock it on the head damn soon, it's gonna kill you."

"I know. I'm sorting it out."

"I could tell last night at the gig when you were playing the harp. You've lost that edge of yours. It's because you were pissed, that's why."

Another barb for Mike. He hadn't realized….

"And when you're pissed, you end up with white trash, like that tart in the car."

Mike raised his hand in defence, "I know, I know, I know. It's all gotta stop. I know it Melvin."

"Sure you do. Just don't go'n repeat it all in Mozambique. Changing geography isn't going to change what's inside you, Mike. You know that, don't you?"

Mike smiled warmly at his friend. "Ja, I know, Melvin. Don't I know it!"

Melvin grasped Mike's hand and squeezed it. "So you old bastard. I'm gonna come down to Beira in a few weeks. Maybe I can get a gig organized, or something. And I expect to see Michael happy and sorted out. Okay?"

"You got it."

Twelve

Nothing had changed much in Machipanda over the years, apart from the seasons. Today was no different. The heat, the flies and the whiff of urine from the public toilets. The enshrouding languor of the border post was the same as ever. It was here that the bureaucrats could spoil your whole day, your whole week or your whole life—and to a degree, invariably did.

As was customary, a group of people, stateless and illegal, sat without emotion in the no-man's land between the two booms of Zimbabwe and Mozambique. The Zimbabweans wouldn't let them in and the Mozambicans wouldn't let them back. They were stuck in an international vacuum. Stoically accepting that their future was fateless, they sucked lethargically on mangoes, and supped tepid water out of plastic Pepsi bottles.

Mike parked his pick-up truck in the lee of a massive pantechnicon, its motor running, belching billows of diesel fumes into the customs and immigration hall. Unperturbed, the officials inside went through the motions of processing the new arrivals. Thankfully today, there were only a few, and Mike was grateful. Normally, he managed to time it so that he arrived just after a bus had disgorged 40 or 50 passengers.

Today was orderly. There was no hurry, no urgency and Mike had learned to accept this. Frustration and impatience did not accelerate the work rate.

He queued behind two German road engineers. He knew they were working on the Chimoio road because they were wearing CAT caps and gave Chimoio as their destination to the immigration official. A fair deduction. Moving on, Mike stepped up to the counter at the same time as the immigration official vanished behind a wooden screen. It was as if it had been programmed to happen.

Mike coughed loudly, but knew it was futile. Depositing the plastic supermarket packet on the counter, he coughed again. To no avail. The man was out of sight. He could be heard, chatting vigorously to a colleague behind the screen. In the packet were a loaf of bread, a packet of sugar, some Madison cigarettes and a bar of soap. Not a bribe, but a gift. After all, the poor man was probably earning a paltry ten US a month. Mike felt sorry for them. He had an identical packet for the customs man on the adjacent counter.

Rustling the packet did not help either. The man undoubtedly was aware of its presence, as he was confident that it would still be there in ten or 15 minutes. For Mike to remove it now would prove disastrous. So he didn't, and instead rustled it some more.

After an age, the man emerged. Without looking at Mike, he clasped his weapon, his immigration stamp, in his right hand, and at the same time lifted the supermarket packet off the counter and slid it out of sight beneath.

"*Bom dia,*" he muttered. "*Com esta?*"

"Good morning. I'm very well, my friend. How are you?" Mike noticed with a trace of annoyance that he'd picked up Melvin's habit of addressing black officialdom as 'my friend'.

The man nodded imperceptibly, which Mike took to mean he was okay. He handed the man his passport.

Hauling out a large grubby ledger, the immigration man laboriously began to transcribe Mike's passport details. At least now, the Mozambicans had done away with those old forms, which took forever to complete. At least now, they had realized that your mother's maiden name and her date and place of birth were of no consequence.

After another age, the man was done. Taking the entry tax, a handful of US dollars, from Mike, he stamped the receipt and the gate pass with a resounding double tap. The climactic conclusion to his work.

"*Obrigado, senhor.* Thank-you," Mike smiled, as he moved aside for the people queuing behind. But the man had vanished again, behind the wooden screen.

The two Germans had a problem. Mike could see it. They were gesticulating and talking loudly with the customs man, who was shaking his head slowly from side to side. Grabbing a customs form from the public counter against the back wall, Mike could see they would be a while. Germanic discipline confronts Afro-Latin *amanha*.

Needing to relieve himself, he stepped through the swinging fly-screen door to be met by a wall of heat. Inside at least, there was an overhead fan, grudgingly moving the air about. He negotiated his way through the diesel fumes and another sedentary crowd of *deslocados,* to the public toilets.

Taking a deep gulp, he held his breath as he tip-toed across the urine on the floor. Undoing his flies at the overflowing urinal, he wondered why he'd bothered. He should have just pissed into the lake. Today he didn't time it right and ran out of air as he was doing up his trousers. He was forced to take a small breath and almost gagged at the stench.

It was a relief to be back at the customs desk. The Germans had finally resolved their problem, or rather, the fistful of US dollars had. A flurry of rubber stamps and it was Mike's turn. His papers were in order, he had the exact amount and type of currency to hand, for the insurance, the road tax and the vehicle entry tax. The customs man recognized a professional traveller and gave him no aggravation. The plastic supermarket packet had helped a bit.

Stamp, stamp, stamp. Next.

Mike stepped back into the wall of heat and diesel fumes. If he were careful, he'd be able to get his pick-up around the front of the pantechnicon, between the mango trees and the mesh fence. The truck driver was nowhere to be seen, a fact which greatly irritated the two Germans who were hooting angrily from within their Range Rover. Unfortunately for them, they did not have the option of the mango route, as their path had now been blocked by a newly arrived bus.

Opening all the windows of the scalding pick-up, Mike turned on the fan and was rewarded with an equally hot blast of air. He was soaked with his sweat, as he manoeuvred the truck between the pantech and the fence, narrowly avoiding an open manhole en route.

There was one final hurdle—the man at the boom. The man at the boom was a god, and he knew it. No matter how precise and how clinical one might have been with the customs and immigration, it may have all been for nought should the man at the boom so deem. He was powerful enough to override any rubber stamp. Any stamp and any signature.

Mike approached the boom with feigned confidence, his right hand holding the gate pass and a carton of Madison, both peeking discreetly out of the window. But today was okay. The man at the boom was in a less than truculent mood, and barely glanced at the white man in the pick-up, as he took the gate pass and the cigarettes. Still jabbering on to a group of Frelimo soldiers, lounging on the edge of the tarmac, he swung open the boom and waved Mike through.

Sedately pulling away, Mike waved back and engaged second gear. He felt good. It was always an accomplishment. He looked at his watch. Forty-five minutes—both sides. Good going.

It was midday. He should make Beira by fourish. Say five, to allow for roadblocks, roadworks, detours and pit stops. He hadn't made any arrangements with Kurt for the caravan and wondered whether he should stop off at his smallholding outside Beira, or whether he should push on through and hope to see him at Club Nautica. He lit up a cigarette. It was a long way to go. He'd see how the journey unfolded.

It went reasonably well, at least until he got to Chimoio, the capital of the Manhica Province. Chimoio, or Vila Pery as it had been known in the Portuguese days, was still an attractive city. If you looked beneath the grime. Of course, the squatters, the refugees—the *deslocados,* were abundantly evident. The town had become a centralized magnet during the civil war, being the halfway point between the Zimbabwean border and Beira. Chimoio was a key town for Frelimo, and thankfully for them, the Zimbabwean Army had bolstered the city's defences. But more importantly for the residents of Chimoio, the Zimbabwean soldiers had brought with them their Zimbabwean dollars, which to the Mozambicans in those times were as valuable as any hard currency.

It was Zimbabwean money that had kept Chimoio alive. Businesses were thriving, by Mozambican standards. The cotton gin was still there, still limping along. But now, the cotton was starting to come back in from the surrounding areas, fertile as they were. This time the farms were managed by Portuguese ex-pats, by white Zimbabweans, and by the more bullish multinationals. And now there was talk that the South Africans were coming to invest. It was ironic, but it was good for the region. Tobacco, citrus, cattle and maize. Maize as far as the eye could see, rolling over the gentle hills, to and beyond the horizon. The rains had not arrived in force. The rainy season, therefore, had not formally begun. But there had been enough of the early intermittent showers for the local peasant farmers to take their chances and plant. Varying in height from two-inch buds, peeking out of the rich alluvial soil, to the sturdier plants a foot in height, the maize crops were now at a crucial stage.

Mike guessed that if the rainy season did not arrive within the week, the crops would be lost. Already some of the maize was tinged blue around the edges, a sure sign of moisture depletion. The hurdles of the future season were academic at this stage. Drought, floods and the ubiquitous locusts were all in the future and, therefore, meaningless. Rain within the week was all that mattered.

The sheer vastness of the panoramic greenness around Chimoio impressed Mike. Here were people who wanted it all to work. They wanted to work, they were tired of war, of starvation. They wanted to grow maize for a better life. The greenness was their statement to the world.

Mike had not been concentrating on his driving as he approached the first roundabout in the town. The revolutionary graffiti, tastelessly daubed on the walls next to the road, was an iniquitous reminder of the past. An immoral anomaly when compared to the pastoral productivity outside of the town. '*A luta continua!*', the Maoist slogans, the crude drawings of the AK-47s. The childish portrait of Samora Machel, the architect of Mozambican communism, euphemistically the one-party dictatorship. Why hadn't anyone painted over the sins of the past? Mike chuckled to himself. Because they were too busy planting their crops. They couldn't be bothered.

He heard a squeal of brakes somewhere to his left. A flash of grey and the smell of burning rubber.

"Shit!" he spat, as he jolted to a halt. Right in the middle of the roundabout and he hadn't seen the vehicle filtering in from the left. He knew without doubt that there'd be a traffic policeman somewhere in sight. There always was at the roundabout.

The driver of the grey van leaned out of his window and shouted at Mike, waving his fist angrily. Mike gave him the finger, and the grey van driver returned the gesture as he sped off, his tyres screeching and spinning.

The traffic policeman, loitering under the graffiti, had seen it all. He ambled across towards Mike, indicating that he should pull off onto the verge. Resignedly Mike did so. He sighed. This would take forever.

The policeman, his ill-fitting navy blue trousers hanging loosely over his worn and laceless shoes, had his notebook out long before he'd reached his victim. It was bizarre, Mike thought, as he switched off the tape. The country was dying, the people were starving, but the traffic police never faltered. Perhaps it was the inherent bureaucracy of the Portuguese.

Taking a chance, Mike pulled out his wallet and extracted a couple of ten-dollar bills. United States bills. If he was going to bribe the man, then bribe him with US dollars. Don't risk it with Zimbabwe dollars or South African rands. The man might feel insulted.

"*Boa tarde, senhor*," said Mike, as he popped the notes into his half-finished packet of Madison. Look at the man directly. Do not show nervousness. Do not show fear.

"Good afternoon," the policeman replied. With a glance he had assessed the white man, who appeared unafraid, yet respectful. He wandered around to the front of the pick-up and noted down what appeared to be the registration number. He wandered back around to the driver's side and noted down what appeared to be the gross vehicle mass, the GVM. Standard traffic police *modus operandi*.

After several minutes, he came back to the driver's window and positioned himself a pace rearwards from the door. It was a tactic.

"Papers," he demanded.

Mike began to panic. No opportunity had as yet presented itself to give the man the packet of Madison. The man was being too thorough. But perhaps that was a good sign. A bribe, if any, would need to be thorough. He grabbed the papers out of the glove compartment and handed them to the policeman. Mike knew they were all in order.

"*Cigarro?*" Mike took the initiative and offered the man the cigarette packet, its lid flipped open with the money well visible.

The man glanced up from the papers and stared blankly at the cigarette packet for a long time. Mike held his breath for a long time. Without looking at Mike, the man slowly took the packet and put it in his trouser pocket. It was done. The offering had been accepted. The fact that he would continue to scan the papers at length, and that he would inspect Mike's passport and his driving licence was of no consequence. It was expected. It was the protocol.

When the man had gone, Mike toyed with the idea of stopping off at The Windmill, that tavern near Textafrica, the textile factory. It was tempting. After all, the journey had been broken. It had lost its momentum and he was in need of sustenance.

He was quite pleased with himself that he didn't stop. It would be easy to wind up spending the night in Chimoio. One *cerveja* would become two or three. And then it would be time to eat, either *galinha* or *camarão*. One could not stop at The Windmill and not sample the chicken or the prawns. The Windmill cooked the finest peri-peri chicken in the Manhica Province. And there would be the wine—Mateus Rose or Lagosta. And of course, there would be the disco ... and the girls ... Who knew what would happen?

Unbeknown to Mike, fate was taking a strong hold on his life on this journey. Had he not wasted an hour with the policeman at the roundabout, he would have run into Oscar at Club Nautica. And without doubt, if that had happened he would have accompanied Oscar on his planned trip to the Zambezi River, where he was going to explore the agricultural potential of the Zambesia Province.

Further, had he dallied for the night at The Windmill, then the startling chain of events that would shortly be set in motion, would not have occurred.

Like everyone, Mike had his choices. He was not concentrating when he went into that roundabout. But that was his choice, unconscious though it may have been. It was his decision, his choice, not to stop at The Windmill. Yet the life-changing consequences of his decisions were fatefully neither of his making, nor his choice.

The sun was setting as Mike wound his way down the escarpment on to the Pungue Flats, that vast floodplain stretching over 100 kilometres eastwards to the sea. The green carpet of maize followed him down, but here the maize was taller and ranker, bolstered by the heat and the humidity. Palm trees began appearing, and here the mango trees stood over a hundred feet tall, as imposing as the mahoganies.

With the twilight came the midgies, slapping and smearing themselves into the windscreen of the truck. A small swarm of immature locusts spattered against the glass. Mike knew better than to switch on the wipers, which would merely redistribute the fattiness of the insects in a blanket of whiteness, making visibility nigh on impossible. He would stop at the nearest available watering hole and swab it down.

The closeness and humidity of the floodplain combined into an erotic aura that caressed his senses. He popped a bottle of Castle beer that he'd forgotten about under the seat. It was warm and frothy, but that didn't matter. It added to the headiness.

A feeling of complete abandon came over him as he crossed the meandering Pungue, a still sheen of water in the moonlight. Candles and lanterns flickered in the doorways of the makeshift huts that crept up to the very edges of the road. He slowed down. Children, dogs and chickens were scampering all about in a general babble.

He'd always had this feeling when he approached Beira. It was another world where life was celebrated, cheap as it was. Where feelings and emotions were more vivid, unrestrained from the confines of a so-called civilized, or westernized society. Where life was death—and life.

He came into Beira around the top end, along the five-kilometre causeway that cut across the swamps and rice paddies to the north of the city. The palm trees that lined the road bent inland, buckling under the vigorous sea breeze, buffeting in from the Mozambican Channel. Mike hadn't noticed the wind until he saw the palm trees. Opening his window, he breathed in the air, salty, swampy and natural.

Twenty kays back he'd made a decision to skip Kurt's smallholding. It was still quite early and the chances were good that'd he'd find the Dane at Club Nautica. After all, it was Friday night. A good drinking night.

Scrabbling around the glove compartment in the dark, he found the Bob Dylan cassette he wanted. The tape was old and stretched, which somehow enhanced the music. It was one of his favourites—*Mozambique*. It reminded him of the time as a younger man when he'd read James Michener's *The Drifters*, the same vintage as Dylan's song. Both writers had obviously spent time in Mozambique, and Mike felt they both captured the essence and quality of the country. That was 20 years ago. But some things never change.

I'd like to spend some time in Mozambique
The sunny sky is aqua blue
And all the couples dancing cheek to cheek
It's very nice to stay here a week or two
And maybe fall in love just me and you

There lots of pretty girls in Mozambique
And plenty time for good romance
And everybody likes to stop and speak
They give the special one you seek a chance
And maybe say hello with just a glance

Lying next to heavenly ocean
Reaching out and touching her hand
Whispering your secret emotion
Magic in a magical land
And when it's time for leaving Mozambique
You say goodbye to sand and sea
You turn around and take a final peek

And you see why it's so unique to be
Among the lovely people living free
Upon the beach of sunny Mozambique.

The song was rough, without the clinical electronic mixing that was the trademark of much of today's music. Without fancy devices and techniques. Honest music with an acoustic guitar, drums, a bass and a violin. And the girl doing the backing vocals, synchronizing imperfectly with the soulful, mournful fiddle. It captured it all, better than a million pictures.

Dylan and Michener, the late 60s and early 70s, the time of Vietnam. The time of Mike's war, nearly a generation before. Somehow, driving along that causeway with the palms swaying and the paddy fields rustling and swishing in the wind, evoked images of Vietnam. He'd never been to Vietnam, yet somehow he almost felt he could hear the crump of mortars and the pervading dik-dik-dik of the Hueys bringing in the airborne troops.

As with the concept of death, Mike had for a long while been pondering the aspect of time. Not as some great meaningful puzzle, but more out of a curious sense of perspective. His war had occurred a generation before, but it was if it had only happened yesterday. He remembered as a young boy of eight, listening in to the wireless, when Ian Smith had announced the Rhodesian Unilateral Declaration of Independence in November 1965. A generation before then, the British Expeditionary Force was evacuating Dunkirk. He was unable to equate the timespan of his generation to that of his father's. It was irreconcilable. A question of historical degrees.

And the matter of history revived the question of time … and death. Time passed and you died. Simple. He felt foolish as he caught himself scanning the black skies for the helicopters. Like *Apocalypse Now*, expecting the phalanx of Hueys to come rolling in from across the horizon. What on earth did he think he was doing … trying to turn back the clock … or what?

He'd reached the outskirts of suburban Beira, the northern end of the city, where the aseptic diplomatic compounds rubbed shoulders with the squatters who had taken over the old Estoril and Dom Carlos Hotels, now icons of putrefaction and decay. He hit the stretch of dirt road between the US Compound and the beach at speed, sliding and careering through the fine beach sand. It was important to keep the revs up.

As he came through it, he glanced to his right, towards the US Compound, clinically fenced off from the rest of the city. A chrome and plastic island of sterile first-world conveniences. With a necklace of monstrous overhead lights scanning the perimeter, it somehow reminded Mike of a luxurious concentration camp. He'd been inside before, to eat at the little Chinese restaurant, and what he remembered above all, were the notices on the advertising board. Transient residents selling off VCRs and dune buggies and wind surfers. And not a kilometre away, the local women with unvaselined legs, were foraging on the beach for periwinkles.

He supposed it was here, in this compound, that the CIA and the various other American 'deskheads' sat and discussed the future of American foreign policy in Mozambique. He'd seen it when he'd been staying at the Polana Hotel in Maputo a few years before. The Americans had arrived *en masse*, having booked out the entire hotel as their base, to monitor the Mozambican peace process. Earnest young men with crew cuts and suits who answered to the name of Chuck and Hank, brown-nosing older men, also with suits and crew cuts, who answered to names such as Marvin and Earle. Having arrived hotfoot from Angola, the American delegation obviously felt the similarities between the two war-stricken, Portuguese-speaking countries were so intrinsically comparable, that within two hours an assessment of the country had been made, and the framework for a foreign policy formulated.

Mike had very nearly laughed out loud at the huddled group of spooks sitting next to him, drinking their Martinis. "Hey!

Don't you Yanks ever learn? Have you forgotten Vietnam already?" he'd wanted to taunt. But he'd said nothing. What for?

There were a lot of cars parked outside Club Nautica when he pulled up. He switched off Bob Dylan, and stowing his bags behind the seat, perfunctorily looked about under the casuarina trees for João. He'd be lurking in the shadows, if anywhere. But he was nowhere to be seen.The fluorescent lighting at the entrance hit him as Jean-Paul nodded briefly. As if he'd seen him yesterday. They exchanged smiles and Mike looked out to see if his normal table was taken. It was. The club was busy. Was Kurt around? He asked Jean-Paul. Yes, he was over there, with the Englishman. That must be Colin.

"Hey, Mike!" Kurt stood up and clapped him on the back. "Where haff you been? Long time, huh!"

"Hi Kurt … Colin. Good to see you."

"Sit, sit. sit, my friend. A beer, huh?"

"Thanks, Kurt. That'd be good." Mike was still feeling unsteady from all the driving. He needed to find his legs.

Colin was grinning blandly at him. He'd obviously had a few too many. The glassy stare of incomplete recognition gave it away.

"So, Mike. You haff come to find zat friend of yours?"

"Who?"

"Zat short one. Whassisname? Ze one with ze curly hair and ze shiny eyes."

"Oh … y'mean Oscar?"

"Ja. Him." Kurt was also a fraction drunk and was speaking loudly, his spittle spraying Mike from time to time. "He was here zis evening, drinking with us."

"Where's he now?" Mike asked without enthusiasm. He wasn't sure he was ready to face any kind of intensity. Not after that drive.

"He's left. With some blacks. He says he was going to ze Zambezi."

"What? Tonight?"

"Ja. Crazy fucker. He was waiting for you, but zen these black guys arrive in zis four by four and … boof! He fuck off. Fuckin' crazy man."

Mike was momentarily confused—and concerned. "Black guys? Who were these black guys?"

"I dunno … I sink Renamo."

Colin nodded his affirmation. "Yeah, they were Renamo. I've seen them around."

"Ja, crazy fucker was saying he was gonna start ze farming in Tete. On ze Zambezi."

"No, Zambesia Province," Colin corrected.

"Ja, whatever. Still ze crazy fucker. Hey waiter! Some more drinks, *por favor!*"

Mike drank slowly. He thought about explaining it all to Kurt and Colin, but then thought better of it. Okay, it was peacetime, but there was a certain amount of sensitivity, particularly when it came to Renamo. But why hadn't Oscar got hold of him? Why had he taken up and left for the reconnaissance of the Zambezi without him? Well … he obviously had his reasons. Not serious. He'd get all the feedback later.

Eventually they got round to the question of the caravan. No problem. He could take it as from tonight. On a month's lease. Renewable.

"Ja, Mike. I take you zere now-now and give you ze keys. An' you get a *puta* in, an' I will take a commission, no?" Kurt laughed loudly and slapped Mike on the back.

At that moment, the eastern horizon lit up in a blanket of lightning, the black cloudbanks silhouetted against the backdrop of the Indian Ocean. Like the commencement of an artillery barrage on the Western Front, the rumble of thunder rolled in to the beaches. The red and white checked tablecloths flapped anxiously, as the candles flickered and went out. Another crack of lightning, this time closer. The roar of thunder enveloped the beaches, invading the esplanade and drowning out the music. The lights went out in one blinding flash.

Jean-Paul and his staff were battling to get the tarpaulin covers down, as Kurt, Colin and Mike stood up to take their leave. It was pointless staying any longer. It would take many hours before the electricity came back on.

Thirteen

The following morning Mike awoke reasonably early. He hadn't been drinking the night before. Well, not that much. For a moment he didn't know where he was. Lying in bed, he took stock. He could hear the rumble of the ocean and he could smell the salty dampness in the air.

Kurt's caravan—that was it. Although it wasn't really a caravan. He hadn't been able to pay too much attention last night. He'd been too busy trying to get in out of the storm, viciously lashing the foreshore. It wasn't so much the rain, but the wind—almost gale force. A preview of what was to come?

He rolled out of bed, and lighting up a Marlboro, took in his surroundings. It was a portavan, not a caravan in the true sense. More of a mobile home. He peered out of the window and looked down into the sand. It was on stilts, jacked-up stilts—not wheels. By the looks of the jacks embedded into the sand, it had been there for some time. Probably ever since it arrived in Beira. He smiled as he noticed the fading sky blue United Nations logo painted on the prefabricated wall. Kurt had guffawed when he told the story.

"Ja, it was my job to organize ze tenders. Y'know, for all ze equipment zat was surplus to requirement. So my boss he tells me, 'Kurt. We don't want zat fockin' caravan. For what?' So I say, 'Ja, okay. We sell it on ze tender. No problem.' So I advertise ze tender and tell ze people zat if zey want to inspect it, zen zey must phone me, ja. An' of course, my boss is a fockin' Swede an' he doesn't understand ze difference between a mobile home and a caravan. In Swedish zere's only one word for both words. So ze people phone an' I say, 'Sorry, but ze caravan is in ze bush on a job.' An' ze people say, 'Zat's no fockin' good. How can we buy something if we cannot see it?' An' I say, 'I don't fockin' know. Zat's not my problem.' So ze people say, 'Agh fockit! No ways. We not gonna buy zat shit in ze bush.' So, of course no one submits a tender, except for me—well, not me, but my wife's brother. For 200 US dollars. So, of course I win ze tender and ze boss says to me, 'Kurt, why no-one wants to buy zis caravan?' An' I say, 'Agh, who wants to buy a shit caravan with no wheels zat is all focked up?' An' he says, 'Ja, okay. Accept ze tender.' So ... I accept."

Mike chuckled to himself and went to the little fridge in the kitchenette area. There was a packet of everlasting milk, half a slab of cheese, a few stale bread rolls, some margarine, an opened bottle of wine and a couple of *cervejas*. Probably been there for weeks, he thought, noticing the blue mould on the rim of the cheese. He switched on the kettle, and digging around in the cupboards, found some teabags (with Hotel Beira on the tags), and a packet of sugar.

While the kettle boiled, he finished his inspection. The portavan was compact, clean and utilitarian. Two small bedrooms, his with the double bed, straddled the living area which was made up of the kitchenette and a small lounge with two easy chairs. A bar counter that doubled as a dining table, separated the kitchen area from the lounge. He noticed there were no pictures but rather, two out of date calendars—one from the *inter franca* duty free shop, and the other from OK Bazaars, a Zimbabwean supermarket chain. There was no TV and no radio. But that was fine.

He found the toilet cum shower leading off from the spare bedroom and relieved himself. It was also clean and smelt faintly of disinfectant.

The kettle had boiled and he made himself a cup of tea. Sitting on the step of the front porch, he assessed the day. It was crisp and fresh, and only a few wisps of cloud brushed the eastern sky. Almost as if God had taken a great broom and swept away the massive black storm clouds of the previous evening. Where had they gone? Stubbing his cigarette out in the sand, he breathed in the fine sea air. It was going to be a good day.

His truck was still parked under the corrugated lean-to off to the side, and the gate leading onto the *avenida* was still chained and locked. The beach was some 50 or 60 metres across the road. Peering under the stillness of the casuarina trees, he could make out its brilliant whiteness, not presently glimmering, the sand still cool and moist from the dew. It was low tide and the breakers rolled in gently and unthreatening.

He took a shower, lukewarm and soothing, and thought of the woman. He hadn't done that since he'd arrived. He'd been too preoccupied with organizing the caravan and ducking the storm. But the sensuous effects of the water had stirred his sexuality. Something that had been dormant for so long. Not lust. Not lasciviousness. Not like with that divorcee back in Harare. He winced inwardly at the memory and unconsciously scrubbed harder with the soap.

But the woman with her beauty and her softness. His gut contracted with want, almost painful in its intensity. It wasn't just the prospect of sex, it was the anticipation of fulfilment. Perhaps that was why he'd come to Beira. For her? He chided himself out loud. "C'mon Mike, admit it. You've come to Beira on a dream. The whole thing's a fantasy. Melvin was right. You weren't running away from Zimbabwe. You're running away to her. Dreaming again! Who says she'll even want you? Who says she'll even be here in Beira? Perhaps she's hooked up with that fat Portuguese businessman, and he's set her up in a little *apartamento* in Maputo, or Jo'burg."

He washed down, and wrapping a towel around himself, sat on the porch and lit up another cigarette, alone with his thoughts. He refused to contemplate any further the idea that she might not be in Beira. It was just too much to entertain. After all, wasn't this going to be the reawakening of Mike? Hah!

★   ★   ★   ★   ★

Phoebe woke about the time Mike was sitting on the porch, smoking his second cigarette of the day. Yawning contentedly, she rubbed the sleep from her eyes, her outstretched body hugging the white silk negligee that a German client had given her a few months before. She'd had another client last night, but it had been clean and quick. Still a mite painful, the residue of the cruelty of that Zimbabwean minister was not wholly spent. She did not feel tainted. He had been a decent sort—paid his money and was gone. A white man—perhaps a Pole, or some other Eastern European. She'd become adept at differentiating between the various nationalities. What an education.

Well, Salim would be pleased, *não*? She was making an effort. She was back in line. For the moment. For the time being ...

She'd missed out on a proper schooling, and although she could read and write to a basic standard, it was hardly anything to be proud of. Dim memories of the class in the bush under the thatched *bashas* in the guerrilla camps. She hadn't understood much of what the political commissars had taught, but the arithmetic and the writing would always be there. There'd been no reason why she couldn't have gone on to the higher school certificate. Well, there was ... the Rhodesian soldiers came and burnt the *bashas* and killed her mother.

There'd been the possibility of furthering her education in the UNHCR refugee camps, after the guerrillas had won the independence for the embryonic state of Zimbabwe. She'd never understood why the refugee camps had existed at all. Surely they were all Zimbabweans and should have gone home to Zimbabwe? Many went, but many stayed. It was confusing. Of those who stayed, many died from the diseases of the camp.

The Red Cross had tried to help. Medecins Sans Frontiers had tried to help, as had the UNHCR. There had even been some white teachers from Unicef. They were nice people, but they were Scandinavians and Australians and Irish and they could not speak Shona. They could not speak Portuguese, and certainly the refugees could not speak English that well, if at all.

They had tried to set up makeshift classrooms, to teach the children at least something whilst waiting for repatriation. But it was disruptive. Every day there would be new children, arriving from the camps in Northern Mozambique and Tanzania. And every day some of the children would leave for Zimbabwe. Sometimes a child would not come to school because he had died in the night. You could not learn in such an environment.

And it seemed that the authorities and the UNHCR officials had forgotten her. Once they came to her and asked her where her parents were. She knew her mother was dead, but did not know her father. And her name? Her name was Phoebe. And her second name, her family name? She did not know.

She remembered lying awake at night on the reed mat, huddled in the thin brown blanket. There weren't enough tents, so she lay outside. It was what she preferred, and what she had been used to in the days of the war. In those times it was normal practice to sleep in the bush. Who knew when the enemy soldiers or their planes would come? The political commissars had told them that the bombers had been attacking the other camps at night. They were never safe.

At times, gazing up at the stars into the clear African sky, she'd cried herself to sleep. But ultimately the tears had dried up with the onset of her emptiness. And the pain had gradually become a dull ache... and then nothing. She couldn't remember how many weeks, or months, or years she'd stayed in that camp.

The UNHCR people came to her only one more time, on that occasion with several black men in smart grey suits, absurd in the heat of the bush. She'd heard some of the other children talking, saying that these men were Zimbabwean 'comrades' who had come back to look for their missing children. The UNHCR people asked her the same questions while the comrades studied her. One even patted her on the head and looked into her face, holding her chin up to his. But they had departed without saying anything. They never came back. Phoebe got out of bed. How long had she been daydreaming? The memories kept flooding back. She tried to keep them out, but it was impossible. A childhood of emptiness, and a profusion of empty memories.

She poured herself a cup of black coffee from the percolator that she invariably forgot to switch off at night. It was therefore scalding hot and very stewed, but that was how she liked it. Sitting at the kitchen table, still in her silk negligee, she fiddled distractedly with the plastic daffodils in the vase.

She thought remotely that Salim's *guarda-costa* might appear at any moment. To check on her. She considered making a decision. It was a decision of great import, yet contemplated without distress. But she deferred. The time was not right.

★ ★ ★ ★ ★

There was a freshness about the sea today. It was not cold. But nor was it the usual warmness that always felt good, but somehow slightly dirty. Something to do with the muddiness that spewed out from the Pungue estuary. It would have been the rain last night, Mike thought, as he plunged under again. He surfaced and sniffed in the salty water. Almost immediately he felt his sinuses clearing, his head cleansed.

It was still relatively early for the citizens of Beira. Mid-morning on a Saturday and the beach was deserted, except for a bunch of black children romping in the surf down towards the crumbling breakwater. Untrodden and virginal, the beach was as smooth as a billiard table, unscuffed by the weekend crowds yet to emerge. Up beyond the lighthouse, black specks of people were busily hauling in their prawn nets from the shore. That was their favourite place. Or perhaps they were forbidden to fish in the bathing areas, although there was nothing, no signs, to indicate that they couldn't.

He lolled a bit, floating belly-up with his head backwards in the water. A sudden splashing nearby alarmed him. Looking around, he saw the group of children coming towards him, laughing and chattering. What did they want? And then he recognized the leader. It was João.

"*He pa!*" João shouted. "You are here."

Mike smiled and waved at the boy. His delight was obvious, his face creased with a wide smile as he pointed out the white man to his friends. This was *Senhor* Mike, my friend from Zimbabwe.

The boy swam up to Mike and circled him closely in the water, almost touching him, as if making sure he wouldn't get away. The beads of water, stuck in his tousled hair, sparkled gaily in the sunshine. His teeth flashed as he grinned happily at Mike.

"*He* João, *com esta?*" Mike grasped the boy's hand.

"I am fine, Mr Mike. How are you?"

"Okay."

"Where have you been, Mr Mike?" The boy's tone was mildly accusatory. He wiped down his face with his cupped palm, as was common with black people in water.

"I have been to Zimbabwe, João." Mike knew what would follow.

"So, why you not take me, huh?"

"I was only going for a short time."

João considered this for a while, and satisfied with the logic, dived under the water in a gesture that said Mike was forgiven. He surfaced a few seconds later and asked, "So, how long you come now to Beira?" He pronounced it 'Bay-ee-ra'.

Mike shrugged. Who knows? "Maybe one month, maybe one year."

"One year?" the boy gasped at the significance, and then cocked his head quizzically. "You work in Beira?"

"I I don't know, João," said Mike. The boy was putting him on the spot. "Maybe work, maybe not … we'll see."

"Ah ha!" João winked at the white man. "You come for the woman, *não?*"

"What woman, João?" Mike instinctively knew that João was aware of the woman.

"That woman at One-Two-Three Rock. She is very beautiful, *não?*"

So the boy was not always asleep in the back of the truck?

"Yes, Mister. She is a very very beautiful woman," he announced. " Maybe you take for wife, *não?*"

Mike chuckled. João was smart. He noticed how the boy had not in any way referred to the woman in anything but glowing terms. There was no mention of her profession, that she was a whore, a *puta*. Obviously it was not an issue. Or he was too polite.

The boy laughed mischievously. Like a porpoise, he splashed and frolicked in a manifestation of his pleasure, that his *patrão* might himself find happiness in the near future.

Mike couldn't resist the opportunity. The boy would know. "João. This woman. Is she still here in Beira?"

"Of course, *senhor*. Where can she go, huh?"

Mike felt foolish for asking, but persisted. "So, where can I find her tonight?" There. It was out. He had declared his intent to the boy and was briefly embarrassed.

For João, it was not a matter of embarrassment. "At the disco, of course. You go tonight?"

"Hmm," Mike tried to backtrack. "Maybe."

"Ha-hah! I think you go tonight, *não?*"

The sun was rising to the vertical as the humidity began to saturate the air. Mike dried off on the sand and allowed João to use his towel when he was done. He lit up a couple of Marlboros and passed one to the boy. A bank of clouds had peeped over the horizon, beyond the ships in the roadstead.

Mike and the boy sat side by side in silence, smoking contentedly, as the faint sea breeze whisked the smoke away on up the beach.

★   ★   ★   ★   ★

It had seemed to Phoebe that she was destined to spend the rest of her life in that camp. But then one day an important delegation had arrived unexpectedly. Not driving the shiny black Mercedes like the Zimbabweans, but Toyota 4 x 4s with Mozambican numberplates. The camp children had studied these new men with curiosity. They spoke Portuguese. Some were black and some were mulatto.

The leader of the delegation was a good-looking man with coffee-coloured skin. He was precisely dressed, almost dapper. Accompanied by the other men, he had engaged in a long discussion with the UNHCR representatives, who carefully studied the papers he had presented. After a while the UNHCR man had called all the children together and addressed them. This man with the coffee-coloured skin was *Senhor* Salim from Beira. He was a very important Frelimo official and he had papers, stamped at the Party headquarters in Maputo, authorizing entry into the camp.

Senhor Salim had come to the camp to look for teenage volunteers. Girls in particular. There was talk of an education camp for young girls, which was being established near Chimoio. It was to be a camp for children orphaned during the war, and as a gesture of solidarity with its Zimbabwean brothers, Frelimo was offering to absorb some of the Zimbabwean children into the programme. It sounded very good. It was an opportunity to get an education in a structured environment. There would also be work in the fields, for it was to be an education-with-production scheme.

The UNHCR man was slightly perplexed. He had not heard of such a scheme ... surely his associate at Unesco would have advised him? But who was he to question? The papers were stamped by the Government of Mozambique, the host country. It would have been an insult to question such protocol. He rationalized that, yes, this was indeed an opportunity for a couple of dozen homeless girls with no future.

Asking for volunteers, he shepherded the girls who had stepped forward to the processing office where they would be signed out. Phoebe had been one of the first to step forward. She had considered the options for a minute or so. What was there to lose? And if she'd didn't like it, she could always return to the camp, could she not?

Senhor Salim had smiled at the girl as she came forward. She knew she had made the right decision. No one had smiled at her like that for a very long time. After writing her name on the UNHCR discharge papers, she gathered up her blanket and boarded the waiting lorry. Apart from the blanket and the clothes she wore, she had no other possessions. No clothes, no shoes, nothing.

That afternoon they were driven to the derelict agricultural college outside Chimoio. It was deserted, save for a handful of Frelimo soldiers, lounging untidily at the gates. Jeering drunkenly, they had waved the truck through the uplifted booms. It was with extreme dismay that the girls took in their quarters. Evidently the squatters and refugees had only recently been evicted, leaving behind their squalor and waste. The dormitory to which they were allotted was a cesspit of trash and human excrement. The remnants of cooking fires were still apparent, the smoke having stained the walls and the ceiling in black swathes.

Phoebe gagged, and turning away in disgust, was confronted by two leering Frelimo soldiers. They groped at her, fondling her roughly before throwing her back into the room with orders to clean the place up. It would not do for *Senhor* Salim to witness the dormitory in such a state.

Fighting back the tears, the young Phoebe and the other girls had set to it with buckets and rags. The two soldiers had taken up a position of permanence by the door, and sat drinking *cerveja,* all the while taunting and laughing. Zimbabwean *putas.* That's what they were.

By nightfall, the place was as clean as the girls could make it. One of the soldiers came back with a bucket of *sadza* and relish that he deposited in the centre of the room. The girls, who hadn't eaten since morning, scrambled and clawed for the food. The *sadza*, the maize meal that is the staple diet of the African peoples in the region, was barely passable. It had not been freshly cooked and was congealed and crumbling. But it was food, and the girls ate.

That evening as Phoebe sat huddled in her blanket on the cement floor, *Senhor* Salim came for her personally. Like an executioner, he slowly strode the length of the room, inspecting the girls cringing against the walls. Stopping in front of Phoebe, he studied her for a few seconds, before kneeling down to her.

"Do not be afraid, little one. You shall come with me." He held out his hand to her and she followed him meekly from the room.

In his private quarters he ordered her to strip. She hesitated and he hit her, a smarting backhander across her face. She took off the ragged dress and let it fall limply to the floor. He was naked now, and forcing her onto the bed, prised her legs apart with his knees. With little finesse he rammed himself inside her, oblivious to her sobs and the wetness of her blood between her legs. Pumping and thrusting, he pounded away, grunting like a rutting pig. His sweat mingled with her blood. She wanted to scream out as she felt the flesh tearing in her loins. It would never end. But it did, in a grinding, heaving climax.

The man was panting as he raised himself from her body. Glancing at the mess of blood, semen and sweat, the corner of his mouth turned distastefully. He grabbed a towel and wiped himself down. When done, he tossed it at the girl, now curled up like a foetus, sobbing uncontrollably. He dressed and left the room.

That was how her virginity had been taken from her. He came to her every night for many nights. So that in the end, she felt no pain. And as the pain and the shame diminished, he became gentler. Without realizing it, she was slowly beginning to respond, and in fleeting moments had allowed her body its freedom. Still, it was not pleasurable, merely gratifying in the absence of pain.

After several weeks, *Senhor* Salim had spoken to the girls. Peace was coming to Mozambique and they had an important role to play. The international peacekeeping force from the United Nations was coming to the country, and there would be many soldiers based in Chimoio. White soldiers with a penchant for black girls. There was money to be made, and if the girls did their job properly, the Norwegian and Italian soldiers would pay them handsomely.

The following months had become a blur in Phoebe's memory. It was the Italian contingent that arrived first and she found herself taking initially one or two customers a day. *Senhor* Salim had blooded her well and she was perversely thankful. She soon found she could take three or four in one day, and then seven or eight. Sometimes it would be two or more at a time. The Italians appeared to be insatiable and she began to appreciate the commissions that Salim was passing on to her. The value of money had been alien to her. In time, she was allowed out of the agricultural college and introduced to the world of Chimoio's nightclubs where she would recruit more customers—not only Italians, but Germans, British, South Africans and many many more.

The Chimoio days came to an abrupt end when the international press ran an exposé of teenage prostitution in Mozambique's Manhica Province. The Italians were sent home in disgrace and the agricultural college closed down overnight. The girls dispersed, some to live in Chimoio and some back to the UNHCR camp near the Zimbabwean border. A few went with Salim to Beira, including Phoebe, who had by now become one of his prized assets.

Pouring herself another cup of coffee, Phoebe smiled dimly at the memories. Not fondly, yet not with resentment. That was when she had become a woman. That was when she had acquired the clothes and the shoes and the handbag. From a ragged waif to a high-class hooker. She owed much to Salim. But he did not own her. She was now sure of this. Yes, it was certain—she was her own woman now.

★ ★ ★ ★ ★

Unbidden, João followed Mike back to the portavan later that afternoon. Mike had not objected. His mood was carefree. Not for a long long time had he allowed himself a day of nothing, of total relaxation. Possibly the anticipation of the evening ahead had helped, but he'd also made a concerted effort to reject any thought of the influences and realities in his life—his wife, his child, his job…

A few short months before, he'd never dreamed that a little black street orphan would have become one of his closest companions. Opening the gate of the plot, he put his arm around the boy. It was not a conscious effort, and only when he'd realized what he'd done, did he pull his arm away in embarrassment. It was his upbringing, the British in him. The boy understood, and without words, smiled up at the man with great affection.

Sitting on the porch, Mike opened the packet of *pregos* and canned Cokes he'd bought at Club Nautica. He gave a steak roll and a Coke to the boy.

"Okay João. This is my new house. You are still the *guarda* of the truck. It is your job to guard the truck. Understand?"

João nodded vigorously, the juice from the *prego* dribbling down his chin.

"Okay. You sleep on the truck?"

"*Não problema,*" the boy nodded again, his mouth full.

Mike had considered allowing the boy to sleep in the portavan. He'd agonized briefly over this, but decided that it would take away the boy's *raison d'être*, his pride and his self-worth. He was happy in the back of the truck. Leave it be.

Mike sat at the kitchen counter and ate his *prego*. It was better to eat before going out. One-Two-Three Rock was a good nightclub. The music was good, the beer was good and the company was good. The food always smelled good, but to eat it might be a different matter. It was not worth the risk. Besides, by the time he got to the nightclub, his appetite would have gone, eaten away by the adrenaline and the excitement.

He toyed with the idea of adding a dash of brandy to the Coke, but desisted. He had gone the whole day on the beach without liquor. It had been a conscious decision. The woman deserved more than a drunk.

Sliding into the armchair, he lit up a cigarette. He felt drowsy from the sunshine of the beach, his skin still hot and taut. Allowing the feelings of languor to prevail, he dozed off. There was no urgency. Beira only woke up towards midnight. The cigarette burned itself out in the ashtray.

The band was into its second break when the woman noticed the beam of headlights swing across the verandah of the nightclub. Instinctively she looked up to see what type of vehicle it was. You never knew—it might be a South African or some of those British military advisors. They were always very generous. But it was a pick-up truck with Zimbabwean numberplates. Of no consequence. She went back to her drink. It was mineral water.

So at first she did not notice the white man when he came in.

But Mike noticed her almost immediately through the smoke and the crowd. She was sitting at a table off to one side. She appeared to be alone and was more beautiful than Mike had remembered. That was a good sign. Quite often in the past he'd fantasized about a woman, allowing his imagination to run away and embellish the memory, only to be disappointed by the reality at the next encounter.

Mike checked for the signs. No other handbag on the table. Only one glass. No jacket draped over the empty chair. There were two unoccupied chairs at the table. An open invitation ... to someone. His mouth was dry and he swallowed, his Adam's apple bobbing hard. What was his strategy now? He looked about the room and took it in. There were no empty tables and very few empty chairs. And people were still drifting in. Before long the place would be full, with standing room only. There was not much time to waste.

But perhaps it would be better to play it cool? Perhaps he should hang out at the bar and have a beer? Perhaps she would come to him? Hah! There it was again, that dreadful rationalization, which in essence was a fear of rejection.

He looked towards her again. Her back was to him and she hadn't seen him. She was reclining, her slender legs crossed carelessly. The long black hair tumbled across her back, contrasting against that same white dress, low cut and sleeveless.

A man went up to her table and Mike felt his breath quicken with panic. He was too late. The man was going to ask to sit at her table and when the music started, he would dance with her. And then he would dance with her some more, and then they would leave together...

The man was oriental, possibly a Philippino. Dressed in a vest and jeans, he was probably working the docks. Mike observed, his heart in his mouth. But the Philippino did not sit down. He had asked for a chair. She'd nodded and he took it, across to the large rowdy table near the bar. Mike closed his eyes in relief.

He suddenly felt conspicuous. He was standing in the middle of the throng, obviously staring. He took a deep breath. It was now or never.

He approached her from behind, forcing himself to put one foot in front of the other. He must be careful not to give her a fright. Give her a reasonable berth and come in from the side, as the Philippino had done. Give her time to see her predator, but not too much. As if in a dream, he saw himself come to the table. As if in a dream, he heard himself asking, "Is it okay if I sit here?"

The woman looked up. He felt himself blushing furiously.

"It's okay. You can sit." Her voice was gentle, welcoming, coquettish—all at once.

He smiled at her, a smile of relief and happiness. He felt foolish, like a schoolboy on his first date.

She smiled back, a warm smile, worldly yet inviting. Of course she had seen him coming. Who could not notice that silly white man, gawking like a lovesick youth from across the room? As he had that time before. But this time she knew he would come to her. That was why he was here. It did not displease her.

It was something in his eyes. There was kindness and there was sadness. There was pain and there was anger. He had a good physique and a nice face. Okay, he did not look that wealthy, dressed in a black T-shirt that hung loosely over his denim jeans. Yet it was the eyes. Behind the tiredness, behind the resignation, there was a burning fire. He could not hide that.

They sat in awkward silence and watched as the musicians came back on to the stage and began re-tuning their instruments. She was ignoring him, casually casting her eyes around the room. At what, he thought? Other customers?

"You would like a drink?" he asked, bringing back her attention.

She turned and smiled again. That disarming smile. "*Obrigado. Agua.*" She indicated the empty bottle of mineral water.

Mike was in two minds whether he should risk leaving the table to get the drinks. Or should he call a waiter? But the service was lousy and it took forever and a day to get a waiter's attention. That's it. He would leave his cigarettes and his lighter at his place at the table. It was his favourite Zippo. If she liked him she would instinctively keep his place and protect his things. If not, well … it was only a lighter. That's all he would lose. A lighter and a bottle of mineral water.

As he stood up, he caught her looking at him, studying him. An inspection? Was he good enough? He looked back at her directly, finding he was unable to smile through his intensity.

"It's okay. I look after your *cigarros*," she said softly. She lightly patted the packet of cigarettes and shifted his vacated chair a few inches towards hers.

Mike felt his heart surge. Surely, surely that was a sign? Standing tall, he made his way through the bustling, sweating crowd to the bar. In the background hubbub, a guitar chord strummed next to an impromptu clatter of drums. It would not be long now. Shouting at the barman, his hand outstretched with a wadge of *meticais*, he forced himself not to turn and look at her. She would see it as a lack of confidence. Don't rush it. Over-eagerness was just as bad. Play it cool. Pace it. Do it right. Easy does it.

The band swung into the first song of the new set. It was The Mamas and the Papas' *Dream a little dream*. The singer wasn't Mama Cass; it was the bassman, laid-back and gravelly. But it worked well for the song, for the mood.

Stars shining bright above you
Night breezes seem to whisper I love you
Birds singing in the sycamore tree
Dream a little dream of me

Already looking to the next customer, the barman passed the mineral water and the brandy and Coke across the bar counter, sodden with spilled beer and melted ice. Snatching at the handful of *meticais*, he barely glanced at the money and decided there was no change required. It was an accepted thing in Mozambique—the recipient's prerogative to give change or not. It was crass to haggle. The currency did not warrant it.

Say nighty night and kiss me
Just hold me tight and tell me you'll miss me
While I'm alone as blue as can be
Dream a little dream of me.

Gathering up the drinks, Mike carefully negotiated his way through the swelling crowd. The noise levels had increased, competing with the music and pumped up by the continuing stream of new arrivals. With nowhere to sit, a group of men had gathered near the table. Hands in pockets and as yet still sober, they were unhurriedly planning their strategy. As Mike had done. As all men do, selecting their prey. Mike caught one of them eyeing the woman, but her body language was defensive. The chair was taken. Finished. Another good sign.

Stars fading but I linger on dear
Still craving your kiss
I'm longing to linger 'til dawn dear
Just saying this …

He elbowed his way through the group of lingering men. They looked Italian or something. One bumped him inadvertently, apologizing profusely, as Mike hung on to the glasses without spilling. The men could see that the table was Mike's and that the woman was already taken, so they let him through without argument.

Sweet dreams 'til sunbeams find you
Sweet dreams that leave our worries far behind you
But in your dreams whatever they be
Dream a little dream of me.

He put the drinks on the table and squeezed into his seat, pressed up against the body of the person behind him. She had not moved his chair away and he felt her knee brush lightly against his leg, imagining the sensual warmth of her bare leg through the coarseness of his denim.

"Chin Chin," she raised her glass mischievously. "How you say?"

He laughed, "Chin Chin's good. Chin Chin!" He raised his glass to hers and they touched with a 'ting'.

The tinkle of her laughter. Mike took a sip of his brandy and Coke, already heady with her presence. Her smell, her perfume—cheap and musky, cheap and captivating. She could have worn any perfume. It would have made no difference. She was a goddess, nothing less. She leaned over to him to speak, her head resting on his shoulder. To Mike, it was a gesture so natural in its intimacy that he barely gave it a second thought. It felt so good. He tilted his head to hear.

"You speak English, huh?" she asked, the timbre in her voice lilting and rising at the end of the sentence. Her accent was a strange mixture of Portuguese, English and some Manhica dialect, not dissimilar to Shona.

"Yes, I speak English."

"My English, is not so good"

"It's fine. *Não problema.*"

The tinkle of her laughter again as she nuzzled his shoulder playfully. "Ha! You speak Portuguese, *não?*"

"No, no, no. A few words. That is all."

"Oh no! You speak okay. Your accent is good."

"Thank you. I would like to learn some more."

She leaned closer and he could feel her warm breath on his neck. "Maybe I teach you?"

He shivered involuntarily. "And maybe I could teach you some more English?"

"Hmmm … maybe." She leaned away, as if to study him in focus. He noticed a hint of a cast in one of her eyes, but perhaps it was because she was trying to centre on him. It was not unattractive. If anything, it added to her, the more enchanting, the more compelling.

"Where are you from?" she asked, inquisitively. She hadn't been able to work it out. Not this one. There was an accent. South African, maybe?

Mike cleared his throat, "Zimbabwe."

"Oh?" she raised an eyebrow. He was not like the other white Zimbabweans.

"Why d'you ask?"

"Oh, no reason. I am curious, that is all."

"And where are you from?" Mike asked.

She shrugged. It was a difficult question. "Here, Chimoio. My mother was a Zimbabwean."

"Really? Where is she now?"

Phoebe turned away fractionally. "She is dead," she said.

"Oh, I'm sorry," Mike felt awkward.

"No, no. Do not be sorry. It was a long long time ago. In the *Chimurenga* camps."

Mike considered taking it further, but it was getting too serious, too heavy. In all likelihood, she had been killed at the hands of the Rhodesians. Rather leave it. He sipped at his drink.

"We dance?" she added suddenly, more of a command than a question.

"Yes." He was not sure whether he could hold the intricate steps of the other dancers, sliding through the various rumbas and bossanovas with such ease and grace. But he was unworried. The thought of holding her on the dance floor was sufficient. She took his hand, as the group of men made way, casting admiring glances at her. Mike noticed and felt proud.

On the floor, she immediately put one arm around his waist and took his left hand with her right, her thumb resting subtly in his palm. Pressing her body lightly against his, she began to sway to the music, slowly, unhurried, with exquisite sensuality. He moved with her, pressing back to her, so that they became one. The shimmery lurex of her dress rustled softly against his shirt, and through the fabric he felt the rise and fall of her breasts.

Nestling her head into the crook of his neck, he could feel the vibrations as she hummed to the music. He couldn't see, but he knew her eyes were closed. Instinctively he kissed her lightly on her head and he felt her respond with a squeeze as she moved her pelvis closer into his, unashamed with her sexuality.

Turning slowly above, the mirror ball's reflections danced and teased hypnotically across the blackness of her shoulders and her hair, entrancing him, enticing him. He held her tighter, unafraid of the rising desire in his loins. The song came to an end and the crowd applauded. During the song the lights had dimmed, and in the pink glow of the aftermath, he felt himself shivering. She felt his need, his shivering, and clung to him. Turning her face up to him, her eyes half closed, her lips half parted, she slowly moved her mouth to his. He felt her wetness and received her kiss, lightly at first, exploring and brushing. And then with a greater intensity as his tongue found hers, probing deeper and deeper, flicking and twirling and nibbling and touching. Her breasts squashed into his chest, seeking his masculinity and under the lurex he could feel the hardness of her nipples pressing into his body. All at once he felt dizzy with happiness, and a craving so intense that it ricocheted into the very pit of his stomach.

The dance floor was all but empty as the couples slowly picked their way back to their tables. But still she clung to him. For a brief second he felt exposed, embarrassed. But it was not unnatural in this place. A woman and a man. Black and white, white and black. It was the ritual of life, nothing more.

She drew back and looked into his eyes, her squint more noticeable at such short range. Still wet with his saliva, her lips pouted with fullness. "We go?" she whispered, low and evenly. Again, it was more of a command than a question.

He was powerless. "Yes. We go."

Fourteen

João hadn't noticed Mike and the woman coming out of the nightclub. Dozing in the back of the truck, he'd woken with a start to the sounds of the engine. If he had been awake, perhaps he would have noticed the innocuous little policeman, who hung around the entrance with the street hookers, making the call from the phone booth.

The truck was driving fast and it took everything within the boy's control to hang on. A few blocks down he noticed that there were two heads in the front seat. Pressing his face up against the back window he studied the passenger. The long black hair said it all. It was the woman. He yelped with delight and banged jubilantly on the roof of the cab, almost losing his balance in the process. This was truly eventful.

He scampered out of the truck to open the gate and watched as the vehicle pulled in to the lean-to garage next to the portavan. He watched as the woman got out of the cab and followed the man inside. Yes. Without doubt, she was the most beautiful creature on earth. The graceful sway of her hips as she stepped up to the porch. The white reflection of the short dress, clinging to the curves of her body in the muted moonlight. The slender turn of her legs, perfectly carved and surreal in the dimness. It was what dreams were made of …

Mesmerized, the boy hardly noticed the blanket that the man tossed out at him.

"Okay João. *Bom noite*," he heard the man say. His *patrão*.

Perhaps his *patrão* would find what he was searching for tonight. He had been so troubled. João looked up at the sky. The stars were gone, muffled by the low, heavy clouds that had crept inland, unnoticed during the evening. It would be wiser to sleep under the lean-to tonight.

"What is your name?" Mike heard the woman say. He opened his eyes and felt her presence. Was he dreaming? Where was he?

Outside, it was light. But a smothered dull overcast light. The faint caress of a soft squall could be heard pattering against the prefab.

"What … is … your … name?" the woman asked again, deliberately, as if speaking to a recalcitrant child.

He looked at his watch. It was nearly midday. He automatically felt guilty, but realized it was Sunday. In Mozambique. He looked at the woman. She was sitting on the bed, next to him, naked. Her fingers were lightly running up and down one of his legs, splayed out on top of the sheet. It was a comforting feeling.

"Oh … I'm sorry. I was trying to work out where I was."

She laughed, a delighted laugh. The man was waking. "So… you do not have a name?" she teased, her eyes twinkling. Dark brown eyes, almost black.

"Yes, I have a name. Do you?"

"Ah ha! I have asked first. Why? Are you shamed of your name?"

For some stupid reason, Mike felt that perhaps he shouldn't tell her. He didn't know why.

He looked at her. She was smiling, like a kitten. Her hair was awry from sleep, giving the impression of a wild, untamed temptress. Stretching her arms, she yawned, her breasts rising and accentuating the flatness of her belly. He followed her lines downwards, from her navel to the softness of her loins. She was sitting on her buttocks, her legs folded underneath. Reaching out, he put his hand inside her thigh and felt her open to him imperceptibly. He felt himself stiffen as the blood flooded into his penis.

She shuffled closer to him, wiggling herself forward on her backside, at the same time guiding his hand into her crotch. The white hand on the black skin. A contrast in harmony. His fingers gently scouted into her vagina, seeking carefully at first, and then hungrily probing deeper and deeper. She moaned softly and began to move rhythmically, her buttocks grinding against the upturned heels of her feet beneath.

Her eyes were closed as she fell on him, unable to restrain herself any longer. Mike cried out involuntarily as he she took him in her mouth, enveloping him with long slow strokes in the hotness of her throat. He felt his pelvis buck towards her as he manoeuvred himself under her hips, craving with every ounce in his body to devour her. The drugs, the alcohol, the music—nothing, nothing had ever given him such unbridled pleasure. Nothing. Ever.

He was under her, his hands pulling her buttocks downwards, his tongue eagerly seeking out her womanhood. He wanted to, he had to, he needed to taste the very core of her being—the musky, sweaty, sweet substance of her femininity. There was no control now. Some force of nature—a driving, urgent, pounding force had taken over. Licking and plunging, he felt his tongue probing into her sex, as he drank and sucked at her juices, like a vampire feeding on its victim. His senses were spinning, light years from his mind. The bursting sensation in his groin, almost painful in its intensity, as the threshold of pain and pleasure melted into one vast sensory plateau. His whole face was wet as his tongue relentlessly ate into her being. Sliding and grinding, her pelvis wrestled against his face, threatening to extinguish and consume.

In a massive climax, the two bodies came together as one, grasping and clenching and bucking in an angry outpouring of screaming pleasure. Unable to breathe, he thought he might suffocate in the vice-like clamp of her body, but he was beyond caring.

And then the two bodies melted and all that could be heard was the rise and fall of their panting, sated and drained. Their body fluids, mingling together, seeped slowly into the sheets, clammy and warm, and then cold and wet. They lay like that for a very long time, their bodies sucked dry of energy, sucked dry of passion.

He dozed, a half-sleep of absolute contentment. She was softly kissing the inside of his thighs in little darting, puckering movements. She sat up and swivelled herself around onto his chest, her black legs straddling the whiteness of his torso. Her fingers played nonchalantly with the hairs on his chest, distractedly twisting and pulling. Never before had it been like this with the clients, with Salim, with anyone...

She looked at him, her eyes hooded. "So ... *senhor...* After that, I think it is now necessary that I know your name, *não?*" She placed the tip of her forefinger on his lips.

He smiled at her and he knew again that there was no power to resist.

"Mike."

Her finger was tracing the outline of his mouth. "Mike."

"Yes."

"Mike. You are very beautiful."

His tongue darted out like a chameleon's in an effort to catch the finger, but she whisked it away.

"You are also very beautiful. But now, I must know your name."

"Hmmm ... it is not important..."

He glared at her in mock severity. "After that," he mimicked, "it is necessary. Very necessary."

She giggled like a girl. "Okay, *não problema... Não fashmala...*"

"Well? What?"

"Phoebe."

"Phoebe?"

"You don't like?" she asked, alarm in her eyes.

He squeezed her tightly around the buttocks. "No ... Phoebe is a beautiful name. I like it very much. Very much indeed."

She crinkled her nose at him. "Mike ... and ... Phoebe? It's okay, *não*?"

He pulled her down to his chest and hugged her. "Yes. It's okay," he whispered into her hair, smothering his face. "It's fine."

★　★　★　★　★

The rain was beginning to come down harder, splattering loudly against the windows of the portavan as if someone was throwing handfuls of berries against it. They had slept. And then again they had made love—slower, gentler this time.

Mike was smoking a cigarette, his arm around the woman curled up at his side. They lay, listening to the rain.

"Phoebe? he asked tentatively, "Is AIDS a problem for you? I mean ... what precautions do you take?"

She turned her head up at him. "Why? Is it a problem for you?" she countered.

"No. Just that in your line of work ... y'know what I mean," he tailed off, ineffectually.

She knew what he meant. "No. You are right. AIDS, it is not a laughing matter. For anyone. Of course, it is always in my mind, but I take care. I have the condoms."

"But what about someone like me?"

She shrugged. "I don't know. I follow my ... how you say? ... my heart." She patted her chest.

"Intuition?"

"Yes, that is it. In this I am never wrong," she replied as a matter of fact. "You must understand. For the *puta* to get these diseases is to lose her job. A *puta* is a very clean woman."

"I know," Mike said, feeling foolish. "But I was thinking about me. You are taking a risk."

She shrugged again. "As I said, it is a matter of the heart. Am I wrong?" She looked at him intently, her eyes misty.

He shook his head, inhaling the last of the cigarette. "No, Phoebe. You are not wrong."

And they had slept again.

João pretty well knew what was going on inside the portavan. The drawn drapes and the silence. But it was good. It was good for the white man. It would be good for him too, *não*? But he was hungry. He hadn't eaten all day and now the rain was coming down harder. It would not do to intrude on the pair inside. It was more than his life was worth.

Scratching through his pockets, he dug out a few grubby *meticais* notes. If he went quickly, he might still catch the women street vendors on the *avenida* along the beachfront. They would have mangoes and tomatoes and cobs of maize. Perhaps even the maize cooked black over an open fire. If they hadn't packed up for the day, or if they were still braving the elements as a few might, huddled under bits of plastic sheeting and old fertilizer bags, waiting against hope for the occasional starving waif who might miraculously have a few *meticais* in his pocket... like him?

He skipped out of the pick-up and sprinted towards the gate, the rain lashing against his face. Within seconds he was drenched through. Without bothering to unlatch the gate, he scrambled over and in his haste failed to see the white Toyota Hilux parked in the gloom under the casuarinas. There was a bus shelter a couple of hundred metres up the road. That was where the women sought shelter, as he recalled.

He ran up the road as a crack of lightning struck nearby, probably down on the beach. A gust of wind nearly bowled him over, but he scurried on. The bus shelter was in sight, 50 or 60 metres along. But now the rain was whipping down in curtains and the boy had to narrow his eyes to keep the stinging rain out.

It had been foolish to leave the shelter of the lean-to. Better to have gone hungry. Anything was better than this.

Now the bus shelter was no longer visible and the boy was forced to slow down to a trot, negotiating the torrents of floodwaters that were now consuming the road. For an instant he wanted to stop where he was and cry. It was hopeless. Never, never before had he known such fury. The thunder and the lightning continued in a ceaseless roar that drowned out the crashing, smashing waves down on the beach. Blocking his ears with the one good hand and the stump, he felt the panic rising. And now the ocean would engulf him. He looked around blindly for shelter, but there was none.

And then alongside him was the whiteness of this vehicle. Of course there had been no way he could have heard it coming. The passenger door opened violently and caught him a sweeping blow across his back. He cried out in pain, but before he could collapse into the muddy stormwaters, strong arms grabbed at him and wrenched him into the cab.

Too dazed and confused to understand, he did not see the *guarda-costa's* fist slam into his face. He did not feel the blow. He did not feel the blood erupting from his face as his nose and cheekbone shattered. There was only the blackness.

★ ★ ★ ★ ★

The cyclone, for surely that was what this was, continued unabated into the night. The man and the woman huddled into each other under the bedclothes. There was the fear of the storm, with the window panes rattling, threatening to implode. There was the fear that the roof would be ripped off like tissue paper and blown into the sea. So they clung to each other, out of fear, out of desire. In a oneness.

And even through the pounding assault of the storm, Mike could feel the curves of her body moulded into his. A warmth so strong that it gave him strength. He rolled over and turned on the bedside light. Miraculously it was still working. The electricity hadn't been knocked out yet. He lit a cigarette and offered it to her.

"You smoke?"

She wrinkled her nose at him. "*Não* …but okay. One.. how you say? One drag?" She took the cigarette and inhaled lightly. Of course, in her younger days she had smoked. It had been the *chic* thing to do. In her profession, naturally it was *chic*. She passed the cigarette back to him.

Naked, he got out of bed and went over to the window and peeped outside. He could feel her gaze on him, studying him from behind. He felt no self-consciousness. It felt good. Outside, he saw nothing but the blackness and the driving rain, illuminated by the flashes of lightning that tore up the Indian Ocean sky.

"Shit!" he muttered. "João!"

The woman sat up in bed, alarmed. "The boy?"

"I'd forgotten about him." Grabbing a towel, he forced open the door into the storm and stumbled towards the lean-to. But the rain was driving in under the rafters, almost horizontal. There was no sign of the boy. He groped and fumbled around in the back of the truck. Nothing. He wiped the windows of the cab and peered inside. Nothing.

"Shit!" he swore again. He looked under the truck. Where could he be?

But he was gone. Mike went back inside, soaked through.

"He has gone," he said flatly, guiltily to the woman.

She came to him with a dry towel and ripping off the wet one, embraced him, at the same time wrapping the dry one around the both of them.

"He will be okay," she whispered. "He is a street kid. He can survive. He has survived his whole life on the streets."

He clung to her, shivering. And she squeezed herself tightly against him, willing her warmth into his body. And after a while, his shivering stopped and he felt warm.

She was looking into his eyes, unsmiling, serious.

"You are a good man, Mike."

He shook his head.

"Yes. You are a good man. Who would care for a *deslocado?*"

"He is my friend. I am his *patrão.* And now I have betrayed his trust."

"Ssh. Ssh. Ssh." The tip of her forefinger lightly brushed his lips. "Do not worry yourself now. There is nothing that can be done for the *momento.*" She squeezed tighter against him, gently thrusting her pelvis against his.

He felt calmness come over him. There was something about this woman. Something wondrous. Something karmic. It was of divinity. He didn't know what it was, but he could feel the spell. It was almost tangible.

For a brief moment, reality hit him. Or was it reality? What on earth did he think he was doing? A white man. A white man brought up in a conservative, middle-class, white world. Albeit in Africa, but with white values. White, southern African racial values. He almost laughed out loud, imagining how his parents would react if he ever took her home—to their white, middle-class, suburban home in Harare's northern suburbs. Or if he took her to the sports club. Or if he one day introduced her to little George.

"Hey George, I want you to meet Phoebe. And guess what? Not only is she black, she's also a whore. Ha! A black whore! That okay with you? I left your mother for this!" Yes, Melvin had been right. It was irreconcilable. Inconceivable.

Then he felt guilty, as he sensed her eyes merging into his, soft and tender. He forced such thoughts from his mind. She was at that moment the loveliest creature he had ever seen, and in that instant he knew he wanted her forever. Quite how and why, he did not yet understand. It was just so. The rest—he would deal with that later. If there was ever to be a 'later'.

Yet somehow, he could not come to terms with what Melvin had said. Logically, yes, he was right. But what of his emotions, his feelings for this woman at his side? Must he dismiss these for the sake of white propriety? To do the 'right thing'? Surely that would be living a lie? For that was why he was here, wasn't it? To come to terms with himself, to discover his true self, unfettered by the hypocrisy of his white peers.

He felt that wringing feeling in his lower gut again and was overcome by an immense feeling of tenderness. Leaning forward, he kissed her, slowly, in long pouting movements. Wet and gentle. And then harder, with more urgency.

She stumbled back onto the bed, the towel falling away. Again he felt the feeling of hunger, of yearning. As did she. They could both sense it. They both wanted, craved it. Her legs opened to him as he entered her—effortlessly, longingly …It seemed as if it would never end.

And still the storm raged outside. The panes still rattled, the wind still howled and buffeted. And still the flimsy prefab walls shook and buckled.

Fifteen

Norman Mubvunduku wanted that girl. Ever since he got back from that Beira trip, he'd wanted her. It wasn't as if there was ever a shortage of women in his life—to the contrary, there was a never-ending flow of them. But none like her. What was the whore's name? Phyllis? Pauline? Agh! What did it matter? It was only a name. The body was what he craved, not the name. And, there was a point to prove, a very sore point...

He heaved himself out of his maroon draylon chair and wandered over to the window, overlooking Samora Machel Avenue. Across the road was the president's office, the white shutters still neatly pinned back against the red face brick of the old colonial building. He'd yearned for that office on many occasions, but had long since accepted that Minister of State Security was as far as he'd ever get. He was a Manhika, a minority tribe. It would never happen. But it wasn't so bad. After all, it was one of the most powerful positions in the government. Probably number three or four as the hierarchy went.

It was overcast. The weather report had predicted rain. Evidently a cyclone had hit Mozambique and that was what made him think of her. But also it had been the yearning in his loins after lunch. It always happened after lunch, and today had been no different. He couldn't remember who his guests were in the restaurant at the Ambassador Hotel. Some trade delegation from Malaysia, or was it Indonesia? Protocol. They were the president's friends. There were no opportunities there. So it had merely been a case of going through the motions and smiling benignly at the fawning Orientals. Naturally the drinks had flowed and by four o' clock he'd had his fill of South African red wine. That was when the urge had come to him. Uncaring, he'd loosened his tie and had made his apologies to his guests. An important politburo meeting, he'd said. He was the chairman, and of course they would wait for him ... but it was getting late.

He left his guests to it, to wrap up with his aide. Let them carry on until midnight. Till dawn. What did it matter? It was no problem. His chauffeur was there at his side and steadied the big man as he got to his feet. The black Mercedes was waiting outside the foyer to drive him the two blocks back to his office.

"Eunice," he bellowed through to his secretary in the adjoining office."

"Yes, Comrade Minister," Eunice appeared instantly at the door, pen poised over her notepad.

"I want you to get me Beira. I need to speak to *Senhor* Salim at the Hotel Beira. He is the manager."

"I know him, Comrade Minister. I will get him right away."

The volume of traffic on Samora Machel was increasing as the evening rush hour built up to a crescendo. A few drops of rain fell indolently. The sky was now dark, the black clouds rolling in from the east. It would not be long, maybe 30 or 40 minutes before the thunderstorm struck. Commuters scurried along on the pavements below, whipping out their umbrellas in readiness. The sense of urgency contrasted with the stillness of the atmosphere.

The telephone at his desk rang and he picked up the handset, clasping it like a bear.

"*Senhor* Salim is on the line for you, Comrade Minister."

He grunted.

"*Senhor* Salim?" The line was not good. It would be the cyclone. "Yes … it is Minister Mubvunduku. …."

A gust of wind buffeted a shutter, which flapped irritatingly against the window frame.

"Yes. yes. I am very well…. Listen, I better talk quickly. This is a bad line and we might get cut off at any minute."

"Of course, of course. You know our delegations will always stay in your hotel…."

The shutter banged again. "Salim … I need a favour from you … You remember my last visit to Beira? … Yes that one."

He could take it no more and muffled the mouthpiece with his hand. "Eunice," he bellowed, "come and close this bloody window. Now."

"No, no, no. There is a storm coming. I was shouting to my secretary to close the windows."

"Cyclone. Yes, yes. Of course. We have heard this. Is it very bad?"

The big man studied Eunice's backside as she leaned forward, reaching out to close the shutters. This Salim was going on and on about the cyclone.

"Okay Salim. As I say, I must make it quick. There is a storm this side as well, and we might get cut off." Salim did not interrupt this time.

"Yes, as I was saying … on my last trip, there was a woman. She came to my room."

"I know. There were lots of women. It was the last one. She was wearing blue jeans and a white T-shirt. I can't remember her name. Phyllis … Pauline … I don't remember. I think it began with a 'P'."

Salim was talking.

"Phoebe! Yes, yes, yes. That's the one!"

Salim was talking some more.

"My interest? … *Senhor* Salim. You are a man of the world. We understand each other.

Our revolutionary parties fought the struggle side by side… We help each other, do we not?"

Eunice had left the room. The niceties were now superfluous.

"Yes, Salim. I would like to set up an … an arrangement. I would like her to come to Zimbabwe for a while … "

Salim was talking at length.

"What are you telling me Salim? Is she not one of your girls? You will be reimbursed very generously."

The Minister could hear that Salim was not at ease. There was something he was not telling him.

"A passport? That is no problem. Surely you can have that arranged in a day?"

Salim was stumbling.

"What?" Mubvunduku boomed down the handset. "She is a Zimbabwean? … From the camps …?"

Salim rambled on for a very long time and for now the Minister was quiet.

"Okay, Salim. Perhaps you are right. Perhaps it is better that we arrange the passport from our side. … Okay, you will get her passport photo and details sent off to our ambassador in Maputo? Okay… I will phone you tomorrow. … *Bom noite.*"

He put the phone down gently and poured himself a neat scotch from the veneered oak drinks cabinet.

Distractedly, he pressed the speaker phone. "Eunice, you can go home now."

He couldn't place his feelings. He knew he was angry. Angry that a petty party official from Frelimo should deny him; that he should not accede to his request with the utmost expedience. Had he forgotten that it was he and his Zimbabwean National Army that had kept the Beira Corridor open for all those years? Without him, without his soldiers, that rabble of Renamo would have swept into Beira months ago.

He smashed his fist on the desk, spilling the whisky at the same time. What was it? So what if the woman was a Zimbabwean? So what? Salim could still arrange a Mozambican passport. It had been done before, had it not? And now? Now he was getting stories.

But it wasn't merely the fact that Salim was being obstructive. Nor was it the fact that the woman was a Zimbabwean. It was something else. Something more. His pride, yes. His masculinity, yes. But more.

Until that morning in the Hotel Beira, he'd never laid eyes on the woman. Had he? Of course, he'd noticed the trace of the Zimbabwean accent. But then that was common with a lot of Mozambicans from the Manhica Province. They spoke the same dialect. They were in effect of the same tribe. It was nothing new.

He drained the remnants of the whisky as the telephone rang. Snatching at it, he slowly lowered the glass onto the desk. It was the president.

"Yes, of course, Comrade President."

He was silent for a long while, still clutching the empty glass.

"I will see to it immediately, Comrade President.... Of course, there is no excuse. They must be dealt with ruthlessly."

He put the phone down. Shit! Where was Eunice when he needed her? The Commissioner of Police. He needed him too. Where was his number?

First Salim. Now this. The trade unions were planning a general strike tomorrow. And the riot police were still embroiled in running battles with the university students.

"Enough!" he shouted to himself. "It is time for the Army."

And as he poured himself a final whisky, he vowed to himself that he would get the woman. No one would deny him. Not Norman Mubvunduku, the Zimbabwean Minister of State Security. How dare they! The matter was just too pressing.

★   ★   ★   ★   ★

Salim sat calmly smoking a cigar. He'd sat like that for a long time and the cigar, now hot and soggy was down to its last inch. Yet he was not calm. He contemplated Mubvunduku's telephone call. Of course, in any other circumstance it would have been simple. If it had been any other girl he would have obliged immediately. But Phoebe? His best girl? Besides, she was too unstable. It would be too risky to send her.

"*Não*. Not even for the Zimbabwean Minister of State Security," he muttered to himself.. He'd considered lying and telling Mubvunduku that the woman was unavailable—that she was out of town—anything. But Mubvunduku's spies were everywhere. It would only be a matter of time before the lie was discovered. The passport thing was a stalling tactic. Mubvunduku would know that. He would also know that a passport wasn't even necessary. She could be issued a diplomatic visa within the hour, and on the first available Beira Corridor Group flight to Harare. Mubvunduku would know that. He was not stupid.

But these Zimbabweans. They thought they owned the country. Of course, they had been allies, but when does a debt expire? Does that mean they own your women? Does that mean they own your very soul?

There would be repercussions, of that there was no doubt. In fact, he was expecting a call from the governor any minute now. But then, the governor had been bought off by the Zimbabweans. What could one expect?

But Phoebe? His Phoebe, that he had nurtured from the bare-footed waif to the sophisticated call girl? His Phoebe, that the Zimbabweans had rejected in the camps? And now they wanted her?

Any other girl, but not Phoebe. That was final. He stubbed out the last of the cigar in the verdite ashtray and ground the butt into shreds, finer and finer and then into ash.

There was a knock on the door. He looked up with a start. "Who is it?"

"It is I, *senhor*." He recognized the *guarda-costa's* deep voice. "Come."

The *guarda-costa*, that beacon of dependability. The door opened to reveal the bodyguard. He was soaked through, the grey suit hugging his massive frame. Salim noticed the water dripping onto the carpet. Ordinarily he would have torn a strip off the man. But then ordinarily the *guarda-costa* would not come into his office in such a manner.

"What is it?"

The man closed the door behind him. "I have the boy. The *deslocado*. The street kid."

Salim looked up, startled. "Where is he?"

"In the Toyota. It is parked in the service yard at the back. I was not seen."

"Good. He cannot escape?"

"*Não, senhor.*" The *guarda-costa* allowed himself the wisp of a smile. "He is ... how shall we say? He is ... asleep."

"Good. Where did you pick him up?"

"He was with the white man."

"Very good. Take him into the laundry room. It will be empty. I will speak to him presently."

Sixteen

There was a lull three days later. For a few brief minutes the sun tried to force its ways through the heaviness of the clouds onto the city in a surreal spasm of effectual surrender. But in an instant, the clouds closed ranks and the rain continued steadily. The initial violence had subsided. Now it was the relentless onslaught of a steady downpour.

But the fleeting appearance of the sun had been enough to convert the port city into a steaming mass of humidity. The floodwaters had subsided, but still the rainwaters, muddy and filthy from the tonnes of topsoil and human waste, disgorged steadily into the sea. The storm drains, long since clogged, had forced the waters to seek alternative passages, and thus the *avenidas* and the esplanade had become one vast mantle of water.

Mike and Phoebe had stayed in the portavan all this time, unable to move out. The floodwaters had lapped up around the porch and nosed under the floorboards. But thankfully Kurt had jacked the stilts up high enough when it had been installed. Mike was grateful for that.

He was also grateful for the few provisions that Kurt had left in the little fridge, and the couple survived on the stale bread rolls and the beers and the wine.

To Mike, it had all seemed like some crazy kind of dream. This was not happening. This was not real. He should be travelling down Samora Machel Avenue in Harare on his way to work. He should be submitting marketing reports to Lionel. He should be ... what, Mike? Should be doing what?

He regarded the woman. She was asleep, curled up naked with a sheet wrapped around her. Her black hair spilled across the whiteness of the pillow. He'd opened one of the curtains and stared, unseeing, at the rain outside. Finishing the cigarette, he tossed it through the gap in the window and watched as it landed in a momentary hiss in the muddy water.

He desperately sought reality and tried to think it out logically. He lit up another cigarette. He was chain-smoking, but it helped him think straight.

Talking to himself softly, for that seemed to put his thoughts in order. "Okay, Mike. This is the crack. You have no job. You are in a foreign country and you are more than likely falling in love with a black prostitute."

He dragged long on the cigarette. "Firstly. Are you able to separate emotions from reality? Does this woman feature in your life? And if so, do you plan your life around her?"

"Okay ... put it another way. Would you be able to live without her? Are you able to know the difference between love ... and lust ... unadulterated physical pleasure? I mean ... after all, this might just be a passing fancy and you'll tire of her in a few days. Come on, Mike, admit it. Your track record with women hasn't been the greatest. Has it?"

The cigarette had become unpleasantly hot from continual drawing, and half-finished, he tossed it through the window.

"You have to look at the practicalities, Mike. Do you really think you could go back to Zimbabwe with her? Do you really think you'd be accepted ... by the whites ... by the blacks? So what then? Do you stay here ... in Mozambique? What about a work permit? What about a job?"

He stood up and wandered over to the kitchenette where he switched on the kettle.

That had been a marvel—the electricity had only gone off once during the storm. She was still asleep, her breasts rising and falling under the sheet. Her mouth was slightly agape and she was snoring gently. Leaning over her, he softly stroked away a wisp of hair that had fallen across her face. She did not stir.

The kettle whistled, interrupting his reverie and he made himself a cup of black coffee. "And what about her feelings? Have you really given any consideration to that? Maybe she thinks you're just another client and when the storm's finished, she'll hit you with a massive bill. When she gets dressed and walks out of your life. When she walks down the road to the One-Two-Three Rock to pick up more customers.

This had been worrying him the past day or so. After all the sex and the passion and the love—for surely that's what it was? Or part of it? Surely she wasn't faking that? Or perhaps she was. Perhaps he was just another John—a John that she happened to think was a nice guy and would stick around for a few days. Well ... she'd hardly had a choice, had she? Not with the storm.

Sipping at his coffee, he determined he'd address the issue when she woke up. The cyclone could not last forever and they couldn't stay cooped up in here forever. He suddenly felt very nervous. Perhaps she'd laugh at him and tell him he was a nice enough fellow, but she had a job to do and she'd see him around ... maybe. He felt sick in the pit of his stomach at the thought, and in essence, he knew deep down that he wanted to be with her ... forever.

Outside on the road, a truck ploughed its way through the floodwaters, throwing up two large bow waves that cascaded high above the casuarinas. If the rain did not intensify, the roads might soon be passable. Perhaps it would be an idea to take her to Club Nautica, out of this present environment. They could discuss the future over a meal of prawns and a bottle of *Graca*? It was a good idea, and he thought briefly about waking her up.

But he didn't. The nerves were still evident. He knew he was procrastinating.

She shifted and he heard her soft moan. His heart leaped as he watched her. In her half-sleep her arm was reaching out for him across the bedclothes. He went to her and sat on the edge of the bed, stroking her hair. Opening her eyes, she regarded him for a while, unblinking, unsmiling.

He looked into her eyes, saying nothing. It was a serious moment and somehow they both knew that a certain time had come. She held his hand and squeezed it tightly.

"My lover," her voice was low and husky. "You want to talk, *não?*"

He kissed her lightly on her lips and felt her body wriggle receptively under his. "Yes. It is time to talk."

"Okay, we talk," she replied lightly.

But he could sense she was serious. He felt relieved. "I was thinking … I was thinking that maybe we could go to Club Nautica and have some food. It is a good place."

She sat up abruptly, the sheet falling away, revealing her breasts, heaving and inviting.

"*Não.* I cannot go to that place …"

"Why not?"

"I just cannot. It is not possible."

He cupped her face in his hands and kissed her again. "It is possible. The rain is stopping. Club Nautica is a good place. The food is good."

"I know this club. Of course I know it."

"Then why don't you want to go?" he persisted.

"Mike … do you forget who I am? Do you not remember that I am a whore? I … am… a …*puta!*" She spelt it out deliberately, as if to a child. There was an unmistakable trace of anger in her voice.

"So what?"

"So … *putas* are not welcome at that club. That's what." She pulled her hand away.

"I know the *patrão*. He is Jean-Paul. He is my friend."

"Of course, he is your friend. He is no doubt a good man. That is why he does not allow *putas*."

He could sense her anger rising. So, she was stubborn as well. "Listen," he looked at her intently, "you would not be coming as a *puta*. You would come as my woman."

"Hah!" She tossed her hair defiantly. "So while *Senhor* Michael is hungry and desires to eat, the *puta* Phoebe must not be a whore for an hour? Is this what you are telling me?"

Mike was beginning to get annoyed. She was being unreasonable, illogical. "No…. what's the big deal? It's just a meal."

"Yes, and while we will eat, there will be other clients who will see me and come up to me. They will say 'Yes, it is you, Phoebe. Can I make a meeting to see you tonight?' Huh? Huh? Then what you say …. Mr Michael? Huh? What you say then?" The sarcasm was undisguised.

He could feel his temper beginning to rise. "Well, what do want Phoebe? What do you damn well want?"

She reached for his cigarettes and pulled one out of the pack. Her hands were shaking as she lit it.

"You do not smoke. Why are you smoking?"

"I smoke. I drink. I fuck. It is not your business. You do not know me. You do not own me."

He turned away, fighting the anger and frustration welling up inside. "Yes. You are right. I do not know you. I forgot my place." He wanted to say, 'Tell me how much I owe you and we'll call it a day.' It was on the tip of his tongue, but he refrained.

Sensing his anger and his hurt, she softened fractionally. She reached for his hand, but this time he drew away. "Okay, Mike. I am sorry. I did not mean to become angry …" She wanted to say more. She wanted to say how deeply touched she was. She wanted to say that she was in love with him. No man had ever behaved like this to her. Ever.

But this thing was not possible. It would not happen. It was unable to happen. There was no destiny in such a thing. Salim would surely see to that.

He was standing at the window with his back to her. She could not see that he was fighting back the tears. But she could see that he was tensed and hunched into his shoulders. She sensed the deep emotion.

He did not answer her. He could not find his voice. He could not find the words.

The rain had stopped now and again the sun was trying to come out. A shard of light beamed through the window, like a spotlight. She stared at it, mesmerized.

"Mike. I said I am sorry … I will come with you to this Club Nautica."

He turned, his voice shaking. "Phoebe, you must do what is right for you. Not what is right for Mike. It is your decision."

"Hey! You do not listen. I will come."

"Before you say that you will come, we must agree on your price. This basis must be agreed upon at the outset." He immediately regretted the words as he spoke.

She stood up slowly and came to him, her face black with rage, her whole body trembling with fury. Without saying a word she stood in front of him, and then with extreme deliberation slapped him across the face.

"You are the *puta, senhor*," she hissed. "Not I."

He was unable to reply, his hand touching the stinging of his face. Without a word, she turned and went to the shower, slamming the door behind her.

Seventeen

The boy was shivering with cold and fear. He did not know where he was. Touching his face with his good hand, he winced in pain as he felt the sharpness of the bloodied gristle that was his nose. He could taste the sweet smell of congealed blood, and looking down, noticed his shirt was stained pink with his own blood.

The room was in semi-darkness, and after a while his eyes became accustomed to it. Shrouds of sheets were draped all over the place—over boilers, over racks, over the rafters—adding an almost ethereal quality to the gloom. It looked like some sort of washing room, a laundry room.

He heard laughter outside, grown-up, male laughter. And then voices talking. Footsteps approaching. He shrank back into the folds of a sheet. What was happening? What were they going to do to him? The last thing he remembered was running down the *avenida* towards that bus shelter. And then there'd been a blinding flash of whiteness and a feeling of intense pain. And after that, the blackness.

The door opened and for a moment the boy was blinded by the brightness outside in the passageway. Two figures were framed against the light, but he could only make out the shapes—that they were men.

"Stand up, boy," a voice commanded.

He shrank deeper into the sheet, trying to hide. Someone flicked a light switch and a buzzing sound filled the room, as the fluorescent tubes crackled and started up. The room was filled with a brilliant whiteness and the boy blinked.

After some time, João recognized the two men. Of course he knew who they were. The bigger one, the burly one—he was the *guarda-costa*. The one who drove that white Toyota Hilux. He had never heard him speak. And the other? The one in the smart suit? With the coffee-coloured skin? Why, that was the manager of the Hotel Beira. The one whose name was Salim. He had seen them many times. And many times they had chased him away from the hotel frontage—his turf.

The bigger man approached the bundle where the boy was ineffectually trying to hide. He kicked at it and the boy cried out as a boot caught him in his ribs.

"I said to stand up. You will listen."

João untangled himself from the sheet and stuttered to his feet. He was very cold, he was hungry and the throbbing pain in his face would not go away. Regarding the two men directly, it was all he could do to stop himself from collapsing. He was a street kid. He was a *deslocado*. But he was also a human being. He too had a soul.

"*Senhor* Salim would like to ask you some questions about your *patrão*," the big man spoke. A deep, low rumble.

Salim was standing in the background, his arms folded and leaning against the doorframe. Like a spectator, not wanting to get directly involved.

The boy was silent.

"*Senhor* Salim says that if you co-operate and answer his questions in the correct manner, then you will not be punished. That you will be free to go. Back to the streets."

The boy kept his silence.

"*Senhor* Salim is aware that you are the *cão* of this white man. The one that is known as Mike. It is common knowledge that you are his cur. You are his property, *não*?"

The boy did not answer.

The big man turned to Salim who nodded imperceptibly. João was still too dazed to see the fist coming. Again it smashed into his face, and again he felt the sickening crunch of shattering bone. Blood gushed from the wound, flooding into his eyes, into his nostrils, into his mouth.

"You will answer, *cão*, when I speak to you." The *guarda-costa* had still not raised his voice. "Now, I ask one more time. This white man is your *patrão, não?*"

The boy was fighting back the tears, but they came, the saltiness mingling with the blood and stinging in his eyes. He nodded, unable to speak. Why were these men doing this to him? What had he done to them? To harm them? But the words did not come.

"And this white man, he has been visiting the offices of Renamo, has he not?"

João nodded.

"Who is the other white man that he goes with? The short one with the curly hair?"

The boy swallowed on some blood. "I ... I do not know, *senhor* ... I have only seen him the once." His voice was choked. It was painful to speak.

"Do not lie to me, boy. What was the purpose of this visit?"

"I do not know, *senhor*.... I am only the *guarda* for the truck."

The big man hit the boy again, this time in the stomach. The boy doubled over in pain, gasping for breath. He felt himself falling, but the big man held him up, one hand pulling him up by the hair. The boy tried to scream but no sound came. Just the bubbling of the blood in his throat.

"And now this white man. This Mike. He has found a woman?"

João nodded. Numbly. It could not be denied. There was no danger here? Surely? To have a woman? Was this a crime?

"What is the name of this woman?"

"It ... it is, I think, Phoebe. But it is nothing, *senhor*. She works at the One-Two-Three Rock. She is a *puta*. So it is nothing, *senhor.*"

Salim stirred suddenly in the doorway. The spectator was becoming involved and the boy could sense the danger. Salim's slight frame was tensed and even through the mistiness, João could see the clenched fists, the knuckles white and angry. His lips were pursed, but he held his tongue.

"Is this white man fucking this … Phoebe?"

"I … I do not …" João cut off as he saw the *guarda-costa* raise his fist. "Yes, *senhor*. They are lovers."

Salim's fist slammed into the door. In total fury. He came to the boy, his face only inches away. "Now listen very carefully to me, boy," the man hissed. "If you are lying, you will regret the day you were born. You will not die. But you will be craving for death. Do … you … understand me?"

The boy nodded, hurriedly. He was very afraid.

Salim spoke slowly. "Are you saying that this white man, this Mike … and this woman, this Phoebe, are lovers?"

João nodded again.

"And tell me, what is it that makes you think this? If as you say, she is a mere *puta,* then why would you not think that she is not simply selling him a *fuck?*" He spat the word.

For a second the boy wanted to tell them about the joy he had seen in the eyes of his *patrão.* Yes, she was a *puta.* But he knew, he could tell that for the white man it was more than just a 'fuck'. But this man with the coffee-coloured skin? He would not understand. And anyway, what was his interest? She was a *puta,* like any other that hung around the lobby of his hotel.

"With respect, *senhor*. The white man is a man of honour. Yes, they are lovers. What of it?"

João knew then that he had said the wrong thing. He could see the veins in Salim's neck pumping. He could see his whole body shaking, the lips bloodless and cruel. As if in slow motion, the boy watched as the man picked up a galvanized iron bucket. He was about to cry out when the bucket crashed into his skull.

Salim sat in the leather chair in his office, one of his legs draped across the armrest. He was very still, yet inside his emotions were simmering uncontrollably. The burning cigar had rolled out of the ashtray and was smouldering itself out on the carpet, from the dampness and the humidity that had saturated everything.

Looking at it, Salim did nothing. So what? And the sheets in the laundry room would never dry in this weather. When would this cyclone ever stop? He had guests coming, and this weekend he was looking at an 80 percent occupancy. But how could he keep them supplied with fresh laundry? Fresh linen? Fresh towels?

And now that urchin had gone and bled all over one of the sheets. It would have to be burnt.

He was struggling to retain his composure. It had all been too much to handle in one day. The cyclone. The call from that Zimbabwean, Mubvunduku. And now this? The boy telling him that his Phoebe was the lover of this white man. Another bloody Zimbabwean. And they all wanted Phoebe. His Phoebe.

"Damn them all," he muttered evenly.

He stood up and went over to the CD player. Flicking through the rack, he chose Handel. *The Water Music.* Appropriate, he thought wryly. He turned it on loudly, and picking up the cigar from the carpet, relit it and sank back into the leather chair.

"Take your time Salim," he thought. "Do not hurry these things. For every negative, there is always a positive. Out of adversity, always there will come opportunity."

The facts were this.

One. The Zimbabwean, Mubvunduku wanted, rather, had demanded Phoebe. If he did not comply, Mubvunduku could make life very unpleasant for him. He could even arrange for his dismissal, for his expulsion from the party. Of that, there was no doubt.

Two. The white man and Phoebe were lovers. The *guarda-costa* had suspected this, and the urchin had confirmed it.

Three. Phoebe had been behaving strangely of late. At the time, he had thought nothing of it—simply a woman thing. But now ... now that he thought back, it made sense. Of late, she had been behaving strangely aloof. Either she was holding back on the commissions. Or she was planning to go solo. Without him. Without his protection. Or worse ... she was in love with this Mike ... and they were planning on leaving.

Four. This Mike had been talking to Renamo with the short one, the little white man with the curly black hair. Then shortly after the Renamo meeting, the short one had left for the Zambesia Province. Was this coincidence? And why had this Mike not gone with him? Was it because he was in love with Phoebe and wanted to stay in Beira ... to be with her?

And five. Lastly. There was the problem of the boy. It would not be possible to let him go. Not now. He would go straight to his master, like the mongrel he was. And he would tell him about the interrogation. Conversely, if the boy did not return, would not the master come looking for him? Who knew such things?

He poured himself a brandy, a Napoleon's, in his favourite crystal goblet. Swilling it around in the inside of the glass, he studied the golden richness of it, the syrupy pureness of it. Raising the glass to his lips, he sipped and let the brandy sit in his mouth for several moments, anaesthetizing, soothing. He swallowed and let out a deep sigh of contentment.

It was so simple. If one did not rush these things, the solution would always come.

Always.

The *guarda-costa* was standing guard outside the laundry door when Salim returned, as he had been instructed. Salim spoke with him briefly and the big man nodded and went down the passageway, towards the kitchens.

Opening the door of the laundry room, Salim observed the crumpled heap of the boy, curled up and unconscious on the bloodied sheet. The bucket lay nearby on its side. Slowly and with extreme deliberation, Salim took off his jacket and hung it neatly on the door handle. He then took off his tie and rolled up his sleeves, ensuring the folds were of a matching width and that each sleeve reached the same position, with the same number of folds, on each arm.

Picking up the bucket, he filled it with cold water from the nearest basin and slopped it over the boy's head, stepping back adroitly to avoid getting splashed. The boy stirred briefly. He was groaning softly, but his eyes were still closed.

Salim filled the bucket again and was about to pour it over the boy, when he stopped short. Putting down the bucket, he looked about him. Where was the ironing section? Ah, yes. That side. He made his way to the other side of the room, gently weaving his way through the damp sheets that hung like curtains all about. Finding the ironing tables, he picked up the nearest steam iron and plugged it in. They were good irons, industrial irons, specially imported from Germany. It would not take long for it to get hot.

The boy was coming round when he went back, but was still moaning softly, his head now partially raised, slowly nodding and bobbing from side to side. Standing over the wretched bundle, Salim contemplated. He could hear the footsteps of the *guarda-costa*, coming back from the kitchens.

He picked up the bucket and slopped it over the boy. The *guarda-costa* was by his side, a large cleaving knife hanging from his hand.

The boy tried to lift himself up and turned his head groggily up towards the two men standing over him. He recognized the knife, its blade glinting in the glare of the fluorescent light.

The man with the rolled-up sleeves was speaking to him. João tried to understand what he was saying. "Now listen, boy. You understand there is a necessity that you must be punished?"

João closed his eyes. He did not care anymore. He did not know what they were going to do to him. They were going to kill him? That would be a welcome release. Do it, he thought. Do it now.

And then the big man was sitting astride his chest, pinning his arm down with his boot. And Salim was gone, and then he was back a few minutes later. He too was holding something in his hand.

"You understand boy? This is for your own good. You will not die. But you will consider this a warning. If I ever hear that you have talked with the white man. If I ever hear that you have talked with Phoebe, the *puta,* then we shall come for you and you shall die."

The big man moved his boot down João's arm, until it dug into the wrist, just above the good hand. The big man looked up and nodded at Salim.

A blade flashed against the backdrop of the sheets and came down on the boy's wrist, severing the hand instantly. A jet of blood, like an oil gusher, spewed across the floor and the boy screamed and screamed and screamed. Strains of *The Water Music* drifted down the passage as the blood pumped out of the artery to its freedom.

The *guarda-costa* wrenched the bloodied wrist up as the slighter man pressed the steam iron onto the wounded stump. The blood sizzled and hissed in a fury, as the stench of burning flesh, of burning bone and tendon, enveloped the room. Salim closed his eyes, and felt the bile rising as he pressed still harder.

The boy's body had gone limp.

"It is sufficient, *senhor,*" Salim heard the big man say. "The blood has stopped."

Salim removed the iron and gagged violently. The sickly, sweet smell seemed to have permeated his clothes, his flesh. His brain.

"Clean up here. I want you to burn the sheet," he commanded.

"Yes, *senhor.*"

Salim unhooked his jacket and tie from the doorknob. Handel had come to an end. He would put on Wagner now. Slinging his jacket over his shoulder, he turned to the *guarda-costa.* "And throw that trash into the street ... where he belongs."

★ ★ ★ ★ ★

A grey dawn. The boy was lying in a gutter, a pathetic heap, drenched and half-dead. It was still raining and for a few seconds the boy thought he was drowned. He was face down in a pool of water and with a supreme effort he tilted his head fractionally. He gulped hungrily at the putrid air and felt a glimmer of life stir in his body, as the air sucked into his lungs, squabbling with the congealed blood and the muddiness of the water.

He was dreaming, surely? He was dead, surely? But the pounding in his head? The agony in his ribs? The vicious throbbing in his wrist? This was not death. A living death, maybe. But not death.

He opened his eyes and for a very long time stared vacantly at the tiny, whirling eddies of water that encircled his face, invading his nostrils, his mouth, his eyes.

A rhythmic crunching sound came to him. A gnawing and a crunching. As if something was eating something. And then there was a growling. He tried to get up. The feelings were there in his fingers, but there was no response. Through the mud, he dragged his arms up to his face. The freshly severed wrist was white and wrinkled from the hours in the water.

The boy broke down and wept. He wept and wailed for an eternity, flailing the gutter with the stumps of his arms, oblivious to the excruciating pain.

In the middle of the *avenida*, the dogs were fighting over the severed hand, until one mongrel snatched at it, half-eaten, and fled with it down the road, the small, black fingers hanging out if its mouth in an obscene fashion. The other dogs sniffed angrily at the spot where the hand had been, and then slunk off into the shadows.

João did not know of this as he finally managed to haul himself out of the gutter onto his knees. Holding both his arms up to the heavens in supplication, his eyes clouded with tears, he cried out to the God above in a scream of such anguish, of such hopelessness, of such despair.

And then he stood up, unsteady on his feet. A few faltering steps. And then some more. And then faster, with more urgency. And then he was running. Running and running and running.

Eighteen

Apart from a cursory nod, Jean-Paul barely acknowledged Mike and the black woman who came into Club Nautica that evening. He was too preoccupied trying to supervise the clean-up of the club in the wake of the cyclone. But for Jean-Paul's advance planning and organization, it could have been worse. The heavy-duty tarpaulins that shielded the restaurant from the sea had held, battened down, securely tied with thick sisal ropes that had been attached to great wooden stakes, driven deep into the sand.

But even this had not been enough to keep out the deluge of water that had poured into the club through every nook and cranny. Waiters, cooks, barmen and even Jean-Paul's blonde South African girlfriend were mopping and swabbing, baling buckets of rainwater and buckets of sea water out onto the beach. But the club was open for business, and Mike marvelled at Jean-Paul's resilience. It would be one of the few restaurants in Beira that was open.

The power failure was the least of Jean-Paul's problems. Power failures were common, even in the good times. Candles flickered defiantly in the closing darkness, casting haphazard shadows that pranced across the red-checked tablecloths.

Mike led Phoebe to his table near the sea wall. It was vacant, as were most in the club. A few desultory guests sat huddled around tables, speaking in hushed tones, as if in deference to the might of the storm—almost afraid to talk too loudly, lest they incur the wrath of nature once again.

Almost immediately a waiter was by their side, bucket temporarily abandoned, and a menu in hand.

"Is wine okay for you, Phoebe?" Mike asked.

The woman nodded peremptorily. "It's fine. White, *por favor.*" The frostiness in her voice was clear.

"*Vino Lagoste, por favor,*" Mike said to the waiter. He lit up a cigarette, without offering one to Phoebe. She didn't smoke, and if she wanted one, she would ask.

The tarpaulins had been rolled up and Mike looked out across the beach. Phoebe sat in silence, her eyes downcast beneath the long black eyelashes. There was no sunset, and day was becoming night in a sombre, silent merging of gloom and darkness. The beach was a mess, littered with myriad shapeless objects of flotsam and jetsam, tossed up from the depths of the ocean. A palm tree had fallen onto the sand, the muddy breakers pounding and sucking at the bedraggled fronds.

No stars were in the sky. Oppressive and suffocating, a thick layer of cloud hung low over the beachfront. Mike felt claustrophobic and decided that a swim might be a good idea. To wash it all away, all the guilt, all the shame. But that must wait. There was unfinished business to attend to—with Phoebe.

The waiter was filling their glasses, his white napkin soaking up the cold condensation of the bottle.

Mike raised his glass to Phoebe. "*Saúde!*"

She looked up from under her eyelashes and slowly raised her glass, touching it against his with a gentle tinkle. "*Saúde!*"

For a few seconds, he held his glass against hers. "To us … Phoebe."

She did not take her glass away and regarded him steadily, her eyes black and piercing. "To us … Mike."

They drank in silence. The frostiness was fading. Now it was a silence of relief and weariness, from the intensity of the fight, the confrontation and the passion.

It was humid and a few beads of sweat had gathered in her cleavage. She was wearing the short white lurex dress again. She had managed to wash it in the portavan during the storm. It had taken days to dry, but they'd had the days.

Mike glanced at her over the rim of his wine glass. It was as if she seemed to become more beautiful every time he looked at her. More radiant, more lovely … just … more … more everything. He sighed a deep sigh, wanting to hold her at that very moment.

As if sensing his thoughts, she caught his eye, almost shyly. With the glass to her lips, she stopped, her mouth open a fraction, her tongue lightly touching the rim with such a precise, uncontrived sensuality.

She took a mouthful of wine and put the glass down. Her elbows were resting on the table, her chin cupped in her hands.

"Words do not come easy to you, Mike." It was a statement. It was also an opening.

Mike looked at her leaning forward across the table, watching the fine detail of a droplet of sweat slowly trickle down from her throat into her breasts. She was right, of course. She always seemed to be right. "No … sometimes it is difficult …"

She took his hand across the table. "You will talk with me Mike. It is possible to talk with me."

He nodded dumbly, a lump forming in his throat.

"I … I have very strong feelings for you Mike …" Her words were measured.

"Yes … I too," Mike felt awkward, unsure of how to express himself.

The waiter had reappeared with the menu, but Phoebe brushed him aside.

She was squeezing his hand tightly, her other hand distractedly removing a long black hair that had fallen into her glass. With the tip of her tongue, she was methodically licking at her top lip, as if on the brink of uttering something of magnitude.

He could sense it and took the plunge. For once in your life, Mike, take the initiative. Say what you want to say. Say it. Do it. Say it now.

"Phoebe... " He felt her respond by gripping harder on his hand. "Phoebe, I ... I don't know how to say this ..."

"Say it, Mike. Tell me what you want to say." Her voice was low and throaty.

He took a deep breath, "Phoebe ... I think I am in love with you." The words tumbled out.

She took both his hands in hers, her eyes sparkling like pools in a mountain stream. She said nothing, aware that he hadn't finished.

"I ... have never felt like this about anyone in my life. I ... I don't know if it is a dream. I don't know ... All I know is that I have these very deep feelings for you. I want to be with you every second of the day. Every waking minute. Every second. " He was rambling, he thought. He was being foolish. But she was looking deep into his eyes, entranced.

"It is no dream, Mike ... how you say in English? 'Darling'?" She laughed coyly, embarrassed.

He laughed with her, relieved

"Darling. I also say, I ... love ... you," she said softly. Teardrops had welled in the corners of her eyes and she was smiling as they squeezed down onto her cheeks.

The waiter had appeared again, hanging back deferentially, yet persistent.

"Bring two portions *camarão,* queen prawns, *por favor,*" Mike heard himself say.

"Mike ... darling," her voice lilted, still unsure of the word, "I can say is that I have also never had such feelings—about any man. I am not doubting that I have a grand love for you. From the moment I saw you that time in the night-club ... that first time..."

Mike smiled in embarrassment.

"Yes, that time when you saw me and then you left. I thought then that perhaps you were a special man. But you were foolish and you left. I was very sad. But .. I knew that maybe you would come back. I knew."

"Yes. I was stupid. But you are right. I too knew that I would come back."

He refilled her glass, and even across the dancing flicker of the candle, could see that her face was flushed. Wholesome, sensual, exquisitely desirable. Her hair had fallen across her face, partially obscuring her features. He leaned across and moved the hair away.

She smiled and shrugged. "But it was meant to be, *não*? You returned."

"Yes. I am glad."

They drank in silence.

He could see she was deep in thought and after some time, a frown began to crease her brow, her eyes narrowing.

"What is it, my Phoebe?"

"It is .. it is nothing. But it is important."

"Tell me."

She looked up and tossed back her hair. "Mike. What I have to tell you is of a serious consequence."

"Yes."

"I am a *puta, não*? I am .. how you say .. a whore?"

"No, no, no, no .." Mike grasped her hand.

"Darling ... I love you, as I have loved no one in my life. But this is the truth. I am a whore. It is my profession. I can do no else. It is me."

"That can change, can it not?" Mike asked gently. He'd known this time would come, but was not prepared for what came next.

"Yes, of course. Anything can change. Nothing is of permanence. But ... it is not simple. I am a whore ... and I work for *Senhor* Salim." Her expression was deadpan, filled with despair and tiredness.

He felt himself go cold, a shiver running down his spine. For several minutes he said nothing.

"Salim? From the Hotel Beira?" This could not be true. She was making it up. There was some insane reason. But it was not true. It couldn't be.

"Yes. Salim, from the Hotel Beira. It is a fact."

"But ... but, how can this be?"

She regarded him with infinite sadness. "My life, Mike. I am a *puta*. It is simple. I will understand if you do not stay. It will be comprehensible if you walk away. I would do the same."

"Hush, my Phoebe. Do not talk like this. I love you. It is enough."

She shrugged. "Perhaps."

And then slowly she told him her story. From the beginning. It came through. The anguish, the hopelessness, the nothingness. The squalor and futility of the camps. And then this suave, dashing man from Beira had rescued her from it all and there had been hope. The words came and came. There was the prostitution—sometimes violent, sometimes pitiful, often sordid. But it had been a living. The only living she knew ... the burden of her life. And now, now this white man had come into her life. And again there was hope. But this time the hope was different. Real hope, albeit distant. But she was afraid.

What would Salim think of such a thing?

The prawns had long since arrived, unnoticed and cold.

Salim would accept such a thing? Salim would give his blessing to such a thing? Hah!

Salim would fly into a white rage if he were to know such a thing. Salim would kill for such a thing. He was a dangerous man.

There was a lull as she sipped at her wine. They were on the second bottle now. The waiter had appeared, uncalled, with a replacement. At the same time he'd taken away the prawns to get them reheated. Thunder rumbled in the darkness, far away across the horizon, interspersed with faint flashes of lightning. The cyclone had retreated offshore, for the time being, gathering its resources.

She had tears in her eyes, glistening in the candlelight.

"Phoebe ..." Mike's voice was breaking as he spoke. "I ... never realized ...," the words tapered off.

"There is nothing we can do. It is the way of things," she said, defeated, her shoulders slumped.

Passing her his handkerchief, Mike suddenly felt a surge of anger. At Salim, at the war, at their country, their homeland, Zimbabwe. At the circumstances which had lead to this. It was so unfair. It was not right. But it was Africa.

"Well, bugger you Africa, you're not going to win this time," he thought. "Enough is enough. You've had your fair share of victims. Enough now."

He stood up and went to her, wrapping his arms around her. He felt her shaking in his arms, the sobs welling up inside. He hugged her tighter, soothing and whispering into her hair. And after some time, he could feel her quieten and then she was calm.

"Phoebe," he said softly. "You must listen to me."

She nodded, biting her bottom lip.

"I too have witnessed the cruelty of Africa. I fought in the war of liberation. I was one of those white soldiers that came to the camps. I was 18 years old. I was a boy, but I was killing." He spoke deliberately, without emotion, without self-pity. "I did things that I still cannot believe I did. I do not understand them ... but I look back now and see that it was a condition of the time ... it was a conditioning of the mind. The same way you talk about how you condition yourself when you go with a client. It is the same thing."

There was an urgency in his voice that she could not ignore. He was trying to tell her something. She was unsure of what exactly it was, but she knew she was drawing strength from his words. And that was enough.

"What I'm trying to say, Phoebe, is that I am tired of the running. I am tired of living in fear. I am tired of not being in control of my own destiny. I have discovered something in the last few days. Something that I will not let anyone take away."

Her tears had dried on her cheeks as she listened, intently. She had never witnessed such intensity before. Such depth of emotion. It was a wondrous thing.

"Phoebe. For the first time in my life, I have discovered a reason to live. I now understand what all the pain and suffering were for. I have found .. you, Phoebe. Do you not understand that?"

She nodded.

"Phoebe. I will not let this Salim take you."

She nodded again and smiled. In her heart she believed him, she wanted to believe him, but still she was afraid. He could sense her misgivings.

"It is a simple thing, Phoebe. I will not permit it."

And for the first time in her life, Phoebe handed over completely—to this white man she had known only a few, short days. For the first time in her life, she felt the weight of the sub-continent lifting from her shoulders. This man, this good, kind man who had had to fight his own terrible battles, was her salvation. She smiled and passed him a prawn. Even a momentary salvation was something.

"Eat. You must eat."

He laughed easily, embarrassed by his own verbosity. He had never spoken like this before. But it was true. She did not know it, but she was also his salvation. She laughed with him and they ate together.

The waiter brought a third bottle of wine. The prawns were finished and Mike ordered espresso coffees. He felt a freedom he'd never felt before, a giddiness of freedom and happiness. Perhaps it was the wine. Perhaps not.

"Come, let's walk," he took her hand. "On the beach. Leave your shoes here. The waiter will watch the table."

She giggled, from the effects of the wine and the emotion. He lifted her over the low sea wall and they felt the dampness of the sand under their feet. Hand in hand they walked up the beach, towards the lighthouse, two silent figures in the darkness.

They stopped at the wreck, as a few stars appeared above, dimly haloed in rings of iridescent moisture. Taking off his shirt, he laid it on the wet sand for her to sit. The air was damp and warm against his skin. She sat, and he sat by her, smoking a cigarette. When he offered it to her, she declined.

"You have corrupted me enough, *Senhor* Mike," she teased.

She leaned her head against his shoulder, her hands tucked warmly inside his thighs.

"But it is okay. You can corrupt me some more. You are permitted to do this." She craned her face up to his and kissed him on the cheek.

He turned to her, her face misty with desire, with tenderness, and they made love in the shadow of the old Portuguese galleon.

There was a man sitting at their table when they returned and Mike felt a pang of anger.

What had the waiter been doing? The man had his back to the sea and was unaware of their return. Calling for a waiter, the man's voice boomed and Mike felt a surge of relief. He would recognize that voice anywhere.

"Kurt!"

The Dane stood up, taken aback at the voice from the beach. Squinting into the darkness, he finally recognized Mike.

"Ah ha! So, zere you are, you fockin' bastard. What haff you been doing out zere? Fockin' fishing?" He laughed heartily.

Mike took Phoebe's hand, sensing her reticence. "It's okay. He's a good friend. He's the guy who owns the caravan." He felt her body relax as they stepped over the sea wall.

"Ja? So what haff we here, huh?" Kurt looked Phoebe up and down, making no effort to conceal his admiration. "You catch a fockin' strange fish, huh Mike?"

"Kurt. This is Phoebe."

"Ja? She is beautiful." Kurt took Phoebe's hand and kissed it. "I am delighted to meet you. Where did you find zis fockin' old dog, huh?" His laugh boomed across the restaurant. "I haff ordered more *vino*. Sit. We drink."

"You are here late tonight, Kurt?" Mike asked.

"Agh, ja. Ze whole city's a fock-up. Now zere's fockin' cholera and dysentry. Ze city council can't cope and I've been calling in ze relief organizations. But you know, zis damn bureaucracy. People are fockin' dying, but ze fockin' government says zat it's more important zat ze relief workers haff ze fockin' visas first. Sometimes I sink Africa can go fock itself.."

Phoebe sat listening, enthralled by this gruff, jovial man. She liked him. But of course, Mike's friends would be good people, would they not? It was obvious this man cared. As it was obvious he had not yet been home. The exhaustion showed on his face.

As if on cue, Kurt turned to Phoebe, topping up her glass. She tried to resist, but gave in.

"So, Phoebe? Zat is a beautiful name, huh? Why are you with a ratbag like zis, huh?"

Mike could feel her blushes and even Kurt, through his exhaustion, could sense the moment. "Ah ha! Mike, I sink zis is something serious, huh?"

Mike nodded. "Yes, Kurt. It is very serious."

"Good. You need it". Kurt said matter-of-factly.

He boomed for another bottle of wine and a waiter came scurrying. Mike began to feel light-headed and wanted to tell Kurt that they'd had enough, that it was time to go home. But he couldn't. Kurt needed him. He needed them. He needed the company.

Phoebe's head had lolled onto Mike's shoulder and she was asleep.

"Agh. Look. Ze princess sleeps. It is better you go home huh?"

"No, it's okay Kurt. It is good to see you." Mike gently lowered Phoebe's head onto his lap, softly stroking her hair. The white dress had ridden up around her pants and he tugged the hem down.

"Hey, Mike. I forgot to tell you. Zat Oscar sent a message. He is coming back tomorrow."

"Hey? Oscar?" Mike had almost forgotten about Oscar, about Renamo and the agricultural project. So much had happened in the last week.

"Ja. Zat short one. He's catching a lift with Colin out of Zambesia."

"What's Colin doing in Zambesia?"

"Agh. He's flying relief charter for one of zese fockin' aid organizations. Probably some fockin' Swedes. Some fockin' old Dakota zat will probably fall outa ze sky 'cause it's overloaded with fockin' mealie meal. But you know Colin, huh? He doesn't give a damn. So long as he's flying, he's happy. Fockin' crazy Englishman."

Kurt downed his drink. He could see that Mike was yawning.

"Kom. It is late. I give you a lift back to ze caravan. You sink you can carry ze princess?"

Mike nodded. "Thanks, Kurt. I .. I must sort you out with the rent tomorrow."

"Agh. Fock ze rent."

★ ★ ★ ★ ★

It was late that evening when Salim put the call through to Harare. Martha had fallen asleep at the front desk, which had made him very angry. Most unprofessional. And he'd also gotten rid of the lone whore hanging out in the lobby, vainly hoping that a client might stumble in.

"Cheap tart. Get out of my hotel. What do you think this is? A brothel? Bugger off!"

The whore had gathered up her plastic handbag and flounced out.

And where was the *guarda-costa*? He didn't remember giving him permission to go off?

"Where's that idiot?" He snapped at Martha who was now fully awake.

The girl shrugged. "Who knows? Maybe he's upstairs in the night-club, getting drunk."

She was unafraid of Salim. She understood his moods.

The hotel manager stormed off into his office, slamming the door behind him. He poured himself another brandy as there came a soft knock on the door. The *guarda-costa* poked his head in.

"You were looking for me, *senhor*?"

"Yes. Where have you been? I will need you shortly. Don't go away."

The *guarda-costa* nodded in accordance and shut the door.

The phone rang and Salim snatched at it. It was Zimbabwe. Martha had got through. And yes. Minister Mubvunduku was still in his office.

"Comrade Mubvunduku?" Salim's tone changed almost immediately. "I trust you are well?" He knew that all was not well in Zimbabwe and that Minister Mubvunduku would have his hands full trying to control the civil unrest that seemed to be sweeping the country.

"Yes, yes, Comrade Minister. I understand that you are a very busy man."

The minister was in a bad mood. It was plain.

"The girl? Yes. It is being arranged at this very moment, Comrade Minister..."

The minister clearly had no time for niceties.

"Of course. Comrade Minister. I have not forgotten. .... As I say, the matter is in hand and she will be delivered shortly..."

Beads of perspiration were forming on Salim's brow. He had not expected such aggression.

"Comrade Minister ..," Salim's tone now ominous, "... it is important I meet with you. I need to see you urgently. I must come to Harare ... tomorrow."

Salim could tell the tack had worked and that the minister had been taken off guard.

"No, no, no. It has nothing to do with the girl … well, not directly. But it is a matter of extreme importance. I cannot discuss it over the phone…. You must understand, Comrade Minister. It is a matter of state security, that is of mutual concern to both our countries…"

There! He'd got him. Hooked. The 'state security' had swung it.

"Yes, Comrade Minister. I had already taken the precaution. I have reserved a seat on tomorrow morning's flight."

Putting down the phone, Salim took a long slow swallow of his brandy. He smiled, a thin humourless smile, his fingertips lightly drumming on the leather inlay of the desk.

"Martha!" he shouted through the closed door. "Tell that gorilla to come here."

Within seconds the *guarda-costa* was standing in front of his desk.

"Did you follow the girl tonight?"

"I did, *senhor.*"

"Where did she go?"

"To that Club Nautica, *senhor.*"

"With the white man?"

"Yes, *senhor.* With the white man."

Salim's fist slammed down hard on the desk, his face dark with fury. She was guilty. She was playing games with him. Well, she would see …

"Now listen carefully to me. I am going to Zimbabwe tomorrow. I want you to pick her up and detain her. Do you understand?"

The *guarda-costa* nodded impassively.

"But, it is of critical importance that you only pick her up after my flight has left. If possible, she must be alone when you pick her up. I do not want the white man to witness anything .."

"But, *senhor.* That is impossible. She is with him every second …"

"Do not argue with me! These are my instructions." Salim was shouting.

The big man shrugged. "Very well, *senhor*. It shall be as you say."

Salim unclenched his fists. "*Bom*.... And no violence. She is valuable to me. My little export prize," he muttered more to himself. "You understand? I want no harm to come to her?"

"Whatever you say, *Senhor* Salim. Whatever you say."

Nineteen

In four decades, Harare International Airport had not changed. Still the same dull grey facade of the fifties-style architecture, from the boom times of the Central African Airways, that short-lived colonial dream of a central African federation of states, loyal to the Crown.

It was raining as Salim picked his way down the steps, out of LAM Flight 032. A Boeing 737, the pride of the Mozambican National Airline. Two men in dark suits were waiting for him at the bottom of the steps.

"Comrade Salim?" one of the men enquired. "Welcome to Zimbabwe."

Salim nodded curtly and followed the two men briskly across the apron, steam hissing as the raindrops splattered onto the asphalt. He was led in through the VIP entrance as lounging customs and immigration officials opened up a path, then ambled off to the public concourse in anticipation of the arriving passengers. But LAM 032 would not be a worthwhile victim. Except for prawns, there was nothing worth smuggling in from Mozambique.

The inevitable black Mercedes was waiting outside the airport, its motor running, with the chauffeur ready to go. It seemed there was no time to be wasted. Salim was ushered into the back seat, sandwiched between the two men in the dark suits.

It struck Salim how Harare seemed to be degrading—slowly, inexorably, insidiously. You probably wouldn't notice the decline if you lived there, but to an occasional visitor like Salim, it was clear. It had only been a year since his last visit and he could notice the differences. In fact, Harare was becoming like any other African capital city—dirty, seedy and decayed. Once the flagship of African aspirations and prosperity, the approach to the city wasn't too unlike coming into Lusaka, or even Beira.

The verges were overgrown, the rank bush encroaching and spilling over onto the road. Wriggling up through the tarmac, the weeds invaded, cracking into the concrete, smothering the gravel. Great billboards beamed to the new visitors, faded and jaded, advertising Zambezi Lager and Madison cigarettes—homegrown Zimbabwean products.

Springing forth in profusion, the makeshift stalls of the informal vendors littered the sides of the roads. Unlicensed and illegal, but desperate to survive, the babbling, jostling Shona peoples went about their daily business. But still they smiled. It was in their nature, not unlike the Mozambicans. It would take more than an economic crisis to wipe the smiles from those faces. Ironically, the politicians knew this.

Across the vlei of the Mukuvisi River, the skyline of Harare beckoned, the Sheraton Hotel, their destination, gleaming with consummate vulgarity across the poverty of the masses, teeming and sweating below. A golden edifice of aggrandisement.

Stopping at the traffic lights, Salim glanced out the window, across the blank face of the man at his side. There, under a cluster of gum trees, through the scurrying swarm of people, he noticed a crudely fashioned sign, pinned to one of the trees. 'The Siya-So Gum Tree Survival Peoples Co-operative Society'. The sign writer, obviously an amateur, had run out of space midway through 'Co-operative', and the last few letters of the imposing title were squeezed into the bottom right hand corner of the sign.

And above the gum trees, the Sheraton loomed. The Zimbabweans still hadn't got their requisite international airport, but they had the Sheraton, a heroes' acre and an international athletics stadium. Almost there.

Pulling up at the hotel, the Mercedes jerked to a halt, and the two men hustled the Mozambican through the lobby, striding purposefully through the chromed glass illusion of pervasive opulence. Mubvunduku was waiting for them in the private cocktail bar that the manager had specially opened up for him. It was still only nine o'clock in the morning, but this was not an unusual thing with Comrade Mubvunduku. He liked to conduct his meetings in this place.

Slouched in an armchair, the minister did not rise as the Mozambican entered. Clasped in his hand was a large glass of whisky. His eyes were red and bleary, hooded from the excesses and the exhaustion. The civil unrest had taken its toll.

Lazily waving his arm at Salim, he indicated he should sit. The two men in the dark suits stood off near the door, as the lone barman quietly disappeared.

"Salim, Salim, Salim. My good friend. How are you today?" The minister was slurring a mite.

"I am well, Comrade Minister. I trust you are in good health?"

The minister roared with laughter, his great belly shaking. "Yes, yes, yes, my little friend. I am very well. I am always well."

The insult did not go unnoticed. Salim blinked slowly, absorbing the retort. The minister had not offered him a drink. Another insult.

"So, Salim? How is the hotel business? Maybe one day the Hotel Beira shall be like this," Mubvunduku's arms swept around him, expansively. "Or maybe, we Zimbabweans should come and build our own Sheraton in Beira? Hey? Not a bad idea, huh?" He laughed loudly, mirthlessly, at his own humour.

Salim regarded him, unsmiling, trying to keep the anger out of his eyes. "Why don't you?" he asked, coldly.

The minister ignored the jibe. "Okay, *Senhor* Salim, what is your story now with the woman? This Phoebe. I assume it is now organized and that she is on her way to Harare?"

"She is not, Minister. There is a problem," Salim said flatly.

Mubvunduku scowled, his brow furrowing heavily. "What are you telling me, Salim?"

"She has possibly gone over to Renamo. She was lured across by two Zimbabweans who are in league with the rebels."

"What?" Mubvunduku bellowed. "Zimbabweans?"

"Yes, Comrade Minister ... white Zimbabweans."

Mubvunduku was silent, his chest heaving for air, as beads of sweat formed across his forehead. He wiped clumsily with his silk handkerchief, but the smoothness of the silk simply spread the sweat evenly in a sheen across his face.

"I have left instructions that the woman is to be detained," Salim continued, "with the utmost discretion. And with the minimum of violence... She will then be delivered to Harare as you have requested ... after we have conducted our investigations."

Mubvunduku glowered. "You will do no such thing, Salim. You will get her on the first available flight. She is a Zimbabwean national. We will insist on her immediate repatriation."

"She has no papers. Perhaps she is not Zimbabwean. Perhaps she is a Mozambican *deslocado*?" Salim added glibly.

"Do not play games with me, *Senhor* Salim," the minister growled. "You yourself said she was a Zimbabwean."

"Perhaps I was mistaken," Salim shrugged lightly.

Mubvunduku nodded slowly, the corner of his lip curling in a sneer. He changed course. "And these white men. These Rhodesians?"

"We have confirmed with our immigration authorities that they are Zimbabwean nationals."

"Rhodesians. There are no white Zimbabweans. They are Rhodesians, the children of the British and the Boers."

"Whatever you say, Comrade Minister. But we have not done anything yet. Not without your approval. After all, they are Zimbabwean nationals. The one known as Oscar is in the Zambesia Province on a Renamo mission. We don't know what it is, but we will find out. The other, his name is Mike, is in Beira. He is the one with the woman."

Mubvunduku heaved himself out of his chair and waddled over to the bar. He topped up his glass with neat whisky. Check. This Salim was cunning. He had better take more care next time.

"May I suggest, Comrade Minister," Salim continued, "that we proceed on this basis. We will detain the woman and will get her delivered to you as soon as we have completed our investigations. After all, surely you would agree that we should establish her nationality? And if she is running with Renamo, it is vital that we establish her position. My president would insist on nothing less."

Mubvunduku grunted, grudgingly acknowledging the logic.

"Don't get me wrong, Comrade Minister. It is of immediate priority, as a debt of gratitude, that this Phoebe is sent to you. But, you surely must understand that in this instance, the matter of national security must take preference?"

Mubvunduku grunted again.

"As for the two white men ... these Rhodesians, as you call them, I would suggest that we leave them be ... for the moment. They have committed no crime ... as yet. It is better that we monitor their movements... Until they play their hand... as you would say. We would be happy to work together with your agents in this matter... But the decision is yours, comrade."

Mubvunduku heaved, his eyes glassy and empty. Salim had wrested the initiative from him—totally.

"If you would prefer, we will detain them and deport them back to Zimbabwe. We will find a pretext. It is not difficult."

The minister was tugging thoughtfully at his ear lobe. He had no interest in a couple of down and out Rhodesians. So? If they were running with Renamo, what could they do? But ... clearly they were close to the woman. For that reason alone, they would be worth pursuing.

"Okay, Salim. We do it your way ... for now. Detain the woman and leave the Rhodesians."

Salim smiled thinly. "As you say, Comrade Minister."

"Oh ... I almost forgot. Maybe I should come down to Beira next week ... just to see how things are going. Maybe our CIO agents can be of assistance? As you keep saying, this Renamo matter could very well be of interest to us as well. Zimbabwean national security."

Salim's smile vanished. "You ... are always welcome in Mozambique, Comrade Minister."

"Good." It was Mubvunduku's turn to smile. "I shall look forward to the visit."

The meeting was closed and Salim gathered up his briefcase. He had two days in Harare. Plenty of time to get in some good shopping.

"Major," Mubvunduku addressed the shorter of the two dark-suited men, as Salim closed the door behind him. "You are a military man. But first and foremost, you are one of my top CIO agents. You have done well in the Central Intelligence Organization, haven't you?"

"Sir, it is my job."

"You are too modest." Mubvunduku leaned forward from the barstool, earnestly. "You will investigate these two Rhodesians. I want you to find out everything you can about them."

"Sir. We will have their files on record, I'm sure."

"Good. And I want you to visit the UN camp at Chimoio. The refugee camp. You will go through all the records with a fine toothcomb. The snake Salim says she had no papers. But maybe they were overlooked. Maybe she is on record."

"Sir, the UNHCR camp at Chimoio was closed down last year."

The minister cursed softly below his breath. "Well then, Major, you will find out what happened to the camp records. The UNHCR still has an office in Chimoio, surely?"

"Yes sir, I am sure."

"Well then. What are you waiting for?"

★ ★ ★ ★ ★

The major had always taken an immense pride in his job. He was, he believed, the epitome of a professional. With an impeccable war record, he'd soon risen through the ranks of the liberation army during the *Chimurenga,* and at independence in 1980 was a successful detachment commander, operating in the Gaza Sector in the south-eastern corner of the country. That was where Comrade Mubvunduku had first noticed him and invited him to join the Central Intelligence Organization. The rank of major was not an issue in the organization—merely a mechanism of ensuring a reasonable salary and a meaningful pension.

The rain stopped around lunchtime when he'd got back to his office. It hadn't taken long to find the files. He drew to a halt as the traffic lights turned red at the intersection of Churchill Avenue and the Borrowdale Road.

He'd been very polite when he'd phoned this fellow Melvin. That always threw them. The nervousness had been obvious across the phone, but the major took no solace from this. He was there to do a job. Simple. Melvin had been very co-operative, and yes, it would be no problem for the major to visit. That afternoon? Yes, no problem. Lived out in Borrowdale.

He was in the olive green Peugeot 504 sedan, with the white government plates. For months, he'd been nagging away at his superior for something a little less conspicuous, something newer than the '79 model he was driving. But he knew there was no money.

The lights changed and he pulled away. He had the two manila files on the seat next to him. But there wasn't too much in them. A wild goose chase probably. But then again … you never knew. After all, that trip to Zambia with this Oscar and this Mike … perhaps there was something in that …

He wound down the window. The air was fresh and clean after the storm. The one thing common to the three white men was that they had all served in the Rhodesian Army, in the same unit. But was that anything sinister? Probably not. Just good friends. Nothing more.

Melvin had been standing at the front door when the Peugeot pulled into the driveway. He'd combed his hair, put on a shirt and had tried to clean up the lounge as best he could. The boxes of belt buckles, the empty bottles, the records out of their sleeves, the guitar with the white cat asleep on top.

He shook hands with the major, a little too enthusiastically. "Come inside, my friend."

The major followed him in and sat down on the couch. A cat was clawing at the fabric.

"Can I get you a drink? Some tea?" Melvin was very nervous, anxious to please.

The major stifled a yawn. It had been a long day. "Hmmm. Okay. I take Black Label."

Melvin was behind the mukwa bar counter. "Sorry, my friend. I only have Castle or Zambezi."

"Okay. Zambezi. It's a good beer."

Melvin opened the green bottle and passed it to the black man. "Sorry, no glasses."

"No problem." The major drank long and hard from the bottle, downing a good half with his first gulp. "So, Melvin. You were in the Rhodesian Army? With your friends Mike and Oscar?"

"Yes," Melvin answered quickly, "but it was compulsory. Y'know … national service and all that. And anyway … I was only on the admin side …"

"It was crazy, huh? That war?" The major finished the second half of his beer.

"Another," he stated, wiping the froth from his mouth. There was nothing here. May as well enjoy the beer.

"So ... Major. What's this all about?" Melvin enquired, tentatively. "I mean ... Oscar and Mike are my mates. We play music together but they're not here ..."

"I know," the major interrupted. "They're in Mozambique."

Melvin was bending down to open the fridge and stopped dead in his tracks. There was an awkward silence.

"You know they are in Mozambique?" the major persisted, casually.

Melvin gulped. "I ... I heard that ... "He didn't know what to say. Was this a trap? "Yes ... I heard that they were down there, but I haven't seen them for ages. I know Oscar lost his job. That was the last I heard ..."

"Did you hear that they are working with Renamo?" the major asked evenly, his tone flat and uninterested.

Melvin felt the blood rushing to his cheeks. Was this a set-up? "No. I never heard that." He tried to sound incredulous, unsure of where this was heading. I mean ... Oscar and Mike working with Renamo? Crazy, man. But ... why would this man be making this up?

The major shrugged. "It is not illegal to work with Renamo, you know? Mozambique is a free country. Renamo is a legally constituted political party now. The war there is finished."

"But ... why would they work with Renamo?"

The major shrugged again. "I don't know. You tell me." He looked directly at Melvin.

"I've no idea, my friend. Another beer?"

"Okay. One more, and then I must go," the major replied easily. "I have to go to Chimoio tomorrow. I must get an early night."

Melvin felt himself go cold again. Chimoio? What was this all about? What had Mike and Oscar got themselves into this time?

"You going on business?"

"Oh yes. Always business."

"So the CIO is quite active in Mozambique?"

"Of course. We still don't trust Renamo. We have to keep an eye on them. They can be troublemakers sometimes."

"I thought you said that was all finished?"

"It is," the major yawned, "but as you say in English— 'fore-warned is fore-armed'." He smiled, self-indulgently. It was a good expression. He finished his beer and stood up.

"Okay, Mr Melvin. Thanks for the beers. Nice to meet you."

"Ja. You too." Melvin showed him out.

The major turned to Melvin as he unlocked his car door, "See you next time." He got in the car and turned the ignition. "Tell your friends that they should stick to music. I understand you have a good reputation with the whites as a musician. Maybe I'll come and listen to you one day."

Melvin slapped the roof of the Peugeot. "Anytime, my friend. Anytime."

The major reversed out of the driveway. It had been as he thought. A waste of time.

Standing at the gate, Melvin watched him leave. He was shaking and hoped it hadn't shown. The Peugeot disappeared down the road.

He went back inside and poured himself a stiff cane and Coke. No ice. He was still shaking and spilled some of the Coke.

"What stunt are you okes trying to pull now?" he muttered to himself, with disbelief.

He gulped at his drink. He was at a total loss, but he knew that they had to be warned. What should he do? Drive down to Beira? For starters, the red Pulsar would conk out on the way. And what about a visa? The CIO would know if he applied for one. The Mozambican embassy would be on the lookout. For sure. And what if he happened to bump into the major on the road to Chimoio?

Ja, that's it. Get them on the phone. But where were they staying? And was his phone bugged? Probably. What about a fax? They couldn't bug faxes … could they?

He wracked his brain, desperately thinking.

Chris someone? He tried to remember. Mike had often talked about an English guy who ran a shipping operation in Beira. Chris … Charlie … what was his name? Colin! That was it. Colin. But what was the name of his company? What was the fax number?

He poured himself another drink, warm and fizzy. Then he phoned Mike's old boss, who sounded irritated, but had finally found the number.

Scratching around the drawers in the bedroom, Melvin eventually found a piece of paper. He sat at the bar counter and wrote with the felt-tip marker in big black letters.

MIKE/OSCAR.
THE CIO IS ON TO YOU.
SOMETHING TO DO WITH RENAMO.
GET OUT OF MOZ. BUT DON'T COME BACK TO ZIM.
GOOD LUCK. M.

He read and re-read the message several times. He felt relaxed now and although he wouldn't admit it, he was almost relishing the histrionics of it all. His sister had a fax machine. He'd pop round later and send it off from there.

He chuckled to himself. "Hey, I mean … isn't that what buddies are for?"

Twenty

Phoebe needed a change of clothes. She shook Mike as he lay next to her, snoring softly.

"Hey! Lover. It is time to get up."

Mike stirred, his hand automatically reaching across to her body. She snuggled up to him like a kitten, nuzzling her head under his arm.

"I've put the kettle on," she said. "You want coffee … or your English tea?"

Mike felt the stirring in his loins as his hand explored the inside of her thigh, silky and warm.

"Hmmm … I want neither," he said sleepily. "What I want is some of this Mozambican flesh."

She pushed his hand away, firmly. "Later … we must rise. I need to go over to the *apartamento* and get some clothes. You think I can live in this one dress, this white night-club dress forever?"

"Ja, why not? It is a very sexy dress. Anyway, when you need to wash it, you can just stay in bed .. while it dries."

She laughed and got out of bed. The kettle had boiled. "Mike … I need to get my things." There was a sense of urgency in her voice that Mike did not disregard.

"What are we going to do about the apartment … about Salim?" Mike asked.

"I do not know. For the *momento*, I just want to get my things … away from there."

It was all happening too quickly for her. Mike, Salim, her emotions, her independence. Her whole life seemed to be turning upside-down, running away from her.

Again, Mike didn't miss the edge in her voice. As if getting her clothes out of there was the first step in severing the umbilical ties with that Salim. If that was what she wanted. He should have known all along that Salim was a slimebag. A pimp. A whoremaster. Posing as a hotel manager.

"I must also get my mirror," Phoebe muttered, as she poured the coffee.

"Huh?"

"Oh, *desculpa*," she looked up. "My mirror. I paid a lot of money for it. US dollars. But it is not important."

"We will get it. It is important."

They drank their coffee and dressed. The white dress was creased, and lay crumpled on the floor. Mike lent her one of his T-shirts. It was way too big, so she wore it as a dress. He studied her. Hell, man. She could wear anything and look gorgeous.

They drove in silence to *2B Apartamento, Rua de Julius Nyerere 86*. Mike was concentrating on the road, weaving and negotiating his way through the stagnant pools and swathes of silt. In places the asphalt was barely visible. That was the danger. Who knew whether a stretch of water was a puddle or a pothole, two-foot deep?

The sun had come out today, triumphant over the cloudbanks that sulked sullenly across the horizon. The humidity must have been sitting at 100 %. By the time they reached Phoebe's street, his T-shirt was soaked through with his sweat. Midday would be a killer.

Phoebe indicated the flat and he pulled up outside. The bunch of urchins stopped their football game to study the new arrival. Two cars at *2B Apartamento* in the same morning. It was curious.

"Come," Phoebe said. "Come inside. You can help me with my things, *não?*"

"Sure." Mike followed her in.

Unlocking the door, Mike saw her stiffen as she opened it. He peered over her shoulder. The place had been ransacked.

"Salim," Phoebe whispered to herself. "Salim. You ... you ... *filho de puta.*"

Mike put an arm around her waist to steady her. She was shaking with anger and emotion. Tears were welling. Picking his way over a broken chair, smashed on the floor, he gently led her to the bedroom and sat her down on the bed.

"Sit," he ordered. "Tell me where everything is. I will pack it."

"It ... is ... Salim. I know it," she sobbed. "Why? For what? What have I done to him?"

Mike held her tightly. "You have fallen in love with me. That is what you have done to him. Well, one thing's for sure. You can't stay here anymore."

"I will go to him. At the Hotel Beira. He must pay."

"*Não!* That is what he wants. He wants you to come to him." He stood up and inspected the apartment. At first glance it looked as if it had been deliberately trashed. But after some time, Mike deduced that it had more likely been a search, a frustrated search that had revealed nothing. The vase of plastic flowers on the kitchen table was untouched. And that full-length mirror with the Oregon pine border was intact. Such items would have been the first to go in a deliberate trashing.

But what had they been looking for?

Hah! That must be the mirror she was talking about. He went to her. Her face was buried in her hands, emitting animal-like whimpers of despair and frustration.

He put his arms around her. "Hush, my princess. Hush."

She looked up to him, her face wet with tears.

"The mirror is okay," he said, lightly.

She laughed through the tears and he kissed them away. "It will be fine, my Phoebe. It will all be okay. These things. They are only things."

"Yes, they are only things. You are right." And then abruptly she sat up, her tone changing, now business-like. "I could expect no less. I should have known. Salim is a cruel man."

"We will deal with it," Mike replied, admiring her fortitude.

"Yes. We will. Now … let us pack the clothes and get out of here."

Mike found an old suitcase on top of the wardrobe and began stuffing her clothes inside. She was in the kitchen, packing bits of crockery and cutlery into a cardboard box. They worked fast and methodically and within half an hour, the job was done.

Mike lugged the suitcase and the cardboard boxes out to the truck. The urchins were still there. He ignored them and went back inside. The plastic flowers were scattered over the kitchen table.

"My bank," she smiled at him, showing him a fistful of US dollars.

He laughed, and she laughed with him.

"Hey! Phoebe. We mustn't forget the mirror."

She locked the door behind her and stepping out into the street, flung the keys as far down the *Rua de Julius Nyerere* as she could. Like a troop of chattering monkeys, the street kids scurried off after them, tripping and stumbling in their haste to get there first.

As Mike got out of the truck to unlatch the gate, he stopped, and glancing down noticed the tyre tracks in the mud. Not the treads of his truck. Something bigger, like four-wheel drive treads. And they were fresh too. He looked towards the portavan. The tracks had not entered the yard.

Swinging open the gate, he inspected the ground for spoor—bootprints, footprints. But there was nothing. Ag! Perhaps it was Kurt. But then perhaps it was Salim or his *guarda-costa,* the one that Phoebe had been telling him about. The big bodyguard. The goon who did all Salim's dirty work.

Without mentioning it to Phoebe, he drove in up to the lean-to and parked.

"Come on, Phoebe. Let's get this lot unloaded. We've got to get off to Club Nautica. Colin and Oscar should be there just now."

"Okay, okay. But first I change. I will not go in this T-shirt."

Mike sighed to himself. It was no use arguing. She looked stunning. But she had said she wanted to change, so she would change. The way of women.

Jean-Paul smiled a hello at Mike and nodded at Phoebe as they came into the club. Mike sensed it was a nod of acceptance. Phoebe was unsure, but gave him the benefit of the doubt and nodded in return, her back erect and her head held high. It would take some getting used to, this thing of being a partner. Was that what she wanted? It was all so confusing.

The three men were sitting, huddled earnestly at Mike's table over by the sea wall. Otherwise, the club was empty of customers. It was still early. An Elton John song was playing over the PA system. *Sacrifice,* Mike noted. Elton John was immensely popular in Mozambique and *Sacrifice* was probably the song of choice, closely followed by *Nikita.*

He squeezed Phoebe's hand as he led her across to his friends. She was nervous. The three men stood up as they noticed the couple.

"Ag! Romeo and Juliet haff arrived," Kurt's voice boomed forth.

Mike felt himself blushing. "Hello Kurt. Colin. Oscar. I'd like you to meet Phoebe."

Oscar looked weary. His hair was awry, his eyes bloodshot from either the dope, lack of sleep, or both. His clothes were dirty and stained, and it looked as if he hadn't changed in two weeks.

He stepped forward and shook hands with Phoebe. "Hi Phoebe. I'm Oscar. I've heard all about you from Kurt. I think he's jealous." His eyes twinkled. "It's a pleasure to meet you."

Mike could sense that Phoebe was taken aback, pleasantly so. Oscar could always lay on the charm when he wanted to.

Colin waved a hello from across the table. He too looked worn out.

"You look stuffed, Colin." Mike stated. "Been doing a lot of flying?"

"Yeah. Non-stop. We can't get the relief supplies in quickly enough. Been collecting loads from all over the bloody show. Nampula, Beira, Maputo, even Lusaka. Y'know how I love Zambia. But I go where I'm told. Got a million and one bosses—UNHCR, Red Cross, World Vision, Oxfam. Redd Barna, World Food Programme. You name it."

"And flying into where?"

"Generally Zambesia. Also Tete, and a bit up into Niassa and Cabo Delgado. But mainly along the Zambezi. That's where the cyclone seems to have done the most damage. Along the flood plain. Thousands of people are cut off, stranded all over the show. Poor sods. Lost all their crops, their livestock, the bloody lot. Some of them hadn't eaten for over two weeks."

"Ja," Oscar added. "So my little trip for Renamo was a total waste of time. All the estates we were supposed to visit were under water. Ended up helping Colin. Shit man, if I see another bag of mealie meal in my life, I'll scream."

"Yeah. And the bloody powdered milk," quipped Colin.

"Okay, okay. Enough, gentlemen," Kurt butted in. "I sink we haff more important sings to talk about, ja?" He was frowning. "Sit, if you please." He pulled up a chair for Phoebe and she smiled gratefully.

"Why so serious, Kurt?" Mike queried. He'd noticed that the others had gone quiet.

"Jean-Paul!" Kurt ignored the question. "Bring ze whisky. Ze bottle, ja?"

Jean-Paul nodded in the background.

"Because of this, Mike," Oscar thrust the sheet of fax paper at him. "Read it."

The lines on Mike's brow crimped together as he read. Unmistakably it was Melvin's writing. He'd recognize that childlike print anywhere.

MIKE/OSCAR
THE CIO IS ON TO YOU
SOMETHING TO DO WITH RENAMO
GET OUT OF MOZ. BUT DON'T COME BACK TO ZIM
GOOD LUCK. M.

He read it, and then re-read it. Over and over. Disbelief showed on his face. The table was dead quiet, save the tinkle of the whisky bottle filling the glasses.

Phoebe felt the tension. In alarm. Uncrossing her legs, she shuffled her chair closer to Mike's.

"What is it, Mike?" Her hand gripped his thigh.

He handed her the fax, numb with confusion. She studied it closely, her eyes straining with the English. Mike slugged back his whisky and felt the burning in his throat. Without asking, Kurt refilled it at once.

Phoebe understood. She understood enough to know that this was something of serious import. The words 'RENAMO', 'CIO', 'GET OUT OF MOZ', 'ZIM' screamed at her from the page. She passed the fax back to Mike. She knew then. The day of reckoning was coming. Soon. She knew then that certain things would happen. She knew too that she was powerless over it, over everything. It was fate.

For several minutes, no one spoke.

"It's Melvin," Mike's laugh was hollow. "You know Melvin, Oscar? Always the drama queen. Always melodramatic …."

Oscar was silent.

"C'mon Oscar. Tell me this is some kind of sick joke. Melvin being an idiot again. One of his practical jokes?"

Oscar shook his head slowly. "I dunno, Mike, but I reckon it's serious. Melvin wouldn't bullshit about this sort of thing."

"But … but where .. did it come from?" Mike tried not to sound incredulous. "I … mean .. the CIO?"

Oscar shrugged. "Dunno, Mike. But we've talked it over—me an' Kurt and Colin. Reckon it's better to be safe than sorry."

"What d'you mean? Get out of Mozambique?"

Oscar nodded. "Ja. At least until the heat's off."

What heat? Mike asked himself. And then it started to make sense. In a fuzzy kind of way. "Kurt. Tell me," he said suddenly, "did you come to the caravan this morning? In your four by four?"

Kurt looked confused. "Huh? No … why you ask?"

"Dunno. Just do me a favour, will you?"

"Ja. Okay …?"

"Go and ask Jean-Paul if you can use his phone. I want you to phone the Hotel Beira and ask to speak to *Senhor* Salim."

"Ja. And zen what?"

"I dunno. I just want to see if he's there. Just a feeling. Make up something. Anything. Ask if he's got any rooms available … anything."

Kurt nodded and left the table.

Mike felt Phoebe's fingers digging into his thigh. He put his arm around her and hugged her, comfortingly. She smiled at him nervously. It would be all right, wouldn't it? Her eyes seemed to be asking.

"I can understand the Renamo bit," Oscar continued. "We could have been followed to that meeting we had with Dhlakama. Frelimo might construe that as some fairly heavy shit. Know what I mean?"

"But the CIO aspect?" Colin asked.

Phoebe cleared her throat. "It is not my place to say?"

"Speak, Phoebe," Mike urged gently.

"Salim is a Frelimo *funcionario.*"

"An official?" Oscar confirmed.

"Yes. He is a Frelimo member for many years. He has many friends in Zimbabwe. Big friends. The Zimbabwe *governo.*"

Kurt returned directly, frowning. "Ze fockin' bastard is in Zimbabwe. On business."

Mike felt his flesh crawl. A sickening feeling in the pit of his stomach. It all made sense. Salim—buddies with Zimbabwean ministers, who without doubt had access to the CIO. The trashing of Phoebe's apartment. Salim's insane jealousy of Phoebe. A pimp having his whore stolen from him? Of course, he would be livid. But the foreign tracks in the driveway?

"The *guarda-costa.*" Phoebe stated with equanimity. "He is still here. He is searching for me. For us. At this very minute."

There was another silence. They all sensed the inevitability of what would happen next. There was no other option.

"Okay ...," Mike breathed deeply, "so what now?"

"We split," Oscar said flatly.

"To where?"

"Well, we can't go back to Zim. And we can't stay here."

Colin coughed. "Well, it depends a lot on what Phoebe wants to do."

"Why?" Mike snapped.

"Well, she hasn't got a passport. Has she?"

Mike felt a surge of anger. His cheeks were flushed as he spoke, his voice low. "Now listen ... Phoebe comes with me. I go, she goes. She stays, I stay. Geddit?"

"Hey, Mike!" Oscar interjected, "Cool it. No one's saying otherwise. We're trying to help!." Oscar was very angry and Mike felt foolish.

"Okay, okay. I'm ... I'm sorry. I didn't understand."

"Well, just shut up and listen—for once in your life," Oscar chided.

Mike lowered his head, embarrassed by his outburst. In the corner of his eye, he caught Phoebe looking at him. Her eyes were glowing as she winked at him, subtly, and he felt himself relax.

"Ja, you stubborn bastard. Just fockin' lissen," Kurt added, a twinkle in his eye.

Mike felt humbled. These were his friends. They cared, and for a fleeting second it was as if he'd never felt happier.

Oscar was talking. "We have options, Mike. Colin has offered to fly us out of the country—all of us … you, me … and Phoebe." He emphasized the 'all'. "But it's your decision … and Phoebe's … whether you want to come. I'm going … with or without you."

"Where to? And what about Phoebe's passport?" Mike tried not to sound panicked.

"Quit worrying," Oscar said, exasperated. "It's all worked out. South Africa would be a problem. A—the Dak hasn't got the range, fuel-wise, to get there, and B—their radar would pick us up immediately. Not a problem in itself, but the South Africans would want to know why Colin hadn't filed a flight plan. And if he were to file a flight plan, it'd mean he'd have to land at a registered international strip—with customs and immigration formalities. So South Africa is a non-starter."

"Okay, then what?"

"We'd thought about Malawi, but then Colin would have no reason to go there."

"How'd you mean?"

"Well, he hasn't been picking up relief food from there. So they'd want to know why he's there, see?"

"Ja, so that leaves …?"

"That leaves Zambia. Lusaka," Oscar finished, as if labouring with an obstinate school child.

Colin continued. "I've been flying into Zambia quite a bit. There's a massive stockpile of relief food up there, which was originally destined for the Congo. But the UN and the aid organizations have decided to divert it to Mozambique for the time being. The air traffic controllers at Lusaka know me now. I could get in without a problem."

"And what about immigration formalities?" Mike asked.

"No problem. I've got a bunch of UN visas. We get diplomatic status."

"You mean … all of us? You could sort us out with visas?
"Yeah. No sweat."

Mike sipped at his whisky and offered a glass to Phoebe. She wrinkled her nose at it. He smiled. "Well … what can I say? You okes seem to have it all sussed out. Except …"

"What now?" Oscar asked, irritated.

"Where do we stay in Lusaka?"

"Wherever you want … but I've already phoned Connelly. He's gonna meet us at Lusaka Airport and is expecting three guests tomorrow night. He said it'd probably be better if we stayed out at his farm, just outside Lusaka."

Mike was shaking his head. They'd thought of everything … except … what about Connelly … and Phoebe? Did Connelly know that Phoebe was black? He sipped thoughtfully at his whisky. Leave it. Racial attitudes were the last of their worries at the moment.

"Sorry. One last question. When do we fly?"

"Dawn tomorrow," said Colin. "I've already filed the flight plan with the Zambians. And you're all staying at Kurt's smallholding tonight. It's out of town. Safer. He'll get you to the airport at zero 400 hours tomorrow."

Then Kurt slapped Mike on the back, at the same time putting his arm around Phoebe and squeezing her in a bear-like hug. "So, ze little love birds will be okay, ja? Hey! Jean-Paul! Bring ze *vino* and ze fockin' *camarão*. Now we haff a party, ja?"

They all laughed.

The wine and the prawns arrived as the sun was setting. Elton John was on about his 20th rendition of *Sacrifice*. Mike looked at Phoebe. She seemed happy enough sitting there, sipping at her wine.

"My Phoebe," he whispered to her. "Are you okay with all this? I … I didn't really ask."

She squeezed his hand, smiling bravely. "Darling. It is as you say, 'you go, I go'."

"But Salim? Beira? Maybe you'll never come back?"

"Hey, Mike. You do not understand," her eyes aflame. "Salim is no more a part of my life. And Beira .. well … it is just a place. There are many other places, *não*?"

"Yes, but …"

"Silence, Mike. You forget everything? You do not remember that I am in love with you?"

"I know, but still …"

"*Por favor.* You shut up. You are my man. I am your woman. Is this not enough, huh?" she heard herself say. But was she convincing Mike … or herself?

"Okay, okay," Mike smiled. "I'll shut up."

"*Bom.*" she whispered. "It is better you do this." What she didn't tell him was the terror and confusion churning in her stomach. Yes, she loved him. She had meant it. But to run away with a man, a white man, she'd only known for a few days? Surely, this was a thing of madness. Why would she go? Out of love … or out of fear? Perhaps the hand-over wasn't totally complete. She closed her eyes, Mike's hand on her knee. It was of comfort and that was something. He was a good man.

★　★　★　★　★

Mike hadn't intended to kill the *guarda-costa.* He'd always believed he'd done with killing 20 years ago, during the war. But it had happened, and now surely, there was no turning back.

They'd all left Club Nautica at about eight that evening. It was agreed that Phoebe and Oscar would go back with Kurt to the smallholding. Mike would stop by the portavan to collect a suitcase of clothes for Phoebe and himself.

He knew immediately that something was wrong when he arrived at the yard. The gate was open and there in the mud, in the beam of his headlights, were the unmistakable tracks of the four by four. The same ones he'd seen that morning.

Switching off his lights, he felt his heart race. He was here. He leaned inside the cab of the truck and switched off the engine. Crouching down at the gatepost, he listened, his every sense straining. He squeezed his eyes shut for several moments, and then re-opened them, to accustom himself to the darkness. It was a trick he'd learned as a soldier all those years ago. Gulping hard, he forced his ears to pop—another trick. The roar of the pounding breakers and the chorus of cicadas magnified. But otherwise, there was nothing. No apparent danger.

Crouching, he crept forward towards the portavan. A light was on inside. Had he forgotten to switch it off that morning? He couldn't remember. Sloppy, Mike, sloppy, he chided himself.

He was here. He could sense it. He could smell him. Mike paused. He needed a weapon. Anything—a stick, a plank, a tool, anything. He remembered the stack of *badzas*, the hoes that Kurt's work gang sometimes left overnight, normally stashed under that old grader.

Picking out the looming shape of the grader in the darkness, he gingerly made his way towards it.

That was when it happened. For a big man, the *guarda-costa* moved with frightening speed. With a roar of anger, the man leaped from shadows, and in a flash had Mike pinned down in the mud. Giant hands grabbed at Mike's neck and he felt himself choking, suffocating. Struggling wildly, flailing wildly, but still the giant hands squeezed and crushed at his throat. Mike felt the world spinning. He felt the blackness as he vainly gasped for air. The man's breath was hot in his face and for an instant Mike could smell the stale smell of alcohol.

It was irrational, but it was the smell of alcohol that did it. He was being killed by a drunk? His very life was being extinguished by a soak? He bucked and kicked ineffectually, as still the great hands throttled. And then his hand touched something. Something metallic. He could feel his life leaking away as his lungs seemed set to burst. He knew he had only a few seconds.

Desperately, with one final effort, he clutched at the *badza,* grasping the tool mid-way up the shaft. And in one final lunging swing, one final supreme effort, he brought the hoe up with every ounce of strength he could muster. He felt the sickening crunch as the metallic blade struck bone, embedding itself into the base of the *guarda-costa's* skull.

And then he felt the vice-like grip at his throat fall away. He saw the *guarda-costa's* head loll forward, grotesque and macabre. He felt the big man's body go limp, heavier and heavier, until finally it toppled slowly into the mud at his side, in an obscene squelch. Hideous rattles bubbled in the mud as the life went from the man.

For a very long time, Mike lay like that. On his back, sucking at the night air. He felt he wanted to be sick, the bile rising in his throat. He rolled himself onto his side, heaving, vomiting, the pain tearing at the lesions and bruises on his neck.

And then he dragged himself to his knees. He remembered very little of what happened after that. He dimly recalled wrenching the *badza* out of the dead man's neck. The blow had obviously severed the spinal chord. But it took a lot of wrenching, and in the end he was forced to put his foot on the dead man's head as a fulcrum.

He barely remembered discovering the white Toyota Hilux, parked behind the grader. He barely remembered heaving the corpse into the cab. Something had been driving him, some demonic automated instinct of survival. Was it he who drove the four by four down the *avenida* that night? Was it he who slammed the vehicle into that wall?

His memory was blurred. It was all such a savage nightmare. How had he managed to drag the corpse across from the passenger side and drape it over the steering wheel? Had it been he? Had he done that?

And then he'd found that jerry can of petrol. Where had he found that? Slop, slop, slop, slop, slop. He remembered the overwhelming stench of petrol. He remembered the stinging in his eyes, in his brain. From the fumes. And then his Zippo was in his hand and he was running blindly back down the *avenida*.

He didn't remember looking back. Only the blast. He had to escape from the flames, from the rush of flames, licking hungrily at his heels.

Twenty one

With his unerring efficiency, the CIO major had arrived back from Chimoio within three days of leaving Harare. Mission accomplished. It had been relatively straightforward and hadn't taken too much time to find the UNHCR camp, long since closed and now overgrown.

He stood quietly, at ease, in front of Minister Mubvunduku. It would be interesting to see the minister's reaction to the contents of the thin manila folder he was reading. The file was marked Case # 16,042. Presumably this woman, Phoebe, this girl had been the 16,042nd refugee through the camp. Or was that another UNHCR number?

The file was marked 'Top Secret' and had the standard red band running down the centre. The major smiled to himself. It seemed that all administrative files were marked 'Top Secret', but if ever there was a case for it, Case # 16,042 was certainly it.

He'd driven from the border post at Machipanda straight to the camp. The perimeter fence had long since been stripped and vandalized so there was no way of knowing the extent of the camp. But he'd wandered around, more out of curiosity than anything else. Apart from a few unfilled latrine 'long drops', the camp had been picked clean of everything. Not a brick left standing, not a fencing stake in place. Nothing.

The bush was claiming back its own, uncaring of the human misery and despair that only a few short years ago had been so manifest.

The major could see that the minister was perspiring. The regulation government issue fan, a relic from the days of the Federation, creaked and cranked above, doing no more than gently rustle a few papers on the desk. He would be getting to the important bit ... about now.

And then he'd left the camp and driven into downtown Chimoio to what was once the CBD. He'd found the UN headquarters without too much trouble, but had to take a detour to get there. The *avenida* leading up to the building had been closed off, a boom across the road. This was the governor's block and unwelcome visitors had to go round. He'd thought briefly about flashing his CIO card to the Frelimo soldiers at the roadblock, but then thought better of it. They'd have let him through ... eventually.

He parked the Peugeot outside the six-storey building, modern by Mozambican standards. It had probably been built in the early 70s, a year or two before the Portuguese departure. The style reflected the era. Square, angular and faceless. The blue and white UN flag hung limply over the entrance.

Two UN soldiers, with Canadian flashes on their epaulettes, manned the reception desk in the lobby. He showed his card and filled in the visitors' sheet, while one of the soldiers phoned through to the fourth floor.

"Yessir. Zimbabwean CIO. Following up on a refugee enquiry .... Okay. No problem."

The other soldier handed him his visitor's tag, with the crocodile clip. The major pinned it to his jacket lapel.

"Fourth floor, sir. Reception is expecting you."

The UNHCR officials had been extremely co-operative. No, the UN man who had been running the camp had been transferred to Somalia several months before. No ... as far as they knew, none of the UN staff who'd been at the camp were still around. They were all field operatives. This was purely an administrative office, you understand?

He'd asked about the camp records. Were they still available? Oh, yes. Nothing ever gets destroyed. Would all end up in New York or Geneva one day. The UNHCR assistant had taken him into the archives where he'd been confronted by rows upon rows of metallic filing cabinets.

"It's all in there," she said. A to Z. 1980 to 1996. Men, women, children—boys and girls, births and deaths, repatriations, applications, dates. Everything.

"I'll leave you to it, sir, if you don't mind."

"Thank you. You have been most helpful."

"Oh … by the way. Nothing is allowed to leave here without authority. If there's anything in particular that you need, we might be able to photocopy it for you. Okay?"

Undaunted by the massed drabness of the filing cabinets, he'd sat at the small table by the door … and thought … logically, rationally, slowly. One—he was looking for a girl. Two—her name was Phoebe. Three—in 1980 she would have been five or six. Maybe seven or eight, at a push. It was something to start with.

He went to the first cabinet. Girls 0 to 5—1980. There were hundreds of suspension files, bulging with folders, all arranged by surname in alphabetical order. But it wasn't the surname he was looking for. It was the first name—P for Phoebe.

The UN assistant came back two hours later with a cup of tea. She was most kind. He drank the tea and continued, methodically. There was no hurry. At four twenty-five, she returned again.

She coughed discreetly at the door. "Sir, we'll be closing up in five minutes. Have you found what you're looking for?"

"No … not yet."

"You are welcome to come back tomorrow. If it's that important."

"Yes. Thank you."

★ ★ ★ ★ ★

He'd found a room that night at The Windmill. It was adequate. He'd eaten early, shunning the bar, ignoring the pimps and prostitutes, beckoning invitingly from outside the disco. But sleep had not come easily. He'd lain awake for a long time, the pulsating disco beat throbbing away in the background. What was the minister's interest in this woman? She had become some sort of fixation, an obsession. Why? Why? Why?

All that talk of Renamo. Some sinister plot. That was bullshit. It was something more. Something different. For a moment, he allowed his mind to empty itself. It often worked, and the mind would kick in again, uncluttered by preconceived thought process. The germ of an idea. That's it! He would try that tomorrow. Of course ... of course. It was worth a try, wasn't it?

He'd woken early the following morning and driven down to the UN building, waiting outside the glass doors, until the Canadian soldier opened up promptly at zero nine hundred hours.

The same assistant greeted him cheerfully, "Bright and early this morning, Major?"

He wasted no time and went back to the filing cabinets. Girls 5—10. 1980. Surnames. Under 'M'. It took a while, as the vast majority of Shona surnames began with either an 'M' or a 'Ch'. But it wasn't the 'Ch' he was after. Ma ... Mb... Md... Ms ... Mt ...Mu... Mu, Mu, Mu.

The file was so thin that he nearly missed it. He stopped and flipped back again to the 'MUs'.

MUBVUNDUKU—PHOEBE: CASE # 16,042.

Slowly, tentatively, he lifted the folder from its suspension file. Still squatting on his haunches, the bottom drawer hanging open, he read. There were only two pages. Five short entries, written in a scrawling long hand.

21st February 1980

Classification: Juvenile female
Ex: Zanla Camp, Chimoio
Surname: Unknown
Forename: Phoebe
Age: Approximately 7—8 years
Nationality: Zimbabwean
Parents: Whereabouts unknown. Child says mother is deceased. Apparently killed during Rhodesian massacre in 1977.
Health: Fair
Comments: Nil.

24th September 1981

Entry: Efforts to repatriate same juvenile female have proved unsuccessful. Zimbabwean authorities will not grant repatriation status without proof of parentage.

6th April 1984

Entry: As above.

13th August 1987

Entry: Female juvenile Phoebe volunteers to attend a Govt. of Moz. agricultural training programme at college in Chimoio. Released from UNHCR camp. Signed out by Frelimo official. (See Release Register).

30th May 1995

Entry: Two boxes of records ex Zanla Camp, Chimoio discovered in a Frelimo warehouse in Chimoio. Evidently, for security reasons, these records had been smuggled out of the Zanla camp during a Rhodesian attack. After thorough investigation of said records, it is suspected that said juvenile female's assertion that her mother was killed during 1977 Rhodesian massacre is correct.

Mother's name: Christine Chikwama. Zanla combatant. Deceased 1977.

Father's name: Subject to confirmation. But assumed to be Zanla ex-Political Commissar Mubvunduku. We interviewed several camp survivors. Their statements indicate that Ms Chikwama was Mr Mubvunduku's concubine. Firm indication that said juvenile female Phoebe is the daughter of same union.

Comments: Efforts to trace juvenile female Phoebe fail. Govt. Ag. College no longer extant. UNHCR Camp Committee agrees that until such time as said female juvenile is traced, no attempt is to be made to contact suspected father.

The UNHCR assistant was framed in the doorway. "I've brought you another cup of tea, Major."

He looked up, startled. "Oh. Why … thank you." He took the cup. "Tell me. Would it be possible to get this file photocopied?"

"Why, yes. It shouldn't be a problem. Do you think you've found what you want?"

"Yes, thank you." He handed her a file. A different file. File Case # 16,042 was already stuffed discreetly in the folds of the newspaper in his briefcase. It would be better that the minister had the original. "One more thing ... where might I find the Release Registers? I'm looking for August 1987."

"Oh, right. They are kept in those cabinets over there. They're the big ledgers."

He found it. On the 13th August 1987, 23 people were signed out from the camp. Mainly teenage girls. Under the column 'Name of Signatory' was a Government of Mozambique stamp. The signature in the right hand column was barely legible. But the flamboyant flourish of the forename was enough. 'Salim'.

For what seemed like an eternity the major stood respectfully at Mubvunduku's desk. It was as if the minister had gone into some sort of a trance, unaware of his presence.

The major coughed politely. "Excuse me, sir. But have you finished with me?"

Mubvunduku, his eyes glazed, looked up at the form of the major. Unfocused and dream-like, his voice a whisper. "Yes ... you can go."

The major turned on his heels. "Thank you, sir."

He was about to close the door behind him, when the minister called after him.

"Major," his spoke slowly. "I need to go to Mozambique. On your way out, ask my secretary to get me onto the soonest flight to Beira."

"Of course, sir."

"And, Major ... I don't need to remind you how sensitive this is. You understand, don't you? This information is not to leave this office. Is that clear?" There was no menace in his voice. It was not necessary.

"Of course, sir."

★ ★ ★ ★ ★

It was dark when Minister Mubvunduku finally stirred. He'd been sitting in the same position, his hands clasped in front of him on the desk, the manila folder lying opened to the side. Those words, those hand-written words in the scrawling longhand, screaming out at him from the yellowing pages, haunting him.

Christine Chikwama, his mistress. Killed by the Rhodesians in that raid. He'd always suspected as much, but had never been able to prove anything. At the time of the attack, he'd been away in Tanzania, on some political education course. The High Command had refused to let him visit the camp. In any case, it would have been futile, as a raging bushfire had swept through the camp after the battle, consuming the corpses, charring them beyond recognition. He'd always assumed the child had been killed as well…

But no. According to this document, she was alive. Alive and well, somewhere in Mozambique.

He slammed the desk with his fist. Why on earth had the UNHCR people not contacted him? When they suspected he was the father? The rules, that would be their reason. Always the rules. He could have done something about it. He could have put his own people onto the case.

And now, now it had come to this. His own daughter, a prostitute. And he had used his fist … on this prostitute. He had fist-fucked his own daughter! Fist-fucked her because he'd lost his erection. It didn't bear thinking about.

He stood up and bellowed, an agonized moan of futility, of what might have been. He had hardly known the child, in fact he'd hardly known the mother. Fraternization with the ranks had been strictly prohibited. He vaguely recalled the woman, Christine Chikwama. Like him, she was a Manhika, having come from the Old Umtali Mission area, near the border. And like many Manhikas, she been one of the first to volunteer for the struggle. Apart from similar tribal affiliations, that was why he'd been attracted to her—her dedication, her determination, her grit. It had come through in the daughter.

The daughter. What to do now? He poured himself a stiff whisky as he pondered. It went without saying that this whole mess should never see the light of day. There was just too much at stake. His position, his career. The consequences were just too horrific to bear contemplation. Expulsion from the party, from the government, but more so, the social stigma, the scandal of it all. So sordid. A sordid, incestuous rape. That's what it was, nothing less.

He slurped at the whisky.

"Stop prevaricating, comrade," he whispered to himself. "You know where this is heading. You know what has to be done. You have no choice ... there is simply too much at stake. Everything, everything you have ever worked for will be destroyed. Nothing is worth the risk. Nothing!"

He finished his whisky and opened a drawer. The 9mm Parabellum gleamed dully in the gloomy confines. He took it out and put it in his briefcase.

Twenty two

The flight from Beira to Lusaka was a frightening experience, as the ageing DC3 Dakota struggled valiantly into the might of the cyclone, still heavily blanketed over the Zambezi valley. They'd taken off at dawn as planned, direction north-west. Colin warned that it was going to be a rough ride and that they'd better find somewhere secure to sit. Unfortunately all the seats had been removed, to make room for the relief cargo.

Mike, still heavily sedated from the tranquillizers that Kurt and Oscar had pumped into him the previous night, lay semi-comatose amongst the sacks of mealie meal and powdered milk. His head was resting in Phoebe's lap, and to him, at that moment, he felt cocooned in a dream-like state of euphoria. She was playing with his hair, looking fixedly ahead into the cockpit where she could see Colin, that gentle Englishman, wrestling with the controls.

Like a cork at sea, the aeroplane bumped and buffeted against the weather. She thought she was going to be sick, but swallowed hard and closed her eyes, willing it away. She had to be strong—for Mike, this man, lying cradled in her lap, like a baby. Her man. Her life.

On the other side of the aisle, or rather the passageway that separated the bags of dried food, Oscar had his guitar out. His hair, still unwashed and uncombed, flayed outwards in all directions like a deranged Rasta. Phoebe smiled to herself. Mike's friends were surely different. But he'd chosen well.

Oscar caught her looking at him and winked at her, "Enjoying the ride?" He was softly strumming an E-minor/A major chord combination. It was a Santana song, *Evil Ways*. He didn't know the words, but the chords mesmerized, repetitive and soothing.

She shook her head, patting her throat. "I think maybe I be sick."

Oscar laughed, "Hey, no problem. Just puke outa the door. But be careful. The slipstream whips it around and it comes right back at you. In your face.Yech!"

She didn't understand what he was saying, but smiled anyway.

"How's Sleeping Beauty?" Oscar indicated the figure of Mike, lying curled up against the woman.

She shrugged, "So so."

It had been very bad the last night, she thought. They had waited and waited and waited, but still Mike did not come. She knew intuitively that something terrible had happened. Kurt said to hang on 'til midnight and then he'd go and try to find him. It was as the Dane was getting into his truck that they saw the vehicle headlights come into the driveway, weaving drunkenly, sliding and careering through the mud.

Mike had slumped out of the cab, as the men grabbed at him. What was it? What had happened? She stood frozen, her hands at her face, in alarm. He was mumbling, almost delirious with insanity, laughing through the tears and the sobs.

"He is dead. I killed him. I killed the son of a bitch ..."

Kurt and Oscar carried him into the house.

"Maybe he went and got himself blind drunk," she heard Oscar say. But it was not true. It could not be true.

Then in the light, as they lay him down on the couch they saw the blood on his shirt. They smelt the smell of gasoline, the sweet smell of burnt flesh, the smell of mud and sweat ... and death.

Kurt had got out the medic case, as Phoebe sat at his side. And ten mills of valium, intravenously, had done the trick.

"What's he on about?" she heard Oscar ask, as Mike floated away in sleep.

"He killed the *guarda-costa*," she said, flatly. "What else?"

Kurt nodded slowly. "Yes. You are right."

Mike slept like that for four hours and then they'd had to leave for the airport. Getting through the security at the gates was no problem. Colin had seen to that, with a handful of US dollars. The sleepy airport guard barely even glanced at the truck as he opened the gates.

Colin turned around to them from the cockpit. "Hang on tight," he shouted over the roar of the engines. "We're heading up over the escarpment. There's going to be a shit-load of turbulence."

Oscar smiled again at the woman, unperturbed. "That means we're in Zambia. We'll be there soon."

The engines were screaming as the plane struggled to climb. She could see Colin hunched over the yoke, his body taut, his every sense, his every muscle straining at the controls. The plane was rattling, threatening to fall apart, to disintegrate into a million pieces.

Yet she felt a great peace of mind. Of course she was afraid. Of course, she could smell her own terror. But if they were to die … well it was fate.

And then they were through it, up on to the highveld of the Zambian plateau. Through the storm, above the storm, away from the storm. The engines subsided to a drone and Oscar started strumming his guitar again. The sun was shining and they were safe. She kissed Mike on the forehead and gave thanks.

"Where … where are we?" His eyes were open and he tried to sit up, but she pushed him back down.

"Hush. Be calm."

Oscar was rolling himself a joint. His celebration of life. The sweet smell permeated the aircraft and Phoebe could see Colin shaking his head up in the cockpit. From the back she could sense he was smiling.

Mike tried to raise his head again. "Hey, Oscar. When are you ever gonna quit smoking that shit?"

Oscar smiled. "Who rattled your cage? A syringe-full of valium is okay for some. Why don't you go back to sleep?"

Phoebe laughed out loud with relief. Her body seemed to melt, the tension seeping away as they came in to land at Lusaka International. Mike was okay.

The undercarriage dropped with a thud. She gripped at his arm as the wheels screeched and bit the tar. Oscar, unfazed, was packing his guitar away in its case.

"Mike," she whispered, "It was the *guarda-costa,* wasn't it? You have killed him, *não?*"

Closing his eyes, snatches of recollection clawing back into his memory, he nodded.

"Yes, Phoebe. I killed him. He had been waiting for us … I did not mean for it to happen … but … but …"

She could feel his body convulse. The plane had come to a stop. "Hush, my darling. Hush. It is done."

★　★　★　★　★

Connelly was waiting for them, leaning against his long-wheel base Land Rover outside the Lusaka freight terminal. His hands in his pockets, he watched as the four people, three white, one black, came down the steps of the Dakota. Three men, one woman. He recognized Oscar, guitar case slung. And then he recognized Mike. It was the black woman who seemed to be helping him down. What was the matter with him? Oscar hadn't said anything about a black woman. Perhaps she was the flight attendant. But on a Dakota?

The other guy must be the pilot. Connelly waved at the group and saw Oscar wave back.

"You must be the pilot?" He shook hands with Colin. "Name's Connelly."

"Yeah. Tough flight. I'm Colin. Pleased to meet you."

"Bloody rotate! They still flying those crates? Must've come outa World War Two."

"More than likely."

"Great landing. You're turning around and heading straight back?"

"Yeah. Refuel, and then may as well top up with cargo while I'm here. Expected in Nampula this afternoon."

"Howzit, Oscar?" Connelly said. He shook hands with the short man. "You wanna start getting all the shit into the Landy? Don't wanna hang around here for too long."

"Ja, no sweat."

Connelly could see Mike and the black woman hanging back, nervously, as if embarrassed.

"Hey, Oscar," he said, quietly. " What gives? Is Mike pissed or what? And who's the nanny?"

Oscar tossed the guitar into the back of the Land Rover. Taking Connelly aside, he hissed, "No, he's not pissed. Just pretty beaten up. Nearly got himself murdered last night ... in Beira."

"Oh hell."

"Ja ... I'll fill you in at the farm. Long story. Couldn't say too much on the phone."

"And the nanny? The kaffir? Where'd she come from?"

Oscar felt himself tense, his voice low, his teeth gritted. "Listen here, Connelly. We're bloody grateful for what you're doing. You've saved our butts. That girl is Phoebe. She is not a nanny and she is not a kaffir. I can't ask you to change your racial attitudes, but please, for Mike's sake, just cool it."

"What do you mean—'for Mike's sake'?"

"She's Mike's chick," Oscar breathed.

"A *munt*!"

"Just ... just do me one favour. Please. For Mike. You don't have to like her ... but just show her a little bit of respect. That's all."

"Okay, okay, okay. No sweat." Connelly was shaking his head in disbelief. What would his wife think about all this? Joyce had never had a black person staying with them.

Even in his state, Mike knew that Connelly and Oscar were talking about them. So did Phoebe. He could sense her, tense at his side, her body quivering … with nerves, with anger.

"Okay, boys and girls," Connelly shouted with feigned jocularity. "All aboard."

They said their good-byes to Colin. Phoebe had tears in her eyes as she hugged him. So did Mike. He was a good friend. One of a kind.

"Hey! Cheer up," Colin said lightly. "I'll be back. Mark my words. I'll be in touch."

They watched in silence as the tall Englishman strode off towards his aircraft. Just like that, Mike thought. In your life one minute, then out of it the next. Didn't emotion count for anything? He put his arms around Phoebe, ignoring Connelly's quizzical glance. She was crying.

They drove to the farm. Oscar sat in the front, updating Connelly on all that had happened over the past few weeks. Mike and Phoebe sat in the back, saying nothing, sensing Connelly's discomfort, his disapproval. But Mike was too tired to care. And Phoebe had fallen asleep against his shoulder.

The Land Rover bounced aggressively over the dirt road. Connelly didn't slow down for the potholes; just rode on at them at full throttle. Phoebe's head bumped against Mike's shoulder and he held her tightly against him, cushioning her against the violence of the road.

He caught Connelly looking at him in the rear-view mirror. The two men regarded each other, saying nothing, showing nothing.

It was Joyce who took Phoebe into her bosom when the Land Rover pulled up in front of the Cape Dutch homestead. Ignoring her husband's mutters, she put her arm around the black girl's waist and led her inside.

"Connelly, I suppose you've been driving like a maniac again? What have you done to this poor thing?" Joyce shouted over her shoulder. "Come, dear," she said to Phoebe, clucking like a mother hen, "we're going to get you into a nice hot bath. A hot cup of tea and then into bed with you. No arguments."

"Women!" Connelly mumbled under his breath. "All the bloody same. Sometimes, I reckon I should've married a whore. At least you know where you stand. Fuck 'em and pay 'em. Only snag is, they can't cook."

Oscar looked at Mike, his eyes imploring him to hold his tongue.

Mike smiled back at him, his eyes saying, "It's no big deal. Connelly is Connelly. He'll never change. But he means well."

Connelly was still muttering to himself, unloading the luggage from the Land Rover.

"Where's that bloody houseboy? LANGTON! ... Damn *munts* are never there when you want them ... LANGTON!"

From nowhere, Langton came running.

"Sorry, baas. I was feeding the dogs."

"I'll feed you to the dogs, zot," Connelly said, clipping the servant around the head with a not unfriendly slap.

Langton was evidently used to this. "Baas. You always say the dogs not eat kaffirs. Don't like smell."

"Humph!" Connelly snorted. "Don't get stroppy with me, zot." This time Langton ducked in time, narrowly avoiding the white man's open palm that had been zeroed in on his left ear. "Langton, get this stuff inside. *Checha!* Hurry up. And then bring the drinks onto the verandah. These *mulungus* need a drink."

That evening Mike and Oscar got drunk. So did Connelly. As in the old days. It was good. They talked about the old days. They talked about the Rhinofest. Man, what an event that had been. What a rave! They didn't talk about Phoebe too much. Every time Mike tried to broach the subject, Connelly would quickly move on to something else. But Mike was not concerned. He'd come round to it in his own time ... or more likely ... in Joyce's time.

Joyce came out on to the verandah at about eight to announce that dinner was ready. She also announced that Phoebe was fast asleep and was not to be disturbed under any circumstance. She glanced pointedly at Mike.

"Mike, you're sleeping in the other spare bedroom, with Oscar. That girl needs to sleep for 48 hours." There was no argument.

After the initial relief of their escape from Mozambique, the reality of the situation slowly came to them all ... in different ways.

Connelly would still not talk to Phoebe, but began to acknowledge her presence after a few days with the occasional grunt.

Oscar reacted by getting stuck into the farm work. The tobacco was knee-high now. It needed weeding, spraying, suckering. It needed supervision, and Connelly was more than delighted that his friend was lending a hand.

But for Mike and Phoebe, it was different. They'd both soon learned to ignore Connelly's grumpiness. But it wasn't that. It was more. It was the vacuum of living in no-man's land. Yet, it wasn't living. It was an existence, an empty existence, marking time.

Not even Joyce's bubbly enthusiasm could alter the fact that they were in a state of transience. She'd taken to Phoebe from the outset and would spend hours with her in the kitchen, drinking tea and coffee, talking and laughing. She'd take her round the farm, to the sheep, to the vegetables. She'd take her down to the farm clinic where Phoebe would help out with the inoculations. But it came back to the same thing.

A crossing over. But to where? To what? What next? Where to now?

It was troubling them both. Joyce could sense it and one evening she came to them as they sat silently on the verandah. Connelly and Oscar were out in the lands.

She plumped herself down in the wicker chair, as Langton came with the drinks trolley.

"I want to talk to you two," she said firmly. Like a matron.

Mike and Phoebe sat up.

"I want to know what's the matter. There's a problem and it's got to be sorted out. You two have been moping around like sulky brats for days. Especially you, Mike."

Mike was taken aback. It was true. Something had come between him and Phoebe. He couldn't put his finger on it. But it was there. They'd hardly said a word to each for several days now.

"It's nothing, Joyce ... well, I guess ... it's the uncertainty of everything .. y'know ...," he finished lamely. He felt Phoebe's eyes on him.

"That's nonsense, Mike. And you know it," Joyce stated.

"It's .. ag! It's just that ... it's all such a mess."

"What is, Mike?" Joyce wasn't letting up. "Tell me, Mike. What is it that's such a mess that can't be sorted out?"

"Well ... everything ... my life ... my child ... everything."

Phoebe was still looking at him, her eyes burning into him. But he did not look at her.

"Can I tell you something, Mike?" Joyce said. "And you listen in good, y'hear."

"I'm listening."

"I think you are a self-pitying, self-centred, sulky young man. I don't think for one minute you realize quite how lucky you are. You have your life. You've escaped from a potentially nasty situation in Mozambique. Even now, right at this very minute, you could be languishing in a Mozambican ... or a Zimbabwean gaol. But no. You sit around and mope all day."

"But ... you don't understand."

"Don't interrupt. Let me finish, y'hear?" Joyce heaved a deep breath, as she took a sip of her gin and tonic. "Mike, you've got something so special. Something so beautiful. It's something that only happens once in a lifetime. If you're lucky."

Mike guessed where she was leading, but was embarrassed. "What?"

"Are you blind? Can't you see, man?"

"What, Joyce? What d'you mean?"

"Oh for heaven's sake, man. Do I have to spell it out for you? She's sitting right next to you. Yes … that gorgeous creature you've been ignoring for the last few days. Wallowing in your own self-pity."

Mike glanced at Phoebe, her eyes misted with tears. His heart ached, but he looked down at the floor, ashamed.

"There you go. Look away, damn it!" Joyce said, exasperated. "Can't you see that she's in love with you? She adores you. You're her whole life. She lives for you, Mike. Can't you see that?"

"Yes … I think I can."

"No you can't. You're too busy feeling sorry for yourself."

"But … I can't offer her anything. Nothing. It's all … it's all so futile. What future is there?"

Joyce stood up, her hands on her hips. She was angry. "Absolute rubbish! She's not asking a thing from you. Look at her, Mike. Does she look like the type of woman who wants fancy cars, fancy clothes? Is she asking for you to map out her future? Huh? After all you two have been through together? You think she expects you to miraculously sort it all out? Wake up man!"

"I .. I didn't realize."

"Of course you didn't. Typical damn male." Joyce poured herself another gin and tonic, her hands shaking with emotion. "May I ask you one question, Mike?"

"Yes."

"Do you love her? Do you love Phoebe?"

"Yes. Of course."

"Well, tell her! And show it! 'Cause I'm telling you right now. If you don't, you're going to lose her and she's going to go right back to Mozambique … without you."

Mike felt the panic rising. He'd never looked at it like that.

"And can I tell you something else?" Joyce added. "You'd damn well deserve it if she did." Her anger was subsiding. "Mike, Phoebe is the best thing that has ever happened in your life. I don't need to tell you that, do I?"

"No. I know."

"Well, behave as if it is. She wants you. You … Mike. You. I don't know why, she must be sick in the head or something, but the only thing she wants in the whole world is .. you." She stabbed her forefinger at his chest. "So, do something about it."

Phoebe quietly stood up, her face wet from the tears. She walked down the verandah steps onto the lawn, her hips slowly swaying, hugging the blue jeans— towards the bed of cannas by the security fence.

Mike stood up to follow, awkwardly.

"Leave her," Joyce ordered. "For the moment …"

"But … I should go to her?" He was puzzled.

"In a moment. I haven't finished. Are you going to marry her?"

"What?" Mike's voice cracked.

"You heard me. Are you going to marry her?"

"I … I hadn't thought of it. I .. don't know … I can't … I'm still married."

"Well, get a divorce."

"I was planning to. Just .. hadn't got round to it."

"Is it because she's a prostitute? Sorry … was a prostitute?"

Mike felt himself shaking. "You know?"

"Of course, I know. What d'you think we've been talking about in the kitchen for these last few days? Recipes? She needed someone to talk to … and you weren't there for her."

"It doesn't worry you?"

"Mike," she said patiently. "I'm not like my husband. I'm not here to judge. All I see is this beautiful, fragile creature who's had shit thrown at her all her life. And then she meets someone she thinks she's in love with. Someone who will take her away from all that ugliness. But what happens? Nothing. Typical male."

"I never knew … I never realized."

"Have you got any idea what sort of upheaval you're putting her through? Have you? Do you realize, that effectively she's been forced to take her chances with you? The fact that she loves you helps a wee bit. But with the way you're behaving, well, she's just swapping one form of slavery for another."

"What d'you mean?" Mike asked, perplexed.

"Think about it, Mike. She's going from prostitution … to you. And it's not a hell of a lot different."

"Now, come on Joyce. That's ridiculous."

"Really? You haven't thought that she might be prostituting herself to you? The fact that she isn't charging, doesn't change anything."

Mike listened in silence.

"She's always been controlled by domineering, sadistic men. You're not sadistic, but you've been treating her like some kind of plaything. Your own sexual toy! I'd call that domineering, wouldn't you?"

"That's not true," Mike argued. He was getting irritated. "She loves me!"

"Yes, she loves you and that's a start. But now, how about a bit of respect? Like treating her as an equal, a partner … in the true sense of the word."

"Ag, Joyce. That's ridiculous. You're just being … dramatic," he finished lamely. He couldn't think of anything stronger.

"I don't think so, Mike," Joyce shrugged.

Mike was shaking his head slowly, " I never thought of it like that …"

"So you keep saying. Now go to her. Now!"

The sun was setting, blood red, across the tobacco lands. She was sitting, cross-legged by the cannas, her head bowed. One of the rottweilers was lying down on the grass next to her, its head resting on its paws.

He went to her and sat down next to the dog, distractedly stroking its ears. She did not look at him, but directly ahead, through the cannas, into nothing. They sat in silence for some time.

"Phoebe. I want to say I'm sorry," he felt his voice catching. He didn't know how to continue, but forced himself. It was very important. He knew he would lose her if he didn't. "I have been very selfish, wrapped up in my own little world. I've had so many problems lately, that I kind of got bogged down in myself."

She said nothing, her face still wet from crying.

"I ... I don't want you to feel you have any kind of obligation to me."

"I don't," she whispered. "But I love you. Yet sometimes love is not enough." She was still staring fixedly ahead.

"I know. But it's a start. I would like to build on that."

"Yes. I too."

"I would like to spend my life with you, Phoebe."

She turned to him, "Do you mean that, Mike? Do you really mean that?"

Mike coughed, nervously, "Yes, Phoebe, with all my heart."

"I too want to live with you forever. But perhaps our future is not in our hands. There are so many other things that want to stop this."

He studied her as she was speaking. The pain, the suffering, the abject loneliness of her life was never far from the surface and now it was coming out, slowly, pitifully. She was crying as she spoke. He felt foolish, inadequate. His troubles seemed so meaningless now.

She continued, without malice, without accusation. "Mike, it's as if everything is against us. The colour of our skin. Salim. Your wife and child. Our histories. Our cultures. From the days of my childhood, we were enemies. You were with the soldiers who came and killed my people in the camps ..."

Mike started. It had been something that had been nagging away in the back of his mind. Something he had been too afraid to confront. But now she'd brought it up.

"Which camp were you in Phoebe?" he asked softly. "When your mother died?"

She focused on him, the cast in her eye magnified under the tears. "It was Chimoio. That was where my mother was killed. Your soldiers came through the bush. She was holding me in her arms, when a soldier lifted his gun and shot her."

The sun had but set, the last defiant rays clinging vainly in the darkening sky. He took her hand and held it against his cheek. It felt small and helpless. He drew her to his chest and she came to him, seeking out his warmth, his strength.

Mike felt the dryness in the back of his throat. A harsh dryness, like a dagger. He knew what he had to say next. It could not be delayed.

"Phoebe," he whispered. "I was at Chimoio. I remember telling a soldier to leave a little girl. He had just shot a woman …." He was fighting back the tears.

She turned to him, shaking violently, and he clung to her, squeezing her, protecting her, protecting himself. He could see that she was biting her lip, looking at him imploringly, her face smothered in tears.

"I know, Mike," she sobbed. "It was your voice."

He felt weak and very tired. He could do no more than cling to her in silence.

★　★　★　★　★

Mike awoke with a pounding headache. It was cold. Where was he? There was a cramp in his arm. Instinctively he looked at his watch. It was after midnight. He felt something furry against his head and put out his hand. The dog stirred. Phoebe was curled up on the lawn, her head in his lap. He could see the wetness of the dew on her jeans. Putting a hand to her check, he felt the coldness of her skin.

"Man, now she'll go'n catch cold," he muttered, gently shaking her shoulder. "Phoebe, we must go inside. It is late."

She lifted her head and opened her eyes. "We have been sleeping here? For all this time?"

"Yes, it is after midnight, my princess." He helped her to her feet and put his arm around her. The dog was shaking itself, yawning noisily.

She huddled into the shelter of his body, her head pressed against his chest. "Mike? You will not leave me?" It wasn't so much of a plea, as a statement.

Mike smiled inwardly. "My princess, I was going to ask you the same question."

The house was still open. A light came on in the passage, as a head popped out from a doorway at the other end.

"I've run a bath for you both and there's a thermos of hot chocolate in Phoebe's bedroom ... with two cups," Joyce smiled at the couple. "Now get out of those wet clothes and into that bath before you catch cold. Sleep well. There's no rush in the morning." The door closed.

"Well, you heard the lady," Mike shrugged. "Into the bath with you."

"And you," Phoebe retorted.

Twenty three

Ordinarily there was very little that ruffled Martha. But today, this morning, she was cowering behind the front desk. Never had she seen Salem in such a blind fury, pacing the lobby like an agitated leopard one moment. And then bellowing in rage like a wounded buffalo the next. Two guests checking in, nervously backed away, edging themselves out again onto the street, past the concierge.

Only a few minutes before, he'd arrived back from Zimbabwe, triumphant, buoyant, laden with shopping bags. And only a few short sentences later he had flipped.

The *guarda-costa* was dead. Yes, most tragic, but evidently he'd killed himself. Driven into a brick wall ... head on. Yes ... he had been drinking. He'd started in the morning ... not long after *Senhor* Salim had left for Harare. And no ... she hadn't seen him that entire day. It was not her place to enquire. Naturally, she'd presumed he was on hotel business for the *senhor*. What else?

And yes. The *policia* had come later the next day ... to the hotel. It had taken them some time to identify the vehicle. Totally burnt out. Seemed that it had exploded on impact. And the body ... well yes, that was another thing. If you could call it a body, that is. Tragic, but true. Burnt beyond recognition. To a cinder. The heat must have been very intense.

Witnesses? Who knew? It had happened around midnight, in one of those alleys that lead off the esplanade. The *policia* had not mentioned anything about witnesses. They had merely come to the hotel with the charred numberplate from the vehicle ... seeking someone to identify it.

Well, no. She had not remembered the registration number for the Toyota Hilux. But she'd opened up the safe and found the registration papers. They had matched. Had that not been a wise thing to do?

"And what about the woman?" Salim spat, leaning aggressively over the reception desk.

Martha retreated, backed up against the banks of wooden pigeonholes. "Woman, *senhor?*"

"Yes. You know who I mean. That *puta,* Phoebe."

"*Senhor,* I am aware of this woman. But what of it?"

"Have you seen her? Did not that gorilla, the *guarda-costa,* escort her to the hotel?" He was shouting, ranting. Wisely, the concierge had locked the front doors of the hotel.

"*Não, não, senhor.* I have not seen her since that day she was in your office."

"And those two white men ... those Zimbabweans? You know the one, that Mike, who has stayed here before? And his friend, that short one who always carries the guitar? They have not been here?"

"*Não, senhor.* It has been very quiet of late ... you know .. with the cyclone."

Salim slumped across the counter, burying his face in his hands—with infinite frustration, infinite weariness. It was all going wrong.

"Oh, *senhor,*" she warily touched his shoulder. "I almost forgot. *Senhor* Minister Mubvunduku is arriving this morning. He demanded that he be collected from the *aeroporto* and brought directly to the hotel."

Salim closed his eyes, without acknowledging the girl.

"*Senhor?*"

"Tell him … tell him if he phones that I am otherwise engaged. Tell him to take a taxi. Or tell him to get one of his Zimbabwean puppets from the trade mission to pick him up."

Martha gasped. "But, *senhor*? We cannot do this … it is very dangerous."

"Just do it, woman. Do not disobey me." He looked up at her, from under his eyebrows. "Just do it."

"Very well, *senhor*. It is as you wish."

"I shall be in my office. I do not wish to be disturbed."

Yes, it was all going wrong. Very wrong.

★ ★ ★ ★ ★

Down at the docks the prawn boats had come in. Only a few, braver than the rest, had ventured out the previous night. The fishing would be good, but the risks would be high. The beast could return at any moment.

The small-boat harbour was a hubbub of activity, with the boats unloading their catches beneath a churning white ceiling of a thousand gulls. Preparing for the next evening's trip, deckhands and fishermen whistled and shouted and swore and sang, competing with the screeches of the birds, the honking of the klaxons.

The boy was sitting propped up against a capstan on the foredeck of the small wooden prawner, ignorant of the activity around him. The boat, like most, was nameless. What was a name? Of course, each vessel was obliged by law to have a registration number. But that was different.

The boat heaved and creaked at its mooring, cushioned against its neighbour with old car tyres bound to the gunwales. The boy was gnawing on a cold mealie cob, cooked black over an open fire the last evening before the boat had gone out into the channel. He struggled to maintain his grip on the cob, but it dropped from his grasp onto the deck and rolled into the water with a plop. Peering over the railings, crusted with salt and rust, the boy regarded the cob without emotion. It would not be worth retrieving, not in that scum, coated with a heavy film of oil and diesel fuel.

"Hey! João!"

The boy looked up. Who was calling?

"Hey, João! *Com esta?*"

He squinted up the quayside, through the throng of people and saw his friend.

"*Hé, pa*! I see you," he shouted back. "I come now. *Uma momento.*"

He hitched himself up off the deck, the stumps of his arms grappling clumsily against the capstan. He winced as the recent wound chaffed against the steel hawser. It had still not healed entirely, but at least the pus was gone. The skipper of the boat had been good like that. Although he'd treated it regularly with meths, for that was all he had, he'd told the boy that there was no substitute for plain honest sea water.

Steadying himself on the railings with the crook of his arm, he timed his jump with the motion of the boat. Landing awkwardly on the stonework of the quay, he felt his friend's arms around him.

The seawater had become a ritual. Hour upon hour, day after day, the boy would sit with the festering stump immersed in a bucket. He still did not fully understand why the skipper had taken him on board. He did not know him. There was no clear reason.

João remembered that dawn, that appalling dawn of terror, when he'd run and run and run. In the drizzle, that ceaseless curtain of rain, he'd run blindly, and perhaps his instinct had led him to the harbour. The seaman, huddled in his cabin, had seen the small bundle of humanity collapsed on the quayside. The wounded stump was tucked into the boy's armpit, and at first the seaman did not see the terrible wound. But what could he do? He could not leave the boy like that, urchin, trash that he was. For surely he would die of exposure. So he stumbled out, and gathering the boy in his arms, took him on board.

João's friend was speaking, breathlessly, excitedly, as he dragged the boy to his feet.

"Come, João. Come and see what we have discovered."

Curious, João followed the other boy, darting and ducking through the bustle. He followed at a brisk trot until they came to the disused rail siding by the old docks. Not the smart new docks that the Scandinavians had built. No, not those docks with their gleaming cranes and shiny container-handling facilities. The old docks, where rolling stock, derelict and rusted through, lay rotting and dying.

This was their turf. The street kids' territory. This was where they came at night to sleep in the shelter of the freight wagons. No one came here. Not even the *policia*.

The other boy was panting as he hoisted himself up through the open door of a wagon.

"Come, João. Up here." He grabbed at João's arms and hauled him up. "There ... see there in the corner?"

"What?" João squinted into the darkness of the wagon. "I see nothing."

"The sack. The bag in the corner." The boy was still puffing from the exertions, but João could sense the urgency in his voice.

"A sack? What of it?" João stepped forward, to inspect the sack.

"*Cuidado!*" the boy said in alarm. "Be careful. There is much danger!"

João stopped where he was. "You have found this thing?"

"Yes, João. It was what you were seeking, *não?*"

★　★　★　★　★

Salim's equilibrium had returned after a few stiff shots of brandy. Yes, he would go to the airport and pick up that Mubvunduku. It had been foolish to think otherwise.

So he had gone, and in retrospect it wasn't such a bad thing. The Zimbabwean had been pleasantly polite. None of the bluster, none of the arrogance. Something had changed. Had he found another woman? A better one?

The big man had talked lightly of Phoebe. Perhaps it hadn't been so important after all. In reality, she was just another woman, huh? Just another *mahori*? A whore. Naturally, Salim would have plenty more lined up. Not so?

Salim had laughed easily. Of course, it was no problem. He could take one now. At the Hotel Beira, should he so wish.

But Minister Mubvunduku did not want a woman just then. Tonight ... yes, he would take a woman. But not now.

"As a matter of interest, my friend," Mubvunduku asked casually, "have you established where this Phoebe has got to? Is she still with the bandits, those Renamo people? And have you any idea where those Rhodesians are?"

Salim was able to answer truthfully that he had no idea where any of the fugitives were. They had simply vanished off the face of the earth, though he was able to tell the man sitting next to him in the car that his *guarda-costa* had died in an accident. Yes, his right-hand man. It was a tragedy.

After all, what purpose was there in lying? What was there to be gained by fabrication?

He did not notice the dark shadow come over the Zimbabwean's face.

"Where would these people go? If they were here in Beira?"

Salim shrugged. "The One-Two-Three Rock, Club Nautica ... sometimes even to the Hotel Beira ...anywhere. Why do you ask?"

"I am curious, that is all."

"We can go to these places, if you wish."

"Hmmm. Maybe we could. Just to take a beer."

Salim knew then that the minister's demeanour was a pretence. It was not simply 'just to take a beer'. The big man did not trust Salim. He had to see for himself. Well ... so be it. It could do no harm. Let him see. Let him.

But he felt it was necessary to reinforce the point. "We have searched the city for them, Comrade Minister. The *policia* still search. Even now."

"I have no doubt on this," the Zimbabwean said distractedly. "But it is a way of passing the time. Is it not? I have the time ... I am only seeing the UNHCR Provincial Director tomorrow." He cast a surreptitious glance at the Mozambican.

"*Não problema,*" Salim replied hurriedly. He had gone cold inside. Did it show? "We can start at the One-Two-Three Rock, and then if you like we can go to Club Nautica."

"Okay, whatever. Maybe we will find some friends of this Phoebe at these places. Just to chat, you understand?"

"Of course. She has many friends in these places ... *putas.*"

Norman Mubvunduku smiled. The beads of sweat, nervous sweat, were forming on Salim's brow. What is your move now, Salim? What now?

He settled back in the seat as Salim accelerated down the esplanade towards the nightclub. He was driving too fast, his knuckles white on the steering wheel. Yes, it was going to be an interesting evening.

The car pulled up in front of the nightclub and the two men got out.

"You can leave your briefcase in the car, Comrade Minister," said Salim. "It will be safe. *Não problema.*"

The big man smiled. "No. It is better I keep it with me."

★ ★ ★ ★ ★

João sat patiently across the road from the One-Two-Three Rock. He had seen the man go in. The hotel manager, the cruel one who had done these things to him. He didn't recognize the big man with him. But that was not important. Salim was the one.

João had considered these things for a long time. He'd had the time, plenty of time, down there by the docks on that boat. Days on end, in fact, with the wounded stump soaking in the bucket of seawater. It wasn't so much a question of revenge, but more a question of practicalities. The man, this Salim had forbidden him, on pain of death, to collaborate with the white man, his *patrão*. Did not this Salim understand that this was his livelihood? He was the *guarda*, after all. What would he do if he could not be a *guarda*? Go back to begging, like the *deslocados*? Like the dogs on the streets? *Não, não, não*, Salim. You do not understand—I have no choice in this thing. Would you, Salim, accept such a thing? I do not think so, *senhor*. *Não*, you would not.

So with childlike simplicity, the boy had taken the decision. Salim, or João.

It was high tide. A light breeze rustled through the casuarinas as the boy shivered, wet from the spray of the waves. He huddled against a tree, trying to shield himself from the sea at his back. The stumps of his wrists were tucked into his armpits. It had become a habit, a comforting habit that masked his deformity from the world and from himself.

It was dark. The two men had been in the club for over three hours now. Would they stay there all evening?

The band had started up and the boy recognized the familiar strains of *The Girl from Ipanema*. He was very tired. He had run a long way that afternoon … all the way from the docks. Firstly to the Hotel Beira. But Salim's car had not been there. Where would he have gone? Where? He could not ask the concierge; he was the enemy. He would try the esplanade.

At the first roundabout, he'd seen the car, driving very fast. Good. He had found him.

He felt himself nodding off when he heard the loud booming laugh of the other man. They were coming out of the club, silhouetted against the lights. There was no mistaking. João stood up, anxiously. He felt the weight in his pocket, dragging his pants down. Was now the time?

But the men got into the car and reversed out onto the *avenida*. Then they were gone, up the esplanade.

The boy cursed. Where now? It could only be Club Nautica. There was nowhere else open tonight. He hitched up his pants and started jogging. It would be better to run on the beach. The beach would be empty of people. No one walked on the beach at night.

The grenade in his pocket flopped rhythmically against his leg as he ran. It was awkward and heavy, worsened by the exertions of running in the sand. His friends had done well to find the grenades so quickly. Yes, abandoned weapons were everywhere, relics from the war, hurriedly discarded during the general amnesty by the Renamo cadres and the ubiquitous *bandidos* that roamed the towns and villages in those times. It had merely been a matter of time before one of them stumbled on something.

How far was Club Nautica? Maybe 2,000, maybe 3,000 paces up the beach.

He came to the club, breathless, and collapsed in the sand, gasping for air. Pray, the two men were there. Pray, they were still there.

He found the shadows and crept around onto the *avenida*. The car was there, parked near the end of the pavement. How well he knew that pavement. How many hours had he spent there, sleeping in the back of his *patrão's* truck? In the days when he was a *guarda,* when all the other street kids had looked up to him. In the days when he commanded respect.

But now this Salim had taken all that away from him. It was all gone. Salim, the cruel one. Now, Salim, the cruel one, you must pay the price for that cruelty.

The street was deserted. No *guardas,* no street kids, no *putas.* He went to the car and peered inside. The passenger-side door was not locked. Lifting his toes up to the handle, he wriggled his foot under the lever. With one of his stumps pressing upwards, he managed to open the door.

Sliding across the seats to the driver's side, he manoeuvred his upper body onto the floorboards. Again with his stumps, he worked the grenade out of the pocket, praying desperately that it wouldn't fall and roll under the seats. It squeezed out onto the seat next to him and he managed to clasp it in his forearms, ensuring that the length of fishing line was firmly clenched between his teeth. Panting from the exertions, he carefully directed it down onto the floor. Now was the crucial moment. The pin had been straightened beforehand. It would take only the slightest jolt, or tug from the line, for it to fall out. Finally, satisfied with the positioning, he let if fall gently, wedging itself behind the brake pedal.

Perfect!

He squirmed into the back of the car and huddled himself on the floor, ensuring the fishing line lay free and unsnagged between the two front seats.

He cursed softly to himself. He'd forgotten the back door. Lifting himself up on his elbows, he popped the doorknob with his teeth and then pressed down on the handle. The door clicked, half-open. He pressed down again, at the same time pushing with his shoulder.

The door clicked again, open. Pray God the big man would not notice when he got in.

Bom! It was done.

It was now only a matter of time.

How long had he waited? Had he fallen asleep?

He woke with a start. He could hear the two men. They were getting into the car. They were talking loudly, drunkenly, and he could smell the alcohol. Something landed with a thump on the back seat and João almost cried out in alarm. But it was only a briefcase. Shrinking deeper behind the seat, he crimped his teeth firmly on the end of the fishing line in his mouth.

He felt himself shaking. Surely they must see him? Surely they would sense his presence? Would they not feel his shaking?

The hotel manager started the car. The boy heard the other man belch loudly.

Now. Now was the time.

He pulled his head back, taking up the slack in the fishing line. He could hear the vibrations from the line, twanging inside his skull. Tighter, tighter. And then he jerked his head backwards in one violent wrench.

From somewhere, Salim heard a strange grunt as he was about to engage reverse gear.

It was as he was letting let out the clutch, that he felt the small ball-like object rolling under his feet.

Twenty four

The Dakota flew into Lusaka International out of a blue cloudless sky. As the pilot circled the airport at 4,500 feet, awaiting landing clearance, he spotted the little knot of people standing by the Land Rover, parked near the freight terminal. Yes, there they were. Dead on time.

"That's them, over there," Colin pointed out to his 'co-pilot'.

"Ag, ja. I see zem."

"So, you enjoy the flight, Kurt? Nice and smooth today. Not like the last time. Thought we were goners, y'know. Didn't think we'd make it up over the escarpment."

Kurt had come along for the ride. It would be good to see Mike again—that foolish, impetuous bloody Zimbabwean. Ag, but he had balls, ja!

The flight had been easy. No clouds, no air pockets, no cyclone. The beast had evidently scudded off across the Mozambican Channel and was presently wreaking havoc over Madagascar.

"Ja, fockin' brilliant, man. Like a safari. All zose fockin' elephants."

"Yeah. Amazing. That was Mana Pools we flew over."

A voice crackled over the radio. They had clearance to land.

Kurt buckled his seat strap, turning to the pilot. "Hey, English. You fockin' drive properly now, ja? I get fockin' nervous in zese old planes."

Colin smiled as the runway straightened out ahead of him on his final approach.

★ ★ ★ ★ ★

Mike could understand now that certain events were destined to happen. Of these, he had no control. He also understood that with other matters, he had choices. This much was apparent. And such choices were to be made clearly, firmly, with passion, with understanding.

He'd been sitting on the verandah, attempting to write a letter to his wife. Joyce was right. The time had come to stop running, to face himself. To address his past, his baggage. Langton had brought him a tray of tea.

It was hot and humid. The rain had gone, but still the air was heavy with moisture. He was on his own and relished the solitude. Joyce had taken Phoebe off shopping into Lusaka. A new South African clothing store had opened up recently and Joyce said it was about time Phoebe got herself a few more things for her wardrobe. Well, yes, those short dresses and mini skirts were very fetching. But hardly practical. And well, also… they were a bit too … a bit too revealing. Fine for nightlife and all that, but not really fitting for the farm. She'd also happened to notice that her husband had raised an eyebrow one evening at the dinner table—when Phoebe came in to the dining room, wearing that very short black skirt and the skimpy sleeveless blouse, that was practically transparent. Well, yes, it had been very hot.

But what was of concern—and surprise—to Joyce, had been her husband's reaction. The raised eyebrow had not been raised in disapproval. On the contrary, Connelly had barely been able to keep his eyes off the girl.

Mike smiled to himself as he noticed the trail of dust coming up the road. It looked like the Land Rover. Connelly, obviously back from town. He'd been to see his accountants, or something like that. In a cloud of dust, the vehicle pulled up, with the rottweilers leaping up at their master, panting and whinnying in excitement.

Connelly strode onto the verandah, his khaki shirt stained with sweat. He tossed the newspaper at Mike. Today's edition of *The Times of Zambia*, folded into quadrants.

"Have a check at that lot, Mike, old boy. Front page. Bottom left."

Mike unfolded the newspaper. It wasn't a long article, but the headline jumped out at him immediately.

"Ja, looks like one of your Zimbo zots has gone and got himself blown up into little bits and pieces. Probably all over the Indian Ocean." Connelly was chuckling to himself. "Tomorrow's shark shit, hey?"

Mike read, his eyes straining at the slightly blurred print. But the contents were clear enough.

ZIM MINISTER SLAIN IN BEIRA BOMB BLAST

Beira. The Zimbabwean Minister of State Security, Norman Mubvunduku, was yesterday killled in a car bomb attack as he and his companion, a Mozambican national, were leaving a beachfront restaurant in the port city of Beira. The attack occurred at about midnight, according to the restaurant owner, who was the first to arrive on the scene.

The Zimbabwean High Commission in Maputo has declined to comment on the incident, but unconfirmed reports from Harare indicate that the minister was holidaying in Mozambique.

A Mozambican police spokesman said it was believed that grenades had been used in the killings. The motive for the attack is still unclear, but the spokesman stated that one of the assailants had apparently been spotted, fleeing the scene. Indications are that the assailant was seriously wounded. "He had lost a lot of blood," the spokesman added. "I'd be very surprised if he was still alive." Police dog-handlers are still combing the area, but apparently the suspect had fled towards the beach, where his spoor had been obliterated during the high tide.

The Mozambican authorities are withholding the identity of the Mozambican national, until the next of kin have been informed. But sources indicate that the deceased was a prominent Frelimo official and businessman.

Under his ministry, Mr Mubvunduku headed up the Zimbabwean Central Intelligence Organization, the state's ruthless security wing. Informed sources from Harare have indicated that Mr Mubvunduku may well have been the victim of an intra-party power struggle. As he came from the Manhika area on Zimbabwe's eastern border, it is suspected that he was consolidating a splinter power base within the ruling party on tribal lines.

The Mozambican Government has expressed its deep regret and has sent messages of condolences to the Zimbabwean president. The Zimbabwean president will be issuing a statement later today.

Connelly was still chuckling when Mike finished reading, "Y'know, it always comes back to them, doesn't it? Look at Mobutu. Look at Mengistu. Even Kaunda." He took his veldskoens off, airing his unsocked feet. "LANGTON! Bring the drinks. We need to drink a toast!" He laughed, raucously.

Mike was quiet. He couldn't quite put his finger on it, but he knew that the report was of significance. Straight off, there was the CIO angle. But had Mubvunduku been involved? Had it got that high up?

"Of course it has," Connelly said. "That oke was involved in everything. He knew everything that was going on. He had to … watching his own ass."

And then that evening, Joyce had brought him the e-mail that had come through from Beira.

"Mike. Phoebe. This is for you. It's come through from your friend, Colin. In Beira."

The crickets were chirping noisily outside on the lawn, as Phoebe huddled up next to Mike on the couch, reading over his shoulder. He flicked a persistent flying ant off the sheet, leaving a fatty smudge on the paper.

He read out loud, as Connelly, Joyce and Oscar craned forward in anticipation.

> To: Mike, Oscar, Phoebe. c/o Mr Connelly.
> Fm: Colin/Beira.
> Big news! Salim dead. Mubvunduku (Zim minister) also dead. Killed in car bomb. The coast is clear. Do you want to come 'home'? Pse. revert ASAP as I will be happy to come and collect 'refugee baggage'.
> With best wishes,
> Colin.
> PS. Mike. I'm looking for someone to manage the shipping office. Need someone with a bit of import/export experience. Got any ideas? Would consider equity arrangement for the right person!! (Work permit no problem).

They'd sat still for several minutes, in absolute silence. The flying ants were intensifying, buzzing stupidly into the overhead light and then dropping wingless onto the quarry-tiled floor.

Phoebe spoke first, her eyes clouded with tears, her voice tremulous. "Mike," she whispered, "does this mean it is all okay? We can go home?" The disbelief in her voice was clear.

"I ... I guess so. I dunno?" He put his arm around her shoulder and brought her closer against his body. She was shaking. This was just all too much to take in.

"LANGTON!" Connelly shouted. "Bring some more drinks! We need to celebrate. Again! *Checha, checha!*"

"Well? What are you going to do? What do you want to do, more importantly?" It was Joyce. "Oscar? What'll you do?"

"Shut up, woman!" Connelly interjected. "Oscar's staying here. I've offered him the job of farm manager. It's already arranged. Isn't it Oscar?"

Oscar looked up, surprise etched on his face. "Errm. Ja. All sorted out."

Joyce glowered at her husband, but they could all see she was secretly delighted. "Well, Connelly, thanks for letting me know."

"Well, you're always whingeing that I'm never at home. So I thought we should get a manager. And Oscar knows tobacco ..."

"Okay, okay." Joyce cut her husband short. "And you, Mike? Phoebe?"

Phoebe looked up to Mike, the tears rolling down her cheeks, Tears of confusion and relief at the same time. "I would like to return to Beira."

Mike could feel four pairs of eyes on him. 'Home', Colin had written. Where was 'home'? Zimbabwe? Zimbabwe, the country that had taken away his youth in that war? The country that had forsaken and rejected Phoebe, his Phoebe?

No. Zimbabwe was merely the birthplace. A circumstantial birthplace. It was not home. Not any more.

Mike closed his eyes. Here we go again, he thought. Another groundbreaking, life-changing, momentous decision. But this time it wasn't just him. He opened his eyes and looked down at the woman at his side. He swallowed hard, overcome with a feeling of intense emotion.

"Joyce," he asked softly, his voice cracking. "Can I use your e-mail? I want to see if I can book a flight for tomorrow."

★　★　★　★　★

They all seemed to be talking at once as Mike tossed the bags up into the door of the Dakota. Oscar, Kurt, Colin, Joyce, Connelly. Above the roar of the Boeing 737 that was taxiing onto the runway.

Only Phoebe was silent, tightly embraced in Joyce's arms.

"You're a good girl, Phoebe. The best," Joyce clucked. "I'll miss you, but we'll get down to Beira. Don't you worry about that." Her handkerchief was out, dabbing at the girl's tears. "Now, get on that plane before I start crying too!" She patted Phoebe on the backside. "And don't forget what I told you. You get yourself back to school! You've got what it takes."

Mike was shaking hands with Oscar, with Connelly. He was struggling to find the words. "Connelly. Just … thanks. Thanks for everything. I don't know how to …"

"Ag, shut up, man. It was nothing. And Mike?"

"Ja?"

"You take good care of that Phoebe. You don't deserve her y'know. She's way too good for you."

"Huh?" Mike stood there, his mouth agape, dumbstruck. He watched as Connelly went to the black woman. Taking her hands in his, he kissed her lightly on both cheeks. Kurt winked at Mike as he prepared to haul up the steps. The starboard engine kicked clumsily into life.

Twenty five

Mike felt a certain amount if trepidation coming back into Beira, anxiety mixed with hope. A hope that he was too afraid to acknowledge. There had never been hope. And now that there was this hint? A possibility? It was too much to absorb.

He sat morosely in the back seat of the car as Kurt drove them back from the airport. Phoebe sensed this and squeezed his hand. She was there for him, but he must be alone with his thoughts, alone with his own demons. There were still some things that hadn't been said. They both knew this.

Beira was the same. The same squalor, the same as ever. But in amongst the poverty and the decay, there was also the feeling of anticipation. It would get better. It would always get better. And that gave Mike the courage to face the hope.

A balmy sea breeze blew in off the ocean, that same cleansing, therapeutic breeze that he'd always loved—the breeze of Beira. The women bending in the paddies across the causeway. The palm fronds bowing, the pigs rutting, the same smells. The familiar sight of the breakers, murky, opaque, crashing relentlessly onto the beach. The knots of fishermen on the shore with their nets, hauling and dragging and cussing and sweating. The same as it always was. The same as it would always be.

"Ja, ja, ja, ja," Kurt mumbled wearily, "here we go again. Back to ze cholera. Back to ze typhoid and ze dysentery. Welcome home, huh?"

Home. That word again. Where was home? He'd always thought Zimbabwe was his home. But Zimbabwe did not want him. Or was it that he wanted no part of Zimbabwe, that he'd decided unilaterally there was no place for him? He was tired, he'd always been tired. Tired of looking over his shoulder, of running, of searching. No roots, no security, no home. But perhaps that was Africa. Live for the day. Simple.

Colin, in the front passenger seat, leaned over. "So, Mike. Have you given any more thought to my offer? I really need to spend more time flying. I can't do both. Can't run a business and fly aeroplanes at the same time."

"Can't fly fockin' aeroplanes, period," Kurt joked.

The ice was broken, the fatigue and tension of the past weeks, melting away with a simple wise crack. They all laughed.

"Yes," Mike said slowly. "I think I will take the job. Thank you."

"I'm stopping at Club Nautica for a drink," Kurt said. "You are invited to join me. But if you'd prefer to sit in ze car and be miserable, well zat's okay too."

"Yeah, interesting to see if Jean-Paul's there. Hear what happened to our two friends the other night," Colin quipped.

They parked outside the front entrance, for it was still early and the club was deserted.

Jean-Paul was there and although he merely nodded to the new arrivals, Mike sensed the relief in the man. Perhaps it was the familiarity of old faces.

"*Camarão, cerveja, vino, por favor*," Kurt ordered at the door. "Ze usual if you please, Jean-Paul."

They sat at the table by the sea wall. It was good. Like old times, as if nothing had changed. Elton John still played on.

But of course, some things had changed. For all time.

Jean-Paul sat with them for a while at the table. In the main, his sentences had been short and stubby—monosyllabic. Words were not his strength. Yes, he had been the first on the scene. He shrugged. Why, he had been at the front desk. Not that far really from where the bomb went off, out on the street. He'd heard the explosion. Who could but fail to notice it? The ground had shaken and a rush of air had swept down the *avenida*.

At first Jean-Paul thought that perhaps the war had started again, that maybe the Renamo rebels were mortaring the city. But that was crazy, huh? He had gone out into the street. It had been very dark. No flames, no sparks—no fire. But there was the smoke and the unmistakable smell of explosive. Only under the dim glow of the single street lamp had he noticed the glass and the blood. Glass, millions of tiny shards, scattered over the road like a carpet of diamonds, twinkling and bristling.

He had been afraid that the fuel tank might explode, but the carnage was exhausted. He had been about to approach the car, to get at the two occupants, the two shapeless forms, slumped, ungainly, twisted in the front seat, when a flash of movement caught the corner of his eye.

Without doubt, it was the figure of a person. He squinted through the shadows and for a moment, he thought he'd heard a moaning sound. Then the figure had vanished and he'd attended to the two men in the car. But it had been futile.

Dead.

And only two minutes before these two men had been his guests in the restaurant. It was crazy. Eating and drinking … and then dead. The eyes gazing vacantly into nothingness. The trickle of blood still dripping, warm and sweet from the mouth of the man behind the wheel.

Jean-Paul shrugged. There was nothing he could have done. Yes, he'd gone back inside the restaurant and telephoned the *policia*. And yes, he told them what he'd heard. He told them what he'd seen. Even the shadowy figure that had fled into the night. A simple statement. The truth. And then, as far he was concerned, the matter was closed. It was no business of his. Those men? Well yes, he'd seen them before. But what of it?

Mike could feel Phoebe at his side, her body taut, as she listened. Unconsciously her fingernails were digging into the bare flesh of his legs under his shorts. Only when Jean-Paul got up to check on the kitchens, did she release her grip.

Had it ended?

It was later, as the sun was setting over the Pungue estuary, that Mike stood up to go to the toilet. He did not notice Jean-Paul follow him in.

Standing at the urinal, his heart jumped as he heard the low cough at his back. He turned with a start, still clutching at his zipper.

Jean-Paul was holding something in his hand. A large white envelope, A4 size.

"*Monsieur*, I did not mean to frighten you. But it is important." He glanced behind him, towards the door. "I could not mention this thing at the table. It is very sensitive."

Mike did his zipper up. "What are you talking about, Jean-Paul?"

"After the explosion, there was debris all over. The contents of the car, you understand?"

"Like what?"

"There was a briefcase. It had been blown apart and there were papers everywhere. Like confetti."

"Yes?" Mike asked, guardedly. "What about it?"

"An old habit, *monsieur*. From *La Legion*, *tu compris*?"

Mike regarded Jean-Paul. Yes, he understood.

"I collected a few of the papers—in order to establish the identity of the dead. Naturally, I gave them to the *policia* when they came. All ... save one dossier."

"Yes?"

"I have it here, *monsieur*." Jean-Paul offered the white envelope to Mike. "I have no use for this thing. But it is of direct concern for you, *monsieur* ... and your girl. Phoebe."

Mike felt himself go cold, as he nervously took the envelope.

"Open it, *monsieur*. But I suggest you keep it well hidden. For me, myself ... I would burn it. I almost did this thing." Jean-Paul nodded as he turned to leave, "Naturally, *monsieur*, this thing is between you and me … alone. It would not do for the *policia* to discover this. *Compris?*"

Mike tore at the envelope and pulled out the manila folder. It was bloodied and torn. But there was no mistaking the bold print at the top right-hand corner. MUBVUNDUKU —PHOEBE/CASE # 16,042.

He felt himself stumble against the cold porcelain of the urinal. The bile rose in his throat and he vomited with extreme pain. Hunched over his knees, squatting on the floor, he retched and heaved as the sweat poured from his body. After some time he was able to stand. Stuffing the folder into the back of his shorts, he returned unsteadily to the table.

Phoebe gasped in alarm when she saw him, "My Lord! Mike. What is it? You seem to have a fever." She went to him, feeling his brow, clammy and cold. She felt the panic rising.

"Yeah, he's as white as a sheet," Colin added.

"It's nothing serious," Mike said feebly. "Probably one of the prawns was off. …"

"Kurt, *por favor*," Phoebe implored. "We take him home? Back to the caravan. Now?"

★ ★ ★ ★ ★

Mike had woken just before dawn. Where was he? The taste in his mouth, acrid and furry. The smell of vomit in the back of his throat. He remembered. Sitting up with a start, he threw off the sheet and padded through to the bathroom. It was still there … the manila folder, tucked in behind the toilet cistern.

Phoebe was fast asleep, curled up, with her back away from him. He brushed his teeth and immediately felt better. Scrabbling through the drawers under the basin, he found the headache pills and swallowed a handful, blitzing the pounding out of his brain.

He slipped on a T-shirt and a pair of shorts, pocketing his cigarettes and the Zippo. Then he took the manila folder from behind the cistern. With one last look to make sure she was still sleeping soundly, he carefully opened the door of the portavan as the sun began to creep over the horizon. The morning would be fresh, he thought, as he closed the door behind him and walked down to the beach.

He'd sat like that, his back against the palm tree, for an hour. Smoking and reading. Then he'd light up another cigarette and read again ... and again and again, until he knew it by heart. It was fully light now. The day had come to the city of Beira.

A woman with a baby strapped to her back came down to the beach from behind the casuarinas. In her hands she held a plastic bag. With hardly a sideways glance at the white man, she went down to the water, her bare feet leaving a faint line of footprints in her wake.

Surveying the beach about her, she mapped out her strategy. The little bubbles in the wet sand ... the periwinkles.

Reading the manila folder for the last time, Mike stubbed the cigarette out in the sand. Then, taking up the file, he cupped the Zippo in the palm of his hand. The flame flickered skittishly for a moment and then took. Gently lowering the cardboard to the flame, he watched impassively as the Zippo licked at the corner of the folder.

A sudden gust of wind scudded across the beach, extinguishing the flame. He re-lit the Zippo, holding it momentarily in front of his face, mesmerized by the blue and yellow flame. Then abruptly, he snapped the lid shut and placed the folder on the sand at his side.

What on earth did he think he was doing? Playing God? This is not your property, Mike! What right do you have to do this? Joyce's words came flooding back. An equal partner. Treat her so.

His headache was gone. The taste of vomit was gone. He stood up, and taking off his shirt, breathed in the sea air. It felt good. It would be good now to have a swim. Like a baptism, he thought, wryly.

He went to the water and wading through the shallows, dived into the surf.

The woman barely glanced up from her task. It was that same white man again. He was crazy.

Mike was still wet when he went back to the portavan, the drying salt pleasantly itchy on his skin. He returned the folder to its place behind the cistern. She turned sleepily to him as he came out of the bathroom.

"Where have you been?" There was no alarm in her voice. Only a tenderness.

"I went for a swim. It's beautiful," he answered, distractedly.

"Hmmm," she murmured, stretching contentedly. "You're crazy, Mike. Crazy. But I love you."

He noticed the sheet had fallen away as she'd arched her back, her breasts, dark and inviting, stretched firmly over her rib cage. Her arms opened to him.

"Come here, *por favor,*" she said. "I want you."

Mike felt the catch in his voice. "Yes, Phoebe. I also."

He went to her, his skin still wet, sliding and merging into the warmth of her body. She smelt the mixture of cigarette smoke and toothpaste on his breath as her mouth found his. She felt her breasts pressing into his chest, her nipples hard, painful with desire. And then gently she guided him into her as their bodies meshed in union. She felt his rhythm, responding slowly at first, and then with a greater urgency, her fingers clawing at his back. She hitched her legs up as far as they would go, willing him deeper and deeper. She could feel the spinning in her brain, she could hear her moaning, her whimpers.

And then he stopped, pulling away almost angrily. "It's no use, Phoebe. It's just no bloody use ..."

She raised herself onto her elbows, the alarm clear in her tone. "What is it Mike? What is the trouble?"

Mike could feel the sweat in the palms of his hands, sticky and tacky. Again, the dryness in the back of his throat, like a dagger. "Phoebe. There is something you must know now. I learnt of this thing last night ... and I have been too afraid to show you." His anguish was unmistakable.

She sat up, bolt upright. "What is this thing, Mike?"

"I will get it."

He came back from the bathroom with the folder. She had slipped on a T-shirt and a pair of jeans, as yet unzipped. She was standing silhouetted against the window, her hair tousled and angry.

"This is it," he said, offering her the file.

She snatched at it, "What is this thing?" But the irritation in her voice could not mask the fear.

"I think you should sit down."

But she ignored him, staring at the case file details, the name on the cover. Her brow was knitted, her head craning forward, stupidly hypnotized.

Mike stood silently, trying to understand the tumult, the confusion raging inside her. Slowly, very slowly, she opened the folder and began to read, her brow furrowing and contorting, her eyes narrowing and then widening. She read for some time, silently mouthing the words.

And then the folder dropped from her hands onto the floor, her mouth agape, her eyes staring wildly in glazed bewilderment. Her arms flopped uselessly to her side.

"My ... my father," she whispered, inaudibly.

Her legs gave way and Mike crashed forward to catch her. Limp in his arms, she was mumbling incoherently, as he gently laid her on the bed.

"My princess," he whispered, stroking her brow. "There was no other way to tell you."

"You will not want me now. I am finished. I am dead," she murmured.

What was she talking about? "Hush, my sweet. Hush! You must rest. We will deal with this later. First, you must gather your strength."

She clutched at his arm, now snarling, "*Não*! We must finish it now! Everything!"

Mike took a step back, afraid of her sudden anger.

"Okay, so that was my father!" she pointed at the folder on

the floor. She was now sitting on the edge of the bed. "And ... okay, now he is dead." She was trying to articulate her thoughts, but there was only anguish.

She sobbed loudly, a wail of absolute despair. "But did you know, *senhor*? Did you know that my ... father ... had been one of my customers? Huh! Did you know this? Huh!" She stood up, advancing on him, as if the fury of her wrath would sweep away all the pain.

"Stop, Phoebe. You are only torturing yourself."

She was screaming now, in madness. "Did you know, *senhor*, that ... that ... my father used his fist to FUCK me, huh?" And then she was clawing at his face, blindly howling like a rabid jackal.

He grappled her away, his face stinging from the onslaught. He could feel the blood oozing down his cheek. He raised his hand and struck her across the face.

She stopped dead in her tracks, her chest heaving violently, her nostrils flared. "And what now, *senhor*?" she growled through clenched teeth, "What now? You will kill me as well? As you killed my mother?"

He wiped the blood from his mouth. "Phoebe. Stop! That's not fair. Please ... please stop this madness. Please ... for the love of God. Please ..."

But it was of no use. She was gone.

Mike sank to the floor, onto his haunches. The tears came and he cried for a long time.

★　★　★　★　★

During the next few weeks, Mike rarely left the portavan. He went to Colin's office to check in for work, but Colin was away flying and would not return for some time. There was no point in starting without him, the secretary had said. She wouldn't know where to begin.

He did not know where Phoebe had gone. He'd considered searching for her, but was afraid of what he might find, afraid of where she'd be. But what was she doing now? What was she thinking? Was she thinking about him ... at all? Joyce's words came back to him. Yes, perhaps she had merely been exchanging one form of subjugation for another.

Occasionally he'd cross the road and go for a swim in the sea. It was better than sitting around, moping in the portavan all day. It was a therapy that brushed away the gnawing ache in his stomach. But the relief was only ever temporary.

One day, a little man on a Velo came to the property and presented him with a registered envelope. Mike signed for it and watched curiously as the Velo puttered out the yard. He opened the letter. It was a divorce summons from his wife's lawyer in Harare. How had they found him? Who cared? It was not important. Couldn't hide forever.

But it gave him something to occupy his mind. He wrote a letter, replying to the lawyer. He would not contest the divorce. Short and simple. The following day he drove into town and posted the letter. Somehow it made him feel better. After the post office, he went to the Banco Comercial de Mocambique and drew out some money. It was an impetuous thing he wanted to do, but it was worth a try. It was to be a gesture, nothing more.

On his way home, he stopped off at the American Compound and sought out the American UNICEF Liaison Officer. A plumpish, middle-aged woman with cats-eye spectacles, she was very accommodating. It was no problem, this thing. She would see to it immediately. Within 20 minutes, she'd had the forms typed up, signed and receipted. She neatly folded the papers and put them in an envelope without sealing it.

"We look forward to it," she said, smiling. She shook hands with him and showed him out.

He went back to the portavan, trying to suppress the excitement bubbling inside him. Tonight he would go to the One-Two-Three Rock. He would see her—if she was there. Pray God, let her be there.

At sunset he went for a swim. The beach was deserted and he was pleased. Alone with his thoughts, he sat smoking. It wasn't finished with Phoebe. One way or the other, it hadn't been properly concluded. Perhaps she thought it had. But it wasn't.

★ ★ ★ ★ ★

The band was playing *The Girl from Ipanema* when Mike walked into the nightclub. Nothing had changed. Not the couples swaying on the dance floor, not the gaggle of hookers giggling girlishly at the door, not the smells of urine and seafood, not the pall of smoke sitting trapped under the ceiling. He'd prepared himself for the eventuality that perhaps she might not be there, but knew it would still come as a bitter blow.

But she was there.

She hadn't noticed him come in, her back turned away. She was sitting at the same table, alone, wearing the same T-shirt, hanging loosely over her jeans. Her hair was untidy and even from the back, Mike could see her weariness.

He caught his breath at the sight of her, the nerves churning inside his gut. Patting his shirt pocket to make sure the envelope was still there, he picked his way through the tables towards her. Still she was looking away.

"Phoebe," he said softly.

She spun round in her chair, recognizing the voice immediately.

"You are here," she stated, flatly, defensively.

"Yes. I have come to talk."

"What about?" she snapped.

"May I sit down?"

She nodded grudgingly at the chair opposite, the faintest hint of hope in her eyes. Mike did not miss it.

"Phoebe … I will not take up your time, but I must say what has not been said, " he began softly, surely. "I don't expect anything from you. It is too much to hope. I love you and I always will … till the end of my days. But as you once said, maybe love is not enough. I can accept this now, but that doesn't mean there is no hope."

She was looking at him, unemotionally.

"I did not kill your father. I did not kill your mother. Yes, I was there at the camp. Yes, I killed people that day, but I did not pull the trigger that killed your mother. Of course, I would give anything to change the past. But it's done. I am white. I can't change that. You are black and you cannot change that. It's the way things are. But together, we are human beings."

She was blinking slowly, as if fighting some emotion within.

"I will not beg you, Phoebe, but I want to be with you. I want to try ... to make it work." His resolve was waning and he could feel the tears welling inside. She looked so beautiful, so vulnerable. He wanted to take her in his arms and hold her forever.

"But I will understand if you choose otherwise," he tailed off, fearing his voice would crack. He stood up, and he could see she wanted him to stay, but she said nothing.

"You know where I am, if you ever change your mind." He had to go, to get out of there. It was too painful. "Oh, I forgot," he took the envelope out of his pocket. "This is for you. No strings. Tear it up if you want. Whatever you want."

She took the envelope, as he turned and strode away. Only then did the tears come to her.

She opened the envelope, her hands shaking. What was this thing? Unfolding the papers, she saw it. It was an acceptance letter from the International School at the American Compound. 'Dear Ms Mubvunduku', it read. 'We acknowledge receipt of your application to commence studies at the US International School in Beira. We are pleased to advise that you have been allocated a place in our Mature Students' General Diploma Course. Attached is the school curriculum and administrative notes for your information. Please do not hesitate to contact the undersigned should you have any queries. We look forward ...

Holding the letter to her chest, she stared vacantly, unseeing, across the room, her eyes misted with tears. Carefully she folded the letter and put it in the back pocket of her jeans.